"One reads Karen Tei Yamashita's second novel with a sense of wonder at the author's ambition as a writer and awe at her powers as a thinker. The tale of the struggles of Japanese immigrants to the Brazilian rain forest, readable as it is and exotic as it first seems, wrestles with profound philosophical and social issues, and does it with the vivid characterzations and entertaining flow of a historical romance." —*New York Newsday*

"With a subtle ominousness, Yamashita sets up her hopeful, prideful characters—and, in the process, the entire genre of pioneer lit—for a fall." —*Village Voice Literary Supplement*

"*Brazil-Maru* is a historically informative and emotionally complex novel. It describes for us the lives of a people we might not have known existed, but also takes us beyond the small community of Japanese immigrants living in Esperança and teaches us about the dangers of power, greed, ignorance, and vainglory." —*Bloomsbury Review*

"Karen Tei Yamashita has a big talent." —*Los Angeles Times*

"*Brazil-Maru* is warm, compassionate, engaging and thought-provoking. An oddly angled view of immigrants elsewhere, it casts light into many of the darker corners in our own immigrant nation." —*The Washington Post*

"One of my favorite books this year was *Brazil-Maru*." —*StarTribune*

"What makes a good utopia go bad? In a second novel as engrossing as her first, Karen Tei Yamashita takes us inside Esperança, an agricultural commune in Brazil founded in 1925 by a group of socialist Japanese immigrants." —*Utne Reader*

"A splendid multigenerational novel. . . . rich in history and character." —*San Francisco Examiner-Chronicle*

"Yamashita's heightened sense of passion and absurdity, and respect for inevitability and personality, infuse this engrossing multigenerational immigrant saga with energy, affection, and humor." —*Booklist*

"Poignant and remarkable." —*Philadelphia Inquirer*

Brazil-Maru

A NOVEL BY KAREN TEI YAMASHITA

COFFEE HOUSE PRESS : : MINNEAPOLIS : : 1992

The Publisher wishes to thank the following for their support of this project: the Jerome Foundation; Minnesota State Arts Board; the National Endowment for the Arts, a federal agency; Meyer, Scherer and Rockcastle; and Northwest Area Foundation.

The epigram at the beginning of Part II is from *La Nouvelle Heloise* by Jean-Jacques Rousseau, and is reprinted with the permission of The Pennsylvania University Press.

The epigram at the beginning of Part IV if from *The Social Contract* by Jean-Jacque Rousseau, and is reprinted with the permission of Hafner Press, a Division of Macmillan Publishing Company. Copyright 1947 by Hafner Press.

Coffee House Press books are available to stores through our primary distributor, Consortium Book Sales & Distribution, 287 East Sixth St., Suite 365, Saint Paul, MN 55101. Our books are also available through all major library distributors and jobbers and through most small press distributors including Bookpeople, Bookslinger, Inland and Small Press Distribution.

For personal orders, catalogs or other information, write to:
Coffee House Press, 27 North Fourth Street, Minneapolis MN 55401.

Library of Congress cataloging-in-publication data
Yamashita, Karen Tei, 1951-
    Brazil-Maru : a novel / by Karen Tei Yamashita.
        p.   cm.
    ISBN 1-56689-000-4 : $19.95
    1. Japanese—Brazil—History—Fiction.   I. Title.
PS3575.A44B7   1992
813'.54—DC20   92-17857
                                                              CIP

10 9 8 7 6 5 4 3

Remembering my father

Many thanks to the following people and organizations in Brazil and the United States without whose help and support this work would not have been possible:

Thomas J. Watson Foundation
Shinsei-no-jo
Yuba-no-jo
Raymond and Ryoko Narusawa & family
The Takiy family
The Fujii family
The Marques family
Shojiro Matsubayashi
The Lopes de Oliveira family
The Escolano family
The Sakai family
The Yamashita family

From 1975 to 1977, I interviewed numerous people within and connected to the Japanese-Brazilian community in the states of São Paulo and Paraná, in particular, the communities of Aliança, Bastos, Guaraçaí, Pereira Barreto and São Paulo. These people are too numerous to name. I was everywhere received with kindness and the warm hospitality for which the Brazilian people are well known. I am greatly indebted to their support and friendship and to the wonderful stories shared by so many kind people.

Special thanks also to Vicki Abe, David Duer, Ted Hopes, Allan Kornblum, Casey Krache, Mako, Mary Nakashima, Ryan Shiotani, Michael Wiegers and Wakako Yamauchi for reading and critiquing early versions of the manuscript.

It is said that there are more than one million Japanese immigrants and their descendants living in Brazil today—the largest such population outside of Japan. Japanese-Brazilians, well into the second and third generations, participate in every facet of Brazilian life—social, political and economic.

Japanese immigration to Brazil has followed patterns of their exclusion from the United States. In 1908, when the Gentlemen's Agreement was signed to limit Japanese immigration to the United States, the first shipload of some 800 Japanese arrived at the port of Santos in the State of São Paulo. In the 1920s, when Exclusion Acts were passed by the United States government, the slow stream of Japanese immigrants to Brazil became a flood, and thousands came to Brazil to work as contract laborers on coffee plantations. By 1940 more than 190,000 Japanese had passed through the port city of Santos, disembarking from any one of 32 Japanese steamships that crossed the oceans in over 300 trips. While the vast majority of these immigrants came to Brazil as contract laborers, a small percentage came as settlers, buying tracts of land and colonizing farming communities.

The story that follows is based on the lives of a small population of such settlers. It is a particular story that must be placed in its particular time and place. It is a work of fiction, and the characters are also works of fiction. Certainly it cannot be construed to be representative of that enormous and diverse community of which it is but a part. And yet, perhaps, here is a story that belongs to all of us who travel distances to find something that is, after all, home.

Part I: Emile

Emile has little knowledge, but what he has is truly his own. . . . Emile has a mind that is universal not by its learning but by its faculty to acquire learning; a mind that is open, intelligent, ready for everything. . . .

Emile has only natural and purely physical knowledge. He does not know even the name of history, or what metaphysics and morals are. . . .

Emile is industrious, temperate, patient, firm, and full of courage. His imagination is in no way inflamed and never enlarges dangers. He is sensitive to few ills, and he knows constancy in endurance because he has not learned to quarrel with destiny. . . .

In a word, of virtue Emile has all that relates to himself. . . . He lacks only the learning which his mind is all ready to receive . . .

He considers himself without regard to others and finds it good that others do not think of him. He demands nothing of anyone and believes he owes nothing to anyone. He is alone in human society. . . . He has lived satisfied, happy and free insofar as nature has permitted. Do you find that a child who has come in this way to his fifteenth year has wasted the preceding ones?

Jean-Jacques Rousseau
Emile, or On Education

CHAPTER 1: BRAZIL-MARU

IT WAS 1925. São Paulo, Brazil. I stuck my head out the window, straining to see the beginning and the end of the train as it chugged slowly up the side of the mountain. The tepid heat of the port of Santos below rose around us in a soft cloud that silently engulfed my view of the now distant port and the ship and the shimmering ocean beyond. The creeping altitude and the rocking train seemed to lull the minds of the passengers so recently stunned by our first impressions. I had seen it myself from the ship below—the sheer green wall lifting into a mass of shifting clouds, daring us to scale it.

How many other Japanese immigrants had already witnessed this scene? Since 1908, they had arrived at this same port in shipload after shipload until there were thousands of Japanese, the majority laboring on coffee plantations in the State of São Paulo.

I had stumbled down the gangway clutching a bundle entrusted to me. My mother was carrying little Yōzo on her back. Eiji clutched her dress with one hand and Hiro held on to Eiji. My father lumbered down with our heavy bags. Although I was only nine years old, I was still the oldest and had to take care of myself. I saw the scholar Shūhei Mizuoka already on the dock struggling with his bags loaded with books. For a moment I sensed a need to look back at the ship we were leaving, and there at the top of the plank was Grandma Uno still standing transfixed, staring at this idea we all had traveled so far to see, this Brazil.

Below, dockworkers pushed loaded carts or trudged under heavy sacks, their soiled shirts patched with circles of sweat. It was not the first time I had seen people of other colors and features. We had followed a route around the earth, sailing south from Japan through the South China Sea to Singapore, then on to Ceylon and the Cape of Good Hope; the ship had docked on the coast of India and the tip of Africa, but still I stared as the ship traded its human cargo for coffee and bananas.

The din of this activity pitched about us, but we were oddly silent, dumbfounded upon seeing what two months of dreams aboard a plodding ship upon the sea had brought. The dank humidity pressed upon us. I saw Grandma Uno's shoulders stoop; perhaps her old heart hesitated. Her grandson Kantaro nudged her at her elbow. "What is it?" he asked. She looked up at him, so tall and handsome and so anxious to step onto this land.

"Ichiro!" my mother called back to me. I hurried on, but not before I saw Grandma Uno push Kantaro aside and walk purposely down alone to land.

We had borne the heavy humidity of the port of Santos along with all our worldly possessions from the ship to the waiting train, and now we were climbing upward with our burdens, struggling against our better senses to gain the plateau. There was some relief as we climbed; the shadowed air filtered through the dense vegetation but so did the smell. We had traded the salty taste of the sea and the fragrance of coffee and bananas for this other smell. It had flooded the car somewhere below us as we passed through what seemed to be a black swamp of rotting vegetation that had dropped off in disintegrating pieces from the great green wall. We had captured the odor of that putrid rot within the confines of the rocking train. I had not felt seasick those many days at sea, but now suddenly I was overcome with nausea.

For many hours the train plodded upward through the green wall. Occasionally we passed through a tunnel, but it did not seem to clear the air. I struggled with my discomfort until it passed into a kind of dream. Flitting through the green wall and mist, I saw a fox, a horned devil, a white-faced ghost, the monsters of my childhood. And then, they were gone forever as the train emerged onto a plateau, and the land stretched out for miles into the distant horizon—pastures of grazing zebu, fields of corn, coffee and sugar cane spotted by thick patches of the old tangled forest and sweeping mango and avocado trees, and only occasionally disturbed by a lonely brick or mud-thatched cottage—a land spacious and vast, and all so different from Japan.

"Well, Ichiro," my father said. "What do you think? It's beyond my imagination," my father answered himself. "So here we are." We looked around at my brothers huddled around and in my mother's lap. They were all sleeping in a big heap. My father looked at me and smiled, "Ichiro, somehow I knew you'd be awake for this."

The train came to a stop at what seemed to be a rural way station. It was also a marketplace of sorts. Vendors sat with their produce spread on mats or makeshift stands. A few peddlers ran along the train shouting through the windows. They had wares in baskets: dried meats, fresh fish, cakes and sweets, strange fruits like bananas and papayas, and birds—some dead, some alive. A great wall of chickens squawked from their cages. I ran out the open door of the car, finally overcome by my sickness, and heaved the contents of my poor stomach onto the new land. My relief was sudden, but my attention was easily diverted by a boy who ran toward me chasing a squealing piglet. He caught the piglet, but it squirmed away and ran off, knocking me to the ground. It had jumped on my chest and over my head, leaving its dirty prints and sour smell behind. I felt an indescribable disgust and joy all at once urging me to join the boy in his chase, scurrying after the slippery pig and running toward that great wall of chickens. Just as it was about to slip between the cages, I dove upon the squealing pig, pinning it beneath my chest. I looked up at cages teetering above to see the face of the pig's young owner, a mixture of relief and gratitude and comedy glowing in his features. For a short moment that boy and I were locked in some middle space where our two curious minds stared at the unknown.

I remember that face as if it were yesterday, the golden sun-bleached burnish at the tips of his curly brown hair, the dark olive skin beneath a healthy glow of sweat, the richness of his deep brown eyes. The boy spoke in a language I could not understand, and yet, I was sure from that moment on that I would soon understand everything. Over the years, I have thought from time to time that I had caught a glimpse of that very boy again, but of course, it could never be the same boy. If he is indeed alive today, he must be, like me, another old man with memories.

*　*　*

There were six of us in my family in 1925 when we arrived in Brazil —my father, Kiyoshi Terada; my mother, Sei; and my three younger brothers. As I said, I was the oldest son, although only nine years old. My mother was pregnant when we arrived in Brazil. Everyone spoke about her next child as being doubtless a girl, that so drastic a change in our lives on this earth would surely change the pattern, but this did not happen. Interesting to recall that with all the changes of place and fortune, some things did *not* change, and it was finally expected that my mother would always give birth to boys.

My family was originally from the town of Matsumoto in the mountains of Nagano Prefecture in central Japan. My father came from a family of pharmacists, and he too had a license. My mother, who was actually a second cousin to my father, was a trained mid-wife. Their marriage must have seemed a logical one to their families, and there was, indeed, a quiet understanding between my parents about everything, or so it seemed to me. When Momose-sensei came to speak about starting a new life on new land in Brazil, they seemed to agree almost immediately that this was the destiny God intended for us.

By the 1920s many Japanese, especially second sons without rights of inheritance, had left to find a livelihood abroad. We knew of several men from our town who had left for California at the turn of the century. My mother knew the fish market family whose oldest sister had left to join her husband in San Francisco. But that was the last anyone had heard or seen of these people. By the time I was born, these stories seemed like the distant past. And yet, every year more and more poor tenant farmers who complained of high taxes and no future looked for opportunities far away. The recent Kanto earthquake of 1923 had left many homeless and unemployed. In cities and towns, students were unable to find work after their schooling, and strikes were rampant among the urban industries. Now my parents discussed their plans to leave too. Everyone came to share their thoughts on the matter.

"Momose-sensei has lived in America, but he was very clear in his meaning. He said our future is in Brazil."

People remembered the 1918 Rice Rebellion when 25,000 peasants protested the high price of rice. This and pro-communist and proletariat movements later provoked government repression. For people like my parents, educated Christians with socialist sentiments, Brazil would be a new beginning.

"Anyway, we've missed our chance to go to America now. The Americans signed an Exclusion Act that won't allow us in."

"I heard that most of Brazil is virgin forest, not like America at all. Brazil is looking for people to develop the country."

"What about those ads calling for contract laborers to harvest Brazilian coffee?"

"This is different. We won't be contract labor. We'll have our own land from the very beginning. Momose-sensei has arranged for a concession from the State of São Paulo. We saw the maps and the allocation of the lots."

"Imagine, sixty acres of land for one family! How much land is that? More than an entire village, and then there are two hundred such lots available—more than 120,000 acres!"

"And," my father confided to his closest friends, "There will be others like us. Christians with the same convictions. We will be able to create a new civilization."

A new civilization. This perhaps sounds strange today, but in those early years, that is the way we used to talk about colonizing Brazil, especially about the particular Japanese colony located on the far northwestern corner of the State of São Paulo, founded by the Christian evangelist, Momose-sensei, and where my parents chose lot number thirty-three: Esperança.

*   *   *

We left Japan from the port of Kobe on a ship named the *Brazil-maru*. The voyage on the *Brazil-maru* lasted some sixty days. Most of the 600 emigrants on the ship were going to Brazil as contract laborers to work on coffee plantations, hired on by the Imperial Immigration Company. The Brazilian government required that contract labor enter Brazil in family units, but this was not always how things worked out. Unknown to government authorities, immigrants, when necessary, created family units, oftentimes mixing and matching relatives and friends and strangers.

For example, I met a boy named Kōji on the ship who was borrowed by his bachelor uncle to complete a family unit. And Kōji confided to me that the woman who was traveling with them was not his mother; she was a stranger from another village. In the beginning, she was mostly seasick, and her eyes were always red from crying. I heard my mother say that this woman was running away because she did not want to marry the man her family had chosen for her. My mother, being a midwife, naturally met many women on the ship and heard the gossip. She also went to comfort this woman.

"I've made a terrible mistake. I didn't realize how far away Brazil is," she sobbed to my mother.

"You must make the best of this situation," my mother said. "What about the poor boy? He's not your own, but he's only a child. He doesn't say so, but he's probably as homesick and afraid as you are." I didn't think much of Kōji's situation then, but now I wonder what ever became of him. He was not much older than me.

My family was different from the other Japanese on the ship. We had paid for our passage and were destined to settle land we had bought, while the contract laborers were committed to several years of labor to pay for their passage. But we were all alike in our expectations of Brazil: the promised wealth of the coffee harvest, the vastness of the land, the adventure of a new life. And I think most of the immigrants were alike in thinking that they would return—after their contracts were up or in a few years, however long it might take —to Japan with certain wealth, stories of adventure and the pride of success. I believe my parents thought that surely they would see their homeland and their families in Nagano once again, at least to visit. As we watched the port of Kobe disappear on the ocean's horizon, I thought *I* would return. But my father said to me, as I turned with the others on the deck, "Ichiro, we're going to a new country, a new life. Everything begins from this moment. Don't look back." I think my father knew I would never return. He did not believe, like so many did, that Japan was the only place in the world to live.

From that moment, my memories of Japan faded; visions of my birthplace became to me a blur. And yet, I have a very clear memory of everything from that moment on: the movement of the ship upon the sea, the snap of cards and the laughter of men gambling, the banter of immigrant talk in different dialects, quarrels with my brothers and our tireless exploration of every nook and cranny in the ship— and the camera.

*   *   *

"A Carl Zeiss box camera," Kantaro Uno boasted proudly to a crowd of interested observers who had little else to amuse themselves on the long trip at sea. "I've always wanted one." He turned the camera in his hands, examining its mechanisms, blowing dust from its surface and carefully polishing the lens with a handkerchief.

"So, Kantaro, I suppose you'll be busy documenting our trip," said Mizuoka, who briefly put his book down to make this observation.

"Yes, that's so," said Kantaro rather too seriously. "I think it's important to remember this passage. It's the beginning of a new life for my family."

"And you'll never again be here on this ship with the same hopes and expectations and the same youthfulness. It's something to record," Mizuoka agreed.

Kantaro smiled, pleased with the attention. He was then no more than twenty years old. His closely cropped schoolboy's head of hair was growing out in an unruly mass, adding a slightly wild edge to his handsome features and the eager intensity shining in his eyes. His forehead was burned by the tropical sun as we slipped over the

Indian Ocean, Kantaro having spent hours on deck studying his photographic compositions. His white shirt hung limply about his broad shoulders, and something about his demeanor exuded strength and certainly the vigor of youth to which Mizuoka referred.

Shūhei Mizuoka was a scholar of sorts, an intellectual, professorial in his manner. He spent much of his time immersed in his many books. I heard that he had completely stuffed his baggage with books and papers, clothing being incidental to his needs. At other times, Mizuoka seemed to emerge from his reading to discuss at length some obscure subject or another with Kantaro's father, Naotaro Uno. My father was sometimes led into these discussions, not always because of a genuine interest in the subject matter, but because my father, like Naotaro Uno and Shūhei Mizuoka, was a Christian. Our three families were brought together on the ship by the simple fact that we were all destined for Esperança.

Mizuoka's interest lent an added but immeasurable value to the possession of the camera. Quite suddenly, it had been raised to a special function in the living history of our travels to Brazil. Moreover, the owner, young Kantaro Uno, had been raised to the prominent position of a photographic reporter.

However, I heard the talk of other passengers on the ship who were perhaps either unimpressed or jealous. They muttered their feelings over interminable card games, looking out to the endless sea, turning the evidence over again and again to confirm their original prejudices without having to face a thousand misgivings about leaving their homes and families behind.

"Where did they get the money to buy such a camera? Do you know what that thing is worth? You could buy a passage on this ship for the price of that camera."

"Kantaro insisted that his father buy the camera for him when we docked at Singapore."

"A spoiled son, no doubt. Where will this get them in Brazil?"

"That Uno family is from Hyogo. Kansai people who like to show off. Naotaro was the village head. I heard they sold everything to pay a debt. Now they're going to Brazil with what's left."

"I heard that too. Naotaro lost his money over some religious retreat in the mountains," the man snickered. "Good Christianity. Bad business."

They all laughed and shook their heads. "These Christians have other ideas."

"Intellectual types with university educations."

"They say Naotaro graduated from Keio University. His family were the only Christians in his village. His uncle is a Christian priest."

"What are these people going to do in Brazil—pick coffee? Ha!"

"I wonder. They even brought their old grandmother. Poor old woman. Imagine bringing such an old woman along."

"Have you talked to her? A very proud woman from an old family. She told me that she was convinced to come by her grandson Kantaro."

"Of course. The spoiled one with the camera."

"She dotes on him. Be careful. You can't say a bad word about that grandson of hers. Do you know what she said? She said that, at her age, eighty-eight, Kantaro convinced her to go to Brazil to start a new life."

"I'll admit I admire an old woman with spirit like that."

"A new life. Such nonsense. Taking a poor old lady away from her birthplace. It's a crime."

So the gossip went. The Unos seemed oblivious to all of it. Kantaro took his photographs, and old Grandma Uno, Naotaro and his wife Waka, their other sons, Jiro and Saburo, and their daughter Ritsu, all went about their business on the ship as if some invisible power had anointed them with a certain special prestige. Other people accused them of having airs, of being snobs, of pretending to still have money when everyone knew that Brazil was a distant solution to their real destitution. At that time I did not think so much about these things, but perhaps the Unos were different, at least different from my parents and their quiet and humble manners. My parents were in no way conceited about their religious beliefs, their education, their social rank or their proposal to start anew as colonists in Brazil. That they were endowed with any special mission would have seemed presumptuous to them, no matter what they believed when Momose-sensei had come to talk to them about starting a new civilization. I knew even then as a young boy that we were somehow different from the other immigrants on the ship. I knew, in part, that it was because we were called Christians and because we were going to Brazil with our own money to settle on our own land. The Unos were proud to be different, flamboyant in their talk and gestures, all in a way that seemed appropriate to a great adventure. Kantaro's new camera seemed to me to represent the future, a great gamble at

great expense, a wonderful exuberant spirit, so different from anything that I had known before.

The youngest Uno son, Saburo, was two years older than me. Even
in those days, Saburo wore a cap. It was a blue cap which was always
tilted rebelliously, I thought, to one side. Later it would be a baseball
cap of one sort or another, but always a cap and always crooked.
Saburo, being older but also an Uno, treated me with friendly disdain. And yet, as time wore on, we became inseparable partners.
With Kōji, we made a threesome and spent many hours planning
adventures to forbidden areas of the ship. We had been chased out
of the kitchen several times. We had also gone down into the hold of
the ship to inspect the furnace, but we were especially curious about
the officers' quarters; so one night, after making a series of careful
plans, we were able to sneak up as far as the door. There was loud
drunken laughter and singing coming from the room. I was afraid to
look in, but Saburo of course was bolder and crept up to the door.
He motioned to us, and we all came forward to look.

I must admit my embarrassment at what I saw. Even though the
woman was not Kōji's real mother, I felt ashamed for him. When she
saw us, the woman jumped up, sending the man on top of her
sprawling. "Kōji!" she cried and rushed toward the door.

We scattered away like mice. I turned around to see her naked
figure at the door, her distressed look of shame, and heard the continuing laughter of the men behind me. After that, Kōji did not join
us again in our escapades around the ship. He became sullen and
distant with both Saburo and me. I realized that he had come to think
of that woman as his new mother, or at least that he had grown to
like her. I felt sorry for Kōji, saying to Saburo that I would not like
to be so alone as Kōji. Saburo shrugged, pushing his cap to one side,
and said pompously that he himself would not mind.

After this, Saburo and I lost interest in exploring the ship. We
would wander around aimlessly with little to do. I often questioned
Saburo about his brother's camera, and Saburo joked that we might
have taken a picture of the woman in the officers' quarters that night.
I couldn't understand this sort of joking; I thought that the camera
was something special, something noble, that naturally, it would
only record important and noble things.

I had heard Saburo's oldest brother, Kantaro, talking with Mizuoka and my father, discussing the camera, discussing Brazil, discussing so many things I could not understand then. They spoke of

something they called the true Japanese spirit and the possibility that this spirit could best be raised in a new country, free from the old ways. Once they pointed to me and said something about a French writer named Rousseau. "Here then is our Japanese Emile."

My father laughed and said, "We will make an experiment of you, Ichiro, in Brazil."

I was puzzled by this talk.

Mizuoka smiled, "Don't be frightened by this talk, Ichiro. All of us must be changed by life in Brazil. It is all for the best, but children naturally absorb change. You'll see. Language, customs, manners, everything. You watch!"

"A new start," nodded Kantaro, looking at me with a significance I could not measure. I was an innocent child, and somehow Kantaro matched my innocence. It was as if he knew something important about me, and I was undeniably attracted to this secret that Kantaro must alone know.

"Look, Ichiro," Kantaro pointed suddenly from the deck. "Land! Brazil!" At that moment, I felt quite as important as the Carl Zeiss camera. A Japanese Emile. This might be a very important function indeed. Suddenly I sensed in myself the feeling that I had been envious of, that feeling of importance that the Unos seemingly all carried so well. I myself, a nine-year-old boy on a ship bound for Brazil, was suddenly someone among many. And feeling singularly important, I disembarked the *Brazil-maru* with my family at the Brazilian port of Santos, nodded proudly to Saburo and caught a glimpse of Kōji disappearing with his uncle and the woman into the receding surge of the crowd.

*   *   *

The train sped on, the red dust rolling in clouds through the open windows at intervals. I did not know it at the time, but we were headed on the Noroeste Line to the far northwestern corner of the State of São Paulo on the very edges of a vast virgin forest whose borders were gradually receding with the cultivation of coffee, sugar cane and pasture. In the 1920s, Esperança was one of many Japanese farming communities scattered in outlying areas throughout São Paulo and Paraná, and there was a growing community in the city of São Paulo itself. I watched the seemingly endless stretches of planted land and pasture, plantations of coffee trees and sugar cane and corn and scores of laborers bent at their tasks, scrawny dogs and children running down dirt paths, mules and oxen pulling heavily laden wooden carts, herds of frantic zebu flowing in long muscular rivers, everything and everyone churning that red earth. Sleepy towns and settlements spun past, and other passengers got off here and there. But we went on and on until we came to what seemed to be very near the end of the tracks. Where the train stopped did not seem to be a place for stopping at all. There was not even a platform built up next to the train. My mother and my brothers were all hoisted off the train, and our bundles and bags, except for a heavy suitcase with Mizuoka's books, were all tossed out the windows.

The Uno family and the scholar Mizuoka also disembarked at this strange place. We stood in a huddle at the side of a small red brick structure, which apparently marked the train station, watching the train pull off and chug away into the distance. There was a silence among us, as if we were watching the departure of our last contact with civilization. The morning sun was high in the sky and a damp humidity settled about us. My littlest brother, Yōzo, began to cry.

A dirt road crossed the tracks and stretched out and disappeared into the forest. Saburo and I followed Kantaro, who stood in the middle of the road, trying to decipher which direction to take. Perhaps a map would have been useless. We were somewhere slightly north of the Tropic of Capricorn in the middle of a country that covered half the South American continent. We had traveled across the rich agricultural center of Brazil. Further to the west was the great forest of the Mato Grosso and Bolivia beyond, and to the north were the mining towns of Minas Gerais and beyond that, the rain forests of the Amazon. To the northeast were the dry brushlands and cattle ranches graced by a long Atlantic coastline. To the south, the flat grasslands extended to Argentina and Uruguay. But I was unaware of this vast land of which we had become a part. We were a small inconsequential dot on a virtually unmapped area. We were the tiny seed of small beginning, one story among many.

An old Brazilian man emerged from the brick house and yelled something, something we could not then understand.

My father motioned to the Brazilian. "Esperança?" he asked the man.

"Esperança. *Sim. Sim*," nodded the man, pointing across the tracks and down the road.

From that direction, I could hear a creaking sound and the thump of hooves upon the dirt, and very soon we could see a man in a cart pulled by oxen coming down the road.

"A Japanese isn't he?" Saburo nodded, squinting at the man in the cart.

The old Brazilian waved at the man in the cart. "Okumura! Okumura!" he nodded and pointed.

Takeo Okumura pulled his oxen to a halt and slid down from the cart. He pulled a handkerchief from his pocket, wiped the sweat from his darkly tanned forehead and replaced a straw hat on his head. The old Brazilian came forward, and both men spoke cordially for a moment, shaking hands. This shaking of hands seemed very strange to me; I had never seen anyone do such a thing. Then we were all introduced: the Unos, Mizuoka, and my family, the Teradas. Soon the luggage was piled high on the cart alongside my pregnant mother, old Grandma Uno, and a few of the youngest children. The rest of us walked a certain distance behind the cart to avoid the dust churned up in its wake. The great forest arched above us, and we were alternately engulfed by its great density and surprised by large expanses of clearing, newly cut and charred by fire. We walked several miles before we reached a long but simple wood-slat house. Okumura's wife, Tomi, emerged from this house and helped my mother and Grandma Uno from the cart.

When we had all arrived at the house, Okumura stooped to the ground and grasped a fistful of dirt. He placed a bit of the dirt in everyone's hands, and then he prayed. While Okumura prayed, I looked down at the soft red powder in the small palm of my hand. So this was Esperança.

CHAPTER 2: ESPERANÇA

MY BROTHER KŌICHI was born just as my father tapped the water level in our well, and by chance I saw Kōichi at the very moment of his birth.

My brothers and I had been given the task of packing mud into one remaining wall of our house. We were making a mess of it, but it did not seem to matter. Meanwhile, my father was busy digging a well. Kantaro Uno and Akira Tsuruta, another young man recently arrived in Esperança, had come to help us. Kantaro was pulling buckets of earth from the hole for the well, and Tsuruta was supervising our work on the mud wall. All of us, including my mother, were caked in red mud.

There is a photograph of us taken by Kantaro of this very day. In fact, there are a great many photographs of this early period taken by Kantaro. It is a wonderful record of our lives and labor in those days. Kantaro would think nothing of stopping everyone in the middle of their tasks to record the felling of a great tree, the planting of a field of corn or rice, or in this case, to show us caked in mud in an effort to build our house and dig our well. In this photograph, you can see my mother literally moments before she lost that great burden in her belly.

It was little Hiro who called down to my father at the bottom of the well. "Papa!" Hiro leaned over the edge looking down at least forty feet into the dark hole.

"Get away from the edge!" My father yelled. "You'll fall in!"

Hiro moved back, but insisted, "Mama says not to worry because the water is already boiling."

My father tugged at the rope holding a bucket and called up to Kantaro, "We've hit water! It's seeping in!"

Kantaro started to crank the muddy contents of the bucket to the top of the well but found it much too heavy. He looked over the edge and saw my father climbing the rope hand-over-hand and scaling the walls. He emerged at the top and excitedly asked my little brother, "Water boiling?"

Hiro nodded. "She said the baby is coming."

Kantaro ran off with Hiro saddled on his back to get his mother, while Akira Tsuruta gathered me and my brothers Eiji and Yōzo about him and showed us how to make animals and small people with the red clay mud. I began to enjoy this activity, but my father called me and washed me down as best he could—rusty water dripping away from my hair, face and arms in a clayey puddle. "We might need your help, Ichiro," he said. "It will take Uno-no-okaasan a while to get here. You keep clean and stay nearby in case I need you."

I stood outside the house, watching enviously from a distance as my brothers, under Tsuruta's instructions, built a castle modeled, he said, after the great Himeji Castle itself. There was soon a road leading to a small village with houses and temples surrounded by fields of rice. "This is the house of a famous samurai," I could hear Tsuruta say, "and here is where the sake merchant lives and here, a famous woodblock artist. Oh, yes, and here is the school." Then they created soldiers on horses, nobles, merchants and farmers and small animals. Very soon, drying in the hot afternoon sun, was a tiny complicated red relief of an old world left behind not so long ago.

I felt angry about being left out and walked sullenly around to the back of the house, where we had been patching the wall with red mud. Here and there the damp mud had fallen away from the bamboo slats, and I could see into the house. I peered through the gaps in our handiwork, poking here and there with my fingers. Suddenly I stopped short. Through the wall I heard my mother's low groan, and then I saw my new brother—Kōichi, my father would name him—emerging from my mother in a thin film of blood. My father said, "Ah, it's a boy. It's a boy. Born in Brazil! Born in Brazil!"

*   *   *

About this time too, Grandma Uno became very ill. My father was called upon as a pharmacist to prescribe medicine, and Kantaro Uno came often to our new house to get medicine or to ask my father to see his grandmother.

One day, Kantaro came by on a horse. In those days, none of us even thought of buying such an animal. Once again, the Unos had expended money for something most people thought of as a luxury, and even my parents, who weren't ones to talk, thought that the horse was an unnecessary expense. "A mule would be put to better use," commented my father, "but this horse can only be used for riding." Kantaro's horse was a beautiful spirited white Arabian with a long mane and tail. I heard that Kantaro had made some sort of deal with a local Brazilian fellow who had lost a bet in a game of craps.

Kantaro rode that horse everywhere, no matter the distance, even though most people thought nothing of walking several miles to accomplish some task or to deliver some message. The Unos were in fact our neighbors, and you could see, though distantly, the back of their bathhouse from our back door. But I admired Kantaro on his horse, trotting down the dirt paths and across our newly cleared fields, the horse's long tail swishing in long silver strands in the sunlight. Despite the backbreaking labor of those early years, Kantaro seemed invigorated and even charmed by the challenge of the work. Some people would have said that this was because Kantaro himself did not labor, that he left the real work of the Uno farm to his parents and to his younger brother Jiro. But to me, Kantaro fulfilled a kind of dream for a young boy, and in those days, I wanted to imitate that particular combination of pride and freedom that Kantaro had so easily adopted.

"Terada-san," Kantaro would call, walking his horse up to the house.

"How is your grandmother?" my mother asked, tiny Kōichi now strapped to her back.

"Not so well. She hasn't been up since yesterday."

"It's the heat," my mother said. "Make sure she takes sips of cool water as often as possible."

Kantaro nodded. He handed my mother a bundle of green leaves. "Mustard greens, cabbage and green onions. My mother sends them. There might have been more if it weren't for the ants."

My mother thanked Kantaro. "I've never seen such large leaves," she exclaimed.

"It's this land. Everything grows quickly and bigger here. Isn't it something!" Kantaro declared. "If only my grandmother would recover enough to let me take her around this new country. I've been riding everywhere, and there is infinite space for the spirit and the imagination."

My mother smiled at this talk of Kantaro's, but I wondered then what he could mean. "Yes," my mother agreed, "we are very fortunate. Very fortunate."

"Well, I promised to see Mizuoka this afternoon. Tsuruta and a group of us are thatching his roof." And Kantaro was off in a gallop down the road to Mizuoka's.

Shūhei Mizuoka had been slow at getting his land cleared and his house built. Although he was a bachelor without a family, he had invested as everyone else in a plot of land. Having neither wife nor children with their more immediate needs, Mizuoka felt that clearing land for planting and a house was of secondary importance. He liked to walk over to see his particular piece of land, observe its dark green and foreboding density in a wistful manner from the road and then walk back to Okumura's long house and spend the rest of the day reading. He was, everyone said, a scholar, more concerned with the expected arrival of a large shipment of books he had personally packaged and mailed himself from Japan than with building a house. "I can't get on with my work until those books arrive," he would say.

"Well," my mother would laugh, "perhaps Mizuoka can be convinced that he needs a house to shelter his books."

When our well was dug and our bathhouse built, my father, too, went off to help Mizuoka complete the preliminary needs of people settling new land. By then, Akira Tsuruta had joined Mizuoka as a sort of hired hand, but Tsuruta, like Mizuoka, was an intellectual sort, a poet, and while full of good intentions, not what one might call a good workhorse. Kantaro Uno soon befriended the young poet Tsuruta and could always be found working at Mizuoka's place with one or two additional young men. Traveling about Esperança on his horse, Kantaro had a way of meeting people and convincing them that they could spare a day or two to help Mizuoka raise a roof or put up a fence. With the additional help of so many concerned neighbors, Mizuoka's place began to take the shape of a small productive farm, despite the fact that Mizuoka himself took little interest in it. I had heard that Kantaro's father, Naotaro, complained of Kantaro's absence from his chores at home, but then, as time went on, Kantaro left more and more of his work at home to his brother Jiro. It became common to hear that Kantaro and his new group of friends had cleared so-and-so's land or dug so-and-so's well. In those early years, we all struggled together as a community, and I think Kantaro, wandering about on his horse with his personable ways and his positive talk, somehow bound us together by bringing us news and collective help.

*   *   *

Every so often, even now, I dream of our first house in Esperança. Perhaps because it was built of mud and sticks which I myself pressed together with my own hands—like Tsuruta's miniature mud village—I have an especially fond memory of that first house.

The house was considered temporary, but nonetheless, we lived in it for several years and for many years after that used it as a shed. The house was made of wood and bamboo slats between which we packed mud. Despite its limited size, this house was built with divisions: two bedrooms and a kitchen, where we spent most of our time. My father built crude but functional beds, chairs and tables. Okumura's wife, Tomi, showed my mother how to make mattresses by piecing together flour sacks and filling them with dried corn husks. At night I liked to settled down into the rustle of the corn husks and stare at the thatching in the roof above.

Takeo Okumura came by personally to assist in building the clay wood-burning stove, which was then torn apart and built up several

times again until it would work without smoking the entire house. I
do not know what the secret was to making a good stove, but there
was a Brazilian who finally came and built such a good stove that my
mother would later often remember the skill of that stove man. Even
when she was able to use a modern gas stove, she mentioned with a
certain nostalgia the taste of food on the old clay stove of our first
house.

In the first days after we arrived in Esperança, we lived in a long
wood-slat and tile-roofed structure which housed our three families
together. The long house was built by Takeo and Tomi Okumura
and two other of the first families to arrive in Esperança. It had already housed several families before us and would house many more
new arrivals after us. It was constructed as temporary housing for
newly arriving settlers until they could clear their lots and build their
own dwellings. In those days, such a house was considered luxuri-
ous. The materials—wood and tile—were transported in at great
sacrifice and on several loads by cart and bull. Okumura felt that
new immigrants needed simple but comfortable and safe housing in
their first days in Esperança. The mud structures we would build to
live in were known to harbor insects with infectious diseases. In later
years, the long house would be transformed into the co-op offices.

Takeo Okumura had been chosen by Momose-sensei to pioneer
the initial clearing and construction of Esperança. He was a quiet but
very firm man. He made deliberate and very careful decisions, spoke
little, and worked tirelessly to help new settlers. He was very relieved
to see my father and mother arrive in Esperança and mentioned this
many times in his very curt and direct way. As soon as we were established in our own house, Okumura brought over his supply of
medications and gratefully turned the responsibility of the settlement's health over to my mother and father. "It's about time you
arrived and took care of these things for me, Terada-san," Okumura
said gruffly.

I had heard many stories about the difficulties of that first year,
when Okumura, his wife, and three other men first came to live in
Esperança, then entirely forest. Okumura was not one to talk about
it much, but Tomi Okumura told my mother, "At first we built a kind
of roof to live under, but that was all. Just a roof. When it rained, it
rained into our shelter, and there was no place to go. What could we
do? We slept in wet blankets. In the daytime, we were attacked by
bees, but at night, it was worse. Grasshoppers and rats crawled all

around and even on top of us. I could never sleep. In the morning, their droppings were everywhere."

My mother shuddered as she spoke."Thanks to you, we don't have to suffer that way."

"Do you know I was all alone in the camp while Okumura and the others set fire to the area? A big boar wandered into camp and I killed it myself with a big stick."

My mother wondered at the courage of this woman, who added as she smiled,"It was very good eating, you know." She paused to think."Things are changing for the better. Especially since you are here now. We've only had this book about first aid." Tomi Okumura showed my mother the book."Here is the chapter on childbirth." She sighed,"It's such a relief that we can depend on you now."

My mother turned the pages of Tomi Okumura's book and smiled. Already she had seen two expectant mothers. Her work as a midwife in Esperança had already begun. Most likely anyone who was born in Esperança between 1925 and 1950 was brought into this world by my mother.

*   *   *

An important part of our lives in Esperança was invested in the co-operative. The co-op naturally evolved from the very structure of our settlement, which was something of a Japanese village. As soon as there were enough families congregated in Esperança and producing more than their personal needs, family heads gathered to pool resources for proper storage, seeds and tools, and to bargain for the best prices. And from the very beginning, all families in Esperança joined in association to make and get loans. The co-op became the economic and political heart of Esperança, and Takeo Okumura was its director. As time went on and Esperança grew to some 250 families, the activities of the co-op grew, and the Esperança Cooperative itself became a very important and profitable entity in the area.

When Okumura first went out to show my father the boundaries of our new land, I went along. He pointed out the measurements across the front of the land along the road. The lots were all measured out in long strips of sixty acres, each lot having access to one of several roads which crisscrossed Esperança. Now we were only a handful of families, but soon there would be over 200 of us. Our lot was several miles from the long house which marked what became the center of Esperança with its co-op offices, store, warehouses and eventually a school and church. Okumura's house was located in this center, and soon, so were the houses of others who worked at the co-op.

My father and I looked at the acreage. It was a green wall of dense forest, trees and vines and brush rising high into the sky. We could not see farther than several meters in from the road. What might be behind that wall of green life, we could not say. When we set fire to the forest, droves of yellow and green parakeets and clattering orange-beaked toucans swept up in great clouds above the flames, while small animals, armadillos, snakes and lizards stumbled and scurried from the smoke. From time to time, wild boar and even a panther might be seen. When the fires died down and the earth was only warm to the touch, the men took long saws and hatchets and cut down the large trees that had not succumbed to the fire. Across the road could be seen the results of the labor of other settlers further along in this enterprise—the charred stumps of enormous trees now hidden in a field of green rice. Soon everything would be very different.

When I think about the old forest, I invariably think about the incredible variety of insects in those days. Along with the occasional appearance of some unusual bird, the great variety of insects that yet remain are a reminder of the wonderfully complex living space the forest once was. When the forest was still intact, you could not light a candle or a lamp at night without being visited by a small dense cloud of moths, butterflies, beetles, mosquitoes, flies, crickets and spiders of every color and description. They flew and crept through our open windows and doors in the hot evenings or congregated near the seeping lights on the walls of our houses. They seemed to us a terrible nuisance, lighting on our bodies to suck our blood or buzzing frantically around, falling into our food and clothing. In the mornings, my mother was forever sweeping out their brittle carcasses. As more and more of the forest was cleared, the number and variety of insects slowly diminished.

Every immigrant remembers the *bicho-de-pé*, an insect which laid its eggs, usually, in your toes or the balls of your feet. We were plagued by these tiny foot worms which grew in soft blisters under the skin and itched terribly. In the evenings, we would gather around a lamp with a needle or the sharp point of a knife and extract the larvae from our feet. When I speak of the *bicho-de-pé* to young people, they always grimace, but old-timers like me became used to this evening occupation. It was something like getting a good massage, if not a new pair of feet.

Berne, however, is something more painful. It too will lay an egg somewhere on your body, and the resulting larva will then penetrate the skin. The skin in that area becomes raised in a painful bump containing a tiny hole in its center. My father was called upon to treat a child with *berne* in her eye, but that was a very extreme case. *Berne* was treated by the locals with a compress of nicotine and soap which would, after a few days and some pressure on the spot, force the *berne* to literally pop out. The Japanese called *berne* the *takenoko* bug because the larva looked very much like a tiny sprout of bamboo, or *takenoko*, about the size of a grain of rice.

It's not possible here to name all the strange bugs we had never before seen. There were the giant *sauva* ants, who came in small armies and could destroy in one evening an entire crop of anything we might have planted. There were poisonous caterpillars whose furry bodies burned our skin. There were giant hairy spiders, sometimes as large as fifteen or twenty centimeters across. There were large ticks whose hard bodies were the size of large watermelon seeds. Those insects that could find food despite the clearing of the forest can still be encountered today, but the strangest and most interesting of them have disappeared with the trees.

Looking out on these endless fields of pasture and planted land today, it is hard to imagine this land as it was then, known only to the wild animals and the Indians. In those days, we thought that the forest was so wide and so deep that it would never end, that carving out our small piece of it wouldn't make such a great difference to something so immense. Besides, we had come to create a new world, and starting on new land was a special and sacred gift given only to a chosen few. Perhaps it was a great sin to destroy the forest in this way. Ever since, we have tried to replace the forest with a new life— growth, sustenance, call it what you will. I have lived here a mere lifetime, but the forest had peacefully existed here for many centuries. What we have taken from the earth will, I think, take many more lifetimes to return in kind. When my father talked of the sin of the immigrant, I believe he meant this sin of clearing the forest away forever.

*   *   *

Toward the end of that first year, Grandma Uno died. Just a month before she died, however, she seemed suddenly to recuperate from a long period of ill health. Just as she had pushed Kantaro aside to walk down the gangway alone to Brazil, she seemed to make a decision to leave her bed. Everyone commented on having seen her riding sidesaddle in Kantaro's lap on the white horse. You could see the two of them riding slowly down the road, Grandma Uno, a gaunt and emaciated remnant of her former self, sitting in Kantaro's lap like a small child, happily looking over the countryside as Kantaro pointed to one thing or another. These rides were never very long or very far, but people still commented among themselves that this must have quickened the end for Grandma Uno. My parents did not support this view, and I myself think that Grandma Uno found great pleasure in these excursions with Kantaro. Sometimes, as I went to the bathhouse near the end of the day, I would see Kantaro and his grandmother slowly returning. Kantaro would stop the horse a little way from the house, and they would both watch the sun set over Esperança, the soft rising swarms of mosquitoes and fireflies speckled against the glowing tones of orange and purple spreading across the darkening sky.

CHAPTER 3: BASEBALL

AFTER WE ARRIVED in Esperança and had settled on our own plots of land, I missed seeing my friend Saburo Uno. Even though we were neighbors, we were separated by sixty acres of land and many chores. But as life settled into certain consistent daily tasks, my parents and other parents in Esperança began to talk about the need for a school and for a proper education for the children. As always, everyone came together to build the school, which they decided to locate a short distance from the old long house. Benches and tables were all hand-carpentered. When the school opened, I could, happily, be with my friend Saburo during a part of each day.

All agreed that Shūhei Mizuoka must be the person to create and maintain our school. I myself now wonder at this unanimous decision (although Saburo, even in those days, contested in his childish way the worthiness of Mizuoka as a teacher). Indeed, Shūhei Mizuoka was a man of tremendous learning, but he was essentially immersed in his own philosophical pursuits. He enjoyed acquiring students in order to talk about his own studious interests, which we often found confusing and thus uninteresting. As Saburo would argue years later, many of us simply needed to learn to read and write and count, and then to learn the skills that would make us good farmers. But Mizuoka insisted that the cultivation of the mind and spirit was essential to the creation of a new civilization, that we, the youth of Esperança, were part of a wonderful new experiment. It was the old Emile experiment: a new breed of youth with clean slates, natural men from a special handful of young Emiles. Mizuoka had the grave responsibility of building the foundation for a cultivated and educated people who took their sustenance from both the fruit of their labor on the land and the joy of their educated minds. Well, Saburo and I had been exposed to this sort of thinking. Even from the time we arrived, Saburo liked to taunt that I was the Japanese Emile. That's how I got the nickname "Emiru."

"Oh, Emiru," Saburo would address me after school as we walked together, "how about this!" He pulled his cap tightly over his head and proceeded to mimic Mizuoka's manner, "Young students of Esperança! A new world of your own making awaits you!" However, other children often wondered what to make of Mizuoka's long digressions into the nature of the Mormon Church as established in the state of Utah in the United States or Tolstoy's asceticism and spiritual beliefs as they developed in the later years of his life or a comparison of the lives of Rousseau and Voltaire. After all, we were farming children, and our ability to survive depended on our skill in turning and sowing the earth's surface.

Still, as the years have passed, many an idea from Mizuoka's old digressions have come to mind and have sustained me in ways I did not expect. Saburo would probably laugh at my example, but the other day while milking a cow, I recalled a few lines that Mizuoka had taught us from the English playwright Shakespeare:

> To thy own self be true,
> And it must follow, as the night the day,
> Thou canst not then be false to any man.

I now wonder at this statement, but Saburo is no longer around to talk of it.

It was Mizuoka's assistant, the poet Akira Tsuruta, who understood our perplexity and who painstakingly worked with each of us to help us read and write and count. Because of Tsuruta, most of the children of the Esperança of those days, unless they were kept away for work at home, received a very refined education. We were taught to read from the works of all the great Japanese poets and writers. And when Mizuoka's great library arrived, we had, I believe, access to all the great literature, philosophy and history of the world that had been translated into Japanese at the time. In addition, Mizuoka, who could read in English, French and German, often produced significant translations of his own, readings to which I politely listened while Saburo nodded off to sleep. Often, people—especially Japanese from Japan—are surprised by the sophistication of my Japanese, my grasp of ideas or my knowledge of foreign countries and writers, but these are largely due to my unconventional tutelage under Shūhei Mizuoka and Akira Tsuruta. Many of the children educated in those early years in Esperança were no different from me.

I think I had greater respect for Mizuoka's learning than did Saburo because of my admiration for his brother Kantaro. When Saburo saw Kantaro, he saw only a young man who happened to be his oldest brother, but I, who was the oldest in my family, felt a great attraction to Kantaro, to the idea of having a strong older brother who rode a horse and recorded our life on a Carl Zeiss box camera. I knew that Kantaro and Tsuruta were close friends and that Kantaro had great respect for Mizuoka. Kantaro thought of Shūhei Mizuoka as his personal teacher, and though he might not have admitted it in later years, I believe that Kantaro received his formal education and established the pattern of his ideas during those many long afternoons and evenings in concentrated discussion with the thinker Mizuoka.

*　*　*

My admiration for Kantaro Uno was perhaps singular until the advent of baseball. It was Kantaro who was responsible for starting baseball in Esperança. Until then, baseball in Brazil was only played by a few Japanese living in the city of São Paulo. These Japanese played in open soccer fields among themselves and occasionally with American businessmen who also enjoyed the game. Baseball, unlike soccer, has never gained general popularity among Brazilians, and it is considered by many in Brazil to be, curiously, a Japanese game. It is odd to discover those things that become a part of one's immigrant heritage. Baseball became a kind of cultural trait to be passed from generation to generation.

I am not sure whether it was Kantaro who promoted baseball or baseball that promoted Kantaro; it was one of those fortunate combinations that makes heroes of athletes and actors. However, I am sure that it was Kantaro who tied baseball to our way of life in Esperança. That the sport of baseball should become part of our immigrant dream sounds strange, but it is true.

"There are many of us young men in Esperança who would be united by baseball," Kantaro affirmed emphatically. "Yes, it's only a game, but it's a game with many virtues."

Tsuruta nodded. "Teamwork . . . Concentration . . . Competition . . . Spirit . . ."

"Recreation," said Mizuoka, closing a book and looking up from his reading. "Leisure!"

Kantaro and Tsuruta looked at Mizuoka with some confusion.

"Why are you afraid of speaking about having fun? You, Kantaro Uno, of all people?" Mizuoka laughed.

"Well," Kantaro said seriously, "there is such great labor to be accomplished in Esperança, it just doesn't seem that we can be encouraging people to spend their time playing baseball without a good reason. So I am thinking of good reasons."

Tsuruta nodded and repeated, "Teamwork, competition, spirit."

Kantaro continued, "The yearly *undokai* when we get together for outdoor games is about our only excuse for fun or leisure."

"Why should you make any excuses?" Mizuoka sniffed. "Do I make excuses for my studies? I know. I know what people say about me: 'That Mizuoka hasn't got his seeds in. Late again this year. All he does is read. If it weren't for our paying his wages at the school, where would he be?' Do I care? What is my answer? My answer is: I came here to Esperança to live! So why do you need to make excuses about wanting to play baseball? Play baseball!"

And so Kantaro Uno played baseball. We all did. It was not as if there were anything to play with. We had to carve our bats from hard Brazilian woods and pack sand and cloth into leather pouches for balls. My three brothers and I marked off a small field and imitated everything that Kantaro and his friends did in their games. Pretty soon there was a commotion over baseball that was to last for many years in Esperança. It was a sort of fever that spread among all the men and boys. Kantaro had soon gathered all of us into teams of varying ages and abilities, and Okumura and the Esperança elders were forced to designate an area of land to be cleared for a legitimate baseball field. On weekends, the baseball field was occupied by a constant string of games, and so many arguments broke out over the use of the field that it had to be carefully scheduled.

As it happened, Kantaro Uno was an excellent baseball player. In Japan, he had taken a team from his school to the prefectural championships, and he was considered, at the time, one of the best young pitchers in the country. Perhaps people don't realize it, but baseball has been popular in Japan since the turn of the century. The Japanese in the city of São Paulo had been playing baseball as early as 1916. Playing baseball was a very serious business with Kantaro, even though Mizuoka called it recreation. Kantaro invested all his time and energy into it. For many years, everything that he participated in somehow involved some aspect of baseball. In a very short period of time, Kantaro had formed a representative Esperança team of our best players. Kantaro's brother Jiro played on the original team as did Tsuruta, who was most likely a bench player. There were others who played on this team, but the player remembered best, besides Kantaro himself, was a young man named Hachiro Yōgu.

*   *   *

Yōgu just seemed to have appeared one day in Esperança. I had heard that he came from a very respectable family; his father was a Christian pastor in Japan. Yōgu must have been a difficult and rebellious youth, and it was said that he had tried to leave Japan as a stowaway three times. Three times he had been caught until his father had taken the advice of Momose-sensei and finally paid for Yōgu's passage to Brazil.

What Yōgu had done in those years previous to appearing in Esperança was something of a mystery to everyone. Some people said that he had lived with the Indians in the Mato Grosso and wandered around with no clothing. Others said that he had been a hired hit man in Pernambuco and had killed a man who'd trespassed on the land of a powerful colonel. Others said that he had been mining gold and diamonds in Goiás. He had a small scar on his forehead which you could see when his hair blew back. People said he got that scar in a knife fight; that he had barely missed losing his eye in that fight. Now that I think of it, everything surrounding the life of Hachiro Yōgu has somehow been exaggerated, even the parts that we knew intimately. Years later, Yōgu himself would probably not know what to make of these stories, but then his memory in later years was something of an enigma.

Whatever Yōgu had been doing in those early years before he came to Esperança, it seemed to have been a rough business, for he arrived with knives in his boots, a pistol in his belt, and a rifle slung over his shoulder. He was dirty and mean and had a habit of spitting when he was nervous. He swaggered about and generally said very little. When he did speak, it was in a rough crude manner which relied on a liberal use of Portuguese epithets. That a colony of Christian intellectuals could adopt such a young man is testimony to our brand of intellectualism. It was Mizuoka who welcomed Yōgu as a sort of noble savage. This was what the Japanese race, unfettered by the tight island society of their past, might produce.

Yōgu had arrived with a very worn, dirty, barely readable letter of introduction from Momose-sensei himself to Okumura. One day on our way to school, Saburo and I witnessed a strange scene: Okumura bowed in prayer with a smelly Japanese *pistoleiro* who grimaced at a mound of dirt in the already grimy and sweaty palm of his hand.

"He's one of us," Saburo remarked in his rather smirking way and not without some delight. We watched with curiosity as Yōgu sulkily divested himself of guns and knives of every description before entering Okumura's house. Beyond the door, we could see Tomi Okumura's eyes pop out round as saucers.

Okumura managed, somehow, to make Yōgu more presentable. After a bath and a shave, Yōgu seemed at first sight just one more young Japanese immigrant looking for a future in Brazil. But Okumura was unable to convince Yōgu that weapons were an unnecessary appendage in a place such as Esperança. After a great deal of measured reasoning, Okumura was able to limit him to a single pistol, which Yōgu wore on a large belt and holster at his side. He had about him the rugged look of a cowboy, the sort I have seen in American movies, but he probably got his demeanor from his rough Brazilian companions from outside the colony. Some newcomers often mistook him for some sort of sheriff or deputy and derived a distant sense of security from his presence. But those of us who thought we knew Hachiro Yōgu saw a volatile and violent man whom Okumura had, by the grace of God, miraculously tamed.

For many days after Yōgu's arrival in Esperança, people wandered in and out of the Okumura household, convinced that Yōgu would commit some sort of horrid crime. My mother went boldly over to spend the evenings with Tomi Okumura under the pretext of Bible studies. She wrapped up her Bible in a *furoshiki* of purple silk and encouraged my father to go with her. "That person is a madman. The Okumuras shouldn't have to shoulder the responsibility of housing such a person, even if he is Japanese, but if this is God's will, then we must show some support." As far as I could tell, Okumura himself did not share my mother's concern.

Saburo's mother, Waka Uno, came to gossip with my mother. They agreed to trade off visiting with Tomi Okumura, each arriving on alternate nights with their Bibles in *furoshikis*.

"I was so reluctant to leave last night," shuddered Waka Uno. "Poor Tomi-san. And he eats so much and has no manners, and he orders her around to get this and that. He puts his feet up on the table and eats right from the cooking pot. And then, when he gets mad, he throws things on the floor. He has already broken dishes and cups, so now she only serves him in metal things. She is such a brave woman."

However, Hachiro Yōgu became daily more manageable. This is not to say that he ever became civilized; he did lose some of his wildness although there was always, it seemed to me, a slightly crazed look somewhere in his eyes. Most people attribute the change in Yōgu to Okumura's unyielding persistence, in this case to integrate Yōgu into the productive life of Esperança. But I suspect that the true reason Hachiro Yōgu began to change was because of Haru Okumura, Okumura's pretty seventeen-year-old daughter.

In those days, there were few young and marriageable women in Esperança. Most women came married with families of their own. On the other hand, Esperança was teeming with young men looking for adventure, fortune, or at least a livelihood with a good future. Most of these young men were attracted to baseball and consequently to Kantaro Uno and his growing group of friends. They gathered in a large group at the Uno farm. They were not only attracted to the camaraderie of Kantaro's group but also by the opportunity to talk frankly with Waka Uno who was, it soon got around, a very willing and able go-between in matters of the heart. If Waka Uno happened to like a particular young man, she would go to great lengths to send his credentials around. Of course, the young man would then have Kantaro take a presentable photograph, and Waka would send the photograph along with a carefully worded letter to an appropriate contact in Japan. Just as my mother was responsible for most of the births in Esperança for many years, it can also be said that Waka Uno was responsible for many of the marriages.

Haru Okumura was special. Being only a boy at the time, perhaps my judgment is askew, but I am inclined to believe that she was special because a rarity, one single woman among so many young men. Yet many people assure me that Haru was considered a great beauty. This must have made some sort of impression on the noble savage, for Hachiro Yōgu began to remove his feet from the table when she entered the kitchen.

By this time, my mother and Waka Uno had also found an answer to the problem of protecting the Okumuras: they sent a strong young man to visit every evening and make his presence felt as a sort of bodyguard. The strong young man they chose was Kantaro. And that was how Kantaro met Hachiro Yōgu.

It must have been a strange meeting. Kantaro was becoming a very intense young man with a manner of talking much akin to Mizuoka's philosophizing. But Kantaro was different from Mizuoka in that he seemed to be able to remove the scholarly dust from Mizuoka's ideas and invest them with a sense of freshness and vitality. And more interesting yet, Kantaro somehow had tied baseball to Mizuoka's philosophy about the New World and a new civilization. Yōgu shrugged at all of this as so much nonsense. Kantaro was a youthful positivist full of exuberance, dancing about a Yōgu who sulked warily, peering into shadows like a hunted animal. "Baseball?" Yōgu snickered. "You gonna play baseball in this hellhole of a Brazil? What stinking nonsense. Ha ha ha!"

Kantaro walked around the room, measuring the distances, and set his box camera on its tripod. Unaffected by Yōgu's words, he insisted, "Well, you can laugh, but I came here to make a new home. When you can make something anew, you have the freedom to experiment. Why don't you give it a try?"

"Experiment, he says. Experiment? Ha! Idiot. You wanna know why I came to Brazil? You wanna know why? I hated Japan. I wanted to escape from Japan. And don't try to take my picture."

"Well, that may be," Kantaro nodded and continue to position his machine. He looked through the lens at Yōgu. "But that's all the more reason for you to want to take advantage of your freedom. That is what Esperança is all about."

"Esperança? I don't know why I ever came here. It looks like Japan here. All you Japanese walking around like you are God's gift to Brazil."

"As a matter of fact . . . " Kantaro looked up and smiled.

"God's gift from Japan!" Yōgu roared, laughing hysterically.

"Why did you come here? I mean, besides not liking Japan, why did you come to Esperança?"

"Do you really want to know?" Yōgu leaned over meaningfully. "I'm hiding," he hissed between his teeth. "What better place? Esperança, a loving Christian colony of Japanese intellectuals and communists. Aren't you all hiding? I fit right in, don't I?"

"I suppose so," Kantaro nodded.

"Why don't you take my picture with me holding my gun?" Yōgu produced his pistol and pointed it at the camera."

"Don't move," Kantaro ordered.

Yōgu sat back and posed arrogantly.

"But why are you all so afraid? You think I don't know? You think I think this is just Esperança's way of greeting a newcomer: come sit in the parlor with poor Okumura-no-okusan and her sweet daughter, Haru, every night just to chat? Now they send you—a rotten excuse for a real man—Esperança's best, to watch the animal in Okumura's house! Well come watch if you want, but I don't want to hear your foolish talk about freedom. You don't understand anything!"

"Have you ever played baseball?" Kantaro insisted, unperturbed.

"Baseball! Baseball! Is that all you can think about? Of course I played baseball."

"Well, I'm the best," remarked Kantaro.

"Is that so?"

"We practice every afternoon at five until the sun goes down. If you can really play, I'll expect you at the field." Kantaro snapped the shutter. It's the portrait of the Hachiro Yōgu we all remember.

As it turned out, Yōgu played baseball. He played with his pistol at his side, and despite what should have been an impediment, Yōgu was extremely fast. It was soon apparent to Kantaro that Yōgu was a natural shortstop—nothing seemed to slip by him. There are many stories about Yōgu and baseball, the truth of which no one is sure. But Saburo and I were there the day when Yōgu joined the team, and I can testify to this particular story. Saburo and I had run over to the field from school that day as we often did. Saburo stopped short and nudged me as I ran into him, "Look, Emiru. It's him. Is he really going to play?"

Yōgu stood at one end of the field in the stance of a man who had come to accept a duel. He watched while Kantaro put the team through a series of preliminary exercises: stretching, sit-ups, push-ups, jumping jacks, running in place. Kantaro had an extremely efficient and regimented method of baseball training, which he did not veer from. As time went on and the stakes became greater, the program became even more severe in nature.

Kantaro seemed to ignore Yōgu at first, and the team formed units to field, catch and bat. Kantaro began to pitch and, after pitching to several batters, motioned to Yōgu to join the line of batters. Yōgu sauntered up with a bat, spitting territorially around the plate.

Saburo squatted down to watch, but I stood anxiously. There was a wonderful tension in the air, and Kantaro played that tension very coolly. I watched my hero eye Yōgu coldly, assessing his competitor, collecting energy from within. Yōgu spat nervously. I held my breath. Kantaro snapped the ball, and it seemed to me that it spun to its mark like lightning.

"*Filha da puta!*" growled Yōgu in Portuguese.

A second pitch came homeward.

"Strike!" I spoke out loud in spite of myself.

This time Yōgu had spun around as he wildly lashed with his bat. I could not help but suppress a smile of glee, but Saburo pulled his cap over his forehead and muttered glumly, "Hit it. Why can't you hit it?"

After that, there was a series of pitches which Yōgu popped foul. "That's it," prompted Saburo. "Hit it." And then, unexpectedly, Yōgu slammed the next pitch high into the air. Kantaro himself ran beneath the ball, waiting for it to fall neatly into his glove. Suddenly there was an explosion which made Saburo jump up, and the ball shattered in the air. Then we all looked with astonishment at Yōgu, who was calmly examining the hot barrel of his pistol.

CHAPTER 4: HARU

THERE HAS BEEN MUCH DISCUSSION over the years as to how beautiful Haru Okumura really was and what exactly attracted Kantaro Uno to her side. Now, when you look at that old grandmother, it seems astonishing that she could have been the participant in a great love story told over and over by the old-timers of Esperança.

There are many photographs taken by Kantaro of Haru, and she appears in the them with the innocent bloom of life and the same happy smile recognizable today. As I have said, some people believe that it was the dearth of women that made Haru so attractive, but I am also inclined to believe that it was Kantaro's passion that singled out Haru from all others. Certainly, when Kantaro was an old man, he himself wondered at Haru's former reputation and concluded that he himself had made her beautiful. That aging men like myself and Kantaro should talk so callously about the former beauty of a woman is, of course, laughable, if not unforgivable. Yet, I am reminded of my own uncontrollable passion for a young woman of great beauty; the anxiety I suffered is now only a memory. Like Kantaro, I myself wonder at the madness of my youthful attraction.

To my boyish mind, Kantaro Uno was a marvelous hero on a white horse, and it seemed impossible that anyone could resist that wonderful image. Of course, my best friend Saburo had very little concern for the great exploits of his older brother and passed off my admiration with scorn.

"Tell me about the darkroom, Sabu. I want to know," I asked Saburo. "What does Kantaro do to make the pictures turn into pictures?"

"Emiru, who cares? I don't want to hear any more about that camera or those photos or about him." This seemed to be a case of sibling envy, which I put aside as I did so much of Saburo's growing cynicism. However, when I heard that Haru Okumura had rejected Kantaro's offer of marriage, I felt a great deal of confusion. Perhaps women had a very different perception of what is wonderful. Besides, marriages were arrangements, decisions by parents and families which no young man and, especially, no young woman would reject. But Haru had rejected Kantaro. This created a flurry of gossip in the colony and much speculation. If Haru could reject the most eligible young man in Esperança, the captain of the baseball team, the documenting photographer with the Carl Zeiss box camera, the personable and charming young man on the white horse, a person who many treated as a sort of aristocratic prince from a formerly well-to-do but fallen family, and a man who was beginning to articulate a newfound exuberance among the young men of Esperança, then who does Haru want to marry anyway?

The colony buzzed back and forth with new developments, but Haru remained impassive. Kantaro, on the other hand, seemed oblivious to his failure, which he deemed temporary in nature.

Meanwhile, Waka Uno and Tomi Okumura had run into some mis-understanding and were now not talking to each other. I heard all the gossip in my mother's kitchen; pregnant women steadily descended upon our house, keeping my mother informed of new de-velopments.

"Do you think it could be that Yōgu?" someone considered with some outrage.

"Haven't you noticed the change in him? He takes a bath every day now."

"Maybe he is holding the Okumuras hostage."

"Nonsense. He's become a very close friend of Kantaro's. Kan-taro has brought him around all right."

I heard Haru is secretly interested in that shy one who works for the co-op."

"The accountant?"

"No. The little driver."

"Ridiculous. He's too skinny. If he picked up a bat, he'd fall over on his face!"

"That Kantaro is so handsome. What's the matter with Haru any-way?"

"Have you thought about it? Maybe it's not Haru. Maybe Oku-mura-san doesn't like Kantaro."

In the meantime, Kantaro visited Haru every evening after base-ball practice. He was relentless in his visits. He could be found in the Okumura kitchen each night without fail, his horse grazing quietly beneath a great *paineira* tree at the side of the house. Kantaro was often accompanied by other young men, all hopeful of being recog-nized by Haru in some manner, believing that their chances were just as good as Kantaro's. Often the entire baseball team was seen milling around Okumura's place, spilling out into the yard, washing vege-tables for Tomi, resetting a fallen fence or patching a barn roof. Haru politely greeted all the men, serving coffee, baking large sheets of cake and patting hot rice and pickles into balls.

Not only did Kantaro visit Haru daily, he spent his evenings at home writing Haru long letters. No one really knew what these let-ters were about. All they knew was that Kantaro presented Haru with a letter almost daily. It is said that she herself never responded, certainly not in a written form, to any of Kantaro's letters. Many people have since expressed a curiosity to read the contents of those passionate missives. Kantaro himself felt that they were a special document of this period in his life, of romance and purity of feeling and the youthful energy that portended a great future. I have imagined these letters as if I myself had known Kantaro's thoughts in those days. I am sure that they were not love letters in the ordinary sense nor even proclamations of Haru's beauty, but that they were an outpouring of belief, a testament of ideals. The letters carried, I am sure, Kantaro's sentiments about his life in Esperança and must have been sprinkled with the principal ideas of those writers Mizuoka had encouraged him to read, the Russian writer Tolstoy and the Japanese philosopher Mushanokoji, for example. I would often see Kantaro ambling home from Mizuoka's on his horse. If it were still light enough to see, Kantaro would be immersed in a book, the horse left to bring its traveler home without direction from the rein. I believe it is fair to say that Haru could make little out of those letters and that they must have confused rather than impressed her. Haru was, after all, a simple girl; she had come to Brazil with her parents when she was twelve years old, before she had completed her education. The Okumuras had had no time to bother with the education of a daughter, even if they believed in such an extravagance. They had struggled tirelessly to build a Christian colony for Japanese settlers, the benefits of which were certainly far in the future. Takeo Okumura was an educated man, but he was also a man of few words—Haru would not have gleaned an education from him—and Tomi Okumura was a hardworking woman from a farming family whose reading must have been limited to delving occasionally into a puzzling scripture in the Bible. The most Haru could have done with Kantaro's letters was to count them occasionally and arrange them by date. When you consider Kantaro's passion from Haru's point of view, it is easy to see why she might have rejected his offer of marriage. While flattered to be the center of so much attention, Haru must have felt unequipped to manage such fervent outpourings, much less the minutiae of his philosophical wanderings.

But there was, I later discovered, another reason why Haru first rejected Kantaro, a reason considered but immediately discounted by everyone: Hachiro Yōgu. Yōgu lived in the corner of a small shed outside of the Okumura house. Like other young bachelors attached to families, he was hired to do the chores around the farm. He was, at first, as I've said, an impossible man, creating havoc in the Okumura household. Only such a stubborn man of solid faith as Okumura could have ever kept Yōgu. Tomi Okumura bit her lip and smiled frailly, obedient to her husband's intentions, but Haru was never such an easy woman. One day, Yōgu sauntered into the kitchen, his muddy boots dragging in clumps of red dirt. Haru was washing dishes in a large basin of soapy water near an open window. "Hey you," Yōgu growled, swinging his boots and all the mud onto the kitchen table. "Coffee. Make me some coffee."

In the next second Haru began throwing soapy pans, cups and dishes, the entire contents of her basin at the surprised Yōgu. "You want coffee?" she screamed hysterically. "Here is coffee!" She flung the dark muddy contents of a large pot at Yōgu, who had by then drawn his pistol and was shooting angrily into the kitchen ceiling. "Kill me!" screamed Haru. "Kill me!" she threatened, grabbing a large knife from her basin.

Yōgu backed warily out of Haru's kitchen and sulked around the house. As he passed her window, Haru flung the remaining dirty dishwater out the window at Yōgu. Yōgu stood for a long moment under the window, looking through the stinging suds at Haru as tears of anger spilled from her eyes. Her face was flushed, her breasts heaved beneath a calico dress, all outlined perfectly by the wooden frame of the open window. He could see her in a rainbow, a picture he would never forget. Yōgu fell in love with Haru Okumura, and he fell in love with the real Haru, the strong, angry, stubborn, often foolish but certainly courageous Haru.

On the day that this happened, Saburo and I were walking home from school, and we could hear the shots from the road. We ran toward the house, and when we got there, we saw Tomi Okumura and Haru outside of the house struggling with a large hoe between themselves. "Mother!" Haru yelled. "Stop it! Nothing happened! Nothing happened!"

Tomi Okumura fell back with a thud into the dirt with the hoe. She had run from the field with the hoe, which she must have intended to use on Yōgu. Yōgu was standing in the doorway of the shed with his wet hair and his shirt plastered to his body. Tomi Okumura flew at him like a protective mother hen, but Yōgu closed the shed door in her face. Before he closed the door, I thought I saw his gaze wander to Haru, who now wore a queer smile on her lips.

If Haru reciprocated Yōgu's affections in any way, no one really knew. She seemed to have the same smile for all her admirers but an intimidating scowl for Yōgu. Saburo and I walked as always, passing the Okumura's house every day to and from school, and on several occasions I saw Haru looking out her window or sitting and staring from her porch. On those occasions, Yōgu was always nearby working, chopping wood or digging and setting posts for a new fence. Several times Saburo and I paused to watch Yōgu at his target practice, a series of bullet-ridden cans flying from a fence railing. In the distance, I could see Haru's figure wandering to and from her window.

One day, my father sent me to deliver a package of medicine to the Okumuras. When I arrived at the house, there was a young Brazilian sitting at Okumura's table. It was the Bahiano himself. I stood shyly near the door with my package, somewhat intimidated by the Bahiano, but Tomi Okumura sat me down with a piece of cake. The Bahiano was a young man in his twenties, but he already had a fierce reputation for being easily angered, and it seemed no mistake that despite his youth, everything in the nearby town of Santa Cruz d'Azedinha was under his control. The Bahiano's real name was Floriano Raimundo, but as it was said that he had come from Bahia in the northeast of Brazil, everyone had taken to calling him the Bahiano. When the Bahiano came to Santa Cruz d'Azedinha, he was only seventeen years old but already had earned his reputation. He had been bequeathed a large section of land surrounding Santa Cruz, which was, when he arrived, a mere outpost in the forest. The Bahiano, people said, had received this land from a wealthy colonel by whom the Bahiano had been employed, everyone suspected, as a skillful applier of pressure. The stories that surround the Bahiano of this early period are similar to the ones you hear about Hachiro Yōgu. Both were schooled in the rugged ways of the men who came to open this frontier. The Bahiano was not a physically large or imposing man; at seventeen, he could not have looked very impressive, a young upstart at best. I can only speculate that he must have seemed mad, an intense glint of craziness swirling in his eyes that made people very wary.

The Bahiano had spread out a large map of Esperança and the surrounding area. There was a red line drawn across an existing dirt road and cutting through the forest to the town where we had first arrived by train. "Okumura," he spoke with authority despite his youth, "I estimate three months of hacking away at that forest. If you can get your crew together, I'll get mine. You start from this end. We start from our end. Meet in the middle. This road is essential to the development of this area."

Okumura nodded and answered in Portuguese, "I will bring it up at our next meeting, but I think everyone agrees that a road is needed. Now, will you join us for a modest meal?"

Okumura stepped outside to wash his face from the well, but the Bahiano remained in the kitchen. His eyes turned to a large bowl of some strange meat. "Dona," he addressed Tomi Okumura, "what might that be?"

At this moment, Yōgu stepped into the kitchen, his face glowing from his evening bath. He seemed to enter the kitchen rather warily.

Tomi Okumura answered the Bahiano's question. "Frog legs. My husband likes them very much," she said in halting Portuguese.

"Frog legs?" The Bahiano repeated with a certain disdain. "You will excuse me, Dona, but rattlers, armadillos, alligators—I know there's people who swear by them, but it's never my preference. Only meat I'll ever put between my teeth is beef." The thought of eating frog legs obviously dismayed the Bahiano. "You Japanese are more adventurous than most." He shook his head.

Yōgu said nothing. He hated frog legs. Yōgu moved his gaze toward the door of the kitchen and watched with some expectation as Haru moved into the kitchen with a large basket of washed vegetables. Haru ignored Yōgu and smiled graciously at the Bahiano. Then she did a funny thing which I will never forget. She walked over to the large bowl of skinned frog legs, the shiny pink meat glistening in her mother's concoction of lime juice and salt. Right there, oblivious to the astonished stare of the Bahiano, Haru picked up a raw frog leg and began to chew noisily, ripping the meat off the tiny bones with her teeth and swallowing everything with great relish. The Bahiano, who had a reputation not unlike Yōgu's for killing men and beasts that might get in his way, watched Haru with a morbid interest, and when the Bahiano later recalled this incident, he compared it to several stories about animals he had seen eating other animals.

A bright dancing look of delight flashed across Yōgu's face as Haru continued to chew and pick at the frog legs. She might have eaten several more except that Tomi Okumura removed the bowl from Haru's hungry reach. I was never quite sure why Haru had eaten those raw frog legs, whether it was to shock the Bahiano or to impress Yōgu, or because she was very hungry. In speaking of a woman who was considered to be at one time the beauty of Esperança, this incident must indeed seem strange. Of course, Yōgu thought Haru all the more beautiful because of it. I do not, however, think it stranger than Yōgu's attachment to his pistol or Kantaro's devotion to baseball. All of us who came to and grew up in Esperança were roughly hewn, completing our education with life in quite unpredictable ways. That Haru could be beautiful and also slightly wild is hardly surprising.

Kantaro, wrapped up in his reading, his passion and his outpouring of ideas both spoken and in his voluminous letters, never, I believe, quite saw Haru as Yōgu must have seen her. Had Kantaro lived with the Okumuras as Yōgu did, perhaps his perception of her might have been very different, but perhaps not. In baseball, Kantaro showed himself to be a young man of great determination; he did not like to lose. He had set his heart on what he determined must be the best and most beautiful: the lovely daughter of the leader of our community. Certainly, like all young men, he must have seen the small things in Haru that teased his desire—the wisps of fallen hair, the curve of her lips, the movement of her body, the music in her voice—but at the same time, this Haru that Kantaro saw was a Haru that he imagined, a Haru that lived among the pages of Tolstoy's great romances, flirted in distant ballrooms, lived, laughed, suffered and felt greatly.

This is not to say that there were not in Esperança women of learning; perhaps even more astonishing than Shūhei Mizuoka's scholarship in this backwoods Japanese farming colony in Brazil was the degree of education held by a few of the women. Kantaro's mother was educated at a famous women's Christian college in Tokyo. My own mother was educated and trained in midwifery. There were women versed in tea ceremony and flower arrangement, and there was a club of women who gathered occasionally to write poetry. In those days, when most Japanese immigrants—men and women—found themselves on coffee plantations struggling from daybreak to darkness in backbreaking labor, it seems more than amazing. I saw my mother struggle with her duties on our farm, care for five rambling and rambunctious boys and work tirelessly with pregnant mothers and their growing children. Unlike the men, who could abandon their work on the weekends for baseball, women had to accomplish innumerable chores—washing, mending, cooking—in those spare moments after the work in the field was done. Women like Waka Uno saw their education and cultural talents put to quite different uses, and I doubt if anyone really practiced tea ceremony or flower arranging. Still, it was the nature of Esperança to brag of this basis for a new civilization, and for this reason, we were called the *ginbura* or Ginza-strolling colonists, as if to say that we had come to Brazil much in the manner of a stroll along the Ginza, bringing with us the chic sophistication of that Tokyo district. Visitors were always impressed by two things which seemed to be an outward expression of our cultured inhabitants: the flower beds which graced the humble simplicity of our houses and the sweet song of a woman accompanying herself with a piano.

The piano arrived in Esperança about the same time as Hachiro Yōgu. It was shipped at great expense from São Paulo for Kimi Kawagoe, the daughter of a former banker turned Christian convert. If Haru was slightly wild, Kimi was completely tamed. She had, in contrast to Haru, a very controlled elegance, the sort people seem to admire in the Empress of Japan. Kimi had enjoyed a rarefied education, an education meant originally to prepare her to marry into a fine family. What Kimi was doing in Esperança might possibly be explained, but what she was doing in Brazil is beyond all comprehension. Kimi was slightly older than Haru. She had a younger brother named Heizo, who played second base with Kantaro. In those days, Kimi often seemed like a pretty bird in a cage, her singular expression of freedom from so many self-imposed social restrictions being her voice. Singing and playing the piano was Kimi's way of bearing her life in a rustic setting. There were several young men interested in Kimi at the time, but she responded to them with extremely reserved politeness.

*   *   *

The preoccupations of courting and the attendant gossip were temporarily curtailed by the prospect of taking the Esperança baseball team to São Paulo for a showdown with the city team. This game was accidentally arranged by Takeo Okumura through a boast—thought to be rather uncharacteristic of our stoic leader—about having a strong team of hard-hitting young men who could easily defeat the older and more complacent São Paulo team. Of this victory, Kantaro had no doubt, and he went about training his team with an even more rigorous schedule than before. There was a great deal of excitement generated by the prospect of going to São Paulo to play baseball. For us, living in the rural backwaters, the distant São Paulo was and still is a great metropolitan center. There was a great deal of pride involved in showing our best.

As Okumura had predicted, the Esperança team came away victors, claiming a title we would hold for many years hence. From this time on, baseball rapidly spread among the Japanese settlements, and wherever a new settlement grew up, a new baseball team was naturally formed. Kantaro and his teammates traveled as far south as Três Barras and Londrina in Paraná and as far west as Campo Grande in Mato Grosso to play baseball and garner points for a much disputed series. And everywhere the Esperança team went, people remembered Kantaro Uno, the determined young pitcher with the fastest pitch in the colony, the young Japanese immigrant who played baseball because he had come to live in Brazil. "People always ask the same questions," said Kantaro. "How is it that people in the rural backwoods, pioneering a new settlement and opening virgin forests, have the time to play baseball? I always answer that we in Esperança have come to build a new life, and sports, like other cultural pursuits, must be a part of this new life. In the mornings, we open new roads and clear new land. In the afternoon, we play. Without this element of leisure, how could we be a whole people? We in Esperança have come to Brazil to settle and to create. We are unlike others who have come here to make money and return with monetary wealth to Japan." Many people thought this talk so much nonsense, the justification of Christians and socialists who had not found acceptance in Japan, but many others were impressed.

It was said that after Kantaro returned from that first victory in São Paulo, there was a definite change in his demeanor; he returned more aggressive, more certain of himself. This seems natural enough for a young hero and team leader, but years later I heard an interesting story about the team's visit to São Paulo. It was during this visit that Kantaro first met Shigeshi Kasai, the defiant young publisher of the first Japanese newspaper in Brazil, the *Brazil Shimpo* (News). Kasai was a journalist with a very witty and often wicked pen. The establishment within the Japanese colony was horrified that anyone could write, especially in Japanese, the sort of editorials and stories Kasai delighted in. This establishment quickly financed a second newspaper of a more conservative tone, which haughtily flaunted its respectability. But Shigeshi Kasai was, among other things, an occasional gambler, and he gambled that this competition would help sell an even greater number of newspapers for him. In fact, people, despite their private or public opinions, were always curious and amused by the newspaper feud. Kasai also played third base for the

São Paulo team, but he was immediately impressed with the captain of the Esperança team, the mean pitcher from the backwoods whose head was filled with romance and high ideals. There was later some gossip that Kasai entered a pool of bets favoring the Esperança team over his own.

Looking back into the old issues of the *Brazil Shimpo*, there is an interesting description by Kasai of the Esperança team:

> I have had the honor of meeting the fine team of men from Esperança. If ever the São Paulo team, of which I myself am a member, deserved to lose a game, it was this one. There is no comparison to their worthiness as opponents, their force of spirit, their intuition as a team. Exceptional men are to be found pioneering and opening the virgin lands of the rural interior.

What Kasai did not mention was the short excursion he gave the innocent Esperança team into the basement print shop of his newspaper business. This was a dirty, cluttered place splattered with black ink, type set into tiny pigeonholes everywhere, paper piled in stacks. "Please excuse the mess," he apologized to the team, wiping his spectacles with a handkerchief soiled with ink. "It's really unforgivable to perform a ceremony of this nature in such an environment, but certainly the Emperor will forgive his poor subjects on the other side of the world." The team members stood soberly before a velvet-covered box supposedly housing a photograph of the Emperor.

It was common in those days in schools and public ceremonies in Japan to pay homage to the picture of the Emperor. A command was given, the veil lifted, and everyone bowed before the picture. Kantaro and his team hadn't had to bow before the Emperor's picture since leaving Japan. They supposed that this must be the sort of thing that you do in the city after winning a baseball game. They had not questioned this act in Japan, and they were not about to question it in São Paulo. Only Yōgu fidgeted nervously in the crowded print shop basement. "I'm not doing this, Kantaro. This is not baseball," he growled under his breath.

"Do it anyway," murmured Kantaro.

"I should have brought my gun."

"What for?"

"I don't like this," he complained.

Suddenly Kasai had the velvet curtain removed from the box, and all the team members bowed their heads, never daring to look at the revered face. Kantaro felt Yōgu nudging him from the side. *"Filha da puta! Filha da puta!"* he cursed.

Kantaro turned to see Yōgu snickering at the box which contained, of all things, a chamber pot. Inside the chamber pot was an erotic drawing in the style of *ukiyoe* of a man and a woman, their larger-than-life genitals exposed between the layered folds of their clothing. What significance this rebellious moment might have held for the innocent and earnest Kantaro I have often wondered.

In a photograph made of the team before leaving for São Paulo, you can see a kind of purity in the eyes of these serious and determined young men. Was there something I did not see or understand behind those expressions even then? I do not know. You cannot blame the playful and more mature Kasai for this odd moment, in which Kantaro's vision of the world possibly became tainted and skewed. The wry journalist had a strong political vision, which he felt at liberty to express, but his dreams were no less ideal than Kantaro's. Shigeshi Kasai was a man who loved to do political battle; he had come to Brazil for that very reason. Suddenly, for Kantaro, the freedom of this New World became quite stretched. Politics and sex: it was more than Kantaro had imagined, different from Yōgu's rustic rebellion or the power of a mere pistol, and certainly different from baseball.

* * *

When Kantaro returned to Esperança, he was full of new ideas. The city had, as he would say again and again, refreshed and redirected his outlook. He was more determined than ever to spread baseball among the young Japanese men of Brazil, to create a strong connection among them which would eventually forge a powerful unity. Kantaro had the idea that someone should return to Japan to get special baseball training, buy badly needed equipment and return to Brazil.

The baseball team, its fans and stragglers all met one evening at the Uno farm. Even I was there with Saburo, despite Saburo's sullen attitude about anything to do with Kantaro.

"Even if we make a choice about who will go to Japan," said Tsuruta, "where will we get the money for passage, not to mention money for the baseball equipment?"

"Maybe we can convince the co-op to create a baseball fund," someone laughed.

"We will hire ourselves out," said Kantaro. "Okumura needs a crew to open a road into Santa Cruz d'Azedinha. We will offer our services."

"Okumura has no money in the co-op to pay for a crew. He expects us to volunteer."

"Then we can hire ourselves out to farms all over. The big plantations pay daily wages for clearing land."

"I can charge for photographs," suggested Kantaro. It had been said he'd spent all his money in the city on photographic developer and paper. "People always want photographs of themselves to send to their relatives."

"The rice harvest is coming in another few weeks. A lot of people will need help. Working together, we can certainly make enough money."

"As for baseball equipment," said Kantaro, "I've been talking to several team captains from other settlements. Everyone is interested in getting equipment. They'll be happy to send our man with money to buy what they need."

After much talk and discussion, the choice of who would return to Japan on the great mission of bringing back expertise and actual equipment had been whittled down to a few team members. "Now we draw straws," announced Kantaro. "A long straw goes to Japan." What strange fortune played in this drawing of straws, I do not know, but the winner of the long straw was Hachiro Yōgu.

By now, it was true, the people in Esperança were all quite used to Yōgu, but this choice did not seem to anyone except the members of the baseball team to be a wise choice. When Kantaro came to collect a donation for the team to send Yōgu to Japan, my father spoke honestly. "I've my reservations about this. It's one thing to praise a man for his talent, but to reward him by sending him to Japan and then to entrust this person with hard-earned money to buy baseball equipment . . . I'd think you might have chosen someone more trustworthy than Yōgu."

"I have lived and worked with Yōgu, Terada-san," Kantaro argued. "He is like a brother to me. No matter what people see or hear, I can vouch for the honesty of this man. I would not endorse this trip if I were not sure."

My father shook his head. "If you want to come to work for me, I'll be more than happy to pay you for your labor. I've got a field that needs to be weeded, and I could use some help threshing rice. But until I get some better assurance about the character of the man you will send with my money, I won't have any part of it."

"I'm sorry that's the way you feel, but I am sure that Yōgu will prove that you and the others are wrong."

When Kantaro left, my mother said, "Weren't you a little hard on him?"

"His own father wouldn't tell him any differently, if he has," my father quipped. "If he has," he repeated.

Most likely Naotaro had said something to Kantaro, but Kantaro was not the sort of son to listen. I had heard that Naotaro Uno had often complained that Kantaro contributed less and less around the family farm, leaving most of the work to his younger brother Jiro. I had also heard Naotaro accept people's praise of his oldest son, saying that perhaps it was true, after all, Kantaro belonged not to the Unos but to Esperança.

This sounded generous, this giving up of one's son to the greater cause, but on the other hand, I also remember the day Naotaro ran after Kantaro with a shotgun. The rice harvest had been in full swing in Esperança, and it would prove to be our largest. Everywhere the golden grain ripened in the tropical sun. The new settlers had planted it in all available soil, between the charred stumps of fallen trees, right up to their houses and skirting the roads like a great waving carpet. After it was cut, my brothers and I pounded the small bundles of rice to thresh out the grains until our arms ached. Kantaro's team had gone everywhere to hire out for the harvest, but they still needed a great deal more money to send Yōgu to Japan. One day, the team pulled up at the Uno farm with a large truck and began to fill it with the drying bales of rice. Jiro came from the field in surprise. "Where are you taking the rice?"

"I've found a buyer!" exclaimed Kantaro.

"But this rice is not for sale. We are going to store it for the year for ourselves," contested Jiro. "I've been working on the silo for several days now. Father has decided—"

"But this price is unbeatable," Kantaro interrupted. "And it will put us over the top in our campaign."

"Campaign?"

"Yes. Now we'll have the money to send Yōgu to Japan."

At this moment, Naotaro came running from the house. "What's happening?" he demanded.

Jiro ran up to his father trying to explain. While Kantaro loaded the truck, I could see Naotaro run back into the house and emerge again with a long shotgun. The rice was now loaded into the truck; Kantaro jumped onto the back as it pulled away. Naotaro, still a spry man in his fifties, ran down the road after the truck, shooting angrily at the tires, but the truck sped off, coughing up a cloud of red dust. Naotaro slammed the shotgun into the dirt in frustration, his chest heaving angrily. He looked across his fields, empty of rice, a dry patchwork of earth and stubble. "Where is he taking our rice?"

Jiro ran up from behind, his words spilling out in short gasps. "Esperança, Esperança," Jiro wheezed. "Kantaro said it wasn't our rice. He said it belonged to Esperança."

A few weeks later, Yōgu left Esperança with several carefully worded letters of introduction, some very detailed instructions and a large amount of money to buy baseball equipment.

And Kantaro asked Haru, for perhaps the third and final time, if she would marry him. Once again, Haru refused.

CHAPTER 5: KIMI

AFTER YŌGU HAD LEFT FOR JAPAN, a kind of sigh seemed to pass through Esperança, the subject of all our gossip and disagreements having slipped from our very lips. Those who had contributed money to Kantaro's campaign to send Yōgu to Japan faced off against those who had not. Those who had supported Kantaro's idea suggested that those who had not were people who lacked imagination and vision, people who lacked the stuff that Esperança was founded upon: dreams. And those who had refused Kantaro's request wondered at the sanity and good reason of those who entrusted hard-earned money to a ruffian like Hachiro Yōgu.

And now with Yōgu gone and the money gone as well, even among the believers there was a sudden sense of misgiving and doubt. Some wondered sheepishly if they would ever see their money again, in the form of baseball equipment or in any other form for that matter. And those who had held on to their money wondered if they had misjudged Yōgu and therefore lost a chance to buy into a dream. Little did we realize that the judgments which divided us in this matter would harden into more serious disagreements in later years. For the moment, however, all of us felt a mixture of relief and nostalgia in Yōgu's absence.

I could tell that my friend Saburo, although he would never admit it, was especially depressed by Yōgu's absence. I think that Saburo had found in Yōgu a man to challenge Kantaro. There was something in Saburo that would never accept his brother. Yōgu had taken a liking to Saburo, who was, like Yōgu, a sort of loner. It was Yōgu who had taught Saburo to ride Kantaro's horse, something of which I was extremely jealous. I felt that Kantaro's horse was something attached to Kantaro both personally and physically; that Saburo should have the opportunity to ride this magnificent beast was more than I could bear. For many days I would not speak to my friend, believing foolishly that he had betrayed a special trust. My hurt feelings were suddenly banished one day when Saburo and Yōgu chose to surprise me in the most unforgettable way.

On this particular day, Yōgu had come to us after school with two mounts, Kantaro's horse and another I did not recognize. "Come on, Emiru," Yōgu had invited gruffly. "You ride this one."

I was much too proud to accept his invitation. I did not even look to see Saburo mount the horse, set his cap, tug the reins and press the animal proudly into a gallop down the road. Now I feel ashamed to have ignored my friend's happiness, knowing how elusive Saburo found that happiness to be. As I walked home alone filled with anger, I thought that I could never again be reconciled to our old friendship. I walked slowly, knowing that every step brought me closer to a series of chores I would be expected to do when I arrived. My steps were heavy with the thought of this drudgery. From our house, I could hear the clatter of pots and pans and the stirring of voices within. I felt mute with my own anger and ran toward the house, hoping that no one would notice my recent tears. As I stepped over the threshold I was caught unaware by the smell of fresh manure and the high surprised whinny of a horse. There, squeezed into the space of our kitchen, were Yōgu and Saburo, still astride their mounts, pacing about with all the aloofness of being in a stable. The horses had dipped their snouts into a large basket of vegetables and bananas, and Yōgu neatly speared a large piece of cake with his knife.

"Emiru!" announced Saburo, tugging his cap to its traditional angle.

"We thought we'd surprise you," said Yōgu, leaning over and spearing another piece of cake as the horse reared, upsetting a pot of beans stewing on the stove.

"This was the only place we could find to hide," suggested Saburo happily.

I looked around the kitchen. There were broken dishes and toppled tins and a mess of vegetables and horse droppings all over my mother's kitchen floor. I felt a sense of panic and delight.

"Come on," said Yōgu. "Now you ride. You ride out of here before you get in trouble." Yōgu hoisted me up behind him. "Hang on!" he ordered. The horses slipped daintily through the doorway and set off in a delicious gallop. We spent the rest of that day riding through distant countryside I had for so long only imagined. We wandered into the neighboring town of Santa Cruz, down the cobblestoned main street, along the rows of shops and across the plaza in front of the church. We skirted the Bahiano's enormous holdings, acreage enough to pasture maybe five hundred head of cattle. In a matter of years, he had planted several acres of coffee trees; this year for the first time, laborers were picking and sorting the beans on the mature trees. Then there were the smaller holdings planted with corn and beans, little plots of vegetables, pigs and chickens, children and dogs running through the simple houses.

After Yōgu left, I asked Saburo if he knew in fact whether Yōgu would return from Japan.

"Emiru," Saburo said, knowingly, "he told me that he would not promise anything. He's not the sort of man to promise, he said, but he did say I could trust him."

"That's the same thing," I insisted. "Trusting and promising."

"I don't know, Emiru. I don't know." Saburo was sad, and I was confused. We wondered what Yōgu meant. We wondered if he would return.

Someone else who must have wondered whether Yōgu would return was Haru. Had there been any sort of understanding between Yōgu and Haru? Perhaps it was the same sort of understanding that Saburo and Yōgu had, this not promising but trusting. I do not know. Certainly an understanding of this nature could not be very clear. An entire year had passed, and there was no sign of Hachiro Yōgu. There were no letters either, but I wonder that anyone might have expected Yōgu to actually write a letter. The passing of time seemed to convince us that, indeed, people like my father who opposed Kantaro's campaign from the very beginning had been correct in their suspicions. Kantaro seemed to hide his disappointment behind his usual confidence. At first he suggested, as others did, that we could not expect Yōgu to return in three months or even six;

Japan was, after all, on the other side of the world. Discussions among the team members went around in circles, and Saburo and I searched for some clue.

"It is quite possible that he became ill," suggested Tsuruta. "For all we know, he may be stuck in a hospital somewhere."

"Yōgu, sick? What nonsense."

"Then there's the possibility that he's having difficulty gathering so much equipment. Perhaps there's a shortage of materials."

"That's it! He's gone to America to buy everything. Of course."

"He couldn't get into America. They've got a no-Japanese policy."

"Yōgu would find a way."

"If it were me who had the chance to go back to Japan, I would go back to my hometown, see my mother, see my old friends. I think I would take my time, enjoy it a little."

"You know what Yōgu said. He said he left Japan because he hated it. He's not like you. You can't judge Yōgu by what you'd do."

"Yes, but think of it. If any of us had the opportunity to return, what would we do? There's no telling whether we would or wouldn't return to Brazil."

"If I could go home, I'd get myself a wife."

"Perhaps Yōgu is trying to get himself a wife!"

"That would take forever!"

There was much laughter over this possibility, a possibility which Haru must not have found comforting. As time went on, even Kantaro, who had long defended his wild friend, began to doubt that Yōgu would ever return. He began to turn his thoughts and energies to other projects, hoping to renew the old confidence lost to Yōgu's disappearance. It was at this time that Kantaro met a young man new to Esperança, a graduate from a farming college in Japan, an agronomist named Seijiro Befu. It was also during this time that Kantaro began a new series of nightly visits, hoping to capture the imagination and love of another woman, the woman with the sweet voice and the piano.

* * *

Kimi Kawagoe, as I had mentioned, was slightly older and far better educated than Haru. Although older by only two or three years, Kimi had the advantage of a certain maturity. She had graduated from a Japanese girls' finishing school before coming to Brazil, and she had been used to a very refined company of friends. Her father's abrupt but impassioned decision to move to Brazil was a rude awakening for both Kimi and her mother. Kinu Kawagoe rarely ventured outside her home and was said to be a very frail woman. The tropical climate did not agree with her, and she was often said to be ill. It fell upon Kimi to care for her family's needs within the household; these things she accomplished without complaint, caring for her sick mother, cooking and washing and sewing for her brother Heizo and her father and their hired help. Shinkichi Kawagoe, on the other hand, thrived in the tropical heat. He was soon tanned a deep brown from working in the fields, and his banker's hands had grown rough and grimy as any other farmer's. Despite Kawagoe's enthusiasm for rural living, there were certain amenities of his old life in Japan that he continued to maintain, most of which surrounded his love of music. This was, of course, the reason why he had, at great expense, bought and shipped the piano from São Paulo. Kawagoe also had a gramophone and a large collection of classical records, which he enjoyed playing every evening for his attentive young guest, Kantaro Uno.

Kantaro began once again to write letters daily, this time to Kimi. Now it was the case that Kimi could read and understand Kantaro's long philosophical digressions, and it was said that Kantaro began to receive from Kimi some letters in response. That Kimi responded to Kantaro's letters was certainly a sign of some kind. Kimi had had several admirers, all of whom had drifted away, unable to make any impression upon Kimi or her father. It was especially important that the suitor make an impression on Shinkichi Kawagoe, who seemed genial enough to anyone attentive to his interest in music but who was quite protective of his daughter. Kantaro knew very little about music, but he was, after all, Kantaro Uno. Kantaro had a way of talking about life and the future which made people feel at once expansive and fulfilled and full of hope. He spoke of projects, both great and small, with fervor and optimism, as if the tasks we took on in our daily lives, no matter how trivial, were part of a larger more important scheme. He spoke of Esperança as if it were the seed of a great dream, a special experiment which would change the world.

Kawagoe, who had left a harried although comfortable world for a rustic and simple one, was more than pleased with Kantaro's verbal expression and philosophical expansion of his own ideals. Years later, Shinkichi Kawagoe admitted to me his enthusiasm. "Yes, yes!" he had exclaimed to Kantaro. "This is exactly why I have come to Esperança! Every day I am outside in the natural world, planting, hoeing, digging, turning God's earth. Look at my hands. These used to be the hands of a man who counted money. Some will say that these hands are dirty, but I know that these hands are only now becoming clean. How many years will it take to cleanse these hands, Kantaro?"

"Kawagoe-san, you have more than cleansed your hands, and you have long since cleansed your spirit," said Kantaro, somehow wise beyond his years.

Kawagoe continued, "I think that God has spared me, spared me from what is happening out there in the world of money. Men have lost their fortunes in the stock market crash. I read that some have committed suicide, and for what? For money! But I'm alive! Now I sweat, I toil. I'm no longer a young man like you, and my body aches at the end of each day, but I'll tell you this: I've never been so happy. This is the life every man was meant to live."

Kinu Kawagoe, huddled in a darkened room with a cup of luke-warm tea, perhaps did not agree with this talk, but her husband and Kantaro were soon gripped in mutual admiration. It soon became apparent that Kantaro was more than a welcomed guest, and the talk began to go around that Kantaro was again in love.

This conquest seemed easy, as I thought the conquest of a woman by my hero should in fact be, but it did not seem to excite Kantaro in the same way as did his pursuit of Haru. In many ways, Kantaro seemed subdued, perhaps even humbled by the disappearance of Yōgu. Pushing the thought of Yōgu's betrayal from his mind, Kantaro turned away from baseball.

The plans for Kantaro's marriage to Kimi were finally negotiated. Waka Uno went to see Kinu, who sat up weakly in her bed and smiled wanly for the occasion. The two women delicately worked through the details, and a date was set. Now I don't know but I suspect that this news must have certainly upset Haru Okumura, who had received no news of Hachiro Yōgu and who must have begun to wonder what this trusting-but-not-promising business could possibly mean. Haru must have heard the gossip, as we all did, that Yōgu had probably run off with Esperança's money and would never, if he knew what was good for him, show his face again in our part of the world. A great number of aspersions were cast on Yōgu's name, and no one, except maybe Saburo, thought Yōgu was ever coming back. I thought that, at least for Saburo's sake, Yōgu should return. I imagined him returning in the dead of night, whispering to Saburo and

me and taking us for a last ride through the moonlit countryside.
Yōgu began to have for me a sort of dark and confused image.
"Sabu," I would say to Saburo, "maybe Yōgu is dead."

"Nobody could kill him," said Saburo, as if killing Yōgu would
be the only way he might die.

"I had this dream," I insisted. "It must have been his ghost."

"What did he look like?"

"Like Yōgu. He spit all around my bed, then he left."

"Emiru, did he have feet?"

"I don't remember."

"If he didn't have feet, it might have been his ghost. But if he had
his feet, it was just a dream."

I nodded. Ghost don't have feet.

If Yōgu had somehow passed into another world for me, I suppose
that he may have simply disappeared for Haru. A kind of despera-
tion seemed to set in. All the fascination and attractive luster about
Haru had somehow left with Kantaro. The crowd of young men
who had once lounged around Okumura's porch in the late afternoons after baseball practice were no more.

It now seemed that it had been Kantaro who had brought the visitors, the charming and gentle Tsuruta and the numerous other comrades who always followed Kantaro. And when Yōgu had also been
around, there was that sense of competition, the wonderful opportunity for Haru to flirt with all of them but to scorn Yōgu. I speculate
that Kantaro did not know, at the time, of Yōgu's attraction to
Haru. Who could have suspected it from the way she treated him?
As I said, Kantaro was wrapped in his own passion; he could not *see*
anything.

Occasionally, a new young man would appear to make his bid for
Haru, but there were none to compare with the bold and insatiable
young Kantaro. And certainly Haru would never know another like
Hachiro Yōgu. Life became tedious and lonely in Esperança. As long
as Kantaro had been there, not just wondering if but assuming that
he would conquer her heart, Haru had felt, if not special or the center
of attention, at least occupied and entertained. It was more than dull
to be passed over for another woman; Haru felt crazy with jealousy.
If Yōgu were not coming back, then she would at least get back the
attention she deserved. In a manner completely ungraceful and as-
sertive, Haru let it be known that she had changed her mind—Haru
would now accept Kantaro's offer of marriage.

It was my mother, Sei, who became the go-between in this odd turn of events.

"Kantaro," my mother began, unsure of how to approach the subject, "it's a rather delicate subject since you are already promised to Kimi . . . The date is set I hear?"

"That's so," Kantaro nodded.

"Of course, Haru spoke to me in confidence—"

"Haru?"

The part about Haru speaking in confidence was of course not true, but it just didn't seem right saying that Haru had pleaded with my mother to convince Kantaro that he was making a terrible mistake in marrying Kimi Kawagoe. My mother marveled at how pushy Haru could really be.

"Yes," my mother continued. "I thought you should know. She was quite upset."

"Haru? Upset?" Kantaro rose slightly from his seat.

"Yes." My mother poured tea quietly.

"Why? What is it?" Kantaro pressed with some exasperation.

"Well, confidentially, of course . . . My, my . . ." she paused with some difficulty. "Haru confessed that she made a mistake in turning down your offer. I mean—"

"She will marry me?" Kantaro stood up in the middle of our kitchen, his face suddenly aglow.

"But what about Kimi?"

"A man must marry for love! Excuse me, Terada-san, but . . ." Kantaro could not finish his words; his heart was so completely filled with the thought that Haru had finally said yes. He ran out the door, flung himself upon his horse and flew away at a mad gallop.

My mother stood in wonder at the door of our house.

"What was Kantaro doing here?" My father looked down the road as he came in from his work.

My mother did not answer. She turned from the door in wonder. "But what about Kimi?" she asked herself again.

The Kawagoes, I heard, were devastated, but they were much too sophisticated to show it. Shinkichi Kawagoe was clearly offended, but he would not speak of it. Kantaro's decision was in no way intended as a snub; it was simply Kantaro's way of doing things from the heart. However, a great deal of conjecture and gossip traveled about, and Waka Uno was seen patching up her recently spoiled relationship with Tomi Okumura while relinquishing her frequent tête-à-tête with the sickly Kinu Kawagoe.

In the meantime, Kimi was talked of as being older than Haru, getting along in years, as if Kantaro might have been her last chance for an appropriate marriage. She was talked of as being too educated and too talented for just any young man, and wasn't it a shame. People also compared Haru to Kimi and Kimi to Haru, and everyone had their preferences for the best wife for Kantaro. It amazed us that Kantaro had the bravado to choose a wife for love. But on the other hand, it seemed to me that Kimi had really fallen in love with Kantaro, and she was hurt and embarrassed and ashamed to be the center of so much gossip. All of a sudden, the piano was silent and the sweet sound of her voice was no more.

Waka Uno simply transferred the plans for the wedding to a new bride and went happily about with the arrangements. To add to the excitement, Jiro Uno also announced his engagement to Toshiko, one of the Sato sisters, an arrangement Waka had been working on for months. Jiro would be married on the same day as Kantaro in a double ceremony. Indeed, it was a great triumph for Waka Uno. This was going to be a big event in Esperança. Everyone was invited. A great deal of commotion was raised over this wedding. It was to be done in a manner commensurate with the largess and boldness the Unos were accustomed to. Almost everyone in Esperança had some participation in the details of this wedding. All the young men and baseball team members spent several days at the Uno farm raising a large extended thatched roof to shade the guests. Then tables and benches had to be arranged or built. Just about every woman in Esperança seemed involved in some aspect of Haru's dress. My mother was responsible for baking several pieces of the enormous wedding cake, which was somehow to come together as a whole from several different ovens. For a few days before the wedding, my mother, Tomi Okumura, Waka Uno, all the Sato daughters and their mother devoted themselves to pickling vegetables, making sweets, and mixing enormous amounts of rice into sushi. There was a festive air about Esperança. Everyone was talking about the wedding, what they were going to wear, how they were participating. You could hear people practicing the songs they would present to the wedding couples, a man blowing a typically plaintive air on the *shakuhachi*, a woman going through the steps of a dance. But the sound of the piano and the sweet lilt of the voice that always accompanied it were noticeably absent.

When the day arrived, I, like everyone else in Esperança, got up early and finished my chores. My brothers and I got spruced up as best we could according to our mother's satisfaction. We all headed over to the Uno farm. I could see Saburo shuffling uncomfortably near his mother, who was looking very nervous. I noticed that Saburo had on a new cap, but on closer inspection, I realized the old one had been scrubbed and bleached white for the occasion. I sidled over to Saburo, who rolled his eyes with his characteristic disgust over the much-ado about his brother's wedding.

Okumura presided over a short marriage ceremony, after which everyone settled down under the open-air roof made for the occasion. All glimpsed with a certain awe the enormous cake to which my mother had contributed. It was one of the biggest wedding cakes I can remember—a gigantic rectangle fifteen centimeters high and perhaps a square meter in size, slathered with white frosting and decorated with pink flowers. My mother was quite proud of this baking achievement, which she claimed required twenty-six dozen eggs and six different ovens. The wedding couples, Kantaro and Haru on one side and Jiro and Toshiko on the other, sat behind the giant cake, oddly dwarfed by its tremendous size. Haru and Toshiko were powdered heavily, awkward in their white headgear and satin dresses; they huddled behind the cake, shyly staring into the pink flowers.

Naotaro Uno got up to welcome the guests and admitted the pleasure he found in the thought that Kantaro's marriage would mean that his son would be found at home from now on. Then Okumura got up to make his speech.

Before Okumura got any further than his opening greeting, Saburo nudged me and pulled me from the table. We ran out of the crowd under the large open-air roof in time to see a figure of a man on a horse galloping at a tremendous speed toward the party. I thought that the man would stop, but he seemed to be speeding up, forcing the horse in our direction, clumps of dirt and dust rising all around him. "It's Yōgu!" yelled Saburo, taking his clean cap and slamming it into the dirt with obvious pleasure. "He's back! Emiru, he's back!"

So it was. Hachiro Yōgu. He never stopped his horse; the pounding hooves on the dry earth and the sound of gunshots was the only warning. People scattered in every direction, rushed into the open or huddled under and behind fallen tables. There were people screaming and yelling and weeping as Yōgu rammed and pranced the horse about while firing wildly into the air.

Then as suddenly as it had happened, the gunfire ceased, and Yōgu sat somewhat dazed, looking at the shambles of Kantaro's

wedding all around him. Haru and Toshiko were huddled under the
wedding cake, which had miraculously escaped Yōgu's abuse.
Kantaro stood over the cake in bewilderment, saying nothing. At
that moment, I saw Haru peek out from under the table to look at
Yōgu, her eyes wild with fear. Yōgu took a long look at Haru, her
disheveled hair, her headdress askew, searching for the woman behind the facial powder that he had known and loved. He said nothing, spit angrily on the earth and raised the horse onto its hind legs.
The horse stood grappling the air before the big cake and came down
threateningly.

I saw my mother, in a protective gesture, suddenly jump up just as
the horse reared its muscular hindquarters into that remarkable
cake. A cry of dismay parted my mother's lips, and the horse with its
rider pranced off, frosting pasted to its derriere, the tail haughtily
flapping the sweet sticky stuff into the heated air.

CHAPTER 6: ON THE LAND

THAT EVENING, hours after the wedding, Saburo threw stones at my
window, and as agreed, we crept out into the moonlit night to find
Hachiro Yōgu. "Emiru," said Saburo excitedly when we were a
short distance from my house, "I found out. Yōgu's at the
Kawagoes'."

I nodded, and we headed quickly down a path cutting across the
Uno fields. Along the path, I could make out the shape of Kantaro's
new cottage, built a short distance from the Uno's main house only
recently for Kantaro and his bride Haru. Suddenly, Saburo pushed
me into some tall weeds, motioning me to silence. Lying there peek-
ing through the weeds, we could faintly see two figures running in
the dark. As they approached us, I could see that they were both
naked, the moonlight gliding over their white bodies.

"Haru!" one of the figures called breathlessly, "Wait! Come
back!"

But Haru ran on, short shudders of panic issuing from her heaving
breasts as she raced toward us.

"Oh no," Saburo muttered. He pulled his hat, dirty but still white,
from his head and stuffed it under his chest. We remained as still as
possible, knowing there was nowhere else to hide.

Haru came so close to us that we could see her full face, black hair matted to her wet cheeks, frightened eyes filled with tears.

"Haru! Haru!" Kantaro's body was shiny with sweat, his penis flapping wildly between his legs. He grabbed Haru several times, but she pulled away hysterically, running in one direction and then in another, once coming so close to us that we could have reached up and touched her prancing legs.

"No! No!" Haru cried as Kantaro caught her suddenly and fell with her. Haru struggled frantically, her legs and arms flinging every which way on the cool earth. "A sin," she wailed. "A sin!"

I could feel my own heartbeat quicken and a familiar sensation that I only vaguely remembered as a recent dream pulsate excitedly through my body. I glanced at Saburo, who lay on the earth beside me, his body tense with the same expectations. I could feel Haru's fingers clawing the earth, her sobs muffled under Kantaro's muscular body. There was a long moment of silence, all of us panting in quiet unison. Then Kantaro rose to his knees, pulled Haru up from the damp earth and carried her slowly back to their cottage.

As soon as they had disappeared, Saburo jumped up and broke into a wild run across the fields. I chased Saburo through the woods and down the road toward Esperança's center, racing until our lungs might burst through our chests, until our legs wobbled precariously beneath us and we fell from exhaustion. Rolling over, I could see a hint of purple light in the east. It would soon be daybreak. "Emiru," Saburo reminded me. "Come on. It's not far now."

The Kawagoe house was at the end of the main road that ran through Esperança. It was surrounded by a pretty garden with flowers which Kimi had carefully tended. Certainly as houses went in Esperança, it was the most elegant, sporting a large veranda and glass windows with shutters and drapery. We could see lights within. Kawagoe was the first to wire his house for electricity.

Outside we saw the horse tied to the fence, shifting from leg to leg, and a cart piled precariously high with wooden crates. The Kawagoes had been noticeably absent from Kantaro's big wedding celebration. It was Kimi's brother, Heizo Kawagoe, who saw and greeted Yōgu wandering into Esperança on a squeaky horse-drawn cart. Esperança on this day must have seemed a ghost town; everyone was at the Uno farm under the big open-air roof looking forward to generous amounts of food and drink and cake. We paused a distance from the house. "Now what?" I asked my friend.

Saburo shrugged. "He's still here."

Suddenly Hachiro Yōgu himself appeared. He walked swiftly to the cart and began pushing and tossing the crates onto the ground. Crate after crate fell with a thud. One crate broke open, and to our amazement, dozens of white baseballs rolled across Kimi's garden, into the neat flower beds and out across the dirt road. I was tempted to rush out to collect the balls, but Saburo gripped my shirt, holding me back. One ball rolled within reach, and I grabbed the precious thing with a delight I could hardly suppress. But Saburo stood watching, unimpressed by the treasure rolling to our feet. He seemed to be waiting for his chance. "Emiru. Yōgu's leaving. I'm going with him."

I felt a chill of loneliness. "What?"

"Don't tell anyone. Let them figure it out." Saburo was not inviting me to come.

"What are you talking about?"

"This is my chance, Emiru. You can't stop me." Saburo was about to rush forward when a woman appeared in the doorway with a bundle in her arms. It was Kimi Kawagoe. She ran toward Yōgu and threw her belongings into the now empty cart.

"Please," Kimi whispered before Saburo could make the same request. "Please, take me with you. It doesn't matter where. Please. I promise I won't be a nuisance. Please," she repeated with determination.

Yōgu said nothing but hitched the horse to the cart silently. He tugged the horse down the road, kicking at the spill of baseballs, which collided about unpredictably. The horse spooked from side to side, unsure of its step. Kimi followed deftly behind while Yōgu seemed to ignore her. Saburo and I watched, unseen by anyone. When they were some distance down the road, we could see Yōgu stop with some purposeful decision, hoisting himself onto the seat of the cart. Yōgu seemed to nod, and with a gracefulness peculiar only to Kimi, she lifted herself into the cart. Saburo watched them travel away until he could see them no more, but I ran to examine the crates filled with baseball equipment and pretended to be occupied in pocketing another ball or two to spare Saburo the embarrassment of his bitter tears.

The next day, a troop of soldiers came through Esperança. We were forced to give them food, and they took Kantaro's horse. A few weeks later, we heard that President Washington Luís had fled the country and that a man they called the Gaúcho from the South, Getúlio Vargas, was now President of the Republic. Several months after that, representatives from the new government came with stores of food in return for our "contribution" to the cause, but we never saw Kantaro's horse again.

*   *   *

With the advent of his marriage, Kantaro's thoughts seemed to return to the land and the labor that would make it productive, rather than leisure. It was Seijiro Befu, the young agronomist, who gave Kantaro a new set of ideas on which to form the great project that would eventually occupy all of us in some way or another.

Momose-sensei, far away in Japan, had convinced a man of wealth and standing of the great potential of Brazil. Baron Tamaki had bought an enormous parcel of land in Esperança for the purpose of creating an experimental ranch. This was akin to a similar experiment the baron was attempting in Manchuria. The baron was an absentee landlord, sending funds and hiring men to administer plans formed a half-world away. Seijiro Befu was hired especially to work on Baron Tamaki's ranch in Esperança. He had specialized in small farm animals: pigs, goats and fowl, in particular, chickens. Befu had become disenchanted with the prospect of working in Japan, where the smallness of the farms prohibited the modern large-scale projects of the United States and Europe, projects Befu had studied intently but without hope of ever implementing. The opportunity to work on the baron's enormous ranch in Brazil was a dream come true.

It had been such a dream that when Befu met Kantaro for the first time, he could not contain the intensity of his satisfaction, his words spilling out with emotion. It was a moment, they later said, marked by fate. Befu somehow knew, upon meeting Kantaro, that this was the friend and the companion with whom he must share his dream. It is not as if Befu would have shared his ideas with just anyone; these ideas were carefully guarded, as one might guard the secret whereabouts of a vein of gold, too precious, too personal to divulge to a stranger with the wrong motives. But Kantaro Uno was a man who understood dreams; his talent was in his ability to articulate visions with the exuberant assurance of a future that must, we thought, be captured in his very movements. If Kantaro knew your dream, it seemed that he must also be capable of making it a reality. Seijiro

Befu told Kantaro everything. "Of course, it's nothing new; we have been doing this with our so-called intensive agriculture in Japan for centuries. Can you imagine the same principle applied to a land like Brazil using modern equipment and innovations? We can operate on a much larger scale."

Kantaro listened intently. "Our production could be enormous. But most important, it would mean a commitment to the land, to Esperança, to regenerating the soil. Why hasn't anyone thought of it? Chicken manure by the tons! Enough to fertilize, well, what would you calculate?"

"We'd have to make a projection, but I'd say two hundred chickens will easily fertilize four acres of land."

"Every year we seem to need more land to produce the same amount. The Brazilian method of cut and burn and plant is no longer feasible for us."

"A sixty-acre plot of land, subdivided, can easily house an operation of two hundred chickens and provide an ample field of corn with any number of diverse cultivations."

"A single family could probably operate it alone," speculated Kantaro.

"It would require some large machinery—tractors, incubators," Befu wondered, but Kantaro brushed his doubt aside.

"The cooperative could provide that sort of assistance. This is exactly the kind of project the cooperative should be involved in."

"If there were some central incubation center to research a strong strain of poultry and produce chicks for distribution to farmers ..."

"Why not? What would it take?"

"Well, at first, not much. A generator of some sort for incandescent lights would be the best, but we can incubate off the heat of smoldering compost. Then, we'd need shelter and an enclosed pen and feeders and—"

"The physical part we can build," Kantaro interrupted with growing excitement. "What about the chickens themselves? Do we pull these red hens off the road?"

"We can ship a strain in from the United States. One with a good record of disease resistance and which would adapt to the climate here."

"How long would it take to generate a base population?"

"Well, you can get a hatch every twenty-one days and maturity in three to six months, depending on the strain. It would be slow at first, but it would only take a few to start."

Kantaro stopped for a moment to mentally add the population growth of chickens over a period of a year. "In a year, we'd be in business!" he exclaimed. "Meat, eggs and manure!"

Although this conversation seemed to be but the bantering of two farmers, with each word Kantaro and Befu bound their separate destinies together. It was a blood pact like no other; the intensity of feeling between these two men cannot be fully described. And to those who listened to this talk, the ideas indeed sounded revolutionary. This was at a time when neither eggs nor chicken meat were produced in quantity for sale in Brazil. Many people simply fattened chickens and gathered their eggs in their own backyards. Or they went to the open-air market and haggled for live chickens or a basket of eggs. The production of eggs and chicken meat for large-scale sale, as we know it today, did not exist. Befu and Kantaro were the first to think of it in our corner of the world.

Seijiro Befu was a small intense young man with dark eyes under a set of very thick black brows. He had an unusually thick head of blue-black hair which he never quite combed in any particular direction. When he arrived in Brazil, he began to grow a beard which soon bloomed into a thick bush about his face, giving him the appearance of a black bear. As Befu never again shaved his face, his distinguishing feature continued to be his tremendous beard, which grew slowly down his chest to his waist. In later years, Befu's beard and hair continued to flourish, an uncontrollable tussle which would one day become white. As such, Befu was an impressive sort, a young man inflamed with his own discoveries, eager to pursue new ideas.

I soon took Befu's ideas about recycling the land's resources and creating a self-sufficient way of life for granted. They became the physical basis for our life on the land. Then, with the coming of agribusiness and the use of chemical fertilizers and large machinery over vast areas of land, those ideas were set aside as antiquated. Yet much of what Befu said then has recently returned to vogue. After all, Kantaro and I and many others like us embraced a plan that was simple but sensible with timeless value.

The talk went around and around, and the excitement over Befu's ideas and so many other proposals began to take shape. "Land. We need our own land," announced Kantaro. "Okumura has not partitioned the area to the north, where there are plans to link another road into Santa Cruz d'Azedinha. When that road is opened, it will be the gateway to Esperança, and this land will double in worth. That is where we must try to get an option to buy."

"We need a down payment. How are we going to get that much money?"

"We can draw our resources together. We've done it before," Kantaro smiled without embarrassment. "We can do it again."

Kantaro Uno, Seijiro Befu, the poet Akira Tsuruta, Kantaro's brother Jiro and oddly, Kimi's brother, Heizo Kawagoe, became the core of the group. There were others of course. There were always others, but these men formed the foundation for Kantaro's next project, a project that sprang from Befu's ideas about chickens and manure and Kantaro's ideas about human beings and the earth. Each of these men seemed so very different in character. Tsuruta was an extremely refined and gentle person who gave our rustic setting an air of timeless elegance, while Befu was a small intense man who never quite rested. Heizo Kawagoe was the youngest. He was a quiet sort who said very little and seemed overpowered by his family—his exuberant father, his invalid mother and his talented sister, of whom he did not like to speak. He would simply say that Kantaro had made a choice a man must make. Kimi's disappearance had cast a long shadow over his parent's lives. Unable to remove this shadow or to replace his sister's presence, Heizo tarried further and further from home, spending more and more time with Kantaro. Then there was Jiro, who was committed to Kantaro. Unlike my good friend Saburo, Jiro—only two years younger than Kantaro—was devoted to his older brother. It was as if Jiro had relinquished his own personality to be Kantaro's shadow. If the truth were to be told, Jiro was actually rather silly. This was not something I noticed as a young boy. In fact, Jiro got along quite well with the young boys like myself, and in later years, when he did not carry the burden of the Uno family farm, a troop of boys was always following him around. Jiro organized baseball games and expeditions and seemed happiest among the youngsters.

*   *   *

Yōgu's brief return to Esperança produced a mixed reaction, but it satisfied everyone's sense of being in the right. Those who had sent Yōgu to Japan with money were able to say that he had returned with the baseball equipment he had promised, and those who had refused to participate in Yōgu's venture were able to say that his conduct at Kantaro's wedding was just an example of the things they feared and had long warned others about.

One thing that Yōgu's return accomplished was a renewed interest in baseball. Once again, the Esperança men and boys were vying for field time in the late afternoons and on the weekends. Everyone was anxious to try out Yōgu's new equipment, to feel the touch of a real baseball falling from the sky, to swing the unmarked ashwood bats, and to fit the neatly sewn gloves over their hands. Kantaro himself returned to the field to coach Esperança's team. Word came that a new player on the São Paulo team by the name of Susumu Kubo was beginning to be the talk of the town. Kubo was the new baseball sensation, and people were saying that Kantaro's era was over. Kubo was now king. Kantaro was not oblivious to this challenge. He knew that his days with baseball were numbered, but he would not leave the field on anyone else's terms but his own. Everyone was anxious to see a big showdown, and a date for a final game in São Paulo was set. Outside Esperança, bets were made all around; Uno versus Kubo, Esperança versus São Paulo. But for those of us of Esperança, beating São Paulo became a matter of honor.

Once again, Kantaro set up a rigid training schedule. During the last month of training, the team camped out on the north side of Esperança, clearing large areas of land in the mornings and practicing ball in the afternoons. Kantaro's purpose was twofold: to train for the baseball game and to begin clearing the land he and Befu and the others hoped to establish as their own. Saburo and I went up to the campsite several times to bring messages and food to the team. I liked to imagine I was part of the team and observed the training closely. Saburo and I often settled down with our tins of food to watch. Everyone had come to accept the rigidity and hard physical exertion of any training with Kantaro, who had never asked anyone to work harder than he did. But this time, I saw Kantaro box ears, slap heads, as he pushed and punched his men into shape. There seemed to be, in the middle of the forest, a small tough army of men training for a war. The team members accepted this treatment as natural to the preparation for a baseball game; in fact, we thought nothing of Kantaro's violent methods in those days. I believe now that that violence in the mid-1930s was a sign of the times. On the other side of the world, young men like Kantaro and his teammates were preparing for a long war.

While we were removed by distance from these events, we were not untouched. My father read Shigeshi Kasai's paper the *Brazil Shimpo* with great interest. "Kasai is right," my father said. "The

Japanese preparations for a war are the first steps to suicide." But others did not agree. "Japan deserves greater respect in the world. We showed the Russians; now we will show the Americans." War seemed to be a way to show the world something, but I was not sure what that something was. Young men who had arrived recently from Japan spoke of something called national socialism, a man named Hitler and the proper worship of the Emperor.

For the moment, the coming tide of war was set aside in favor of the coming showdown between Kantaro and Kubo. Many people in Esperança were preparing to go to the game in São Paulo. After a great deal of persuasion on my part, my father agreed to take my youngest brother Kōichi and me to São Paulo to see the big game. He thought that he might also be able to replenish his medicinal supply on this trip, and my mother sent with him a shopping list of goods and material that she needed.

Those of us who saw this most controversial of games can never forget it. The tension in the air and the suspense of this game made all others pale in contrast. Kubo was indeed a wonderful pitcher and hitter, a young man with superb form and speed. From the newspapers and gossip, everyone knew that Kubo lived for no other reason than to play baseball. Kantaro Uno was not the same sort of athletic machine, but he was not to be knocked aside by a young upstart. For Kantaro, winning that particular baseball game was more than a display of physical talent, it was proof that Kantaro had chosen the correct path. Winning at baseball sent an important message to everyone: that Esperança was not just an idea, but that we were alive and well and strong. Baseball was a test of worth and spirit; Kantaro would not treat it any other way—he *would not lose*. And of course he did not. He struck Kubo out. The crowd went wild. My father lifted my brother Kōichi into the air, and we all ran onto the field, following the team members as they held Kantaro aloft over their shoulders. It was a triumph we would never forget.

While in São Paulo, Kantaro once again met Shigeshi Kasai, the publisher of the *Brazil Shimpo*. Kasai, who had discovered Kantaro's enthusiasm for photography, made him a gift of a reporter's camera—a folding-bellows-type Voightlander with a Zeiss lens. That Kasai should make such a gift in such an automatic and generous way certainly impressed Kantaro. The forming of friendships was a ritual bonding to Kantaro, a bonding so complete in the minds of Kantaro's friends that they would later be able to assert unquestionably what they felt to be his deepest feelings or his true thoughts about this or that matter. This tying of spirits, this sensation of great love transmitted, was no simple matter. But it seemed even more complicated for Kasai, who had by nature a very critical mind. Yet it was Kasai who ultimately came to know more than all of us about Kantaro, and because of this friendship and his own deficiencies of character, he could not later lay judgment on his friend.

It was Kasai who introduced Kantaro to the founders of what would become the largest and most powerful cooperative in Brazil: Sarandi. Sarandi began as a Japanese farmers' potato co-op on the outskirts of the city. Gradually, more and more small Japanese co-ops joined forces with Sarandi in an effort to get better prices for their produce. The leaders of the Sarandi Cooperative immediately took an interest in Kantaro and Befu's talk about poultry farming. Sarandi agreed to make the inquiries and arrangements to bring a small sample of initial chicks from the United States for breeding in Brazil. Befu would return to São Paulo and coordinate everything. It was a small but auspicious beginning. Indeed, it was the beginning of everything. Baseball had brought Kantaro and Befu to São Paulo. Now they would return to Esperança with a promise of the future.

* * *

When the team returned to Esperança, Kantaro and his companions immediately went to work, clearing, building and preparing for their chicken investment. Befu, who had originally been hired as an agronomist for Baron Tamaki's ranch, made his apologies and left his contract. There was a flurry of activity on the north end of Esperança. While in baseball training, the team had already cleared a sizeable area of land and built a spacious bunkhouse with a kitchen to one side. A well was dug, and in a short period of time, three houses went up, one for Kantaro and Haru, the second for Jiro and his wife Toshiko, and the third a dormitory which housed Befu, Tsuruta and Heizo and a varying number of young bachelors who came and went. The old training bunkhouse was turned into a sort of dining room, conveniently attached to the old kitchen. By now Haru was pregnant, and she and Toshiko could be seen busy at work, preparing meals for the men, sewing and washing in the yard outside. According to Befu's careful plans, barns and pens were built and several acres of land were cleared for planting corn.

In Kantaro's large collection of photographs, there is one photograph in particular of the five men who first cleared and founded what we initially called New World Ranch. Kantaro had set up his Carl Zeiss camera and run back to pose with the group. Heizo and Jiro can be seen smiling at the two ends of a long saw poised across the trunk of an enormous tree. The wistful Tsuruta is seated on one end of the fallen trunk, his legs dangling from his tall seat, while Befu is standing powerfully atop the trunk with his arms folded across his chest. Kantaro stands in the foreground, fists on his hips, on the tree's giant stump. They all look the part of young lumberjacks, white cotton shirts and work pants hanging loosely from their wiry bodies, tanned dark by the tropical sun. A youthful intensity is reflected in their eyes, a genuine and innocent moment captured for memory. When people talk about the founders of Kantaro's original ranch, they point to this now famous photograph.

A few days after this photograph was taken, the same men, while clearing this field, found a large mound of earth. "We're going to have to borrow the co-op tractor to push this earth aside," announced Kantaro. But when it was done, the tractor unearthed a cache of what seemed to be buried Indian remains. Saburo and I, who had been standing around watching, were sent off to find Mizuoka. Now Shūhei Mizuoka had for some time been interested in archeology. As always, he had been doing a considerable amount of reading on the matter, but it was said that he had also worked very briefly for an American archaeologist who was studying the Japanese aborigines, the Ainu, in Hokkaido. Mizuoka had learned a little about classifying pottery shards and how to dig for artifacts and bones. He had once lived in Utah, visited the American Southwest and knew a slight bit of American Indian history. He now thought it worthwhile to study the Brazilian Indians and make comparisons between them and the Japanese aborigines. He thought he might be able to find connections between the Ainu and the Brazilian Indians which would prove the thesis that the Asian aborigines crossed the Bering Strait into the American continent, eventually moving far down into South America. To prove that the Brazilian Indians were our distant relatives became an ongoing study which Mizuoka pursued for many years. From time to time, Mizuoka would simply disappear from Esperança, abandoning his responsibilities as a teacher, gone on an expedition to find Indians in the Mato Grosso.

When Mizuoka arrived with us to see the large mound, he was delighted. One other family had discovered a similar site, but the tractor had largely destroyed the contents of the mound. This mound was virtually intact, an excellent opportunity for study. He was sure that Esperança had long ago been inhabited by Indians and that these hidden mounds were burial sites. He excitedly applied the techniques of excavation he had learned in Hokkaido, carefully digging and picking to unearth ancient pottery and bones and tools.

Saburo and I became very interested in his work. Saburo's older sister Ritsu, too, became interested. She came out, usually with lunch for us, and stayed to watch. Saburo and I were there every day helping Mizuoka dig himself into a large hole, pulling shards and bones from the earth. One day he handed a small human skull to us. Saburo and I examined the thing in amazement. "Small," he remarked. "A child's skull." Saburo and I realized that our schoolmaster was after all a whimsical romantic sort. While digging around the mound, he liked to talk and tell long involved stories about Indians. It was from Mizuoka that I learned that the land we lived on had a past of unwritten words, a silent spirit that lived in the forest we cut and burned and changed forever.

After several days of careful digging, Mizuoka pulled a large urn from the earth. Mizuoka reverently turned the old thing in his arms, his eyes wandering over the designs that appeared after careful brushing. "This is a real find!" Mizuoka announced triumphantly. "And there is more. So much more." Mizuoka sighed. It was already growing dark.

We left the mound, but as I walked into the house, my father was at the door looking into the skies. "Looks like a downpour is coming," my father shrugged. "It's that time of year."

As my father predicted, the rains came that night. I suddenly remembered the Indian mound, and ran out into the increasing downpour to see Saburo. "Go home, Emiru," said Saburo. "We can't do anything about it. It's too far from here, and we'd never find our way in the dark."

I nodded and sloshed back to the house, tiny rivulets of water now washing down the path in a small muddy river.

That night, Kantaro came all the way from the north end on a tractor. "Terada-san!" he yelled above the sound of the rain. He had come to get my mother to deliver Haru's baby. In the rain, my father hoisted my mother and her satchel up beside Kantaro. The lumbering machine with its giant tires cut deep gashes into the slogging road and was soon swallowed up by a dark curtain of water.

Anxiously I waited for the daylight, and holding my shoes under my coat, I ran barefoot through the mud to get Saburo. It was still raining when we got to the site. Mizuoka was already there. He was looking sadly at the place where the mound had once been. The mound had caved into the hole we had helped Mizuoka dig. Every trace of our work was washed completely away. We ran around searching in the puddles, but we could find nothing. Saburo pulled his cap over his forehead and punched his hands into his pockets. "Emiru," he shrugged, "It's useless."

Mizuoka nodded unhappily, "Useless. Such a shame. Such a shame," he repeated hopelessly.

We walked down the road, all of us soaked to our skins, saying nothing. The rain was now a thin mist, and we could see the brightening lines of a complete rainbow before us. Behind us came the chugging sound of a motor and voices. Kantaro with my mother seated next to him on the tractor passed us along the road. Kantaro's face displayed a glow of exhilaration and triumph which could not have comprehended our disappointment. "A boy!" he announced happily. "A boy!"

But I could not forget that Mizuoka's carefully wrought work had been washed away in the torrential downpour, the invaluable contents of an unknown past lost forever. Had it not been for Mizuoka's inexperience with the Brazilian seasons, many precious artifacts of the peoples who lived long ago on the land we settled as Esperança might have been preserved. Nevertheless, Mizuoka was able to salvage a few shards and some bones and that one good pot in its entirety. Mizuoka built a room for his collection and a shelf for the special funeral urn. Every now and then, I visited the collection of pots and shards, ancient tools and feathered headdresses which he began to collect and bring back to Esperança with every trip into the Mato Grosso. I would look at everything, touch the things Mizuoka said we could touch, and wonder if anything of me would, like this, be left behind when I have become an ancient ancestor in my grave. Would my bones be unearthed, my skull displayed, my story told?

CHAPTER 7: NEW WORLD

EARLY IN 1935, ten years after our arrival on the *Brazil-maru* and on my nineteenth birthday, Saburo came to tell me that he was leaving Esperança. "I don't believe you," I said playfully. "You've been saying the same thing for years, probably since the time we first got here," I laughed.

"This time I'm really leaving, Emiru. I've got to get out and see the rest of Brazil."

I didn't understand what Saburo could mean about the rest of Brazil. Of course, it is far bigger than I could ever have imagined, and we were one isolated colony in the middle of nowhere. We were connected to other Japanese colonies by occasional communications from travelers, but we lived great distances from each other, many days over dirt roads or by train. The closest Brazilian town was Santa Cruz d'Azedinha, but we only occasionally found need to go there for medical treatment or supplies, which we usually found in Esperança at our local co-op store. It was possible to never leave Esperança, to never speak Portuguese, to ignore the rest of the world. This sort of life was much too confining for my friend Saburo. So he announced to me, "I met this man from Palma. He's here visiting. He's got a big commune of people, something like this thing Kantaro and the others have got going. They want someone to go over and see what it's like, so I've volunteered. I'm leaving with this Palma man, Gustavo, tomorrow morning."

Palma was a large commune of Latvian immigrants. These people had come from Eastern Europe to escape the First World War. There were many people who had lost their families in the war. They had come together to Brazil to find a new life. Like us, they were a Christian community, and they had come to live in the rural outlands of the State of São Paulo. Kantaro had met and visited these people while traveling with our baseball team. He was very impressed by their way of life and their productivity. We heard that Palma had electricity generated by a water mill, a large dairy industry producing milk, cheese and butter, and that all their needs, including woven cloth for clothing and a cobbler who made shoes, were taken care of within the community.

That Saburo should be sent to study Palma's way of life was no coincidence. Kantaro, I believe, was looking for some way to be free of Saburo, who paid Kantaro none of the respect an older brother might expect. I knew that Saburo had more than once gotten into arguments with Kantaro. Saburo's disagreeableness always put Kantaro's leadership into question. Saburo hated to be compared to Jiro. "Jiro! Jiro!" Saburo laughed scornfully. "If it weren't for

Kantaro, Jiro would shrivel up and disappear!" In the years after Yōgu's disappearance, Saburo gradually became more and more vocal about his differences with Kantaro. I did not like to argue about these things with my friend. Once I suggested to Saburo that his disagreement with his older brother was nothing more than jealousy. "Emiru, you don't understand," Saburo turned to me. "You don't live with Kantaro. You don't know. One day you'll see what I see." Saburo stomped off; he would not talk with me for several days after that. That Saburo would one day leave Esperança seemed to be inevitable, but when the day came, I did not really want to believe it.

"Will you be back?" I asked, wanting to be invited to come along but knowing that I would not and could not leave Esperança.

"I can't promise anything, Emiru." Saburo looked at me significantly and then turned away.

I recognized Yōgu's old trusting-but-not-promising line. I wanted to tell Saburo I trusted him. I put my hand on his shoulder and spat on the ground as Yōgu might have done.

At that, Saburo smiled. He hopped into the truck and nodded at the old Latvian. The truck swung around in a great U-turn and came back. Saburo hung out the window and handed me his old cap. "Maybe you could use this?" he asked.

I nodded. Saburo looked suddenly naked, defenseless without his old covering. He was twenty-one, older than me and, I always assumed, wiser and tougher. In some ways, ours had been an unlikely friendship, pulled together by circumstance, by the notion that we had experienced and seen the same things—or had we? I pulled his cap, still warm with his unspoken thoughts, over my head to reassure him, and watched the truck trundle away. It was a long way to Palma, and I would not see Saburo again for many years.

*   *   *

My father, Kiyoshi Terada, was, for lack of any other person of such title, a doctor to the Esperança community. People still tell me that my father was better than any doctor, that he had more experience than most doctors in those days and that he had cured many ills and saved many lives. My father was very modest about his duties. He was always very careful to say that he was not a doctor, only a pharmacist, and that you could get professional care from the Brazilian doctor in Santa Cruz d'Azedinha. But the Japanese of Esperança were hesitant to go to Santa Cruz and see the Brazilian doctor. They would only go to Santa Cruz if my father strongly suggested it. Many Brazilians from outside Esperança had heard about my father. After a while, Brazilians began to come from far away to see my father. They called him Doctor Terra, probably because they had misunderstood our name, Terada. Because of his name among the people as a healer, my father became rather famous. As time went on, my father became more and more busy helping people who lived great distances from Esperança. There was a great need for medical help, and few to provide it. Poor people knew that my father would not ask for anything in return. They showered my father with gifts and food and often came purposely to repay my father with their labor.

Unlike most other Japanese in Esperança—with the exception perhaps of Okumura—our family formed friendships and dealings with Brazilians outside our Japanese colony. Because of this, my father felt it important that I go to a Brazilian school and learn the Portuguese language. In those days in Santa Cruz d'Azedinha, you could get schooling up to what might now be the equivalent of the eighth grade. After that, only those who could afford it sent their children to São Paulo to get a private education. Unlike other Japanese of my time, I was taught to read and write in Portuguese. This ability to deal comfortably in both languages has since been invaluable to me. I am grateful to my father for this. He urged me to get the tools to live in a new country, a country which he knew and I began to realize would be the only place I would ever call home. "Brazil is a rich, wonderful place to make a home," he would say. "We are very fortunate to be welcome in such a country. It is our responsibility to give it something in return." When I reflect upon these things now, I realize that my father saw beyond Esperança, which seemed to me to be the entire world.

My father died a few days after Saburo left Esperança. It seemed to me that my world was being overturned, my old sense of security tossed away. I thought that suddenly I knew the loneliness that Saburo had always felt despite our friendship. I had been to see Mizuoka, who had recently returned from the Mato Grosso. He had some interesting tales to tell about the Indians there, and I was looking to fill that part of my life which Saburo had suddenly left empty. Coming from Mizuoka's place, I could see a large crowd of people coming from the direction of Santa Cruz d'Azedinha. It might have been a crew of laborers returning from the fields, but they lacked their usually jovial and spirited quality. In fact, an eerie silence hung over them, and I could see that they were carrying something on their shoulders. One of them pointed at me, "There he is! Doctor Terra's son!" I recognized Batista, the man whose daughter my father had treated for malaria. Batista ran out of the crowd toward me, but I could finally see that the thing they were carrying on their shoulders was my father. Blood was splattered over Batista's shoulders, and he was nearly weeping as he approached me. "It was his horse. Down by that swamp near Clovis's place. A snake, I suppose. Spooked the horse. Doctor Terra fell. And the horse . . . and the horse . . ." Batista could not finish, but he did not have to. I could see where the horse's great hooves had fallen upon my father, crushing his ribs. I wanted to grab my father and run with him back to the house, my head flooding with thoughts of medications and bandages, a flashing sense of terror rushing about me. He had given his life to care for people in need, to heal their wounds and to relieve their pain, but I could do nothing for him now. Batista held me securely by the shoulders as I stared in disbelief. "Son," he whispered sorrowfully, "he's gone to God."

Takeo Okumura presided over the funeral for my father. He was buried in the graveyard beside our little church, where Grandma Uno had long ago been buried. Everyone in Esperança was surprised by the large number of Brazilians who came to pay their respects. It was only then that people realized how much my father had done, not only for Esperança, but for the Brazilians in the surrounding areas. I myself did not know many of these people, poor simple folk who stood shyly outside the chapel, crossing themselves in the Catholic manner and leaving small bouquets of flowers with my mother.

After the funeral, Okumura came to talk with me. I felt confused and burdened with his words. "You're the oldest, Ichiro. Your mother and your brothers are depending on you now. You must take up where your father left off." To me, this was an impossible expectation. I did not know how I would be able to continue my father's work—I was only a nineteen-year-old boy. I did not understand what it was that people seemed to want or expect of me. They did not want me to mourn my father's death. Instead, they wanted me to be my father, as if this were the proper sequence of events, as if, in this way, he would not die. I too wanted to see my father alive again, but I could not see my father in myself, as much as I wanted to find him there. I could not be the same man. No one seemed to understand. Perhaps Saburo would have understood, but he was not there.

* * *

By this time, the New World Ranch, which most people simply called "Kantaro's place" and later, the Uno Ranch, was a place of endless activity. Kantaro, Jiro, Befu, Tsuruta and Heizo all put their names on an initial plot of land of some 120 acres. With time, they acquired the surrounding land, and the ranch grew to more than 400 acres. Besides the founding five, numerous other young men and a few families had joined Kantaro and were housed and working along with everyone else. Where Kantaro's and Befu's small wood structures had once stood alone, there was a growing cluster of rustic one- or two-room cottages, each with their flower beds, vegetable patches and red dirt paths to the kitchen and the bathhouse. A longer sort of bunkhouse was also built for young men like me who came and went. The kitchen had already been expanded twice and the dining hall extended. All the structures were built from large boards and heavy beams—timber we lumbered ourselves from the very forest—unpainted inside and out, with shuttered windows but no glass. Some cottages had polished wooden platforms about a half meter off the ground in the Japanese style for sleeping. Others had dirt-packed floors and required Western-style beds. The roofs were thatched until we could afford tile. The basic simplicity of these rustic and simple structures would remain the same over the years. In fact, except for the use of concrete, I would say that it is pretty much the same today.

Befu's barns and chicken pens began to pop up everywhere. Eggs were incubating on compost heaps in every possible corner. Large areas were mapped out for planting vegetables, beans, rice, corn. In time, fruit trees of every species were planted here and there: avocados, oranges, bananas, papayas.

Haru and Toshiko were now joined in the kitchen by other women; they needed all the help they could get to feed the gangs of as many as thirty young men with healthy appetites who filed in and out and lined the long tables and benches. Kantaro had so many men working around the ranch that he could send crews out to clear new roads around Esperança and still have men to work the nearby fields.

My responsibilities at home and my friendship with Saburo had kept me away from Kantaro's projects, but now I wondered why so many like me were attracted to this work. I drifted over to the road crews and found myself hard at work, sawing, cutting, digging, slashing, hacking through the forest. The work was backbreaking, and no one was paid to do any of it. Still, I went back day after day, challenged by the forest and attracted undeniably to the companionship of others like me, all looking for a place in the scheme of things, full of undirected energy and the same confusion about a newfound manhood. I had never worked so hard in my life. In the evenings I returned home exhausted but strangely content. "Tomorrow, we need you here," my mother would say accusingly, but I would rise early, finish the chores she might complain of, and wander back to Kantaro's. I returned to Kantaro's perhaps to escape, to find the proper interlude that youth claims before adulthood. At Kantaro's, I was given assurance that this was an interlude to which I had a right. I floundered into the camaraderie of youthful rebellion, a wild and, to me, new disrespect for old ways and conventions. I remember our irreverent name for the Emperor was *Ten-chan*, or Little Emp, and that I signed my name to a letter sent to the Japanese troops in Manchuria suggesting that they abandon their war and join us here for the work of real men. This mocking attitude toward Japan was unheard of, even though the elders of Esperança were generally thought to be political and social renegades. At Kantaro's place, up until the period of wartime repression, we forced these issues into the open. Kantaro himself represented a new order in Esperança. It was perhaps not so different from the old days when Kantaro attracted members to his baseball team, leaving his familial duties to his brother and selling his family's rice to send Yōgu to Japan. The rice, Kantaro had said, belonged to Esperança. In the same way, the youth—taken from so many family duties and responsibilities—belonged to Esperança, to this new idea, this collective responsibility, this New World Ranch. One day, I did not return to my mother and my brothers. I had found a new home.

It was Akira Tsuruta who came often to see me in these days, wondering if I had made the right decision. "How's your mother?" Tsuruta would ask. "Are you going to see her this weekend?" And without knowing quite why, I would go to see my mother and my brothers on the weekend. But I could not stay, nor could I explain to my mother why.

"My father died just before I came to Brazil," confessed Tsuruta. "I was in a position to inherit everything, but I left it all behind. I suppose it is still there waiting for me to return." Tsuruta shrugged,

"I have one sister. She must be your age now. My mother wrote me to say that she will be married soon. She is hoping that I will return for the wedding, but I cannot."

"What do you mean?"

"No money," laughed Tsuruta. All of us knew the rumors that Tsuruta came from royal stock, and we all assumed that he must have the money to do as he pleased. "Well, I suppose I could ask my mother to send my inheritance, but then, that would be cheating, wouldn't it?" Tsuruta smiled. "You're lucky, Ichiro. You have your family here with you. I haven't seen mine in ten years."

"Do you miss Japan?" I asked, wondering myself what it was I had left behind and had no memory of.

"Yes," Tsuruta admitted.

"But you are here building a new future," I suggested, trying to project the sort of arguments I had heard Kantaro use.

"Well, that's true, but it's hard to be reconciled to the idea that I can't go back."

"But you came here to settle."

"People who come to settle make families, build homes, create children. These are the people who can see the future blossoming before their very eyes. It's a shame to deprive your mother of that pleasure," Tsuruta paused and added, "as I have done."

I did not understand the meaning of this. I had always thought that Akira Tsuruta was an avid partner in Kantaro's great plans, but now it seemed to me that he was really quite lonely, quite fragile. For so many years he had been my teacher, his patience and quiet humor so different from the vibrant and agile Kantaro. Tsuruta placed his gentle hand on my shoulder; his long delicate fingers had been made rough by farm work. His touch both soothed and frightened me. The question in my eyes made Tsuruta withdraw his hand. He smiled and left. A silence passed between us, but strangely, I felt no discomfort in this. From then on, Tsuruta's kindness followed me around as always but expected nothing in return.

* * *

I was still too young to understand much about the life I was on the road to choosing. It was not that my family was less important to me. Perhaps it was the nature of Esperança to give up its youth to great ideas, to the hope that it was possible to live very close to an ideal.

Kantaro had set the example. From the time I joined Kantaro's place, my relationship to my family changed forever. My brothers continued to be my brothers, but my peers at Kantaro's were in some way more than brothers to me. As with other families, each of my brothers is very different in character; we would have in another time and place perhaps gone our separate ways. Fate would have it that they would also come to live at Kantaro's. I do not feel that I can speak for my brothers, yet our collective life has dictated that they would also have the very same memories. Collective memories. I am unable to say, from this time in my life on, that my memories belong to me alone, but can only vouch for the particular filter I applied to the lens of those memories.

For several years, I lived and worked for months at a time at Kantaro's place, returning to my family periodically when they required my labor. My brothers Hiro and Eiji both came at different times to live and work at Kantaro's place. I was glad to see them join me. We became much closer during this time, and I felt that they understood rather than resented my choice. My mother did not oppose us when we left for Kantaro's place. She seemed somewhat bewildered, and I realize now that she must have felt quite overwhelmed by life in Brazil without my father. I am sorry that I did not know how to relieve her of her hardships. I know that it was, in fact, my mother who took up where my father left off. Having a family of five sons, she did not think that she would hold on to all of us; after all, everyone in Esperança had sons at that time who had taken up Kantaro's banner.

Kantaro's place became a natural meeting place, even for those young men who did not take up residence. In small towns all over Brazil, the central plaza has traditionally been a meeting place for young people, but in those days in Esperança, it was Kantaro's place—a rustic outpost at the north end of Esperança—where you could always get a meal, enjoy the banter of friends, toss a baseball, exchange gossip, all this in return for laboring for a cause. Tsuruta might be rehearsing a play, Befu discussing detailed projections for his chicken incubation, and Kantaro talking to newcomers, inspiring youth with a plan. It is difficult perhaps to convey the excitement and satisfaction so many of us felt. It was more than the gathering of youthful energy, it was a gathering of minds. Looking back on it all, I don't wonder at my complete enthusiasm for Kantaro's words. It was a period of youthful idealism, and Kantaro challenged all of us to live our ideals. "The main thing," Kantaro said, "is rejuvenating the land. The future depends on fertilizer. Without it, the land will go bad, people will desert their farms, and there will be no future."

In time, Kantaro took his message everywhere. He began to talk about uniting the Japanese rural youth all around Brazil. There were Japanese colonies as far north as the Amazon River in Pará and as far south as Paraná. I began to see myself as part of a great movement of Japanese rural youth. Already, we were naturally tied to each other by the growing network of cooperatives which the Japanese farmers had created to govern and support their interests. Kantaro saw that we could use this network of farming cooperatives, beginning with the influential São Paulo Sarandi Cooperative. He also knew intuitively that there was a new generation of young Japanese immigrants in Brazil who needed to find reasons and a focus for their energies.

Kantaro organized a conference in São Paulo, and young representatives from Japanese colonies all over Brazil gathered to hear Kantaro's ideas. "Until now, we have occupied ourselves in the great task of clearing the virgin forest. We have used the land, planted coffee, rice and cotton. In a matter of years, we've become guilty of depleting the soil of its natural fertility. Many Japanese have left the land and gone off to the city. We must find a way to keep people on the land. The answer is simple: restore the land's fertility."

And Kantaro had Befu's plan. Perhaps the figures were slightly exaggerated, but the plan was clear. "In Esperança, we have already begun with fifty-two leghorn chicks. Now we have more than twenty times that. Our calculations show that one thousand birds provide thirty tons of manure a year! Six tons of manure produced by only two hundred birds can rejuvenate four acres of land or fertilize two thousand coffee trees! The future depends on fertilizer!"

But Kantaro always thought big. He wanted to spread his plan around, to lead a great team or perhaps an army of young men like me. "Here gathered under one roof are one hundred and twenty young men representing sixty different areas. Until now, each of us has been scattered, working alone with no real power. Today I invite all of you to unite as one movement. My proposal is to create centers in every rural area. Every area will start a poultry farm, plant corn and build chicken yards and houses. In these centers, I propose that we work for free and that the profits from the sale of eggs be kept by the centers. This money can be used to create schools, to educate the youth, to build hospitals, to strengthen our rural colonies." Kantaro overwhelmed us with the possibilities, and then he assured us of our participation in the greater scheme of things.

"We are ready for a change which will ensure our future. Together, we have the potential of revolutionizing agriculture using intensive methods on a large scale. Our productivity will be enormous. What is the destiny of young Japanese men like ourselves a half world away from our homeland? This is our destiny! This is our work! I am not promising that it will be easy. We in Esperança have spent our hard labor on this dream, but we have proven that it is no idle dream, that it can work! Who among you is willing to make this sacrifice for the future?"

I was there. I stood up with all the others and applauded Kantaro, filled with pride and emotion. Saburo called us "Kantaro's communal compost," the human stuff that churned his dreams. But Kantaro's dreams were undeniably my dreams. I had found my place and my work. There was no longer any confusion in my mind. The rice belonged to Esperança. I belonged.

Part II: Haru

Love is accompanied by a continual uneasiness over jealousy or privation, little suited to marriage, which is a state of enjoyment and peace. People do not marry in order to think exclusively of each other, but in order to fulfill the duties of civil society jointly, to govern the house prudently, to rear their children well. Lovers never see anyone but themselves. . . .

. . . a place so different from what it was can become what it is only with cultivation and care, yet nowhere do I see the slightest trace of cultivation. All is green, fresh, vigorous, and the gardener's hand is nowhere to be seen.

You cannot imagine with what zeal and gaiety everything is done. They sing, they laugh all day, and the work goes better for it. Everything is done in the greatest familiarity. Everyone is equal. . . .

Freedom knows no bounds other than honesty.

Jean-Jacques Rousseau
Julie, or The New Eloise

CHAPTER 8: COMPOST

SOME PEOPLE SAY I married Kantaro because of great love, but they all know that it was really Kantaro who had great love. For my part, I married him because I am as stubborn as he. Well, perhaps not as stubborn. Everything Kantaro did in his life, he did because he wanted to. When you think of it, that is not something many people can say. Most people, especially women, are forced to do things because of circumstances, because they have children, because their children are hungry or crying. But Kantaro never cared about circumstances. Funny, but it was because he was that sort of man that people have loved him so much.

Kantaro was a man who was full of life. It was as if there was something in his chest that wanted to burst. He compared it to a cup brimming over. I knew this feeling of his, and I wondered how it could be so. This was something people wanted for themselves as well, this feeling of being full to bursting, this great love of everything around you. At first I was afraid of this feeling of his, that I could not fulfill such a great need to live. But as time went on, I saw that life spilling over can be a troublesome thing. Someone like me is always needed to wipe things up, to clean up the mess.

I had all of my children by the time I was thirty-two. First there was Kanzo. Then Mieko. Then Asa. Then Hanako, and last was Iku. Four girls and one boy. Poor Kanzo was the first and only boy. It has not been easy being Kantaro's son, but it was not easy to be Kantaro's brother or father for that matter. Still, Kanzo was lucky to grow up with so many children. He was a very happy child. Some of the girls are tougher than the boys. My girls in particular are tougher. Some people say that's my fault. Kantaro liked the children when they were about two or three and starting to talk. After they could really talk, he didn't seem so interested and left the rest of their years for others to notice. Maybe Kantaro wanted more boys, but he never said that. I don't think he really thought about it. There were always so many children around; what was one more girl or one more boy? They all grew up together, and we were all one family. Kantaro said they were all the future.

*   *   *

Kantaro's first and closest friend was Akira Tsuruta. Before we knew that Tsuruta would die, he and Befu had a terrible argument about whether Japan could win a world war. Not that I understood any of this, but it always seemed that the true reason for their argument had nothing to do with politics. From the time Befu arrived in Esperança and introduced his ideas about chickens and manure to Kantaro, there were differences that set Befu and Tsuruta apart. To begin with, Seijiro Befu was a small hairy man with dark eyes. He was a very intense sort with a fiery character. Akira Tsuruta, on the other hand, was tall and thin, fair and rather hairless. And he was a very gentle sort; so gentle that sometimes I wonder he didn't break. While Befu was easily excited, full of sudden ideas and actions, Tsuruta was always calm and patient and thoughtful. Befu found Tsuruta's thoughtfulness irritating, while Tsuruta found Befu irrational and insensitive. Tsuruta probably never thought so, but Befu somehow decided that Tsuruta was second-in-command to Kantaro. This sounds strange to me when I think about the man Tsuruta was and how he and Kantaro could be quietly happy together. It was not at all the way Befu saw it, as if we were all chickens with Kantaro on top and then Tsuruta and then someone else below and so on. But Befu always saw things that way. Tsuruta didn't seem to care, but Befu liked to dance about and show his spurs.

People remember that Tsuruta was a scholar, like Mizuoka, and a poet. They liked to think that Tsuruta made Esperança even more special. "Interesting people live in Esperança," they might comment. "Akira Tsuruta, for example, a second cousin to the Emperor himself."

"No, no," another might contest. "I've heard he's a first cousin."
"Do you think the Emperor has plans for Esperança? It is possible, wouldn't you think?"

"Well, Baron Tamaki has a ranch there."

"Esperança—intelligentsia, Christians and snobs."

Akira Tsuruta was a very smart man, but no one wanted to listen when he said that a Japanese victory in a great war against a world power like the United States would be impossible, that it would destroy Japan.

Befu, who was always looking for an argument with Tsuruta, was enraged by this point of view. "What would you know of these things with your simpering sniveling ways?" he screamed at Tsuruta. "You are an insult to the Japanese race! You haven't the courage to fight a man's war, so you speak in feminine tones about the tragedy of war! You are afraid to die!"

"It's not a question of my courage or your courage or whether any of us is afraid to die," Tsuruta retorted coolly. "You have no understanding of history or politics or economic realities. Mizuoka lived for five years in the United States. Listen to what he says about that country." Tsuruta spoke of Mizuoka, his and Kantaro's teacher, but who was Shūhei Mizuoka to Befu? Befu, who had come more recently from Japan, thought he knew the real truth.

"You and Mizuoka are the same. Minds wrapped up in so-called Western history and philosophy, you are blinded to the truth. You think because you read pretty words that that is what America must be, but I heard Mizuoka say that he left America because the Americans called him a 'yellow slant-eyed jap.' What does that mean? It means that all your education and wise talk is for nothing. If we want stature in this world, we must get it by force."

"At what cost? Have you thought of that? To begin with, Japan is an island. How can we maintain a war without natural resources? America has endless resources. How many years, no, how many months can Japan survive without oil or coal? For how many days can we even propose to sustain a war?"

"You are the great thinker? Where are your powers of strategy? The greater coprosperity sphere encompasses all of Asia—"

"What nonsense!" Tsuruta scoffed. "Asia for Asians or Asia for Japan? China? Korea? Indonesia? Do you think they will run to our side to battle the rest of the world? We have not been good brothers for centuries. They do not trust us."

And so the argument went. But in those days, I don't remember that anyone thought about Japan losing a war, and no one could predict the horrible destruction and loss of life that war would bring. There was nothing in our imagination or experience like this. I thought myself that if we were living in Japan, Kantaro would be sent to war, but I don't think he thought about dying. He said that his destiny was to survive and to be productive in Brazil; this was his sacrifice to Japan. When the war was over, young men like Kantaro would be ready to contribute to a prosperous peacetime. The idea that Japan should not go to war did not seem to be a question. They say that most Japanese in Brazil in those days felt this way. Kantaro now says that if you think about it, we were very young, all born in Japan, too foolish to know the cost of war. And while people like us came to Brazil to live and settle, most Japanese only thought about returning. Those in Esperança who thought war was a mistake were among the few. In those days, it was courageous of Tsuruta to speak out loud. Of course, my father always said he was a Christian and a pacifist who did not believe in war, but he was not a man to speak unless it was necessary. Tsuruta's opinions were written publicly by Kantaro's friend, Shigeshi Kasai, in the *Brazil Shimpo*, but Kasai was always that way, so no one paid much attention. Everyone was careful about this matter, careful not to say too much. There were always angry people like Befu, and as we discovered later, there were even spies. People listened carefully and remembered what others said.

Kantaro did not become involved in this argument between Tsuruta and Befu. Kantaro wanted to be a leader, to be outside of this argument. I know he was torn between his two friends, but he did not want to show weakness. Others had gotten into fights; it was better not to take sides. No one knew what to think anyway, so we watched Tsuruta and Befu fight. I know that Tsuruta was very brave. He never backed down, never lost his educated manner. Befu, on the other hand, fought cruelly, attacking Tsuruta personally. He could be very mean. I told Kantaro that it seemed mean to me, but he said that Tsuruta was strong enough to hold his own. It would be humiliating for Tsuruta if Kantaro stepped in to protect him. I told Kantaro that I protected my children no matter what. Kantaro said that Tsuruta was not a child. I still think that this was a mistake. Maybe Kantaro knows this, too, in his heart. Everyone followed Kantaro, and no one defended Tsuruta. On the outside, Tsuruta seemed very cool, but finally I think he must have been hurt very badly.

"This!" Befu held up a large binder of paper at dinner one evening. "This, I want you all to take a good look at!"

Tsuruta saw the binder and jumped from his seat. "What are you doing with that?" he exclaimed.

"I found it," smiled Befu. "I was just wondering what you found so interesting to write about. Here it all is, a confused mass of drivel about us, interspersed with poetry," Befu laughed. "Poetic nonsense! Did I say poetry? And unsent letters to Mother. Poor Mother. What sort of son are you anyway? And what does he write about us?" Befu opened the binder to cite an example.

"What is the meaning of this?" Tsuruta stepped forward to get his binder from Befu.

Befu danced backward. "We might all be in this thing, I tell you. We have a right to know what you have written about us."

"It is nothing that interests you," Tsuruta defended himself.

"Ah, but the poetry. Poetic lyricism. Great poetry. A modern Bashō, no less!"

Tsuruta came forward, but Befu ran around the table, prancing about with the binder like a teasing child with a ball. Everyone was laughing. Befu tossed the binder to another who in turn tossed it away to someone else. Tsuruta foolishly ran about after the binder until it fell into Ichiro Terada's hands. Tsuruta's sad gentle eyes pleaded. I could see a wave of shame running over Ichiro, who held on to the binder until Tsuruta thankfully took it. Everyone jeered and cuffed Ichiro across his ears, but I secretly thanked him. Ever since then, I have liked that boy. Well, Ichiro's not a boy anymore.

* * *

Kantaro's sister Ritsu was always lost among the men in her family. She wasn't like my mother-in-law, Waka, who liked to talk and arrange marriages. Maybe she was more like Jiro, a kind of follower. She never had a mind of her own. I could never understand this, and I told her so. She was content to do what her mother suggested, what her brothers wanted, what her father liked. Time went on, and everyone forgot that Ritsu had grown up, that she was a pretty young woman with a sweet shy personality. Everyone except her mother remembered that Ritsu should be getting married soon. I saw Waka always looking over the new young men who came to our place. Finally, there were three men who were interested in Ritsu: Seijiro Befu, Heizo Kawagoe and even the scholar Shūhei Mizuoka.

Mizuoka got to know Ritsu when he was digging up an Indian mound on our land. He was out there every day with the boys, Saburo and Ichiro, puttering around in the dirt. At first, I went out with hot food in pots to feed them at lunch, but then I was pregnant, and it became difficult to walk very far. Ritsu went out in my place. She would sit on a log with them and eat lunch too. I always thought she was such a cute girl; I remember she was always tugging her pigtails. She liked to listen to Mizuoka tell stories about the Indians. Mizuoka was always the teacher lecturing, but maybe something about Ritsu made the teacher look up from his papers. I was surprised by this change in Mizuoka, as if something had hit him on the head. I could see his gaze following Ritsu everywhere. It was very obvious, but then men are so foolish anyway. Kantaro always laughs that Mizuoka let the rains destroy the mound because instead of looking at the clouds in the sky, he was looking at Ritsu. Even after the mound was destroyed, Mizuoka kept coming around to see Ritsu, giving her little Indian trinkets and telling her stories about going into the forest.

One day, I saw Heizo Kawagoe staring at Ritsu, too, so I said, "Heizo, Ritsu is a cute girl, isn't she? And she is shy like you." Heizo turned very red. His face must have been so hot that he could hardly stand it. He suddenly ran off. Heizo was the sort who had difficulty talking. Everything was locked inside. He never confided in anyone. Later I wondered if Ritsu knew that Heizo watched her, and I asked her about this. She seemed confused to hear this. If you are shy, you think everyone is looking at you. Poor Ritsu. Poor Heizo. They thought everyone was looking, but no one really noticed anyway. I heard that Heizo had bad dreams, that he thrashed about at night. Someone thought he heard him mumble Ritsu's name at night. Some nights he woke up crying. Everyone began to know these things about Heizo; it was very embarrassing to him. No one said anything, but everyone knew. He knew everyone knew, and it made things worse. I said to Kantaro, "Why don't you talk to him. Better to talk than to dream."

"This is something that Heizo has to work out for himself," Kantaro said. "If he is a man, then he will find a way. If he has a dream, he must pursue it."

"But Heizo is shy. Ritsu is shy too. Maybe they are meant for each other. Perhaps if you said something."

"Heizo has to learn that his life is only his own, that only he can take charge of it. If he truly cares for Ritsu, then he will have to take charge of his life. I cannot do this for him."

"But what about Ritsu?"

"What about Ritsu?"

"Perhaps she likes Heizo in return."

"What a nuisance you are. You keep out of this!"

Kantaro was right. I can be a nuisance. I made Heizo get hot in the face. I feel bad about that because after all, Heizo knew what Kantaro knew: that he would not be the one chosen for Ritsu. Even if he could take hold of his manhood and find the courage to speak, he could not be like Seijiro Befu. Everyone knew that Befu liked Ritsu. How could Heizo be better than Befu? Befu the chicken genius, Befu the brilliant, Befu the tireless, Befu the patriot, Befu, Kantaro's second-in-command. Heizo could not compete. What would Kantaro say? What would the others say? They might laugh. It would be humiliating to let the others laugh. Befu had made them laugh at Tsuruta. No. That could not happen to Heizo. Heizo remained silent. Befu boasted and laughed. He looked at Ritsu as if his very thoughts were fact. He spoke winningly with my mother-in-law, who loved Befu's genial talk and quick wit. This was a man who would force some life into her quiet Ritsu. This was a man Waka herself would have liked to marry. A man with power and energy. A man devoted to her son Kantaro.

Maybe after all, Ritsu really preferred Shūhei Mizuoka. Mizuoka wasn't one of us. He came around to our place because of the mound and because of Ritsu. He was Kantaro's teacher, but he was older and out of place, not like the young men on Kantaro's baseball team. He was eccentric and a loner. He preferred books to people. He was nearly forty then, and Waka thought that was already too old, too set in his ways. Maybe that's true, but then when you see how these other men turned out in their old age, Mizuoka was still traveling around, going back and forth to the forest when he was maybe past eighty. Ritsu was shy, but maybe she had her own dreams too. Mizuoka would have taken her away to the forest. It might have been for the better, but it is useless to think about these things now.

People always talk about Kantaro and me as if we made a choice about getting married, but they talk about it because it was not a very normal thing to do. Ritsu did what most women did; she got married to a man chosen for her. Befu was overjoyed, but it was not really because he was getting married to Ritsu but because, in this way, he would be related to Kantaro. Kantaro always said that there is love between men that is different than that between men and women. Well, I can understand this because what was between Befu and Kantaro was like a bonding of blood. It was a fierce thing between men. They would die for each other. I don't think women think that way because they have their children. They would rather die for their children. But Kantaro was that way; he had great love for his friends. He loved Befu because Befu could be angry and passionate.

Mizuoka came around foolishly with his books and Indian trinkets, but Waka was busy making arrangements for Ritsu's wedding. And poor Heizo bothered his companions nightly with his bad dreams.

*   *   *

For several days no one had seen Tsuruta. We were accustomed to having him disappear to study and write, but Toshiko and I noticed he didn't even come around to the kitchen to find food for himself. We went to his room only to discover that he was sick and feverish, his bedclothes soaked in sweat. I ran to Sei Terada's house and made her come to see Tsuruta. What should I do? Tsuruta was so sick. She nodded and came with me. The symptoms I described—the blood in his sputum, his high fever, the cold sweat—could only mean one thing. We quarantined the room and sent everyone away.

Tsuruta knew what it was. "Tuberculosis," he said. "I had it in Japan. I went to the south of Japan to rest, and I got better. But when I went home again, it seemed to come back. Brazil," Tsuruta rasped. "Brazil. They said it would always be warm in Brazil. I've been well all these years."

I nodded. "The rainy weather this season. You must have been out in the damp weather," I scolded. "And it doesn't look as if you've been eating well at all. Look at you. So thin."

"The stigma of the disease in Japan," said Tsuruta. "It was such a burden for my mother."

"What nonsense," I said. "No burden is so great that she would want to lose you. Here. Eat this. What are we going to tell her now?" I held up a large bowl of soup.

Tsuruta sipped slowly, suddenly stopping to cough and sending the hot broth splattering about the bed covers.

As I sopped up his mess and changed the sheets, he said, "I have failed in my duty to my family, to my mother." Tsuruta said sadly, "At least my sister is now married." On the wall was a picture of an elegant family dressed in beautiful Western clothing, a man and a woman and their two children. The little girl, who was perhaps three or four years old, sat in her father's lap. The young boy stood to one side of his father. The gentle eyes and features could only be those of Akira Tsuruta.

Kantaro came to visit. He stared for a long time at the people in the photograph—the man who was now dead and the woman who would never again see her son. I don't think Kantaro really understood until then about Tsuruta's loneliness. Somehow Tsuruta felt incomplete. Kantaro had come to Brazil with his entire family, leaving no one behind. He did not need a photograph to remember people he missed. He saw the weak figure of his old friend in bed and said gruffly, "Tsuruta, be strong. Get well. We are your family, and we need you."

I felt angry at Kantaro about his manner, but Kantaro could not think about death. He only thought about life. Maybe he and Befu and even Tsuruta had pledged themselves to die together, but this was not the same thing. He did not know what to do about Tsuruta who was too young to die. When Kantaro came, he hid his tears from Tsuruta. Tsuruta must die like a man. I felt sad about this. I didn't know what to do. At first, I tried to remember things about Japan, about my grandmother or my cousins, something my mother told me, this or that. Somehow this made Tsuruta feel better. But I thought to myself that I would never see these people again, and that I could not turn back. It was only a memory. This was my home. My parents said so. Kantaro said so.

Kantaro thought Tsuruta didn't understand this. On the day Befu learned that he and Ritsu would be married, he came to Kantaro first. There were tears in his eyes, and he made a promise to Kantaro. "No matter what," Befu said, "I will stand by you. I am obligated to you, friend, forever. I will die with you." But Tsuruta was dying, and he had no such words for Kantaro. His thoughts only wandered back to Japan. I saw that Kantaro felt angry that he found comfort in these memories, as if these years struggling together on this new land were of little consequence.

I cared for Tsuruta until he died. Toshiko was pregnant, so we kept her away, but she took care of my children too in those days. Sei Terada came often to help me. Every morning I opened the shutters, removed his bedclothes and put everything in the sun to air. I would be sweeping the room and Tsuruta would thank me and say the same thing every morning, "You are so kind to me."

And I would say, "I don't know why I'm wasting my time on such a skinny man as you. I'm going to write a letter to that woman in the picture to tell her what a nuisance you are."

In the end, Tsuruta wanted to talk about everything, about his home, his family, his life in Brazil, things that came to mind, things he wanted to share, but all of these things were told in small pieces as he coughed up what remained of his rotting lungs, gasping for air until there was none. Tsuruta began to tire easily and could soon only speak in whispers and gasps. I filled everything in, chattering foolishly, remembering other times, hoping Tsuruta would forget his suffering. Sometimes I read to Tsuruta until he fell asleep. But one day Tsuruta did not awake, and only the sound of my foolish voice lingered on.

* * *

Before Tsuruta died, Befu married Ritsu. It was another one of our country weddings. Waka put herself out to make the cake, and Toshiko and I worked without rest to make the food. Kantaro and the others built a large open-air roof and long tables and benches. I took my old wedding gown and pinched in the sides to make it fit on Ritsu, who was a little thinner than I had been. Like every wedding, the wedding couple sat in front of an enormous cake. There were the usual speeches and songs and poems. Ritsu hardly even looked up from the uneaten food on her plate. Someone had brought several large cases of beer from São Paulo for the wedding. In those days beer was very scarce in Esperança, and it was considered a daring way to celebrate Befu's wedding. But Kantaro and Befu and the others always liked to be daring. Befu had been drinking beer with the others and was red in the face. He sat next to Ritsu with a happy dazed look, so different from his usual look. Since our place was rather out of the way, most people left early in large batches atop tractors, trucks and carts pulled by mules. By nightfall, only those who lived at New World remained, happily passing the beer around. Not too far away I sat in a small room trying to feed Tsuruta a little cake. Mizuoka, people said, had left Esperança suddenly, probably run off to the Mato Grosso. And unknown to anyone, Heizo Kawagoe had wandered off, armed with a small pistol. From somewhere the sound of a shot reverberated through the forest. I wandered out from Tsuruta's room, wondering about this sound, but Toshiko and the few women who lived with us had already wandered off to bed, and all the men had drunk themselves into a stupor, one by one dropping off into a deep sleep. I saw Kantaro sleeping there among them. I thought he had a peaceful smile on his face; he was still so young and handsome then. I remember seeing one young man, perhaps it was Ichiro Terada, staggering from his seat, thinking he would try to find his bed. Instead he fell over into a plate of food, his cheek coming to rest comfortably in a soft mound of leftover cake. And I saw the wedding couple still sitting at the head table. Befu was slumped over, snoring into his fancy silk tie, but Ritsu was still sitting there in my wedding gown, looking around, bewildered. All around were snoring young men, bodies flung across and under tables. I saw their stupid and innocent expressions caught in the soft moonlight. The sweet stench of beer and vomit and sweat rose around them with the drone of cicadas and the hiss of mosquitoes in that hot December night.

CHAPTER 9: WAR

THE NEXT DAY after Ritsu and Befu's wedding, we heard that Japanese bombers had attacked Pearl Harbor and Japan had declared war on America. Brazil was in agreement with America, and suddenly we were cut off from our birthplace. People in Esperança felt confused about this. My parents had left Japan because they were Christians, and they were saddened by these events. They felt, like Tsuruta, that war was a great mistake. Some people said privately that this had always been the reason they left Japan, to escape the military. My father-in-law, Naotaro Uno, remembered his experience in military service. He had been bullied for being a *yaso*, a bad name for Christians. He admitted that he and Waka had decided to come to Brazil so that Kantaro would not have to serve in the military. I know Seijiro Befu must have heard this, but he pretended not to. Waka told me that she was very relieved that her sons would not have to go to war. But everyone spoke quietly and only among trusted friends; there were many like Befu who favored the war and spoke of those who did not as weaklings and traitors. I heard that outside of Esperança, most Japanese felt as Befu did. In the colonies, there was a lot of propaganda about Japan. Japan was a superior nation led by a divine Emperor. Truthfully, people like me in Esperança did not know what to make of the war. We felt torn and confused to realize that we had lost our dearest ties to our families and friends far away. Even though correspondence was always very difficult, it was hard to accept the idea that now we could not even write letters. After a while, people felt resigned to these things. In Brazil, we were so far away from the war itself. Kantaro said we would have to wait and see. I wondered what would happen to us in Brazil, what would happen to us in Esperança. It always took a while for things to happen in Esperança. We were too far away to really matter. Stories reached us first.

My father-in-law Naotaro had an aching tooth. He was feeling terrible pain and decided he must see Takehashi, our dentist friend in São Paulo. Kōhei Takehashi and his family had come originally to Esperança to live. Then he decided to move to São Paulo to build a bigger practice, but he always returned to Esperança to treat our teeth. He and Kantaro were good friends. They liked to talk about cameras and taking photographs. Kantaro was impressed with a new camera that Takehashi had, and Takehashi liked to take photographs of the baseball team when they went to São Paulo. When he came to Esperança, he usually stayed with us, and when we went to São Paulo, we stayed with the Takehashis. People like Naotaro who couldn't wait for Takehashi to come to Esperança would take the train to São Paulo to see him. Takehashi never charged us much, and he always liked to have you pose for a photo portrait in his collection. Everyone liked to joke that Takehashi only asked you to pose if you had nice teeth.

Naotaro did not like to go by himself to São Paulo. He thought Waka should come, but she did not feel well. I felt badly for Naotaro, whose jaw was beginning to swell. Only my youngest child Iku was in diapers by then, and there were always plenty of mothers to look after things. I agreed to go with Naotaro. It was maybe the second time I ever went to the city. We did not know that there would be special wartime travel restrictions, and we left for the city rather innocently.

"You're lucky you came when you did," Takehashi commented to my father-in-law.

Naotaro nodded. He could not say anything with his mouth stretched opened.

The dentist pressed his mirror against Naotaro's lip. "Now we need special passes to go anywhere. I don't know if you'll be able to go back to Esperança. Have you thought about that? And did you hear that the newspapers have all been closed? Kasai's paper closed up a while ago. Kantaro knows that Kasai disappeared, doesn't he? I wonder what happened to him? Is it true Kantaro hid him in Esperança for a while? Where did he go?"

Naotaro shook his head.

"And our money. Money is frozen. Can't take money out of the bank. Only two *contos* per month."

Naotaro's eyes blinked and opened wide.

"That's tender there, isn't it," Takehashi said tapping the sore molar. "Japanese banks all closed. Brazilians took them all over. Sarandi Cooperative too. I heard they were closed down. No Japanese can run anything anywhere. Can't speak Japanese. Most of the Japanese schools were closed a long time ago, but I heard that the headmasters and some of the teachers of the old schools have been put in jail on suspicion of espionage. Japanese can't gather in groups of more than two. How are we going to comply with that? Someone said that there happened to be three Japanese waiting at a street corner, and they were all arrested! The restaurants will all have to close.

I don't think I can survive here much longer. How can I run a practice under these conditions? If I have three Japanese patients waiting out there, we could all get arrested. I'm thinking about taking my family and moving back to Esperança until the war is over. What do you think?"

Even if Naotaro could have answered the question, he would not have had time. Takehashi's wife Shizu and I ran into the office to warn them, but suddenly, we were surrounded by Brazilian policemen. They searched through everything, emptying the desk drawers onto the floor, sifting through Japanese books, letters and newspapers. A radio Takehashi liked to listen to and a box of small but rather sharp dental tools were immediately confiscated. Naotaro gagged on a piece of cotton the dentist had placed between his molar and the side of his mouth. Takehashi held his dental mirror and drill in the air. "You are both under arrest in accordance with the wartime restrictions of Japanese aliens," announced one of the policemen. At this, Takehashi and Naotaro were handcuffed and taken away.

* * *

Many people who were leaders in the community were arrested: Japanese schoolteachers, presidents of Japanese prefecture societies and other sorts of Japanese clubs, business association officers, presidents of agricultural cooperatives, Buddhist priests, newspaper owners. Most people were released after two or three days, but it was still a frightening thing. People feared for their lives and their homes and businesses. Everywhere, Japanese burned letters, commendations, diplomas and books. They buried photographs, heirlooms and memorabilia in boxes under the earth, under their houses. People hid or destroyed tokens of precious memories of their lives and families in Japan. Swords, knives, pistols, rifles, arms of any kind were all buried or destroyed. If the police came, they must not find anything. We heard a terrible story about a man and his son who were shot while police were searching their house. The police found nothing but a small cache of money, which they decided to keep for themselves. It was a very small amount, but it was hard-earned savings and meant a great deal to this poor family. When the man and his son tried to prevent this injustice, both were shot and killed. This frightened many people and caused a great wave of fear and suspicion.

I don't think it really occurred to anyone that the Japanese in
Esperança might be a threat. My father went to talk to the Bahiano.
Everyone said the Bahiano was a dangerous young man, that he built
and controlled Santa Cruz d'Azedinha. But I knew him from many
years past, and it seemed to be an exaggeration. He and my father
worked together to build roads between Esperança and Santa Cruz,
and they had an understanding. I heard the Bahiano say that he liked
"those Japanese." My father said the Bahiano agreed that we were
hard workers who made the land produce. The Bahiano said, "Brazil can't survive without the Japanese on the land. These people produce the food we all eat. We'd be slitting our own throats to deny it."
I know the Bahiano had great respect for my father. Because of this
he said, "I know these people. Takeo Okumura is against the war.
He's a Christian pacifist. I don't know if I agree with that, but he's
got his ideals. These people came here to settle. We've got no argument with them. We're all in this together. What's it to us if those
others want to fight thousands of miles across the sea? I don't want
to hear of anyone giving the Japanese problems. When all of this
business settles down again, we still have to build this town." Because the Bahiano said this, Brazilians in Santa Cruz also agreed.

There were a lot of stories about the Bahiano, and people did not
easily cross him. People were afraid of his deputies. They called them
jagunços which was the same as saying that they were hired gunmen.
My father did not agree with the Bahiano's ways, but he did not want
anyone to get hurt. The Bahiano called the war "political nonsense."
To him, his town, Santa Cruz, was more important. He liked to
come around and ask questions about our cooperative, about how
we sold our produce. My father worked very hard for the Esperança
Cooperative, and it was very productive. The Bahiano liked the idea
of a cooperative, and he wondered how Santa Cruz could use it.

The Bahiano protected the Japanese in Esperança by looking the
other way. First he warned my father, and then he sent his deputies
to search our houses. When the deputies came, we had already buried or burned anything suspicious. The Bahiano knew it was impossible for us not to speak Japanese, so he ignored us. Even
Mizuoka continued secretly to teach Japanese school. We felt sure
that the Bahiano would warn us about any outsiders who might
come to snoop around. Except for only one incident, these years
were in general, I think, a very quiet time.

That is to say, it was quiet for most of us, excepting my father; I
know he felt many difficulties. The wartime law was that no Japan-

ese could be president or director of any business. Mostly, Japanese found Brazilians who were friendly and agreed to be president in name only. Perhaps they got their salaries while the Japanese worked to keep the business going. It was just a formality. In the case of the Esperança Cooperative, my father had to let the Bahiano become the director. At first this seemed like a good idea, but eventually we discovered that the Bahiano really wanted to know about cooperatives. He made my father teach him everything.

This was a very big headache for my father. He said that the Bahiano understood about farmers getting a better price, but it was another problem to explain about sharing. This was not the Bahiano's way. He didn't like to share. I saw my father running in circles to keep the Bahiano and the farmers happy.

"It's not communism," said the Bahiano, "but it comes damn close. Yet I can see how it works. This might well be the answer for agriculture in Brazil. I think we've got something here, Okumura." All during the war I saw my father trying to teach the Bahiano about cooperatives. It was a strange thing to see the Bahiano converted to this new way of thinking. If it is true that the Bahiano was a dangerous man who used violence to get his land, my father did a very incredible thing. Perhaps the Bahiano would have become old and respected anyway. He was a very good man to us. Even Kantaro says so. When others took advantage of our situation, the Bahiano did not. Kantaro said the Bahiano was innocent.

*   *   *

Even though things were quiet in Esperança, it was still a difficult time. Prices were frozen. Savings were frozen. There was a frost that winter, and the harvest was poor. People wondered how long the war would go on, how long we could wait for better times. More and more people in Esperança were in debt. Friends came to talk about their troubles. Kantaro always said that if we worked and lived together, it would be much easier. Many people had sons who already lived with us. Ichiro Terada and his brothers Hiro, Eiji and Yōzo were already with us. Their mother, Sei Terada, could not work her farm alone with only Kōichi, her youngest. Her sons convinced her to live with us. The Teradas turned their land over for planting. Lately, Sei Terada was always at our place tending pregnant women and helping me care for sick people. She felt happiest in this work and was relieved not to have to worry about her farm. Kantaro's parents, Naotaro and Waka, too, decided to move in. They left their land to us for planting. More and more people in Esperança thought about moving in with us—the only place in Esperança where life seemed to prosper. Families had already come from as far as São Paulo to join. One man had worked for a Japanese bank that closed. Another had worked for Shigeshi Kasai's old newspaper, the *Brazil Shimpo*. These people suddenly had no way to live. All of them came with an idea of joining us to survive through hard times. By the end of the war, there were more than 300 of us living together.

Many more houses had to be built. We built small cottages one after another. We had to make the dining hall longer, and our kitchen, laundry and the baths had to be almost twice as large. Many men worked to build a larger water tower. The saws in the lumberyard buzzed all day long to make boards for the new buildings. A man who was a carpenter joined us; he opened a small shop next to the foundry, setting up his tools and saws on shelves and work benches. He was a very clever man. He took the smaller pieces of wood and built simple furniture for everyone.

Of course, Befu continued to build his barnyards for his poultry project. This chicken operation of Befu's was beginning to spread out in every direction. There were pens, feeding troughs, and chickens and roosters cackling and crowing everywhere. I saw the new chicks every day and said, "Befu-san, what are we going to do with so many chickens?" But he and Kantaro were already talking about plans to clear the forest to the northeast for six new chicken houses.

Well, everyone found some job they wanted to do. One man brought his special breed of watermelon and spent all his time growing watermelons. He told me that perhaps his misfortune had been a blessing in disguise. Now that he had joined us, he could spend all his time developing a perfect watermelon; he didn't have to worry about so many daily matters of running a farm by himself. Very soon, our New World Ranch was a small busy world. For the moment, we were a large active family protected from another world torn by war.

*   *   *

Shizu Takehashi and I did not know what to do when we saw her husband and my father-in-law taken away by the police. We tried to go to the jail to find out about them, but it was no use. Then, three days later, they came home. They were mostly very hungry, and nothing bad had happened except they'd been interrogated.

"What is your name?"

"Naotaro Uno."

"Where were you born?"

"In Hyogo prefecture in Japan."

"When did you come to Brazil?"

"In 1925, on the *Brazil-maru.*"

"Where do you reside?"

"In Esperança, near the town of Santa Cruz d'Azedinha. I immigrated here with my entire family, my wife, my children. I have grandchildren born in this country. We have our own land, a sixty-acre farm. We have come here to live. Brazil is our home now."

"What are you doing in São Paulo? Don't you know that your travel is restricted?"

"We are Christians. We are honest people. I do not believe in this war."

"Do you profess loyalty to the Japanese Emperor?"

"We came here to create a new civilization based on the ideals of Christianity and freedom of religion. We came to start a new way of life."

"Do you profess loyalty to the Japanese state? Would you renounce your Japanese citizenship?"

"I am a citizen of the world."

"Crazy Japanese! What's he talking about?"

After this, Kōhei and Shizu Takehashi decided that life in the city would not do. They only talked about how Esperança was their true home and how it would be safer there for them and their children. Naotaro said immediately, "You must come home to Esperança. You must join us. You are a dentist, and we need your skills."

Naotaro and I helped the Takehashis pack their belongings. Shizu was like Waka; she liked to gossip. She said, "I heard an interesting thing. Hachiro Yōgu is in São Paulo now. He came back from the Amazon." Shizu looked away. She pretended to be busy with her packing, but she was waiting for me to say something. All these years and somehow I had forgotten about Yōgu. I knew people liked to gossip; they liked to tell about Yōgu and his horse at my wedding. "Why did he do that?" they always wanted to know. "Why?"

"He ran away with Kimi Kawagoe," I said.

"I heard they have eight children."

"Eight?" It sounded impossible, but I had five.

"It was too difficult to live up there, so they came back."

I thought about the Amazon. When people heard these rumors, no one was surprised. They all said, "Yōgu was a wild jungle monkey anyway, but poor Kimi." I asked Shizu, "What will they do now?"

"That's just the problem. As soon as Yōgu got back, he took a long bath in the hotel. The fumes from the burning charcoal heating the bath went to his head, and he fell over and banged his head. Well, when he woke up, they say he couldn't talk. Can't remember anything." Shizu shook her head.

"Yōgu? Can't talk? Can't remember?"

"No. They say he looks at Kimi and their children like strangers. Scratches his head. Stares around all day. I didn't believe it myself. A completely different man. Can you imagine? Totally helpless."

"What will Kimi do?"

"She's too proud to ask for help. I think she should go home to her parents in Esperança, but she's probably so ashamed. Her money is going to run out; then the hotel will throw them out."

"Eight children?" I thought about this. What sort of life did Kimi have in the Amazon with a man like Hachiro Yōgu? I always heard people say that it was such a waste. Kimi could play the piano and sing. She was so educated, they said. Such a waste. What did they mean? What did they expect?

Naotaro heard everything and said, "These are difficult days for everyone. I will go see Kimi at that hotel and tell her to come home with us. You Takehashis are coming to join us. She and her family must come as well."

*   *   *

Naotaro convinced Kimi to come home to Esperança with us. All of her children followed behind in a big huddle. I did not know what to say to Kimi, so I looked at her children and said things like, "That little one there has a cold. I know some good medicine for him." Then I saw Yōgu. It was true what they said. He did not know me or anyone. He wandered this way and that. One of his children always had to run behind to grab him and bring him back.

When we arrived, Naotaro and I went first to take Kimi to her old home. Her mother Kinu was still always in bed. People rarely saw her. I heard that her father Shinkichi Kawagoe spent all his time listening to his records and caring for Kinu. I knew that he and Kinu would not talk about their children. Heizo was dead, and Kimi had disappeared. When Shinkichi saw Kimi and all her children, he was so stunned, he could not say anything. Kimi looked away. She was so ashamed. I felt ashamed too. I had been stubborn. I had never thought about how Kimi felt. But that was already twelve or more years ago. Kimi's father did not know what to do; he went to the back of his house and sat under the giant mango tree and wept.

Kimi saw that eight children was too much. Kinu did not like the noise, and Kawagoe was too old. Naotaro insisted that she should come to New World. We were a big family, and her family would make us bigger. The past was forgotten. Naotaro could say that, but it was still a problem for Kimi. When she saw Kantaro, she turned red. We were all older now. Kantaro always said that he married me for great love. It could not be otherwise. Kimi made a choice too. It was a hard life in the north. Now she was a worn-looking mother with lines creeping from her sad eyes. And her hair was like mine—striped with strands of grey. Now Kimi was tough, but not tough like me. I guess she could never be tough like me. Everyone noticed her callused hands, and we wondered if she still remembered how to play the piano.

It was a great shock for Kantaro to see Hachiro Yōgu. Yōgu was like another child, staring around blankly. He seemed to be staring at something inside his head. We wondered if Yōgu could hear; maybe not. He did not respond to any questions, and he did not speak. The only thing we recognized about him was his old habit of spitting; this alone had not changed. Everything about Yōgu was completely different. Suddenly he was dependent, childlike and silent. Gone was the old Yōgu, the fiery, blustering, angry *pistoleiro*. Someone remembered that my father had to take Yōgu's guns and knives away and tame him when he first came to Esperança. They laughed, "If only Okumura had known. All he had to do was to hit him on the head!"

For those who had known Yōgu, it was hard to believe that such a change could occur. Those who had only heard of Yōgu thought the tales told were false exaggerations. Befu, who did not know Yōgu in the early years, scoffed at the stories. He only remembered that Yōgu had shot his pistol and ridden his horse into our wedding party. "Why did he do that?" Befu asked out loud, checking to see Yōgu's response. "Disrupted everything. The horse sat in the cake." He laughed. "Eh, Kantaro, was it because of Haru?"

Befu and Kantaro looked at Yōgu carefully. Befu suggested that maybe Yōgu only pretended to be dumb. Kantaro said, "Do you really think that Yōgu liked Haru? All that time he was at the Okumuras with a thing for Haru? I wonder."

Yōgu stared past Befu, past Kantaro. There was no recognition. Befu sneered, but Kantaro smiled. I shook my head. All this foolish talk so many years later. Men had nothing better to do.

At first, Kimi or her oldest daughter Akiko had to dress and feed Yōgu. It seemed strange to see Yōgu sitting patiently at the table in front of his food as if he had forgotten what it was that he should be doing there. Yōgu had also become incontinent, so Kimi fashioned large diapers for Yōgu. The diapers bulged under his clothing. Kimi had to watch Yōgu constantly because he might wander into mischief or danger. One day I found Yōgu opening a hot oven full of baking cakes. Another day, we spent all afternoon trying to get him out of the top branches of an avocado tree. Then there was the time he chased Befu's prize hens out of their pens and scattered them into the vegetables. Befu was furious. We didn't know what to do, so we all treated Yōgu like another child, always scolding, always instructing. This was probably good for him. After a while, he could take his diapers off and feed himself. The world was a new and strange place. Some days I saw Kantaro staring at his old friend and wondering. Maybe Kantaro missed the old Yōgu, too.

*   *   *

One day, Ichiro Terada said, "Haru, I'm going into Santa Cruz with the truck. What do you need?" I had a list: a sack of salt, several of flour, cakes of soap and thread. Ichiro took the list and said, "Why don't you come with me and get these things?" I didn't usually go to Santa Cruz, but Ichiro liked to take me. He thought I would like a change. Ichiro was nice that way. He said, "Let's take Yōgu with us, too. Then Kimi can have a rest."

Ichiro stopped the truck in front of Abdala's store. Yōgu sat quietly between us, staring out onto the street. We got out and went into the store to talk to the old Turk. Kantaro said the old Turk was really not Turkish; he was Lebanese. Abdala didn't like it, but everyone called him "the old Turk" anyway. Abdala was grumbling about something. "Outsiders," he muttered. "Come here just to make trouble. Sons of prostitutes. I don't give no credit to outsiders. No credit. Sons of—" When he saw me, he closed his mouth. Well,

I can understand that much Portuguese, but he spoke to Ichiro, "Ichiro, your people I can trust, but these outsiders never come back. I got a family to feed."

While we were inside, Hachiro Yōgu got out of the truck and wandered away. He must have been attracted to the sounds of laughter in the bar at the corner. A small crowd of afternoon customers were drinking and playing cards at the sidewalk tables. A man who was passing through town was talking loudly, impressing everyone with his outsider's news. He saw Yōgu wandering toward the bar and pointed. "Now look at that. You've got a Japanese coming down the street. These are the people you gotta contend with I say. They're all spies for the Japanese Imperial Army. You ever wonder why the Japanese work so hard? Working day and night? It's because the Emperor has ordered it. They're all working like little ants, having lots of children, thinking they are going to take over this place. I heard you got a whole colony of these people nearby. What are you doing about it? You gonna let these people quietly take over everything?" By this time the man was yelling these words directly at Yōgu. But Yōgu only smiled stupidly and walked over to look around the bar. He examined the tables and the people with curiosity. "These people should all be put in jail. Rounded up!" the man continued. "How can all of you sit here in the same bar with this scum?" The man approached Yōgu, now sitting silently at a table. "What do you have to say about that, eh, *Japão?*" the man shouted. Yōgu looked through the man and said nothing.

This created a great deal of amusement among the other people in the bar. "The Japanese are inscrutable. You won't get a word out of this one!" they laughed.

This angered the man further. "You bastard! Son of a yellow bitch!"

Yōgu blinked and spat on the ground. To the man, this must have been the ultimate offense; he grabbed Yōgu by the shirt. This man was a large strong fellow, but at another time, I am sure that Yōgu would have killed him on the spot. Sadly, Yōgu did nothing to defend himself. The people in the bar, eager for some excitement, did not come to Yōgu's rescue. Instead they passed bets around while the man pummeled Yōgu with his fists, throwing him onto the dirt road and kicking him again and again.

Ichiro saw the commotion in the street as he loaded the truck. From inside the store, I heard him yell something. The old Turk looked up from his books and muttered, "Trouble out there. Better go see." Suddenly I remembered Yōgu. I ran out, the old Turk huffing behind. There he was curled up in the middle of the street, writhing in pain. A circle of hysterical drunken men caroused around his beating. Ichiro threw himself into the center, trying to pull the attacker away. The man looked crazy. He threw his big fist into Ichiro's eye, and poor Ichiro fell backward into the crowd. Still, Ichiro was brave and pulled himself up, staggering blindly around. I saw the big brute coming at him again and yelled, "Ichiro! Watch out!" Suddenly, the man seemed to fall on his face. Someone pounced from the crowd and pinned the raging man to the ground.

A shot was sent into the air, and the crowd quickly dispersed. Abdala had sent for the Bahiano's deputies.

I tried to push my way into the crowd to get to Yōgu. He was folded in a sorry heap on the ground. I wanted to cry. Someone was picking Yōgu up from the ground, lifting him onto his strong young shoulders. Ichiro staggered forward to thank him. Then I recognized the sound of a familiar voice.

"Oh, Emiru," Kantaro's younger brother Saburo said, smiling in that old sarcastic manner of his. "What's this mess you've gotten yourself into?"

CHAPTER 10: KACHIGUMI

YŌGU'S BEATING in town caused a big commotion in Esperança. Although it was forbidden, everyone gathered at New World Ranch to protest. My father came to personally calm everyone down. "This is an isolated incident by an outsider. The Bahiano has run the man out of town." But everyone had heard about incidents much worse in other parts where Japanese homes had been looted and people beaten up and thrown into jail for no reason at all. There was that story about the man and his son shot to death by police. Everyone was afraid that these things would soon happen in Esperança as well. Some people thought that everyone should move into our place for protection, and people like Befu thought we should secretly train the men for defensive action.

My father was now in his sixties. My mother and I knew how hard he had worked over the last twenty years for Esperança. He was not just the director of the co-op; people came to him for advice about everything, about their lives and their beliefs. They sometimes also came to pray as well. My father was not a very talkative man, but when he talked, people listened. This time we heard him speak in his usual slow and deliberate manner, pausing to think carefully. He pleaded to the part of all of us that must be reasonable and Christian. These were difficult times for everyone, but these difficulties would not be resolved by panic or fear or hatred. Forsaking the ideals we had brought with us to settle this land would be the destruction of Esperança.

For the first time, my father was challenged; people grumbled unhappily about this being more of the same talk. People privately scoffed that Okumura could trust a man like the Bahiano, and many people were angry that he had allowed the Bahiano to participate in the cooperative. Some people even said that he let the Bahiano infiltrate our business. They said that they did not know when the Bahiano might be taking over everything in Esperança; Okumura must be involved in something devious. Somehow people forgot that the war had forced this situation on us and that the Bahiano had taken advantage of it. My mother and I saw my father stripped of his leadership and forced to run messages between the Bahiano and the colonists of Esperança. It was an unfortunate situation, and we felt embarrassed to see my father fumbling helplessly for respect.

That day, Kantaro made a speech which moved many people to tears. Some people who had only wondered about moving to New World made their decision to join on this day. For Kantaro, this day was perhaps a turning point. Everyone, I think, remembers this speech. I listened to Kantaro, and I knew his energy. It was a powerful speech. He began with the hardships of our journey to Esperança and the sacrifice of my parents and the early families. He recalled the pride of our baseball days and how we worked and planted on virgin land. He reminded everyone that my father Okumura had sacrificed his life for Esperança. He said that he did not say these things just because Okumura was his father-in-law; he said them because they were the truth. He reminded everyone that it was Takeo Okumura who placed a little of the precious soil of Esperança in each of our hands, blessing the land and our arrival. The memory of these simple beginnings touched a soft spot in people's hearts. How could they forget?

But then Kantaro continued to talk about other things, about our purpose in the war and the promise of Esperança. He said, "At New World Ranch, we have been quietly but industriously bringing together people for the great work ahead of us. We are experimenting in new technology and making new discoveries in the farming of poultry. New World Ranch is a progressive place, the farming of the future. The war has not stopped anything. That Yōgu has been beaten only demonstrates our need for stronger resolve. We cannot depend on the Bahiano or anyone else for protection. We cannot call attention to ourselves, but we must be patient. When the time comes, we will be ready. The combined production of so many people of resolve is indeed formidable. Everywhere, people will have to recognize the dawning of a new day, a new era." That was Kantaro's speech. I remember that it made me feel both happy and sad—happy and proud for Kantaro, but sad for my father who had lost his place.

* * *

Kantaro said that when we came to this land, we were blessed with the freedom to create our own lives. This was a blessing from God, not to be squandered on small visions of the future. Kantaro said most immigrants thought only about returning to Japan, about their day-to-day survival. While they were busy thinking of the past, their lives passed them by. When I think about it, my life has passed me by as it has any other immigrant, living day to day—cooking, washing, feeding, sewing, planting, weeding. I have tried to think like Kantaro that I have been a part of something special, but every day, people want to eat at the same hour. Children need their diapers changed. Old people must take their medicine. The dirt comes in with muddy feet.

There was a long time when I could not sleep at night. I would lay in bed and stare into the dark. Every night it was the same—Kantaro snoring, me staring into the dark. One night I thought about it. I am a part of Kantaro's dream; that is why he sleeps and I cannot. I got up and went into my garden. I worked there in the moonlight all night. I picked the snails off the leaves; I followed the ants and put poison in their hole. The next night, I slept all night. I never had this problem again, but I can never sleep very long. I always get up at dawn.

* * *

Saburo came back. It had been maybe ten years since he went away to Palma. He was over thirty now, and he was much heavier. It was that Latvian food. His broad shoulders had filled out, and now he looked more like Kantaro. He still had his old habit of wearing a cap. The one person who was truly happy to see Saburo was Ichiro Terada. They were always such good friends in childhood. Kantaro tried to show that he was happy to see Saburo, but he worried that Saburo had not changed. Maybe Saburo still could not get along with Kantaro.

One day after he arrived, I went to Saburo's room with a basket of his clothing. All the shutters were closed; I didn't think he would be there. With the slight light from the doorway, I could see a big mound humped up on the bed and covered by a heavy blanket. I could hear some noises and voices under that blanket, so I put the basket down quietly and left. I thought it was strange that Saburo's room was always closed up, always dark and stuffy. Some days I went in to sweep it out and left the shutters open, but he always came back and closed them up tightly. Then one day, I saw Ichiro go into the room. He didn't come out again. Although it was winter, it was an unusually hot day. What could they be doing together in a hot dark room in the middle of the day?

Finally, one day I went in with my basket and saw the same big covered mound on the bed. I turned to leave, but then I heard a funny scratching sound and muffled voices coming from under the blanket.

What's that she's speaking?" whispered a voice.

"Spanish," whispered another. "Weather's cold in Buenos Aires." There were more scratching sounds and a strange whistling noise.

"What's that?"

"English."

"How do you know?"

"Quiet . . . The Americans have taken Iwo Jima."

"Iwo Jima?"

"I heard it this morning in French, out of Cambodia. Japan is losing the war."

"Losing? What do you mean?" I blurted out despite myself.

Someone grumbled under the blanket, "Nuisance." Then Saburo peeked out. "Haru, what are you doing here? Go away!" He hissed with bad humor.

"What are you doing under there?"

"Taking a nap!"

"At this hour? Who's that with you?"

Saburo laughed, "Haru, you are still the same, aren't you. Why do you want to get into other people's business all the time?"

The voice still under the blanket said, "Let her see it, Sabu. Haru can be trusted."

"Haru, you can be trusted not to talk?" Saburo broke out into laughter.

"What do you mean?" I said, trying to look angry, but I liked Saburo. "What is it you are hiding from me. You'd better show me, or I will tell everyone about finding you in the dark with—"

"Ichiro?" Saburo sneered.

Ichiro popped his sweaty head out, and Saburo pushed the blanket away. I saw the thing that made the strange noises: a shortwave radio. No Japanese could have one during the war. They thought we would spy with it. Saburo hid it under his bed and used the blanket to muffle the sounds. "I built it at Palma," said Saburo. "Gustavo helped me. We had to listen to it in secret; if the wrong people found out, I'd have to give it up." Saburo paused. "There are even people here in this place who would destroy this radio if they knew I know the truth about the war. Do you understand, Haru?"

I nodded. "What do you think I am?" I looked at Saburo. "How do you understand what's on the radio anyway?"

"Sabu understands English and French," Ichiro said.

"Everyone at Palma speaks several languages," said Saburo. "Besides Latvian, they speak Russian and German. Some speak French and English, and others Scandinavian languages, Italian and Spanish. I was teaching several people to speak Japanese, and in return, I got some lessons. And Spanish isn't so different from Portuguese. I can't understand everything, but I know enough to follow the war. I haven't gone anywhere, but through that box," Saburo pointed, "the world has come to me."

I felt a strange happiness for Saburo. I had never heard him speak with such enthusiasm. Kantaro once said that Saburo did not have enthusiasm for anything, that he did not have passion or love. Even Jiro had passion and love, he said. How could a man live without these feelings? Kantaro did not know about Saburo's happiness. I felt sad about this, but I had promised not to tell anyone about the radio. I could not tell Kantaro.

Later, we all heard that Saburo discovered that Japan had lost the war. One day, Saburo flung away the heavy blankets that hushed those strange foreign voices. All during the war, the radio was Saburo's constant companion. In this way, I think, he traveled great distances. On that day, sweat must have covered his face while he listened to his radio under the warm blankets. The air would be cold outside. He had heard the Emperor talking in his strange language to the people. The war was over. Outside, we all heard the thunder of fireworks, lighting the sky over Santa Cruz, but only Saburo knew what the celebration was all about.

* * *

No one really knows why it was, but it was at that moment when the war ended that it began for the Japanese in Brazil. It seems impossible that so many of us could believe that the war did not end, that Japan was still fighting, that Japan was winning the war, or that Japan won the war. I have heard that there are still Japanese here who insist that Japan won the war. There is that man Fujii who wouldn't let his daughter marry into a family who did not believe the same. Kantaro said that maybe it is because Fujii feels it is about his honor. Fujii cannot declare such a defeat openly. It would be an act of betrayal, a loss of heart. It might seem impossible that someone could continue to stubbornly believe a falsehood, so it must be a question of honor. But then, some others have traveled to Japan. They say that Japan has a bullet train that travels 200 miles an hour. They make cameras, cars, televisions. No one is hungry in Japan; they are rich and comfortable. How could such a country have been defeated?

Kantaro said that our New World Ranch was neutral, but outside our farm, people became divided, divided between those who believed that Japan was still fighting or had won the war and those who accepted the defeat. Those who believed in victory were called *kachigumi* and those who believed in defeat were called *makegumi*. Among the *kachigumi*, there was a very secret society of men who called themselves the Shindo Renmei. The Shindo Renmei formed death squads and sent out threatening messages to people who were said to be *makegumi*. We heard that bombs had exploded from packages left for unsuspecting victims. A few people were gunned down in their homes. Men whose lives were threatened sent their families away and slept at night behind barred doors with pistols beneath their pillows. No matter what people believed, everyone remained quiet, fearing to say anything in public. No one felt they could trust anyone. Who might be listening? Who might misinterpret what you said? Suddenly the violence and bloodshed of a war we had not known was at our very doorsteps.

Kantaro was not afraid, but he did not take sides, no matter what Befu believed or what Saburo told him about news on his radio. Befu believed in the rumor that anything said about Japan's defeat was an American propaganda trick. Befu decided to read the old Imperial Rescripts before dinner, and we all listened. Kantaro did not complain about this. The rescripts told us to work hard and keep our faith. Great sacrifice was required for victory. Kantaro thought that even if Japan lost the war, we still had work to do, and people were inspired by Befu's readings. There was always disagreement between so many of us, but only Saburo protested Befu's readings. He went to Kantaro and said, "Befu must stop! What is this reading from Hitler's *Mein Kampf?* Are you crazy? How can you put this stuff next to the scriptures and prayers?" I didn't understand Saburo's argument, but somehow it all made sense.

Kantaro would not become involved in these discussions. He had to be a leader while others argued. If he did not remain quiet, perhaps there would have been more trouble than just talk. As always, many people traveled through and stayed with us. We liked to welcome these people who brought stories and gossip. Kantaro was always uncommitted. He liked to watch the people sitting at the same table; eating side-by-side, there might be a man hiding from the *kachigumi* and another hiding from the police. I remember this man Nakashima who received a death threat from the Shindo Renmei. He left his wife and children with relatives in another town and came to live with us. One evening at dinner, I came by with the big pot of soup. Nakashima was quiet; he served himself some soup. There was another guest nearby talking arrogantly to Kantaro saying, "All of you need to be careful around here. The traitors know who they are. They have run away to hide, but we will find them eventually." He lowered his voice to make us afraid and said, "Confidentially, I heard some of those dogs might have come here to hide."

I saw poor Nakashima turn green and choke on his soup.

Kantaro laughed. "What nonsense. Why would anyone come here to hide? Everyone here knows everyone's business. It would be foolishness."

The man nodded. Of course, he agreed, a traitor would easily be spotted in such a place as ours. The man continued, "I am grateful to you for your sanctuary here. The Brazilian police are too stupid to look for me here."

Occasionally the police did come to ask questions, but Kantaro only shrugged innocently.

*   *   *

They said the war was over, so we were allowed to travel again. Befu, Kantaro and the men were always talking about what they would do if they could sell Befu's eggs in São Paulo. Finally, we could do this. Kantaro made a deal with the Sarandi Cooperative in São Paulo, and Ichiro Terada started to drive shipments of eggs to the city. It was a long trip for Ichiro. In those days, it took all day, driving along endless dirt roads. Sometimes these roads were long sun-beaten tunnels of rising red dust or, during the rainy seasons, they became muddy rivers. More than once, Ichiro told us he got stranded on a lonely highway with a flat tire and a truckload of eggs. He was always glad for a passenger to accompany him on these rides. I liked to pack him a thermos of cool water or hot tea with sweet cakes and rice. Kantaro often went with Ichiro on these trips, traveling to the city to make purchases, negotiate deals and meet friends like Shigeshi Kasai, the newspaper man.

Kantaro had to spend so much time in São Paulo he decided to buy a small house. I never went to this house, but then, I never went again to São Paulo. I heard it was a little two-story place on a secluded street. Kantaro said it was nice. He said we were becoming a very lucrative operation; now we could afford small things. Sometimes I wondered about this house, about life in São Paulo. I had only stayed at Takehashi's house. The city frightened me; it was too busy. I was glad to get back to Esperança.

I know there are stories about Kantaro's life in the city. People did not like to say things to me. I asked Ichiro when he returned with the truck from São Paulo, "What is that house like there? Does Kantaro keep it clean?"

Ichiro said, "I don't know about the house. I have never seen it. Kantaro gets a taxi from the warehouse. I just sleep in the truck and come home."

"Why don't you sleep at the house? You are too tired to drive back. You are going to kill yourself."

But Ichiro wasn't concerned. "I don't mind. I don't like that city. I'd rather drive home."

I asked Kantaro, "What do you do in the city?"

"I run around all day making deals."

"What about the house. It must be a mess."

"Kasai's wife, Teru, found me a maid. She's very good."

Maybe I was stupid, but I said what Kantaro said, "There's a maid. Kantaro says she's very good."

Now that we're old, everyone says everything. They don't say it in front of me, but I know everything anyway. Kantaro always did what his heart wanted him to do. I could not change that. He would not say that he was without faults. He said he was a great sinner. But when you reach the end of your life and your life has been as full as his, maybe you can understand how he cannot admit shame. He cannot apologize for the way he chose to live his life. Well, I am old now, too, and have seen so many things. I shake my head; it's just another story. Kantaro said that God did not give him humility. If after so many generations of his ancestors he did not receive humility, then he must accept this result in himself. This was part of his destiny. I have had to accept many things about myself, but then, I am not Kantaro. My destiny was to marry him and to have his children. Perhaps, Kantaro said, it was a sin to take hold of his destiny, but he could not have lived another life. No one, he said, bears greater pain or greater pleasure for the fulfillment of this destiny than he. Perhaps this is true, but who can measure such things? I think all of us have borne the same pain and the same pleasure.

*   *   *

I'm not sure when it was, but Kimi's father, Shinkichi Kawagoe, decided to move to our place. He decided he wanted to be close to Kimi and his grandchildren. He brought his invalid wife, Kinu, and his phonograph and record collection to New World. With Saburo's help, Kawagoe wired the entire commune—every house, the dining hall, the laundry and kitchen and even several acres of the chicken pens and vegetable gardens—with loudspeakers. He wanted to share his record collection by playing it over these loudspeakers for everyone to hear. All the young girls —my daughter Mieko, Akiko and the others hummed classical pieces while filling water troughs and shoveling chicken droppings. Even I started humming the music in the kitchen. All of us were working and humming, working and humming.

My son Kanzo was too young to think about girls, but Ichiro Terada was getting too old not to. I was not the only one who noticed
him following the girls around in the chicken pens. When Ichiro was
not on the road delivering eggs, he was with the girls helping them
with their chores. The funny thing about Ichiro is that he didn't seem
to know why he was out there with the girls. He was always hanging
around watching the girls chick-sexing—tossing the peeping hatchlings into fluffy piles of male and female. I think he was tired of Befu's
talk of war and tired of Saburo's sullenness, tired of men. Everyone
noticed this change in Ichiro and made fun of him.

But Ichiro was like everyone else on our farm in those days, happy
and not knowing really why. We didn't have any cares. We never
saw money. The children did not know what money was; they went
into shops and grocery stores and took what they wanted without
payment. They weren't dishonest; they just didn't know. Here at
home, everything belonged to everyone. If they were hungry, they
wandered over to the kitchen and bothered me for a piece of cake.
Or someone got a big machete and hacked down a bunch of bananas. If anyone needed anything—toothbrush, soap, razorblade, it
was in our big pantry.

All this time Hachiro Yōgu was just like Kanzo, just like Ichiro,
growing up, but Yōgu did it faster. Every day he was changing,
working his way back from childhood. The problem was that Yōgu
was a strong grown man. What do you do with a child that big?
Gradually he began to understand, but he still could not speak. It
was funny to watch Yōgu. Maybe he would be playing with some
toy or staring at something like an insect or a dog. Suddenly he
would stop, his face full of confusion. Everything in his head seemed
to be swirling around. Then everything seemed to settle, and he
threw up his arms and walked away. The other mothers and I
watched Yōgu. "Just like Nobu-chan at that age," Toshiko would
say. Maybe watching him every day like that, we should have known
what would come next, but instead, we were completely caught by
surprise.

Kimi slept by herself. Who would want to sleep with a grown in-
fant? We put Yōgu in a room with his sons. One morning we were
changing the sheets. Kimi stopped suddenly and stepped away from
Yōgu's bed. I went to look at the bed and saw the sheets. Kimi turned
very red, but I pulled the sheets up quickly and said, "What do you
know. Having dreams. Same thing with Kanzo. All turning into little

men." Of course Yōgu still did not know who Kimi could be, except maybe his mother. But he had dreamed something and went around looking for his needs. He liked to spend a long time watching the chickens. He must have noticed the young roosters vying for the hens. One day, I was humming with Kawagoe's music. Kawagoe said it was called the *New World* symphony. Suddenly, I could hear a commotion coming from the chicken pens just behind the incubating barn. The girls were running this way and that. Eggs toppled out of their baskets. Corn feed got scattered everywhere, and the chickens squawked like crazy chasing after the corn and in and out of the way. Feathers flew everywhere. I ran out to see better and saw Yōgu with no pants on running around after the girls. Everyone who heard the commotion ran around trying to capture Yōgu. This was almost impossible because the girls had thrown eggs at Yōgu to keep him away. He was not only fast but slimey with egg yolk. Ichiro was already there, but he was no help in catching Yōgu. All he could do was to bend over in laughter, and he could not stop laughing until Kimi arrived with her angry look. Suddenly Ichiro became serious. He got a funny expression on his face. Yōgu was innocent, but finally Ichiro must have understood why he was always in the chicken pens with the girls. He laughed foolishly.

*   *   *

While Kantaro was in São Paulo, a traveling pots-and-pans salesman had already arrived in Esperança. He came to stay at New World for a few days. He spent most of the time in the kitchen trying to make us buy his shiny new pans, fixing broken handles and mending old pots. In the evenings, the salesman and Befu got into animated discussions about the war. A lot of people sat around to hear the news the salesman had to bring: gossip about Japanese victories in the South Pacific, ships in Santos, spies, traitors to Japan, Japanese planes located somewhere. There was even a story about a Japanese prince who was secretly traveling around visiting Japanese colonies and testing our loyalty. "Maybe he has already been here," the pots-and-pans man said. "Well, you have nothing to fear if you are honest and loyal Japanese subjects." Then he said, "I have heard that Okumura is *makegumi*."

Even Befu smirked, "Okumura is a pacifist. He doesn't support any wars."

"Those are the sorts of people you have to be careful about. The people you least expect are traitors, secretly dealing with the Americans. Didn't you say that Okumura had been to the United States?" The salesman looked around searching for other traitors among us. "Think of this," he leaned over and spoke softly. "Isn't Okumura promoting the production of silkworms here in Esperança?"

"That's true. We are thinking of starting a batch ourselves."

"Where do you think this silk production is going to be sent?"

Befu and the others shook their heads.

"To the Americans of course!" The salesman slammed his hand on the table. "For military parachutes! This silk production has got to be stopped! Anyone who participates in this is a traitor!"

So the talk went.

"All lies and nonsense," Saburo grumbled. I heard him say to Ichiro, "Eh, Emiru, I saw your brother Kōichi listening to that salesman. He isn't being swayed to Befu's camp is he? Why don't you talk to Kōichi?"

Kōichi was the youngest of the Terada brothers, the one born in Brazil. When Sei Terada's husband died, Kōichi was just a little boy. Ichiro and his other brothers wandered off to our place and left Kōichi behind with Sei. When Saburo spoke of Kōichi, Ichiro shrugged. "He just wants to listen in. What harm can it do?" He pushed Saburo's concern aside.

The night after the salesman had left, we could see flames filling the skies on the southwestern end of Esperança. Soon there was a commotion of people jumping onto trucks and tractors with buckets. Everyone in Esperança was headed for the Tanaka farm to put out a fire started in their silkworm barn. By the time we all arrived, the barn had burned to the ground. Silkworms and mulberry branches were a charred sizzle. Lumber and thatching smoldered where the barn used to be. Tanaka's wife was weeping quietly. The Tanakas were having a difficult time, but they were very proud people and didn't want to join us at New World. My father encouraged them in their new silkworm project, and it looked as if they were starting to make ends meet.

"This fire was not an accident," Tanaka insisted. "Cans of gasoline were left behind. You can smell it everywhere." Those of us who had heard the salesman's talk about silk farming and traitors felt a strange pang in our hearts, but we did not say anything. Now people say that the burning of the Tanaka silk barn was the work of fanatics, but it was also part of a plan to create confusion.

At the other end of Esperança, my father had also seen the flames shooting across the moonless night skies. Always a father to our colony, he ran out to the road in the direction of the Tanaka farm to gather help. A car rolled up and stopped on the road. He ran up to the car. "I need to get to that fire! Can you help me?" he cried to the driver.

Five men in black hoods clambered from the car. One of the men yelled, "Okumura! Traitor!"

My father did not have time to respond. Five rifles exploded in terrible unison. Unknown to any of us, Takeo Okumura lay in a pool of blood, his body neatly cupped in the palm of that red earth each of us had once held in prayer.

Part III: Kantaro

You have seen my peaceful youth pass away in a tolerably uniform and agreeable manner, without great disappointments or remarkable prosperity. . . .

The sweet remembrances of my best years, passed in equal innocence and tranquillity, have left me a thousand charming impressions. . . . It will soon be seen how different are the recollections of the remainder of my life. To recall them renews their bitterness. . . .

The real object of my Confessions is, to contribute to an accurate knowledge of my inner being in all the different situations of my life. What I have promised to relate, is the history of my soul.

Jean-Jacques Rousseau
Confessions

CHAPTER 11: NATSUKO

BY THE END OF THE WAR, I was the leader of a large commune of 300 people farming on a ranch of 420 acres and at least another 1,000 in outlying areas. At this time, we had a group of 10 poultry barns and 5,000 laying hens. Seijiro Befu had his trap nests filled with breeding hens stacked three and four shelves high. Befu and I walked through the barns, inspecting our work—the layers all clucking in contentment, nesting in the sweet smelling rice and sugar cane chaff, smooth white perfect eggs peering from beneath the feathers. We were selling eggs in the immediate vicinity, but if Befu continued to breed with such success, we would need to find markets farther away. Befu could easily see our operation doubling in the next few years. Now that money had again begun to flow, it was time to venture out to make deals, to expound on new ideas, to get financing for new projects. Three hundred hard working dedicated people were an immense fortune in productive wealth. It could not be overlooked. Befu and I and others had spoken about so many possibilities, so many grand projections. Now with proper financing and a network of cooperative support, a great dream could be realized. I, Kantaro Uno, would turn Esperança into a great civilization.

* * *

There has been much conjecture over the years about my life in the city. Everyone has a story and a particular perception to tell about this period, but I will set the record straight. Of these things I will be honest. There is nothing to hide. My life is an open book.

In this venturing forth, I renewed my friendship with Shigeshi Kasai, the former owner and publisher of the *Brazil Shimpo*. While Befu was perhaps my closest comrade at home, it was Kasai who became my city comrade.

Kasai had left Brazil before the war, barely escaping the Japanese police who had come to Brazil to arrest him. The Japanese military government had been advised of Kasai's radical views and his outspoken newspaper, and they ordered his immediate arrest. There were few places that Kasai, with a Japanese passport, might be welcome. Kasai went to Germany, mingling with the people and watching the tide of war until one day he was recognized by the Nazi Gestapo. His luck had run out. He was shipped at the request of the

Japanese government back to Japan and into prison. Kasai spent the
rest of the war in a wretched prison cell in Tokyo. All around him,
he could hear Tokyo being bombed. His captors finally left Tokyo
in fear. Kasai found himself locked in a cell guarded by no one, without food or water, rotting in the stench of his own refuse, while the
city crumbled and burned around him. One day a fellow prisoner
managed to escape and excitedly released everyone in the prison.
"Go! Come on! We can go! Get out!" he yelled at Kasai, who stared
blindly in the man's direction. "What is it?" the man asked. "Don't
you understand? The Americans are coming. Save yourself!"

"Americans? Save myself?" A wry smile must have crossed
Kasai's worn features. Kasai fumbled for the broken pieces of his
spectacles to see a little better. "What's there to save?"

"Are you crazy? Everyone has left. There's only you left in this
snake pit!"

"Finally the Americans have come," chuckled Kasai weakly.
"Being a Japanese prisoner or an American prisoner—what's the
difference? If I were you," he eyed his disbelieving colleague through
a piece of lens, "I'd stick around. At least, the Americans are sure to
have food."

"Fool!" the man who would be Kasai's savior yelled in exasperation.

But it was, in fact, thus that Shigeshi Kasai was saved from certain
death, stubbornly managing to get back to Brazil and the old site of
his newspaper office. When I first saw Kasai at Miyasaka's, I didn't
recognize him. Kasai stood for a long moment, staring at me. Perhaps he wondered what the war years had been like for me. I was
now a man in my early forties and must have seemed still youthful
to Kasai, who had been definitely aged by war and prison. I felt in
myself a great vigor and tremendous energy. The passing time had
been to me as a necessary period of growth, and I felt confident, sure
of the maturity I'd gained by these years of experience. Still, I was the
same person, full of the enthusiasm of my old baseball days.
"Kasai?" I asked, finally focusing on the familiar but much wearied
face, the grey hair and eyes squinting through even thicker spectacles
than I remembered. "Kasai?" I felt my eyes well with tears.

Miyasaka's was always filled with people, no matter the time of
day or night. It quickly became a popular meeting place for the hundreds of Japanese who hurried into the big city to celebrate what
they believed to be a Japanese victory. At any time you would find a

crowd of Japanese there celebrating some aspect of the Japanese victory, buying drinks for everyone in the bar and carousing with the numerous young women whom Mama Miyasaka employed to serve and entertain her guests. It was known that Papa Miyasaka ran a perpetual card game upstairs, a continuous flow of gamblers coming and going through the premises. Miyasaka's had originally begun as a small noodle shop with a tatami back room which Papa Miyasaka used for gambling and entertaining special guests. The women who entertained in the back room wore kimonos and played the *shamisen*. Papa Miyasaka had managed to recreate a microscopic piece of an old floating world where, if you had the money and status to pay, you could enjoy the illusion of returning to Japan. Pretty soon, the Miyasakas realized the popularity of their hidden back room and expanded their operation to a large old mansion in the Liberdade. This mansion soon housed three floors of tatami back rooms, a large restaurant, an enormous kitchen, temporary housing for workers, a Japanese garden with a large collection of tropical animals and, of course, Papa Miyasaka's perpetual upstairs card game. In fact, Kasai was headed upstairs with some idea of getting lucky when he met me.

It is said that all the Japanese bar, restaurant and hotel owners in São Paulo and the port of Santos were *kachigumi*, and if they were not *kachigumi*, they all pretended to be anyway. For years, these places thrived on the generous flow of money spent by people celebrating a false victory, people who had sold their farms and houses and settled in Japanese hotels, awaiting the Japanese ships which were said to be on their way to take loyal patriots back to the homeland.

Kasai leaned over the table, looking at the sliding paper door cautiously, "What is going on here?" he asked me. "The hotels are flooded with people. And you go anywhere: Banzai! Banzai!" Kasai threw his hands up. "They're all crazy!"

I shrugged.

Kasai continued, "Yesterday, I was eating my lunch. 'Have you heard the news?' the owner asks me. She shows me a newspaper, a Japanese newspaper printed here. The headline says that MacArthur will be received by the Emperor. 'There,' says the owner. 'Read it yourself. Our Emperor will give the American general an audience. What more proof do people want? Unless we were victors in this war, how could such an event even be considered?'" Kasai snickered, "What nonsense! Pretty soon everyone in the restaurant is reading the paper and buying beer and singing. Someone comes by with more copies of the paper and sells it to everyone. It's historic information! The newspapers are perpetuating this lie!" Kasai was outraged.

"They sell a lot of copy," I nodded.

"I am going to find out who is behind this."

"You might get killed. People have been killed."

"This has got to stop. Look everywhere. It's the middle of the afternoon, when normal people are working. These are all simple people from the interior, country folk like you who should be turning the land into food. Fools all of them! They are spending their money like water!"

"Would you be as indignant if they were gambling?" I asked slyly, knowing Kasai's old inclination for an occasional game.

"Of course not!" retorted Kasai. "Gambling is different. Taking a chance is different. It's the delusion that's wrong."

"They did not come here to settle," I sneered. "They came here to return to Japan. Can you fault them for a little delusion?"

"It's more than a delusion." Kasai shook his head. "It's all gone. I was there in Tokyo while the bombs fell day after day. And then, Hiroshima. Nagasaki." Kasai's voice fell into a painful whisper. "I know. Things too horrible to speak of. I know. These people need to know. For some of us, there is no home to return to."

"You mean Japan lost," I confirmed.

"Of course Japan lost! Are you crazy?"

A shuffle of feet outside the door brought Kasai's voice to a halt. Two young women ushered a man into the private room and then entered themselves with trays of tea and food.

"Ah, Sawada," I motioned to the man entering through the door.

"Excuse my delay," said Sawada, making himself comfortable on the mat next to me.

"As I came in, I met an old friend of mine," I said, introducing Kasai.

Umpei Sawada nodded politely, removing the jacket of his silk suit. He was a very tidy, meticulous man with, appropriately, banker's hands. One of the women poured Sawada a glass of fine brandy without asking. Sawada rolled the thick golden liquid around the glass, tentatively sniffing the stuff. "So," he toasted us, "how do you like it here?"

I nodded. "We don't have anything similar in Esperança."

"Esperança?" one of the women piped up. "They say only intellectuals come from Esperança." She looked at me with interest. "Are you an intellectual?"

"Intellectuals, Junko," Sawada smiled with gracious urbanity, "are people with ideas. Kantaro is not only a man with ideas but a great idealist."

Junko demurred properly, quickly moving to light Sawada's cigarette, but the other woman sat quietly, only observing. I watched the reactions of the two women. Junko was a small lively woman with cute features, but the second woman had a long elegant face and an imperial aloofness. Her strange beauty stunned me.

Sawada continued, "We are here to celebrate the closing of an important deal, and if I am not mistaken, the beginning of a great future and a lasting relationship. Kantaro's proposal is the kind of project the bank needs to finance, the kind of commitment the bank needs to make for the future of this colony."

"You didn't tell me," Kasai smiled.

"It's Befu's old plan," I said, somewhat distracted by the attending women. "Now we will be able to go forward with it. We want to buy trucks, incubating units, new poultry stock. We want to expand our entire operation. We have an agreement with the Sarandi Cooperative to distribute our eggs and, eventually, our meat products. This is just the beginning," I beamed.

"So," Sawada smiled behind his glass. "Shall we?" The two women poured a round of beer, and the deal was neatly closed in a toast. As more beer and brandy were poured, the occasion began to lose its formality, and Sawada relaxed into the more jovial position of a host, initiating Kasai and me into the delights of an unknown and forbidden world. Some people have said that I was nothing more than a country bumpkin who went to the big city and was taken for a fool. Well, that may have been true in the beginning, but I soon learned my lessons well—learned the suave methods of the banker, learned to juggle the arrogance and egos of men who had it in their power to finance my projects, learned to charm and to capture the hearts and minds of the countless people with whom I came into contact. I was no fool. This meeting with Umpei Sawada, the head of the newly opened Nibras Bank, was only the beginning.

Shigeshi Kasai needed no initiation into the forbidden delights of such a place as Miyasaka's. I envied that he could casually sit, accept the attentions of the two women and mentally store information on the journalist's notepad hidden within his head. I sat somewhat stiffly, unwilling to drink a great deal, remembering in part the drunken fiasco of Befu's wedding several years ago. I listened absently, my eyes wandering back and forth between the two women and my thoughts returning to Kasai's assurance that Japan had lost the war. Meanwhile, Kasai filled Sawada's cup several times and expertly pumped the banker for information.

"Now that our capital has begun to flow again, we need to begin to invest in ourselves," said Sawada.

"What about an investment in a restaurant like Miyasaka's?" asked Kasai.

"As a matter of fact, we have invested in Miyasaka's," smiled Sawada.

"Is that so?" Kasai prodded, "It's doing quite well. Was that expected?"

"Well, Miyasaka knows how to do business."

"As long as people keep flooding into the city to celebrate a Japanese victory, I would suppose so," said Kasai dryly.

Sawada ignored Kasai's comment. "Well, you know that this is the way we've traditionally done business. We," Sawada looked significantly at me, "have just done business right now. Miyasaka's serves an important function in the business of the colony. And there aren't just Japanese here, the *gaijin* have been attracted as well."

"Speaking of business," Junko spoke up. "Can Sawada-san tell me the price of yen? Someone said you would know, of course."

Kasai raised his eyebrows. "The price of yen? Who is buying yen?"

"Everyone is buying yen," Junko asserted knowingly. "Don't you know? Every day that the Imperial ships get closer to Brazil, the price of yen goes up." Junko turned again to Sawada. "Sawada-san, I was told that you would know a good contact with a good price. I don't want to wait too long."

Sawada pushed Junko's question aside. "Why should I know such things? My bank only deals in Brazilian currency."

Junko's face fell, yet she insisted, "But—"

Sawada puffed a veil of smoke into the air, deftly changing the subject, while Junko made an excuse to the leave the room.

Kasai observed these things with interest.

"Natsuko," Sawada asked the young woman who remained, "why would Junko want to buy yen?"

"She won a sizeable amount on the lottery. I thought you might have heard. Everyone is talking about it. Someone suggested that she should invest in yen."

I stared at the strangely beautiful young woman who spoke for the first time. I was surprised to hear the sound of her voice. Despite her beauty, Natsuko did not seem to belong at Miyasaka's. All the other women wore thick makeup, chattered and gossiped endlessly, and vied continually with Mama Miyasaka for the biggest tippers. But this woman, Natsuko, seemed quietly aloof and above the clamor surrounding her. I felt a silent communion with this woman, who, I imagined, must also feel the same discomfort in this situation. I wanted to know why she was here serving me beer and tea and waiting for my tip at the end. I thought there must be some mistake, some sad story of sacrifice and inopportune destitution, to cause her appearance, no matter how elegant, at Miyasaka's. "If you had won the lottery," I asked Natsuko, "what would you do with your money?"

There was no hesitation in Natsuko's voice. A quiet excitement made not only of dreams but determination sparkled through Natsuko's answer, "A piano. I would buy a piano."

This might seem to be a simple answer, but to me, Natsuko's words were infused with a special magic. In those days, the only person I had known who had had the luxury of a piano was Kimi Kawagoe. It was not only an item of great expense but an item of great luxury at a time when people labored for food and shelter. A woman like Natsuko, who depended on tips dealt sometimes generously, sometimes meagerly, even after many tedious hours of fanciful conversation, could not hope to buy such a luxury herself. It is true that she might attract a wealthy patron to her side, convince such a man to buy her a house and clothing, and perhaps even a piano. These were the idle dreams of women like Natsuko. That Natsuko would want a piano suggested to me that, despite the cynicism, greed and false opulence of the world surrounding us, Natsuko was a dreamer, perhaps even an idealist like me. My thoughts about Natsuko were a curious mixture of self-recognition, charity and sudden passion. "A piano?" I repeated. "So you play the piano?"

"I would like to," she smiled. "It's only a dream."

"A beautiful and worthy dream," I said, suddenly smitten.

Sawada interrupted knowingly. "Kantaro, you and Natsuko might have a lot to talk about. Natsuko is an avid reader. She is always hiding a book somewhere. If only she could find a patron who would finance her habit for reading," Sawada pouted. I later learned that Natsuko had attracted many men, Sawada among them, at Miyasaka's; no one had so far met the rigid set of criteria that Natsuko seemingly required. Sawada was a man with wealth and power, a man whom several women at Miyasaka's were anxious to snare. "Natsuko is such a snob," her colleagues all laughed, watching the disappointed men bow out before Mama Miyasaka.

Mama Miyasaka commiserated apologetically, always suggesting some other woman. "This one is more fun," she waved to the poor suitor. "You wouldn't have any fun with Natsuko, you know. Pretty, but such a bookworm. Think of it. Life is too short."

I did not know the gossip about Natsuko in those days, but it hardly mattered. For a miraculous moment when Natsuko had spoken the word *piano*, I felt an uneasy stirring which would never again leave me.

Kasai and I walked away from Miyasaka's full of our separate thoughts. "I think we have discovered something significant, don't you think?" Kasai suggested casually.

"The piano?" my thoughts wandered away.

"No. Money. The reason for this entire falsehood. Well, a part of it, but a good reason for some people at least. Don't you see? If people continue to believe that Japan has won the war, then the yen has value."

"What are you saying?"

"The yen is worthless. Someone is buying worthless yen, somehow, somewhere, and bringing it in suitcases. These fools are buying it. If I'm not mistaken, Sawada himself is selling it. Or he knows who does. Maybe, maybe, he is financing the return of the bank on these deals. Can you imagine?"

"Incredible," I murmured.

"I want to start up my newspaper again. Expose them all. That stupid Junko will lose her money anyway, but countless other people are being innocently duped. If only I had the money to buy a press." Kasai shook his head sadly and then suddenly turned to head back to Miyasaka's.

"Where are you going?" I questioned him.

"Upstairs for a little game. How else can I get my press?"

"You haven't changed," I laughed, "but you were never very lucky, you know." I pulled out my new checkbook. "I've got a nice bundle now at Sawada's place," I suggested wryly. "How much would it take?"

Kasai smiled. "Put that away," he urged me, and then thought out loud. "But then again, what if Sawada is involved—" He remembered the way Sawada had blown smoke over the table and changed the subject.

"My loan is more than we need." I was serious. "And if you are right, there is more money where this came from. I have other plans to suggest to Sawada. Why shouldn't we have a decent Japanese newspaper in the colony again?" I signed two blank checks and pressed them into Kasai's surprised hands.

"I'll pay everything back. I promise," he said earnestly. "But you've signed two checks." Kasai looked at me questioningly.

"The second check is for the piano." I looked at Kasai. "Give Natsuko her piano."

Kasai looked speechless at me. "Where are you going?"

"Kodak," I said. "I'm curious about a new Brownie camera. I think I saw one on the São João."

*   *   *

When I returned to the city, Natsuko had her piano. I did not necessarily think about seeing her again, but I saw a poster for a piano concert at the Teatro Municipal. I made a mental note of the concert and went off to Miyasaka's. Junko bumped into me at the door in surprise and then ran off to find Natsuko. I could already tell that I had made an impression. All the women at Miyasaka's looked at me from the corners of their eyes. Mama Miyasaka appeared and led me to a private room. She came in herself and poured tea for me. "Uno-san, everyone is talking about you. Such a generous man."

"Natsuko seems like such a bright girl. I felt sorry for her. It seems a shame that she cannot have a better life."

"Her family has come into difficult times, but what is new? Her father—" Mama Miyasaka lowered her voice, "such a good-for-nothing. Her mother is ill, and there's a younger sister she dotes on. Everyone is living off of Natsuko. Poor child."

"Well, maybe I can do something to help."

Mama Miyasaka smiled and left. When Natsuko entered the room, she seemed so much younger than I remembered her. Perhaps it was because the strange elegance of her features were happily embarrassed. "It is an incredible dream," she beamed. "I am forever indebted to you."

"Yes, now I will insist that you learn to play," I teased.

Natsuko was not sure. "I will try," she hesitated.

I smiled, "You will need a teacher. If you find a teacher, I will pay for your lessons."

"Oh," she gasped.

"We will talk about that later. First you must hear what a piano can sound like. Tonight at the Teatro Municipal. A piano concert. I will come for you at eight," I announced.

When I came for Natsuko, I was surprised by her transformation. Her dress was quite simple, but everything seemed to hang about her with an elegant sophistication, a studied look of refinement. She seemed to me beautiful and graceful as no woman I had ever known. As she was youthful, she also seemed wise. All the young girls on my farm had a kind of innocence that would never end, but Natsuko seemed both innocent and knowing. And it was true what Sawada had said; Natsuko was a reader. After the concert, we passed the evening talking about books we had both read. I suggested this book or that book to read. I would find and buy her a copy. I suggested that when I came again, we would see another concert. I would get her a phonograph to listen to records. She could take singing lessons as well as piano lessons. We would see a play together. The opera. The ballet. Later, I could take her traveling. She could see the world, study voice in Italy, music in Germany. My altruism was boundless; I was saving a human being, creating a new woman. I was impassioned with an idea that Natsuko would become a model for others to follow. I had never seen such possibilities in another woman. I was impassioned.

I bought Natsuko a house for her shiny cherrywood upright and her phonograph, the books and records, her new concert clothing and shoes. I let Natsuko choose and furnish the house herself. It seemed natural to provide for Natsuko in the same way I provided for my people at home in Esperança. I was creating a way to link rural life to city life. Soon there would be a beaten path between two ideals, the simplicity of country life and the cultured sophistication of the city. I would bring the youth from New World to the city, and Natsuko would be their teacher. I would create a new nucleus in the city itself.

I admit that I did not succeed in my plan. As time went on, I could not see who Natsuko might really be. My idea became confused with my passion. I created a vision of a woman who did not fully exist. Perhaps it has been a great failing of mine, but I have been unable to stir the same passion I have felt in the women I have loved. In the end, they did not know what my passion could mean; they felt afraid and distant from my vision. Perhaps I wanted more than they could give. I could not control my great desire, and as time went on, I knew that my life in the city and with Natsuko was only my own, a separate world, distant from Esperança. No one back there knew of my city life. Even Ichiro Terada, traveling back and forth with egg shipments, had never seen the house in the city and probably didn't suspect anything for a long time.

* * *

I knew that Akiko Yōgu had long since become a woman, but it was not until she rode with us to São Paulo that Ichiro must have been helplessly struck with this thought. Akiko had inherited none of her father's old wildness and all of her mother Kimi's delicate elegance. Yet unlike her educated mother, Akiko had the innocent naïveté of a farm girl. Akiko was like the other girls in the commune, my daughters included, who spent carefree and happy days feeding the chickens and gathering eggs.

I announced one day that I needed a housekeeper for my place in São Paulo, and Akiko was of course my natural choice, as she was the oldest among the girls. Kimi and I discussed this. Someone suggested that we depended greatly on Akiko to care for and watch over her father, but Kimi insisted that Yōgu was getting better. It was true that since his run-in with that Brazilian brute, he seemed to be much more prudent and less apt to wander off toward the slightest curiosity. Every day Yōgu seemed to relieve his redeveloping conscience of some new discovery. Some wondered what Akiko would do all day by herself in a house in the city. I waved these questions away. I would arrange all that. Piano lessons, I suggested. French, I suggested foolishly. For a girl who spoke but little Portuguese, the suggestion that she should learn French seemed rather odd, but for some reason, no one questioned this. So Akiko left for São Paulo, tearfully waving good-bye to her mother, her seven brothers and sisters, and all the girls who shared her chores in the chicken pens.

Akiko sat between Ichiro and me in the front of the truck. Ichiro must have been aware of the smell of her hair and her weeping, but he did not know how to comfort her. Akiko wept for a long time until the farms, pastures and forest along the road were no longer recognizable as Esperança. "Everything will be all right," I reassured her. "You'll see. You'll like my house in São Paulo."

Akiko nodded but did not respond. Perhaps she drew closer to Ichiro. I did not notice. Certainly he must have felt the soft touch of her shoulder rocking against his own. She stared down the undulating road, heat rising in an astigmatic mirage, until dizzy with sleep, she laid her head upon his shoulder. Long wisps of her hair were brushed by the warm wind against his neck and cheek. Her breathing was long and deep and soft, and for the first time, Ichiro must have wished that the road stretching out before us might never end. I saw Ichiro's confused look of sadness as he left her behind with me in the city. She was dressed in something Haru had sewn for her, her very best dress, yet it had the quaint stamp of the country all about it. I had been struck by how pretty Akiko seemed in that dress as she lifted herself into the truck between us to leave Esperança. But now, in the city, the dress had no charm; like Ichiro, Akiko was one more awkward rural waif in the big sophisticated city. Akiko in her braided pigtails, with her little bundle of belongings, looked small and lost.

So Akiko came to live with Natsuko in my city house. We gave her a bed in the maid's quarters, and she was kept busy every day following Natsuko's instructions about cleaning house, cooking meals, shopping at the weekly fair, washing and ironing our clothing. Natsuko was very precise about her desires, and she patiently taught Akiko. Akiko, under the rough tutelage of such as my wife, had had a very different education about housekeeping on a commune. Food was cooked in enormous batches for hundreds of people. Washing clothing was not much different. Farm clothing was treated with vigor, scrubbed relentlessly and laid out in the sun to bleach. Cleaning house amounted to sweeping out the floors of our simple cottages, wiping the long dining tables after meals, or washing out the kitchen floor with a hose. There were no windows to wash, glass cabinets or credenzas with bibelots to dust, brass knobs or fine wood furniture or floors to polish, white walls to wash, pantries or linen closets to arrange. Everything, from the finely crocheted doilies on the arms of the sofa to Natsuko's delicate collection of African violets, was new to Akiko. This perhaps was the world that had once been meant for Akiko's mother. I thought often how odd it was that Akiko should finally, even for a short time, encounter the small luxuries lost to her mother forever.

Between Natsuko and Akiko, my city house became a picture of urban domestic tranquility. I would call from the warehouse as soon as I arrived in São Paulo, and Natsuko would have a special dinner prepared, an array of delicate china, crystal and tableware arranged on a white tablecloth with cloth napkins carefully ironed by Akiko. For dessert, I sipped tea while Akiko was called to join Natsuko in a simple duet on the piano. Then Akiko was sent to polish my country boots, to prepare my bath and a change of clothing. Natsuko usually had plans for the evening—the theater, an opera at the Teatro Municipal, a movie in the Liberdade, a soiree of friends in a private room at Miyasaka's. After several weeks of puttering around the house, following Akiko as she did her housekeeping, an occasional shopping spree, her weekly piano lesson, her weekly flower-arranging lesson, visiting friends, putting aside the books of Tolstoy that I insisted she must read, visiting her hairdresser and painting her nails, Natsuko was always ready to enjoy the life of the city.

After years on a commune, where everything I did or said was most likely observed by someone, where all of us ate, slept, worked and even bathed together, I found the private seclusion of my city life a refreshing change. Then, too, there were the attractions of the city, dabbling in cultural events, the opening of a famous art collection, the symphony, a concert. Unknown to my family and comrades hidden away in the deep interior, Natsuko and I were seen everywhere, chauffeured in fancy cars—Natsuko dressed fashionably in haute couture gowns, jewelry and extravagant hats—accompanied by a varied crowd of friends and stragglers who were sure to be treated by my generous purse. I wanted all of it to the fullest, and I did not spare any expense.

Some people blame Natsuko for all of this, but after all, Natsuko had a very different view of what life should be and what she should receive from it. She had come from nowhere with nothing but her beauty and her flair for choosing the fashionable. She had observed the wealthy Brazilian women dressed in fine clothing escorted by handsome gentlemen and chauffeured in expensive cars to the Teatro Municipal. She would be such a woman. She would find the right man, a man with intelligence and charm and the exuberance to offer her a piano.

But it was Akiko, I know, who always insisted that Natsuko was a good person, a woman with a kind heart. Akiko was not much younger than Natsuko, and the two women, isolated in their separate ways, became close as perhaps a handmaiden to her mistress. No matter what people later said, Akiko was always firm in her belief that Natsuko had been unfairly judged. "All lies," Akiko would defend Natsuko. "Natsuko loved Kantaro. She gave up everything because she loved Kantaro."

I was in my early forties when I met Natsuko, who could not have been more than twenty-one or -two then. I was the father of five children, famous in Esperança for the stories of how I courted Haru inexhaustibly. Haru, still the stubborn strong-minded woman of her youth, had become physically strong from lifting children, hoeing fields and cooking in giant pots. She was no longer the vied-for beauty of Esperança, but she was a faithful companion and a hard worker. It was true that Haru and I had never been quite alone to enjoy our married life. Someone—Tsuruta, Befu, eventually a whole troop—was always there to join us for supper. It was not long before all my companions moved onto my place, but Haru did not complain. This was the life she had chosen, and if she had not loved me in the beginning, other things like children and a multitude of responsibilities seemed to suffice.

Twice in my lifetime I have been fortunate to have lived great love, and from that love I derived my tremendous energy to create. Now in my old age, I can say this. Other men would never admit such a thing, but perhaps other men have never felt such passion or have had such opportunity to pursue their dreams. Even in those days I spoke of my passion as the fuel to drive my activities. Whenever someone asked me how I could maintain a wife and a mistress, I jokingly said that Haru was like the gas for a car and that Natsuko was the ignition. Perhaps I placed a great onus on both of these women. Certainly, Natsuko became a woman marked for life because of her relationship to me. For ever after, people would point to her and say that she was Kantaro's woman. Other men of my status and position certainly had mistresses, but perhaps they were scandalized or jealous by the way I flaunted what they considered to be a privilege. No one of them spent or lived their passion with such generosity or flamboyance. Anyone who recalls my days in the city will say that only Kantaro knew how to live in a big way.

* * *

It was about this time that I met Takashi Inagaki, a friend of the publisher Shigeshi Kasai. Takashi Inagaki was an artist. He had left São Paulo with a little money and some charcoal in his pockets and made his way to Rio de Janeiro drawing portraits of people and selling sketches of colonial churches. In Rio, he had entered the School of Fine Arts. With the war, Inagaki was forced away from the coast and returned to São Paulo. When Kasai, with a little help from me, was able to start up the old *Brazil Shimpo* again, Inagaki went to work for Kasai on pen-and-ink illustrations and cartoons. When I met him, Inagaki was struggling to survive by drawing charcoal portraits of passersby on street corners. Inagaki, despite his emaciated appearance, was a man of tremendous vitality and inner resources. He spent all of his money to buy art materials, brushes, canvas and paints, and lived on whatever was left over. A man with such single-minded determination was the sort that I was always impressed with. It reminded me of my old baseball days. That a Japanese immigrant, even one with his extraordinary talent, thought he could shatter the Brazilian art world, such as it was in those days, was about as absurd as my idea about playing baseball in a country that embraced soccer. The two of us immediately got along. Inagaki, Kasai and I were a threesome about town.

In those days, I returned regularly to Esperança with an oil painting or a charcoal by Inagaki, each of which was proudly displayed in our large dining hall. Everyone thought that these paintings were gifts to the commune, but in reality, they were Inagaki's way of paying me back for the rented art studio in the Liberdade, for the canvas and paint, the brushes, and even the models that posed for him. "This is one of my best," Inagaki would promise me. "I give you my word. One of these days, this will be worth a fortune." Then there were those expensive dinners and evenings at Miyasaka's, when Inagaki brought along his artist friends to fill their starving frames and drink the discouragement of being unknown and undiscovered into a temporary but sweet oblivion. My comrades back home did not know it at the time, but they paid for all of this. In return, we got Takashi Inagaki's paintings, and for a while, we got him as well.

Many artists—all of them friends and acquaintances of Inagaki's—came to New World, but Inagaki's stay was the most extended. Ours was a place of refuge, a place with a free bed, a bath, and three square meals. No one ever insisted that anyone who visited New World should work for his or her keep. This was simply an understanding about life on a commune. Sooner or later, even an honored

guest begins to understand that everyone must contribute to keep
things going. It was understandable that a friend or relative might
come to visit and pass the time for a few days; certainly the work of
so many was able to absorb the leisure of one or two. Still, I know
the fact that Inagaki and his artist friends contributed nothing in the
form of physical sweat irritated many people. True, the artists came
every Christmas and organized plays with large painted scenic back-
drops, which were well attended in Esperança in those days. But to
farming people, it seemed odd (although sometimes flattering) that
Inagaki and others could spend their entire days in front of their
easels propped up in places of mundane interest—an old barn, the
laundry area strung with clothing drying in the sun, the old mango
groves, a vegetable patch. It was a curious thing to all. No doubt it
was the pride of being Esperança people, those eccentric intellectuals who thought farming could be mixed with art and culture, that
allowed them to accept Inagaki and his friends. All of those artists,
Inagaki included, are gone away now, some of them famous, some
destined for permanent obscurity. Left behind in Esperança are the
odd remnants of their artistry, impressionistic oils of our chicken
ranching, studies of Haru at work in the kitchen, portraits of Befu
and me, romantic and passionate, precise and blurred, memories of
a past lost forever.

Takashi Inagaki, I acknowledge, was a man of energetic and single-minded opinions. He was always talking about an idea that he
considered extremely radical and innovative, which he convinced
me should be experimented with at our commune. This idea had its
basis in some self-experimentation, some of it experienced on his
long trek to Rio from São Paulo. There was mixed in a certain asceticism and spiritual Zen, none of which was understood. When Inagaki discussed his ideas with others in the commune, I saw people
smile politely and leave to go back to their work. Only Befu seemed
enthusiastic about Inagaki's talk and gave up his only son, my nine-
year-old nephew, Genji Befu, for Inagaki's experiment.

Inagaki's idea was that anyone could be taught to draw and paint.
It was a matter of physical and spiritual focus and careful training.
Inagaki had worked through a series of artistic sessions in which he
elaborated the artistic process and the philosophical basis for his
procedures. The opportunity to teach a child with no prior experience and no special aptitude for art was an enormous opportunity
to prove his theories. So, Inagaki came to live with us for several
years. During the day, he taught Genji to draw and finally to paint

in oil. I generously supplied both Inagaki and little Genji with art materials, and their production was prodigious. In the beginning, Inagaki spent the evenings expounding his theories to Befu and anyone else who would listen. One or two other people tried their hand at drawing for a short period of time, but only Genji remained faithful to his apprenticeship. I, like everyone else, was amazed to see the progress in Genji's artwork. In a short period of time, Inagaki had taught Genji to paint in oils. This news about a nine-year-old child who could paint soon spread all over Esperança and beyond.

Genji quickly became the focus of an unusual amount of attention. Visitors came to see our artistic marvel. We ourselves sauntered over to see the young artist and his teacher peacefully seated at their easels in front of a scene of our rugged dining hall, large *jaca* and flowering *paineira* trees to one side and the tower of our water reservoir to the other. Genji and Inagaki would always choose different perspectives —making it difficult to compare the teacher to the student, but very soon there seemed to be little difference in style or skill. Inagaki had taught Genji to paint in a French impressionistic style, much in vogue in those days, but most of us had no basis for distinguishing styles. We all liked the soft strokes of the brush, the play of light and colors, the romantic presence of a scene we regarded as ordinary. All of this Genji and Inagaki brought, not to life, but to art. When I look back at the paintings that remain of this period, I am reminded of my Carl Zeiss box camera. Both the camera and Genji's paintings became for us the vision through which we saw ourselves at particular times. When I see the photographs and the paintings of this period, I am struck by their romantic and idyllic nature. Perhaps it was because those were the days when all of us were still in love.

*   *   *

When I announced that Akiko would be coming home and saw Ichiro Terada stunned with the sudden pain of anxiousness, I had some misgivings. The protectiveness I felt for Akiko cannot be explained. She was not my daughter. She was unlike any of my four daughters, who all resembled Haru—well, perhaps they also resembled me. They had our assertiveness: Haru's pushy ways, my arrogance. They were boxy farm girls, husky and strong. They could lift bags of feed and load a truck high with large crates of eggs. Akiko had the same strength, but somehow it was arranged differently in her. All the girls of the commune lived together, slept together in one large dormitory cottage. This situation made me forget their parentage, and gave me the feeling that they all belonged to me. But Akiko was special from the moment she arrived with her family. Perhaps because Yōgu was no longer Yōgu, I adopted Akiko away from him for my own.

I tried to ignore Ichiro's interest in Akiko as if it would simply go away. And yet I noticed that he could hardly contain his pleasure and woke several hours earlier to leave for the city. It was dark when he left Esperança, and he must have seen the sun rise in a golden glow that emanated from the place where Akiko was.

I left later, taking a small biplane to São Paulo, as had become my custom, and met Ichiro at the Sarandi Cooperative offices. I got into the truck. Usually Ichiro looked haggard from his long drive and ready for a well-deserved nap, but that day he was especially alert. I directed him through the maze of city streets to my secluded house on a shaded cul-de-sac near the Praça d'Árvore. I avoided talking about Akiko and said, "I won't be returning right away, but there is something I want you to take back to Esperança on the truck. It is packed and crated at my house. There should be some men there now to help you put it on the truck." When we pulled up, two men were squatting near the porch waiting, and Akiko ran out of the house to greet us. She must have seemed older and more mature, for Natsuko of course had made her impression on Akiko. And she must have seemed to have lost her ruddy complexion and to be much thinner. But I remember even now how her face lit up happily when she saw Ichiro; I remember that special glow of expectation and felt jealousy. "How I've missed you!" she cried. "How I miss everyone." Those words must have spun about Ichiro gloriously, but I ignored his joy.

Natsuko came out at that moment, and I introduced her. "Since Akiko is leaving, this is my new housekeeper," I said nonchalantly. Ichiro stared at Natsuko almost impolitely, and she in turn ignored him somewhat imperiously, directing the workmen as they carefully took the crate out to the truck for loading. She spoke in clear and perfect Portuguese, and this must have impressed Ichiro as he continued to stare at Natsuko. "Come on," I cuffed him lightly on the side of his head. "What are you waiting for? Put this thing on your truck."

"What is it?" he asked.

"It's a surprise," Akiko interrupted. "Don't tell him," she cautioned me as she smiled sweetly. "You'll see." She was full of happiness.

Finally the crate was loaded onto the truck. Ichiro scratched his head in embarrassment and said to Natsuko, "I'm sorry, but I think I remember you from somewhere."

Natsuko smiled and nodded, but it seemed impossible to me that Ichiro of all people, who never left Esperança except to deliver eggs, should have ever met a woman even similar to Natsuko. For a long time after, the thought puzzled me, but one day on one of his deliveries, I asked him about this. I remember what he answered: "It's probably just a coincidence. I wondered about it myself. The other day I was looking through the albums of the photographs you took, the very first ones aboard the ship, the *Brazil-maru*. Remember?"

I nodded.

Ichiro continued, "There was a woman who came with this boy I met on the ship. His name was Kōji. In one of your photographs she is standing there in a group behind my friend. You can see for yourself. She is the very image of your housekeeper. Of course, how old was that woman then? A little younger than my mother," he laughed. "She must be a grandmother now."

I felt great surprise. No wonder they said Ichiro never forgot a face. Just like a camera, his mind took pictures of everything that happened.

Later, I rummaged through the photo albums and looked for myself, tried to remember. In the photo, the woman looked sad and distraught. There was some gossip about this woman, I remembered. Hadn't she run away from home? She was discovered up in the officers' quarters. The thought suddenly intrigued me that perhaps, just perhaps, Natsuko had been conceived somewhere out there as we rounded the Cape of Good Hope, as I displayed my Carl Zeiss box camera, and we made the last leg of our journey to a new world. Although we could not foresee the events of our lives in this world, it is true that we had brought with us everything, all the elements, all our cultural baggage, all our wisdom and all our faults, the very impetus to strike out in new directions and all the self-imposed barriers that might deter us from our purpose.

Akiko rode back to Esperança beside Ichiro. I saw the truck pull away and imagined what I did not know I could not prevent. I knew Akiko's innocence to be complete and unspoiled, as complete and unspoiled as perhaps Ichiro's. In this I felt jealousy and yet power. I was not such a fool, and yet indeed I was. Although I felt relief in Akiko's return, I knew the ache of a yearning I could not extinguish in myself. I returned to the house full of my tremendous need, a rising fire groaning within me. I closed the door behind us and pulled Natsuko to the floor, pushing the image of Ichiro's truck, of Akiko beside him and the piano hidden in that large crate, away.

CHAPTER 12: PIANO

ALTHOUGH THE PIANO that I sent home with Akiko arrived somewhat out of tune, its arrival was the cause of much pleasure. Akiko's grandfather came out to inspect the small upright that had, unknown to anyone, once belonged to Natsuko. I wanted to impress Natsuko with a more elegant piano, a baby grand, and I thought this upright would be a fine present to Akiko and the girls. Kawagoe had long ago, I suppose in a moment of despondency, sold his daughter's piano. When he saw this replacement, he became tearful. Kawagoe ran chords up and down the keys with a flourish remembered from long ago, and Akiko's friends from the chicken pens crowded around, passing their fingers over the wood, caressing the keys and asking a hundred questions about her life in the big city. The excitement over Akiko's return and the arrival of the piano spread through the commune.

Ichiro must have felt happiest of all. Perhaps he thought himself responsible for bringing happiness to the commune, as if he himself had bought that piano for Akiko. Perhaps he reveled happily in the thought of his future with Akiko. He knew this was where they both belonged. And of course he was right.

* * *

The Bahiano came in and out of the commune with his deputies, asking questions. I was surprised to see that he was devastated by the death of my father-in-law. He confessed to me that he considered Okumura his mentor and friend. He mourned Okumura's death, but he cursed us all for our foolish war. "Damn fools couldn't participate in a real war, so you have to go and make one up! Well, it's not going to happen in my town. This has gone too far! We're going to get to the bottom of this. I'm going to hang everyone responsible!"

The Bahiano came with his interpreters and searched high and low. Everyone remembered the pots-and-pans salesman, but no one said anything. The salesman had disappeared, and no one ever saw him again. It was determined that Okumura had been killed by outsiders, members of the Shindo Renmei. There was a clandestine group, my friend Befu probably among them, who supported the Shindo Renmei, if not in action, then in words, but Okumura's death could not be traced to them. But the Bahiano was still not satisfied. When the matter of the Tanaka silk barn was investigated, the name of a young man in Esperança came up. This young man was only sixteen or seventeen years old, but he was held for questioning. I suspect the Bahiano had a purpose in holding this innocent young man, whose mother wept and pleaded with the Bahiano to no avail. The mother came to see me. I was now Okumura's undesignated heir. She sobbed and insisted that her son was innocent, that she and others could testify to his whereabouts on the night of the fire. All of us felt sorry for the poor woman. That was when one of the Terada brothers, Kōichi, came forward and confessed that he and the salesman had thrown gasoline all around the Tanaka barn and set it afire.

This came as a great shock to all of us, but most of all to Ichiro. The Terada boys had all joined us at New World. There seemed to be an unspoken understanding among them, but probably Ichiro had never really talked to his brother Kōichi. Each of the brothers was very different, but they seemed to agree that this dream, this vision, was worth working for. Ichiro must have assumed that Kōichi thought as he did, but in fact, he did not know what his little brother thought about anything. He felt a great shame that he had not been a better brother to him. That night I saw the light in the dining hall where the older brothers—Ichiro, Eiji, Hiro and Yōzo— all sat with Kōichi until daybreak, trying to make up for lost but irretrievable time. All night long the five of them sat in the dining hall and talked and argued about this thing they called Kantaro's dream. Maybe it was the first time they really all talked about these things. Were they surprised to learn that Yōzo and Kōichi were both stubborn sorts, that Hiro was romantic and that Eiji blamed Ichiro, the oldest, for everything? And what did they mean by "Kantaro's dream?" Was it not also their own? They saw the dawn throw a soft pink light over the oil paintings of Inagaki and Genji and others on the walls, and Kōichi continued to argue that he had burned the barn for me, Kantaro, that he had acted not only from passion and commitment but from what he believed was a correct interpretation of my words and goals. Ichiro strained unconvincingly in his arguments. In Kōichi he must have seen himself not so many years ago, young and passionate and a believer.

The morning came, and Ichiro drove Kōichi to Santa Cruz d'Azedinha so he could turn himself in to the Bahiano. Before they left, I saw Sei Terada run out from the kitchen with one bundle of food and another of blankets and clothing. I saw Kanzo, my first and only son, come out to see Kōichi leave. Kanzo and Kōichi were close friends, and I suspect Kanzo had known all along of Kōichi's deed. Everyone looked at each other with speechless sadness. Kōichi confessed to Sei that he had known nothing about the plan to kill Okumura that night. He said that he would not have accompanied the salesman had he known. He was not sorry, though, that he had burned the barn, but he would never forgive himself that Okumura had been killed. He said that since that night he had not been able to look Haru in the face. He begged his mother to ask Haru's forgiveness. He dropped his head, and Sei sobbed pitifully on his shoulder. After Kōichi left for prison, I noticed that she was never quite the same. Kōichi was her youngest and last son, and she had held him close for many years after her husband's death. I, like many, felt a special love for Kōichi, the first of us who was born in Esperança, born in Brazil. We all saw him as forever a youngster, the true Emile in a New World.

* * *

Then my brother Jiro's wife, Toshiko, died suddenly. Jiro had succeeded through Toshiko and his three children—gaining a measure of independence from me. It was not a great measure, considering that we were all dependent on the fruits of our collective labor, but it was something. When Toshiko died, Jiro groped around helplessly. It was no consolation to Jiro that his three healthy children remained; he had never participated in caring for them. Like all children on the commune, mine included, Jiro's ran in great bands around the commune, cared for by the nearest mother at the moment. Jiro could hardly separate his own children from the bunch. When they came home at night to sleep in the room adjoining his, he was surprised to discover that they both resembled and reminded him of Toshiko.

Toshiko had fulfilled a special unknown place in Jiro's life. She was a cheerful woman who liked to talk. She was generous and full of caring, and she went to such lengths to do the smallest thing to make Jiro happy. For the first time, Jiro had felt someone who was devoted to him. For such a long time, he had been devoted to me, never receiving anything in return except the acknowledgment of his devotion. Toshiko had made my brother feel, in his own way, important and loved. Jiro was, after all, a rather childish person, dependent on the guidance and instructions of others. Toshiko, in her loving way, guided Jiro through a series of functions, pushing him forward each morning toward his duty. Without Toshiko, Jiro seemed to lose his way. For days, he sat in his house and wept, and long after that initial mourning, he might be found sitting in the dining hall and suddenly bursting uncontrollably into tears. No amount of consoling or talk could bring Jiro away from his mourning. Jiro stopped going out to work and wandered around aimlessly looking for sympathy and stopping to talk with anyone who would talk about Toshiko. When Jiro had exhausted all of us with his mourning, he wandered away into Esperança and then into Santa Cruz d'Azedinha. On several occasions I sent Ichiro to find him in Santa Cruz at the corner bar. Ichiro had to enlist the help of the other customers in the bar to carry Jiro out. More than once, Jiro had drunk himself into a stupor. Once, Ichiro found him passed out in a pool of vomit in the dark alley behind the bar, and another time, he was found sleeping by the side of the road.

In between these bouts of drunkenness, Jiro had taken to terrorizing the young girls in the chicken pens, much after the fashion of Hachiro Yōgu. However, these attacks were not immediately discovered because Jiro, unlike Yōgu, planned clandestine attacks, snatching girls at the edge of the forest or near the tall stalks of flourishing corn. This produced a flurry of hysteria, after which someone was always sent to follow Jiro. The girls never ventured anywhere except in large groups. I knew that one family with two young daughters was appalled by this situation and used this as an excuse to leave the commune. The problem with Jiro gradually became a rather more serious one, for which no one except perhaps my mother Waka had any clear answers. My mother thought that problems of this nature were best resolved by marriage. Of course, she was right.

*   *   *

While Jiro's problems went unresolved, Hachiro Yōgu's reawakening took a new and astonishing turn. Yōgu remembered, or perhaps I should say revealed, his old attraction for my wife Haru. In the beginning, Yōgu stalked my daughter Mieko, who actually did resemble Haru somewhat in her younger days. Yōgu rushed into the women's bath one evening. There was a sudden squabble of voices when Yōgu appeared. Yōgu had rushed in naked from the men's bath and slipped on the wet tiles. Naked women scattered from the bathhouse while others pinned Yōgu to the floor. Mieko, wide-eyed, sank deep into the steaming tub, looking through the clutter of wet and naked bodies struggling with Yōgu's flailing body. It was Haru who hustled in from the kitchen, her apron soiled with soup and grease, and pulled Yōgu out with that muscular grip known to every child in the commune. But before Haru pulled the naked man to his feet, she grabbed a basin of soapy shampoo water and tossed it into Yōgu's dumbfounded face. Yōgu stared through the stinging soap suds at Haru, who was red with the anger of a protective mother. In that moment, I suppose Yōgu caught sight of some distant memory. Whatever it was, the memory was a potent one, and Yōgu grasped it hungrily. Little by little, everything was coming back. Haru. Haru. Yes, this was the woman called Haru. A smile of happiness spread over Yōgu's face as she dragged him from the bathhouse. Before she could say anything, Yōgu looked at her full in the face and whispered the first words he had spoken since he had returned to Esperança. "Haru?" he asked. "Haru."

Those around who heard Yōgu speak for the first time were astonished by this marvelous accomplishment. But my Haru, naturally, was unimpressed. She grabbed a towel off the body of one astonished girl and wrapped it tightly around Yōgu, tucking the end of the towel next to the wet skin of Yōgu's stomach with a perfunctory jab and pushed Yōgu off. "Go," she ordered. "Get dressed! Imagine—a grown man like you!"

But this was only the beginning. From that time on, Yōgu followed Haru everywhere. The only thing he could say for a long time was "Haru." He seemed to use the word *Haru* indiscriminately for everything. *Haru* seemed to mean "yes" or "no," depending on his expression. *Haru* also meant a great variety of food and drink. *Haru* was pain and happiness and laughter as well. Haru herself was both annoyed and pleased. At times she ignored Yōgu, shuffling quickly by with some task and ordering Yōgu to get out of her way. At other times, she went to great lengths to explain things to him. When I think about that old lady of mine, she was always that way. I never knew it. I took her for granted. Sometimes I wonder who I married and why. But Yōgu seemed to know.

One day I saw Haru open a big album full of old photographs, the photographs that I had taken with my box camera. She pointed at each photo, showing Yōgu the past he had forgotten. "Here you are. You with your pistol. Always the pistol. Don't you hear people say you were wild? You are wild now, but you were always wild. Here, my father, old Okumura. Don't you remember? He made you leave your weapons at the door. Here, you used to play baseball. Yes, baseball, just like the boys out there. You were the shortstop. Like little Masao. Yes. It's true."

Yōgu studied these photos with great interest. One day I saw him motioning to the pistol in the photograph and back to his own hand. He wanted one like the one in the photograph. Haru scoffed, "Those days are over." But Yōgu did try his hand at baseball. The movements and the rules came back, and the old agility was more than apparent. All of us watched the old shortstop reappear before our very eyes. I felt great envy because, despite his real age, he seemed to be a young man again.

When Yōgu recognized Haru and began to follow her around, a buzz of gossip went through the commune which Kimi properly ignored. She seemed only happy that Yōgu seemed to be responding to a jolt in his memory. Perhaps he would soon remember that they had been married and that the children he slept with were, in fact, his own. It was not for lack of telling Yōgu. Haru often pointed to Kimi. "Kimi," she enunciated slowly. "Your wife! This one here, that one there: Your children!" But Yōgu did not remember this. What could this wife be? Yōgu needed a confirmation in his mind that was stronger than a simple declaration. He had felt the bat in his hands, and he had known intuitively what he could do with that bat. What was it that he should do with Kimi? But I guess Haru was different. She was the one he remembered. The key to everything must be kept by Haru.

I saw that Kimi found solace from her trials in the piano. It was Akiko who gently urged her mother back to her place before the ivory keys. For a long time Kimi only stared at the keys and shook her head. "It's been too long. Too long," she protested. She rubbed her ruddy hands, thick and toughened by farm work and hid them under her apron.

"Mama, please," Akiko nudged. "Listen. I learned to play this."
Akiko played one side of a duet she had often played with Natsuko
for me. She nodded encouragingly at her mother.

Kimi cautiously placed her hands on the keyboard and began to
join Akiko. By the time they had finished, a crowd of us had come to
listen. We applauded. I looked at Kimi and smiled, and she buried
her face in her apron. After that, Kimi found her way back to the
piano, her old friend and companion. In a matter of time, she once
again found her voice. It was not the sweet voice I remembered, but
a fuller more mature voice, and though Kimi sang from renewed joy,
there was always something sad about her voice. When I was back
in Esperança, I often sat in the evenings listening contentedly to Kimi
and Akiko and, sometimes, Kawagoe play. I could sit for hours listening to Kimi's voice accompanied by the piano. Everyone drifted
away to their houses to sleep, but I alone remained, sipping tea and
urging Kimi to play just one more piece. A quiet communion began
to exist between Kimi and me. In later years, I wondered why I had
chosen Haru over Kimi. Kimi's music soothed and invigorated me
like a good massage. It's true that my attentions to Kimi's playing
were mixed with regret and guilt and pleasure. Natsuko could never
play the piano like this; she never had the drive to learn. I admit she
did not merit a baby grand. Of course, I knew by this time that she
had only wanted a large and beautiful piece of furniture. I knew this,
but it no longer mattered; I had been absorbed by a passion from
which I could no longer extricate myself. I wrestled with my emotions, craved the woman I had left in the city and wrapped myself in
the nostalgia of another woman's music. Meanwhile, my brother
Jiro continued to fall into drunken stupors at the corner bar in Santa
Cruz d'Azedinha. And on more than one such evening, you could
hear the coarse voice of Haru yelling across the dark yard toward the
light in the dining hall, "Kantaro! Come to bed!"

*   *   *

One day, Akiko gathered with her friends. I could hear the flutter of
girls in the dormitory where Akiko and her friends all slept together,
but I suspected nothing. Akiko produced a small leather case she had
been hiding under her bed. The case had been given to her by
Natsuko. It had a small key and a lock and a small mirror on the
inside cover. Inside, the case was filled with tiny brushes, sets of eye

shadow, mascara, false eyelashes, lash curlers, lotions, powder, perfume, lipsticks and pencils. It was an assortment of Natsuko's
tossed-away makeup. All afternoon the girls hid away in the dormitory, looking at magazines that Akiko had brought from the city,
comparing the women in the pictures, and painting themselves with
the treasure in Akiko's little case. Nearing mealtime, the girls were
still ensconced in their activities, and it was boldly decided that they
should appear together in their new faces at dinner. A few of the girls
protested embarrassment, but finally, all were coerced into the idea.
The appearance of the girls at dinner in full makeup produced a mild
sensation of sorts. Some of the girls had gotten carried away in the
project, applying several coats and colors of everything. There was
a distorted theatricality about all of them, and some were quite un-
recognizable. A murmur of amusement and disgust and no doubt
some pleasure filled the hall as everyone nudged and pointed at the
brazen thing they had done. But when I saw the girls, Akiko seated
happily among them, giggling with delight, I jumped up from my
seat in rage. There was within me an emotion I could not control.
Even now I cannot explain my anger. Akiko had revealed something
about my life in the city that should not be shown; she had betrayed
me.

Akiko did not see me thunder down the aisle to her table, but she
could feel the cold silence of everyone around her. In an instant, I had
jerked her from the bench by her hair. I took a long cold look at her
pretty features plastered in false lashes and thick mascara, beet-red
lipstick and ruddy rouge, all powdered and cologned by the cheap
scent of lavender, mocking me. Then I slapped her hard across the
face. She crumpled to the floor. My entire body trembled as I lunged
down to grab her neck. At that, Befu and the dentist Takehashi
sprang up and pulled me away. It was my father who ran forward
between Akiko and me. "What are you doing? What does this
mean?" Naotaro demanded.

I struggled away from Befu and Takehashi. "Fool!" I cried. "Get
out of my way!" At that moment, I struck out at my father's face.
When I pulled back, my fist was covered with my father's blood.
Naotaro was a small feisty man. He had been proud of me; he had
even admitted that I had often been right. Remembering that I had
sold our family rice harvest to send Yōgu to Japan, he always said,
"The rice did belong to Esperança." But Naotaro was also a stalwart
Christian, a man with a kind and forgiving heart. He assumed that I

must be the same. He had long thought of himself as retired. He spoke of his peace of mind, knowing that I would now take care of him and my mother. Now he looked at me in disbelief.

But I had no respect for him. I was in charge. How dare he question my actions. "Get out of here!" I screamed.

My mother came to rescue her bleeding husband, supporting him under her arm. It was a pitiful sight to see my elderly parents limping away like that, but I felt no remorse. I felt only my anger and my power to show it.

Ichiro Terada was not there, but when he returned from his deliveries, Saburo told him of the incident. Akiko hid away in her room and wouldn't come out. She would not see Ichiro, and he could not understand this. He felt anger and pain. What could Akiko have done to deserve such a thing? Why would Kantaro do such a thing? He could not see.

"Talk to Kimi first," suggested Saburo wisely. "She and Kantaro have an understanding."

I heard it all from Kimi. She listened to Ichiro patiently. She nodded kindly and smiled warmly at everything he had to say. But her answer must have struck him as strange, "Ichiro, you are a good man, and I could not wish more for Akiko, but you cannot protect her from Kantaro by simply marrying her. You must forget about Akiko. Pursuing her will only bring you pain." Kimi would not say anything more.

Ichiro did not understand this answer until it was much too late. I saw him wander off in the night to the mango groves, wandering around trying to untangle his confusion. When had I myself wandered the mango groves at night waiting for dawn, waiting for the light and rushing off to pound on Ichiro's door, "Get up! We have a shipment to take to São Paulo!" And all the time full of my expectations of a woman and her piano. And when had I, in a fit of exhaustion, fallen asleep in those groves, only to awake in the dark with the shudder of my own sobbing. I remembered my friend Heizo's hopeless solution and my useless recommendation to secure his manhood. I stared up through the dark shadows moving among the last of the ripening mangos, hanging like so many human hearts. The sweet stench of rotting fruit rose all around me.

CHAPTER 13: BANK

I HAVE ALWAYS lived my life with great feeling and emotion. There can be no other way to live life well. I have trusted my intuitions and followed my ideas. What is considered practical or pragmatic has never been my concern. I have always abandoned what others believed to be sensible or rational; common sense is not a sense that I understand. Destiny cannot be fulfilled by common sense; it is not driven by anything that can be explained. If an ideal is to be achieved, one must abandon all thoughts of failure, all thoughts of impossibility. The achievement of an ideal is a great leap of faith. Nothing truly great has ever been achieved by common sense. Common sense does not drive a man to create a beautiful work of art, to love with great passion and abandon, to pioneer a new life from a virgin forest. The accomplishments of my lifetime cannot be measured or evaluated by common sense.

The struggle to keep faith with one's deepest intuitions, one's greatest emotions, is not easy. The weak fall away from this great task, run away to their predictable lives, daily toil without greater meaning; a lesser place in history is left for them. My companions and I were not called upon for a lesser place; those who remain with me to this day remain with the strength of their convictions, the strength of their great destiny.

* * *

Before Shinkichi Kawagoe left, he played Wagner constantly. It was piped through the sound system to every house, to the bathhouse, to the kitchen, to the dining hall, to the barns, to the lumberyard, to the chicken pens, even to the outhouses. We heard it all day, every day, from dawn to dusk, until we were consumed by it and no longer heard it. Some people broke the wires connecting the speakers in their houses, but others found themselves wailing Wagner in their morning ablutions, while washing clothing, in the bath, turning weeds, gathering eggs, making love, in their sleep. The air we breathed moaned with the Valkyries; the sound seeped from the very pores of our skin, from the living nerves at the roots of our hair, in inert salty drops we could not wash away.

Around this time, a man named Shiozawa was sent from the Nibras Bank by Umpei Sawada, our financial banker, to manage our accounts. He was not just there to look at our books, but to budget our money and supervise our spending and sales. This should have been an indication to everyone of our true financial situation, but even then, no one took the warning very seriously. It was inconceivable to my people that a production like ours—grounded in a work force of 300 people—could be failing.

By now our operation had expanded to 70 poultry barns, each about 40 meters in length. At 500 layers a barn, we had some 35,000 birds producing an average of 33,000 to 35,000 eggs a day. Another 50 or so smaller barns and coops were occupied by hatchlings, replacements, Befu's experimental breeds and young roosters for meat. Ichiro made two or more weekly runs of eggs to São Paulo, plus smaller runs to nearby towns and train shipments to more distant places. Befu was also supplying farmers with hatchlings for their budding operations. Saburo was involved with a team of men building chicken coops for farmers; they went all over Esperança to help establish new chicken ranches. It had once just been talk, that Esperança would one day be the egg capital of South America. Now it was true. We were the first and the largest such operation in South America; some people were calling me the King of Eggs. We had also cleared an area for a butchery with freezing compartments. Everyone had looked proudly on the plans for the most modern equipment, the first of its kind in Brazil. Ichiro had been told that he would get a new truck double the capacity of his present truck and with built-in refrigeration. Befu was talking about new incubators and a new disease-resistant breed of chicken called the New Hampshire which he was anxious to introduce in Brazil. Every day, Befu came up with some new plan for feed which everyone scrambled around to implement. The women had been promised a large new gas stove with eight burners and a double oven. They were also talking about a new sewing machine and even a modern washing machine. My people were all immersed in these plans for a great future. They were sure that the bank's concerns were bogus and, as time went on, that the bank was taking advantage of us, taking a larger, ever more sinister interest in our great production. The bank was an evil force and Shiozawa's efforts must be subverted in every possible manner. This was the only way to get the bank out of our concerns; we would make them throw up their hands and leave the proper business of poultry farming to us.

Some people have said that it seems impossible if not foolhardy that 300 people could have left the entire financial dealings of their operation, the hard-earned product of their labor, to one man. I was the sole manipulator of all our money. But this is not to have any understanding of our operation. Money was always simply a parallel consequence of building a great civilization. What was money after all? The children of our commune didn't know what it was, and had no use for it. We received our life from the land. The land was our storehouse. This was our ideal.

Perhaps the illusion that we could confront the world solely with our production and ideals and my influence seems incredible, but people believed. I obtained enormous loans from the bank and had involved other prominent enterprises, including the Sarandi Cooperative. Sarandi had, based on my projections, also gotten loans to augment their operations to receive and furnish eggs and chicks throughout São Paulo, Paraná, and Rio. Everyone had joined this optimistic bandwagon to bring eggs to the New World. Everyone believed and wanted to believe. Was this such a bad thing?

Some people think that I acted like one of the children in the commune, walking into stores and freely selecting items without a thought to pay. People thought that I was an innocent from the back country. "A great idealist," they called me, an innocent who knew nothing of the rude pragmatic world. It may have been true that I did not know the value of the money I held in my hands, that I thought that the source of that money, the Nibras Bank, was unfathomable.

I spent money like water, denying Natsuko nothing; no small trinket was too expensive, no idea or plan impossible. Nothing was beyond my means. I bought everything: plush hotel suites, motorists at my beck and call for days at a time, plane trips to Rio and Buenos Aires. And who does not remember that I bought out Miyasaka's for an entire evening? Money flew from my hands and lined the pockets of every adventurer with a good story. Takashi Inagaki was sent to Paris to paint. Natsuko's old friend Junko set up a small bar and restaurant. An artist friend opened a gallery. A friend at the Sarandi Cooperative bought land and started an egg ranch. The *Brazil Shimpo* returned in full force. Money was not important; it was only a means to an end. Dreams were had to be realized. And the rice always belonged to Esperança.

*   *   *

Ichiro must have begun to suspect that something was askew when the Sarandi Cooperative stopped handing him checks for payment of our shipments. Usually I would be there to receive our checks, but more often Ichiro took the checks and deposited them in the bank for me. Lately, I had ordered him to hold the checks or leave them at my city house with Natsuko. Then Ichiro was told by Sarandi that they had a directive from the bank to deposit our proceeds directly into our bank account. There would be no checks handed over to him or to me. Only later did he discover that I had not made payments on our loans for almost a year. In the meantime, I had incurred new loans at other banks and used the Nibras Bank as a guarantor. It became a habitual sort of thing for me to enter a bank, often a small rural bank with a small clientele, talk circles around an eager manager and come away with a new loan. But then, who in the vicinity hadn't heard of our modern operation, of the hardworking Japanese who produced 35,000 eggs a day? I had miraculously convinced dozens of banks to release thousands of *contos* to my name, all for the sake of a great plan and the 300 productive people back in the rural miracle called Esperança. In the moment that Sawada toasted our first historic deal, I knew I had absorbed a method to deprive banks and wealthy investors of their money which could be enacted over and over again. Everyone participated in the dream, but the rice still belonged to Esperança.

It should have been no surprise then that the bank eventually stepped in to reorganize our operation to keep money flowing back into the commune rather than into my hands. Shiozawa came with his family and set up house in Esperança. He was a conscientious, responsible and respected employee of the bank, and Sawada trusted him implicitly. Shiozawa was not the sort of person who could be swayed by my sort of talk. He was a man to follow specific orders and carry out specific plans. His honesty and tenacity made us dub him "Sawada's Boy Scout." I treated Shiozawa with bluster and smiles.

The books of the commune were kept by Kawagoe, who had been a banker himself in Japan. Kawagoe and Shiozawa conferred over the books with a great deal of serious thought, but it turned out that Kawagoe had two sets of books—one which Sawada and Shiozawa saw and another which told a much bleaker story. According to Kawagoe's optimistic bookkeeping, it seemed impossible that the commune was not doing better. Everything pointed to amazing productivity. Sawada and Shiozawa could only conclude that I was a poor manager and that if I could somehow be kept at bay, the commune would bring itself out of the doldrums within a year's time.

With these false calculations in mind, Shiozawa went eagerly to work. Nothing could pass in or out of the commune without his signature and approval. He saw to the buying of everything from a single bag of salt to a truckload of diesel. All of our shipments of eggs had to be accounted for. I can still see Shiozawa rising early in the morning to count the crates and check the gas mileage.

Ultimately everyone must admit to sabotaging Shiozawa's work. Everyone believed that this was the only way to convince the bank to stay out of our business. Kawagoe slipped me money as I left for the city, and I secretly signed contracts for more loans, putting Shiozawa's legal name on all the documents. As these deals brewed in faraway places prepared to break the calm surface of Shiozawa's tidy work, he was forced to deal with other problems that I had sent back to Esperança. For example, I closed a good deal on tires for the tractors and sent an entire truckload to Esperança. "Talk to Shiozawa. He'll pay you on the spot," I would say. Shiozawa was constantly kept busy sending my purchases back to where they came from. There was clearly no money to buy any of it, but I kept sending more on: fifty barrels of diesel, a new refrigerator, three new washing machines for the women, a truckload of flour, blankets and bedspreads for thirty families, twenty bolts of expensive cloth. It was a spectacle—Shiozawa chasing the orders around the commune before they could be unloaded, or loading them back on the trucks himself, and then shipping them all back to a dozen different sources.

To make matters worse, I would come back to Esperança only to slap Shiozawa on the back with a new project. I think the last straw was the New Hampshire hatchlings deal. "Shiozawa, I'm glad we're finally getting the managerial help that I've always needed. I really am indebted to your fine work," I said brightly. "Now, I've been talking to Americans in the business, and they are interested in sending us that New Hampshire breed that Befu wanted. I knew you'd approve so I ordered them right away. Even with airfare to Brazil and the customs documentation, it's not much money at all. A real deal!" Shiozawa was then sent into a frenzy about how to deal with a seller as far away as America.

As time went on, Shiozawa became thin and bedraggled, with deep shadows under his eyes. He seemed to suffer from a bad stomach and had to refuse the generous portions of food that Haru dished up for him when he stayed for meals. I began to feel sorry for

Shiozawa, whose hands began to shake when he drank tea. Someone spread the rumor that Shiozawa slept fitfully every night, and that recently he had awakened in a terrible sweat, grabbing his wife's hair and shouting at the top of his lungs, "Stop! Stop the New Hampshire shipment!"

There was no end to Shiozawa's humiliation; we had no mercy. Everyone sent him in circles after illusions while I continued to make deals for our produce. I would slip off, unknown to Shiozawa, to the city. When I came back, I would have an address for Ichiro, a shipment destination and consignee who would pay in cash. In the middle of the night, everyone was rounded up to load the truck full of eggs at the southern corner of the commune. The crates were hidden surreptitiously during the day. Ichiro would drive this shipment to my secret dealer, where I would be waiting to receive his cash. I would count the money with satisfaction, shake hands with the dealer and wave Ichiro on. He had to return before sunup and slip back in with the truck before Shiozawa noticed his absence. Inevitably, Shiozawa would come pounding on his door just after he had returned. "Ichiro!" he'd yell, "Wake up! Let's get that shipment counted." Without even changing his clothing, Ichiro would obediently turn around and go back to São Paulo. His days and nights passed in a blur. He took catnaps between shipments, fell asleep more than once on the road, luckily surviving for lack of traffic. When Shiozawa came to question him about expending twice as much diesel as before, he could only mutter nonsense. Even I don't know how Kawagoe must have justified the fact that we had produced two and three times more eggs than we had been paid for.

In everyone's eyes, Shiozawa and the bank became the villains, the enemy against which we had to fortify our defenses. As the furor surrounding the "Japanese victory" began to die away, we became caught up in a new cause, a new struggle for survival. After a year of this, no inroads had been made securing the stability of our operation, but Sawada had discovered my secret deals, and my extravagance and my love affair with Natsuko became common knowledge.

I do not know when this information about Natsuko became known in the commune. For a while, Ichiro must have been the only one who knew anything. Shiozawa must have quizzed him several times about my trips to the city, and often people made comments when he made deliveries. When Ichiro drove Sawada to the airfield to take his small plane back to São Paulo, Sawada must have told

Ichiro enough for him to realize that that the woman they were all talking about was the "housekeeper" he had seen so briefly at my city house. Yet he spoke to no one of these things, for he was never sure what to think. These things must be rumors, gossip spread to dissuade him from his duty. Besides, in his physical state, he was never sure what it was that he had seen and heard and what he had perhaps dreamed. He must have often arrived in São Paulo not knowing how he had gotten from one point to another, thinking that he had only dreamed that long stretch of road. But the gossip began to come to Esperança from so many different sources that my people all found themselves whispering the same things.

Then one day, Befu heard it too. I was not there that day, but I'm told Befu rose up in an angry rage and growled so that everyone could hear, "If this is true, I will kill Kantaro with my own hands!"

When I came home, everyone was strangely quiet. I sat at my place at the head of the table and sighed contentedly that I was glad to be back, that city life was not for me, that there was nothing more pleasurable than getting back to Esperança and having a bowl of rice with tea. "You don't know, Befu," I continued to wax nostalgic about rural life, "but city life is a rat race. No, people like me and you belong right here."

No one said anything, and Befu glared at me with his dark eyes hidden behind those black bushy brows. "City life?" he asked. "I wouldn't know. Fancy restaurants. Expensive food. Prostitutes."

There was a terrible silence, and they all waited.

I flung my rice bowl suddenly from the table. "Get out!" I screamed. "All of you! Out! Out!"

Everyone shuffled hesitantly away.

But to Befu I motioned, my tone softening, almost pleading, "Stay here. We need to talk."

Befu sneered self-righteously. "I want to know the truth."

"I will tell you the truth," I said. "I have been meaning to tell you these things for a long time. I need your advice."

Befu softened but continued to sit stiffly.

"I met a young woman. It's true that she does not have what people call a respectable background, but I saw from the moment I met her that her spirit could be raised, that she deserved to realize her dreams. I thought in the beginning that she had great potential, that she could rise among young women in the colony and become a leader. This was my only intention—to save a human spirit, to lift her out of her poor situation."

Befu nodded. "So there is nothing. She is just an acquaintance?"

"I cannot lie to you, Befu. You are my best and closest friend. What I am going to tell you I have never told anyone. Only you know these things."

Befu leaned closer.

"I thought it would never happen again. I thought love, this passion, the passion I felt for Haru, that it was gone, could not be retrieved. But I have been blessed again with great love. How could I deny such a blessing? It would be to deny life itself. Suddenly I feel my youth again, my creative powers have returned in full. Look at me, Befu. Can't you see it in me, you who are my closest friend? You among everyone must understand my greatest, deepest needs. What should I do?" I looked hard at my friend for his answer.

Befu felt confused. "You love this woman?"

"It is not just any love. If it were, then you have every right to take my life, to end it now. But you know that I cannot live in an ordinary way for an ordinary love. It would be to betray everything I believe in. Do you understand?"

Befu broke down, his eyes welling with tears. He had heard my confession of love, so he said, as each of my loyal followers would also say, "Kantaro told me everything. He confided in me. After hearing what he had to say, I am convinced that it is a man's right. This woman has stirred in Kantaro a renewed energy and a greater capacity to create. We should be thankful."

I believe even Haru was thankful. She said nothing, but continued to bustle about in her habitual manner, ordering this and that and caring in that general brusque way of hers for everyone's needs. She seemed unaffected by the gossip, and when anyone mentioned the details within her hearing, she would speak out loudly, "That Natsuko is a very nice woman, you know. Kantaro said so."

In the meantime, Yōgu continued to follow Haru about. He was beginning to talk in sentences and to remember other names and faces. "Tsuruta," he said one day. "Tsuruta?" When Haru told Yōgu that Tsuruta had died, Yōgu sat down in a corner of the kitchen and cried like a baby. Slowly but surely the memories returned and with them, emotions. One day Ichiro climbed into his driver's seat in the truck and encountered Yōgu sitting on the passenger side. "City," he nodded seriously. "Drive," he ordered, spitting out the window. "Yōgu go."

* * *

By this time, the Bahiano and I had come to an understanding. This understanding was a long time in the making and to my way of thinking began to take form about the time my father-in-law, old Okumura, began to teach the Bahiano about cooperatives. The relationship cultivated between these two men over the years and certainly during the war became much closer and important to the Bahiano than anyone in Esperança could imagine. The death of Takeo Okumura was a severe shock to the Bahiano, changing and humbling him in ways he admitted to me. "Okumura was a father to me. I never had a father; I was orphaned at birth. I'll never forgive myself for not understanding the danger he was in. I could have prevented his death." By the time the Bahiano had gotten an education in the Japanese way of cooperatives, it was an easy matter to move on to something like our communal operation. We were the next step in a natural evolution of thinking. We didn't just belong to the cooperative, we lived our lives as a cooperative. We weren't concerned with just a better price for our produce, we were concerned with a better life. Well, this is how I explained it to the Bahiano.

There was one other reason why the Bahiano was ripe for an understanding with me. It had to do with Maria das Dores, the woman he married. One day the Bahiano left Santa Cruz and returned with a twelve-year-old girl who clung to him on the back of his horse. I heard the story that the Bahiano had been to see his old patron—the Colonel, they called him—whose wife was dying. The Colonel's wife had called for the Bahiano; she would not die until the Bahiano arrived, and when he did, she made him promise to marry her youngest daughter, Maria das Dores. The Bahiano said that he was not one to argue with the wishes of dying people, and the following year when Maria das Dores was thirteen, they were married. That was the way he was. When he made promises, he kept them.

People say that the Bahiano spent the first several years of his marriage raising his wife. Contrary to what people expected, the Bahiano was gentle and extremely patient with her, and many women in Santa Cruz d'Azedinha wondered what magic the Bahiano had performed to turn Maria das Dores into a proper wife and, soon after, mother. People say that the Bahiano himself taught his wife to cook and sew. Some people remembered the Bahiano making a painstaking effort to teach Maria das Dores to embroider and crochet. They say that the first towels and bedspreads that were used in that household were made by the Bahiano himself.

Maria das Dores turned out to be the sort of person who adopted everyone and everything into her own family. Before long, the Bahiano and das Dores, as she was known, had not only a large household of children, several adopted children and two Indians who wandered in for meals, but animals of every description, tropical birds, dogs, cats, donkeys, ponies, goats, pigs, chickens, a llama from Peru, snakes (among them a large slow-moving anaconda), monkeys, all of which roamed, flew, crawled or slithered in and out of the large spacious house that the Bahiano had built. All of this and the fact of having raised his own wife must have had a domesticating effect on the Bahiano.

It would be easy to blame some bad Brazilian for our troubles. There were unscrupulous people, both Japanese and Brazilian, who took advantage of our situation. I will not name them here, but they know who they are. They must have thought, like me, that the source of the money was fathomless. Well, I cannot blame them. They only thought about their own gain. But the Bahiano was not one of these. He understood our ideal. He was a man everyone respected. He and I initiated a strong friendship on one of those jaunts by air to São Paulo, sharing the small biplane that I hired to make weekly flights to the city. Ichiro drove me to the landing to make my flight and translated for the Bahiano and me. I described our financial problems to the Bahiano, who listened with concern. "I was never aware that you were having these troubles," the Bahiano shook his head. "Why didn't you come to me earlier? You know my feelings about Okumura, God rest his soul. After all, you're his family. This ought to be a concern for all of us in Santa Cruz. From what you are telling me, that bank of yours is playing some serious games. I wonder if that man Shiozawa should even be here taking over your operation. I wonder if that's even legal. It all has the ring of something invasive and underhanded to me."

I nodded my head sadly. "I don't know where to turn for help."

From that moment, the Bahiano was a listener. He began to learn about our dream, and he began to be a believer in this great experiment. He would say to his friends and anyone who would listen, "You ought see the operation that these Japanese have put together. It's marvelous really. These are people with strong Christian ideals, hard working, productive people, the sort of stuff that Brazil needs more of. These people have got an answer to our problems, and they are showing us it can work. Marvelous. Just marvelous. That chicken ranch is something you'll never see anywhere else. The man who runs things, the master over there, is Seijiro Befu. A genius. And everyone works together. Even the children. Hardworking people. These people are going to feed Brazil, I tell you. But the children— you can tell if something is working by the children. Befu's son, just this little shoot of a kid, is an artist. I'm serious. Paints like the stuff you see in the museum. If that doesn't tell you something is right, I don't know what." The Bahiano could not praise us enough. He brought visitors constantly to show off this miracle in the rural wilderness.

Pretty soon, the Bahiano had Brazilian newspapers, ministers of agriculture, ministers of culture and education, social scientists, politicians of every party, Brazilian investors and lawyers interested in my commune. Reporters came through, constantly interviewing me, the King of Eggs, while photographers took quaint shots of Befu sporting his long black beard, the girls in the chicken coops, the women in the kitchen, the men in the fields, 300 of us at mealtime. There were large spreads and articles in every major local and national newspaper and magazine in Brazil. They were exaggerated somewhat. One article said we covered an area of 36,000 acres and had 220,000 laying hens. Well, this was not an exaggeration if you included all of Esperança and meant to say that we were largely responsible for the great production of eggs in the area. Overnight we became famous. All of Brazil looked upon our modern operation, our fabulous production, our idealism, and my leadership and could not but believe that this was a lucrative business of the future.

This brought a great deal of consternation to Umpei Sawada and the Nibras Bank. A famous Brazilian lawyer took me and my commune on as his personal cause; he was quoted in a national magazine saying that the Nibras Bank was illegally taking advantage of Kantaro Uno and that he could prove that the bank had invaded our operations. He implied that the bank was part of a kind of mafia, built on greed, which subjected their clients to unreasonable deals to keep control of lucrative businesses in the Japanese colonies. That I had taken this issue out of the community and had engendered this sort of publicity enraged Sawada.

Sawada gathered with his board of directors and his lawyers. He sent his men out to literally scoop me from the streets and bring me captive to the bank's feet. "This has got to stop!" Sawada yelled and pointed with emphasis at me. "All the evidence is here. You are

worthless! This is Shiozawa's report on your inventory. Here is the
full assessment. It all shows that even if you sell everything, you are
still indebted several times over. This is not only an assessment of
your debt to the bank, but it includes debts to other banks, investors,
the cooperatives, and to numerous shops and hotels and restaurants.
I have personally seen several people enter this terrible mire of yours.
A craftsman named Takemura who built furniture for you. He wept.
He has a family to feed. Then there is a woman who sold several bolts
of expensive cloth to you. There are dozens of small merchants, too
numerous to mention. Have you no pity?" Sawada slammed his
hands on a pile of bills. "And all this. Truckloads of tires, tractors,
diesel, chicken feed, flour, salt, oil, oil paint and canvas! Nothing has
been paid! Your name is mud! You have wreaked a terrible havoc
on all of us. Is this the thanks we deserve for supporting you? Your
manner of dealing with this situation is chaotic! You are nothing!
You must face the fact that you have very few choices in this matter.
Very soon 300 men, women and children will have nowhere to go!
All because of you, Kantaro Uno!" Sawada sat back in an exhausted
huff.

I said nothing. Something that Sawada said gave me hope: "300
men, women and children." Of course, no one could turn out 300
people from their land and homes. It would be scandalous. Sawada
and the bank could never do such a thing without an uproar from
the community. This would be a heartless and cruel thing for which
no justification, especially not one based on money, could be made.
I said nothing.

"We have drawn up the proper papers for an accord which you
will have to sign, for the sake of everyone concerned. This paper calls
for your resignation as leader of New World Ranch, negates your
authority to sign for anything. And it turns over the existing property to the two remaining founding families—the Unos and the
Befus."

"But the others," I protested. "We are not only two families."

"The land cannot accommodate the others, and they have no legal
title to it anyway. You will have to make arrangements to compens-
ate them in the best way you can. I'm sorry. This is the best solution
for dissolving the commune that we can arrange. Give these people
their freedom. They are hard working people. You have influence on
them."

I looked at Sawada in disbelief. "This is the end," I whispered. "Three hundred men, women and children. You cannot do this to them."

Sawada smiled sympathetically and said, "Sign here, Kantaro. You have no choice. My lawyers will take these papers to Esperança tomorrow and get the proper signatures from your brother Jiro and from Seijiro Befu. That will be the end of it."

I signed the document and ran from the room. I still had hope. I would not give up the commune, or the land, or my leadership. I would not give up the future. I knew where to find Ichiro, dozing in the seat of his truck. I rustled him from sleep. "Ichiro, get up! This is important! Everything depends on you! Go home now. Drive without stopping. Get back there and tell Jiro and Befu to sign nothing. When the lawyers from the bank come, tell them to keep quiet and to sign nothing!" He got in the truck and drove all night. He was back in Esperança just before Sawada's lawyers arrived by plane. Jiro and Befu were adamant. They would not sign.

*   *   *

In the meantime, Sawada went about trying to accomplish his objective with another strategy. He hid Natsuko. No one would tell me how he accomplished this, but by the time our relationship had been made public, it may not have been difficult to convince Natsuko to leave me. When I discovered Natsuko's disappearance, I became frantic. I searched all over the city, breaking in on old friends and acquaintances, checking any possible place, following any possible lead. I ran into Kasai's printing shop and accused my old friend of hiding Natsuko, but he denied everything. "Forget her," Kasai said, rubbing his tired eyes beneath the thick spectacles. "This has all gone too far."

"I can't. I can't." I slumped down in exhaustion. "I have to find her."

"If you continue this nonsense, I will have to write about it," Kasai warned. "You know, I've got no strings attached to you that aren't made of friendship. If it takes putting everything in writing to make you come to your senses, I'll do that."

My trembling hands came to my face, and I crumbled into a pitiful heap. "I tried to kill her," I said.

Kasai stirred. "What are you talking about?"

"I tried to kill Natsuko. It was a moment so perfect, so peaceful. She looked so beautiful, so serene. I felt the moment so full, like a cup before it runs over. I felt that I could not come away from that moment without a deep sadness, an ache of disappointment. Have you ever felt that way? I felt so happy, so complete. How can I describe that moment? When I leave, I cannot control my need to return; I am consumed with jealousy. I have fought and suspected everyone, including you. I rush into the house at strange hours, thinking that I will find another man. I smell her clothes. I rummage through her drawers, through her purse. I want to know that all of her time is accounted for, that she is totally mine. But I can never be sure. I can never be sure. We argue uselessly over the slightest thing, the look in her eye when another man appears, a change in her clothing or her perfume, how many hours she has been practicing piano, but it is all the same argument. I am jealous, controlled by my passion, which is gnawing away at my insides, possessing my mind and my spirit. So I thought that this moment was a kind of apex, the height of a great love. I wanted to die. I wanted to die with her. I wanted to have her forever. So I brought my hands around her neck and squeezed. I stared into her eyes all the time, quivering with expectation, my short gasps and her breathlessness, watching her flush, watching her eyes roll, her body heaving, giving, leaving. I did not succeed. I crumbled, wrapping her in my arms, rocking her and pleading, pleading forgiveness. I cannot trust myself anymore. These hands. I might have destroyed the very thing I love." I wept.

"Go home," ordered Kasai. He shook his head. "Go home to Esperança. You don't belong here. You never did. Go home. You still have work to do. Go home."

*   *   *

By the time I returned, Shiozawa had already left. The bank's lawyers had already come and gone with no new results, leaving Shiozawa with the same mess, the same interminable headaches. Shiozawa could see no end in sight. He could not be vigilant enough. There were too many of us to oversee, too many schemes, too many bills to pay. The figures never matched. The books never balanced. Nobody cared. We all smiled and fed him large portions of food he could no longer eat. No one believed him when he talked about the terrible financial burden which had been heaped upon the commune, the awful consequences of not paying your bills, of incurring debt, of bad credit. We only smiled as if he were joking. We slapped him on the back, and said, "Shiozawa-san, you work too hard. You need to relax. Country life is slower. You need to adapt your habits to country life."

He could get no peace, no sleep. Dark shadows surrounded his tired eyes. He was thin and drawn, and his stomach seemed to be a clenched fist of continual pain. He walked around with a bottle of medicine which Sei Terada gave him. He had dispensed with taking that medicine with a spoon; instead he took regular swigs throughout the day, several as he might enter any crisis. All night he wrestled with the enormous figures which daily grew larger. It was an accountant's nightmare. One day, Shiozawa could no longer distinguish the nightmare in his sleep from the one he experienced daily. We saw him in his nightclothes one morning, running down the road, screaming, "Stop! Stop the New Hampshire shipment! Stop! Please! Stop!" Behind him ran his wife in frantic despair.

So they took Shiozawa away. They had to bundle him up in blankets and gag him. Haru went out to sit in the small waiting room at the airfield with Shiozawa's wife while they waited to leave. Haru held her hand and tried to console the poor woman. If Haru felt sympathy, no one else seemed willing to admit these feelings about Shiozawa's demise. There was, in fact, a great deal of rejoicing back at the commune, as if we had won a battle in a longer war. "The Boy Scout is gone!" we all exclaimed. "They've sent him away to the funny farm!"

* * *

Shiozawa's departure must have made some impact on Shinkichi Kawagoe, who could sympathize with Shiozawa's zeal to keep balanced books. Kawagoe had known for years about the commune's real financial situation; he himself had manipulated the books to hide the truth. He admitted freely to doing so, almost as if it had been a sort of experiment, the realization of a hidden desire to manipulate numbers to some other purpose. He had always known that embezzling money by manipulating books entailed a certain skill. In this case, Kawagoe made no real money for himself. He went to a lot of trouble to make things look good for us. He did this while changing the records on his phonograph, humming to Beethoven, Mozart and, later, Wagner. The memories of Heizo's suicide and Kimi's running off to the Amazon with Yōgu had faded. When Kimi returned with her ten children, Kawagoe felt a renewed sense of the old reasons for leaving his comfortable banker's life in Japan for the Christian ideals of nurturing the spirit and the land in the New World. His grandchildren were beautiful and strong, happy children who clambered around him to sing when he played the piano. Their hands and faces were smudged with the red earth, with the sticky juices of tropical fruit. They were bright and curious—quick learners. He loved all of them. He moved onto New World Ranch to be with his grandchildren, to share his love for music with them.

Kawagoe's wife, Kinu, was simply transported to a small house on the commune. She did not like to be near people, so the Kawagoes resided in a small house quite a distance from the other houses, clustered in communal blocks. Many had never even seen Kinu Kawagoe, who was said to remain all day alone in her bed, listening to Kawagoe's piped-in music and sipping tea and broth. Haru and my mother and others felt it their duty to make Kinu feel welcome; they took small trips out to her distant cottage to talk and be with her, but soon everyone realized that Kinu did not really like people and that she did not like living on the commune or in the country. She missed her distinguished life in Tokyo as the wife of a prominent banker, and although it had been nearly twenty years since the Kawagoes had immigrated to Brazil, Kinu had neither forgotten nor forgiven her husband for making that, in her opinion, disastrous decision. She looked wanly on at her grandchildren, each of whom reminded her of Kimi's marriage to Hachiro Yōgu. She could only abide their noisy antics for moments at a time. She complained that the children tired her, so they left her alone, forgetting that they had a grandmother. The memory or the notion of a grandmother faded as before, when they lived in the Amazon.

Notions of many things seemed to fade. The notion of a father faded at New World. Indeed, Yōgu had become another child among a larger band of many children, but the idea of fathers in general was lost upon children raised in a commune. I, Kantaro Uno, was the leader. This was all that most children understood. Mothers were many, some more popular than others, but Haru was a mother to everyone. In the same way, Kimi seemed to lose her identity as a mother and wife to a specific family.

When Shinkichi Kawagoe came to tell his daughter that he had decided to leave the commune, she had somehow lost her notion of being a daughter to this man. Kawagoe did not want to leave Kimi and her children behind. He wanted to take all of them with him somehow, but he could not. He was an old man. He had given up everything to our cause and would have to start all over again, but he could no longer stay, knowing what he knew. "Things are in a very bad way here, Kimi. I know everything. Shiozawa has told me everything. I have heard things from Sawada. I know because I have been keeping the books. Everything is pointed downhill. I don't know where we will go or what I will do now, but I want to prepare a way for you to all leave eventually."

"Leave?" Kimi looked at her father with surprise.

"Yes, leave. We will all have to leave one day. This will all come crumbling down. Kantaro has spent everything several times over, mostly for that woman in the city. I will go first with your mother, and when I can, I will send for you."

"I cannot leave."

Kawagoe looked at his daughter in confusion.

"I promised Kantaro. I promised him that we would not leave, no matter what. And he has promised that we would always be taken care of."

"It is an illusion."

"I must stay at his side. I cannot leave."

"What are you to Kantaro? A woman with ten hungry children and a husband who has lost his mind! You are only a burden on this failing operation."

"Then I will only be a burden to you. Take my mother and leave. It is her only wish, not to die in this place. Take her as she has always wanted to the city, to another life. As for me, there is no other life left to me. Everything ended a long time ago."

"I will call for you. I will not leave you here."

Kimi looked upon her aging father, a man whose dreams had been crushed one by one. When she had returned with her brood from the Amazon, Shinkichi Kawagoe was renewed by the idea that he must once again take hold of the situation, become a father and a grandfather to his family. Kimi could not bring herself to tell her father that this too was an illusion. She nodded quietly and said nothing.

*　　*　　*

That evening Ichiro returned from São Paulo with Hachiro Yōgu. How many days had he been gone? Perhaps two weeks. He was dirty and in need of a shave, reminding us of those days when he first arrived in Esperança. He did not speak a word on the entire trip back. Ichiro must have asked him what he had been doing in the city all those days by himself, but he would not answer. Every now and then, he might spit out the window onto the road speeding beneath the wheels. As the truck arrived, Yōgu dashed out to the kitchen. I could hear the clatter of pans and the commotion of badgering women as Yōgu interfered with their work. I was already seated, sullenly drinking my soup, nursing the wounds of lost love and endless debt, while Befu sat in silence beside me. Suddenly Yōgu burst from the kitchen with an enormous knife, jumping onto the tables and kicking over the large pots of rice and soup. He pranced over the tables in his muddy boots, knocking over pitchers of water, kicking plates into the laps of the surprised diners. From his throat, there came a long loud guttural roar that filled my ears and my heart. Even now I can hear the terrifying sound of Yōgu's roar, the fast heavy thud of his boots against the surface of the long table. Yōgu's features were crazy with rage, his entire body a single muscular weapon of revenge. He held the kitchen knife high in the air, secured in his fist like an old memory. I rose, backing away from the table in fear. But for a moment of hesitation, I would surely have been killed, my neck slashed neatly in a clean and sudden cut, but just as Yōgu was about to reach his destination, Befu slammed his arms across Yōgu's path, sending Yōgu flying from the table. In a second, Ichiro and others pounced on Yōgu, grabbing at his wild arm, the knife flailing everywhere.

"Haru!" Yōgu cried. "Haru! Haru! Haru!" he screamed over and over again, until the knife fell from his hand. Even then, Yōgu shook them all away like so many flies and stood for a moment alone, heaving like a wild bull and staring at me.

Suddenly, he spat onto the ground with a familiar contempt. And I saw the old Hachiro Yōgu turn on his heels and walk away.

* * *

The next morning Hachiro Yōgu was gone. Eggs had not been boiled for breakfast, and we did not wake to the potent smell of Haru's hot strong coffee. Everything was strangely askew.

People wandered out to see Shinkichi Kawagoe and his wife leave. Ichiro helped Kawagoe load his tremendous collection of classical records onto the back of the truck. "I've left the Wagner behind," Kawagoe said. It was true. People could still hear Tristan singing to Isolde.

Some people came out just to see what Kinu Kawagoe looked like. People were not surprised to see that her skin was the color of white porcelain for having never been out in the sun, but most were shocked that Kinu was not, after all, the invalid they had expected. She had come out of her house by herself, walking with a small suitcase packed with her belongings. Certainly she walked slowly and very carefully, but she did walk. She nodded to everyone with dignity. When Ichiro stepped forward to help her into the truck, she refused his help. "I have waited nearly twenty years for this moment," she whispered. "I can do it myself."

Kawagoe looked around and grimaced. The Wagner he had left playing was skipping, Tristan wailing the same thing again and again. He sat for a moment with his eyes shut, his head bowed. With great effort he suppressed the sob that rumbled from the center of his belly. He suppressed everything, turned to smile at his grandchildren clustered near the truck. Then he nodded with a blank face at the road ahead, and Ichiro knew enough to gun the motor and drive away.

That night, Kimi sat at the piano and played all night. People could hear the sound of the piano reverberating endlessly through the night air, and when the cackle of laying hens and the crowing of cocks broke the dawn, they could still hear the unbroken soliloquy of Kimi's rendered heart.

CHAPTER 14: SANTOS

OVER THE YEARS, I have been called many things: a great idealist, a romantic, a dissimulator, a dictator, an actor, even a monster. Shūhei Mizuoka said as much himself many years later, but even he knew that I could not so easily be explained away. The sum of a man's life is more than a mere word. Some have said that I have changed over the years, but who does not change? Who does not grow and grow old? And yet who is not always the same person?

Perhaps the people who have said these things about me are jealous, jealous to see that another man has lived his life and destiny to the fullest. As I have said, at every moment in my life, my cup has been brimming over.

Some may think that I had forgotten Haru, but I admit that I could not live without her. Perhaps I took my good wife for granted, but so did everyone else. If it is true, as I have been told, that Haru disappeared, many things we assumed would happen as a daily matter of course must have ceased to occur in quite the way we had come to expect. I know Befu liked two soft-boiled eggs every morning. This I'm told was forgotten, and he got hard-boiled eggs. No one could make strong coffee the way Haru did, and some people complained about that (some people never liked my wife's coffee anyway). And Haru always had a basket of food ready for Ichiro to take on his trips to São Paulo. She knew he liked hot tea in a thermos and a half-dozen rice balls and pickles. All of this would have been forgotten. I confess I was too busy to even notice at the time, but ever since I gave my old man a beating, he and my mother had taken to eating away from the dining hall in the quiet of the teahouse. My mother had been ill for several weeks, and Haru carried a tray of food out to my parents at every meal. Naotaro had to hobble into the kitchen to ask apologetically about their meals. Some people had special dietary requirements that Haru never seemed to forget. "No!" I could hear her barking. "That's not for you, Takeshita-san! What would the doctor say? This is for you! If you die, I don't want anyone blaming me!"

I heard some say that Haru's special food was awful stuff but that you had to eat it obediently or she would shove it down your throat. Well, I always said that she was well meaning and very conscientious; Haru enforced goodwill. No one crossed my wife willingly, no matter what they thought about her food or her manner of doing things. Haru was always consulting with Sei Terada and brewing special teas for someone with rheumatism or high blood pressure or a common cold. If Haru had left, people would have missed the awful food and teas and her bossy way of administering both things that were supposedly good for them and things they were particularly fond of. "I don't know why you like these soft eggs, Befu-san," she complained. "Raw eggs would do as well." But she cooked them just the same, the very way he liked them.

It was not just food; there were other small things that would have ceased to happen. It was Haru who swept out the bachelors' dorm every morning. It was Haru who gathered their clothing and washed and mended it all. It was Haru who cleaned out the bathhouse and made sure there was soap and a pile of clean towels. It was Haru who watered the flowers along the side of the dining hall. It was Haru who tended the herb garden and dried the leaves for special teas. It was Haru who, with Sei Terada, looked in on all the sick people and made sure that they got their meals and took their medicine. It was Haru who made new clothing for the youngsters and shirts for the men out of the cotton sacks that had held flour and feed.

Of course, I'm not saying that Haru did everything. There was always plenty of work to go around, and no one woman could handle the kitchen and the washing and cleaning by herself. But when I think back about my wife, I know she did some one thing for each of us that touched us in a special and individual way. In a commune where everyone got the same treatment, the same food, the same clothing, Haru treated each of us, not just me, in some singular way. I know Haru's way was usually brusque and heavy-handed, but she was never too busy to forget. I shared Haru with everyone. Because of this, I lost Haru for myself. Maybe it was selfish of me to need a woman for myself, but I did.

* * *

Although all of my people knew that Haru was gone, I myself never did. Even today, Haru denies that it happened. What am I to believe? In fact, I had left Esperança the same morning, not waiting to see the Kawagoes leave, not caring to confront Hachiro Yōgu again, still plagued by the smallest hope that I would return to São Paulo and find Natsuko, still certain that I would encounter the solution to bring us out from under the dark shadow of the bank. What I encountered on this trip to São Paulo was the unexpected shame of meeting our founder, Momose-sensei. Momose had become rather famous internationally as a Japanese Christian evangelist. He had survived the war in prison and had now come to Brazil to see how his brethren had fared in Esperança and to talk of larger issues—the war, the devastation of Hiroshima and Nagasaki, and his campaign for world peace.

Still searching for Natsuko, I followed the crowd of people into a small church to hear Momose-sensei speak. I had met Momose-sensei only once many years ago when he had come to Esperança and made his famous speech telling the colonists, "Make men rather than coffee." This was his way of saying that men were more important than the harvest of coffee for profit. When anyone ever talked about Momose, this is the famous line they always remembered. It was my father, Naotaro Uno, who had known Momose and followed his ministry. I wondered about this man who had inspired so many people to settle in Esperança and yet had spent most of his life in Japan. What could this man say to me who followed his very words and still struggled with this destiny? But as I listened to the evangelist, suddenly his words began to make sense to me; I was led back to the roots of my faith and my belief, and I stood up and confessed in a tearful moment of rebirth. The people who sat there and saw my redemptive moment were also moved to tears; they all left spreading the word that I had repented and changed. They had seen it happen. A new Kantaro Uno was born.

On that same day, a well-to-do businessman from São Paulo named Taro Ōshima also repented and found a new life, and the evangelist, given heavenly intuition, bound before a crowd of witnesses Ōshima's fate and my fate into one. "You, Ōshima-san, who have until today only thought of your own material welfare and you, Kantaro Uno, who have been lead astray by physical passion, are now bound in a higher love, the love of God. I command you, Ōshima-san, to give sustenance to this man, now so broken in spirit, and you, Uno-san, to receive this sustenance as God's love for you."

*   *   *

Meanwhile, back in Esperança, a new drama was brewing. Umpei Sawada had come to the commune with an entrepreneur by the name of José Santos. The two men walked around the commune escorted by Befu. As usual, Ichiro was asked to come along as an interpreter for Santos. "What is this thing you've got going here? Communism, isn't it?" Santos asked plainly, fingering the strap on his camera.

"If that's what you want to call it, but it's simply the way we've chosen to live," Ichiro answered.

"Well, I don't believe in it, frankly. Where's the incentive to work in a situation like this? No. No. You ought to release these people and put them back in the work force." Santos stepped back and snapped a long shot of our sawmill.

"We have a long history," Ichiro countered. "We are a very productive operation. We started this from scratch, and created everything you see here today."

Santos checked the focus on his camera and said, "Yes, but the books say you're up to your neck in debt. Poor management, I say."

To this Ichiro said nothing. By now, people all over Esperança were talking about the things they knew, the things they had heard. After the Kawagoes left, other families came to their own conclusions and decided to leave. I saw these foolish ones leave without money and without a destination—no plot of land upon which to make a new beginning, no promise of work. But if they wanted to leave, I didn't stop them. They were free to leave. We let them go with the few belongings they were entitled to. Most of these people had relatives who would take them on for a while anyway. The rest, who had nowhere to turn and would have been ashamed to beg for charity, stayed. Of course it took some courage to leave, but it would have taken greater courage to stay and fight with me.

Santos turned to the banker. "Sawada, I don't know about this. If I were to take this operation over, first off, I'd trim the work force. It's not necessary to have all these people. I couldn't possibly pay them all. Right now, maybe a family or two. Maybe, in time, the operation could be expanded, and we could call some of them back, but initially, we need to cut costs. All these people have got to go."

Trim the work force? These people have got to go? Befu was in shock. The blood drained from his dark features. "What do you mean by bringing this—" Befu sputtered, "this foreigner here!" Befu attacked Sawada in Japanese. "This is not a simple business operation for profit! It is a way of life! It is a great human experiment! How can you assume to take over such a thing?" All the while, Santos continued to snap pictures of everything—our chickens, our houses, our barns, our equipment, everything—as if it were mere property, things he could later examine at leisure, things to buy and sell.

Sawada calmly took out a cigarette and offered it to Santos. "The bank has done everything possible to try to help, to make the present decision unnecessary. But Kantaro and you people have broken our trust too many times. We can no longer harbor Kantaro's debt. We tried with Shiozawa to forestall this situation, to try to put your operation on stable ground, but everything we've tried has failed. Now we can no longer afford the risk. We have other honest and trustworthy clients to attend to. The bank is not in the business of great human experiments. You have brought this situation upon yourselves. Think about it. You have treated my people, my lawyers and Shiozawa—a very good man—with scorn, as if we were the enemy. When everything is turned over to this man, you will see how good the bank has been to you." Sawada blew smoke from the side of his mouth and sneered.

Befu glared at Sawada. "Kantaro will not stand for this. You will see. We will fight this until death." Befu turned and walked away angrily.

Santos turned to Ichiro, "Now what did they say?"

I imagine Ichiro looking around helplessly. "Befu said that no decision could be made without Kantaro."

"Kantaro? Your leader? Ah yes, well, we will have to work out the final plans, but of course, I will want my own managers. All this talk about Kantaro. I read an article about him. The King of Eggs, isn't he? Well, he may know something about eggs, but as far as business organization—" Santos shook his head. "It's beyond me how all of you can work for this man for nothing."

*   *   *

The idea that José Santos could take over New World Ranch was so appalling no one really believed it could happen. My solution had always been to buy time, to stall our creditors, to march forward boldly with new projects, to talk big and broadly, to speak of our history and the productivity of our great enterprise. Someone with a heart, someone with a sense of history, someone with ideals would understand our plight and save us.

In São Paulo, I found such a person in Taro Ōshima. Ōshima had had some luck in the scrap metal business. He had started a modest business with a small truck and, in the beginning, had done all the work himself, collecting and hauling scrap metal and turning all of it into a good profit. In time, Ōshima had several trucks and employees and was well known and respected in the business. Ōshima was a modest man with a kind heart. He alone had stood up when the evangelist had asked the question, "Who in God's name will answer His calling? Who has seen the light and is cleansed by His message?" Ōshima, who had not given much thought to the question of God and religion, suddenly felt moved to answer.

In the beginning, people were cautious about my transformation, looking at me askance, talking behind my back, scorning my love affair, sneering at my great debt. No one was willing to take the first step toward welcoming me back, but on the other hand, I was openly welcomed into the Ōshima household. I had dinner with the Ōshimas, played with their children, talked of my own family and how the Ōshimas must come to visit Esperança. The Ōshimas became a place of refuge.

But I could not help speaking of my ideas, my projects, my plans for the future, and Ōshima was a kind and inspired listener. It was not long before I had caught Taro Ōshima's imagination with the egg business. "I know what everyone is saying," I pushed aside the gossip. "Well, I have been to the bottom and can go no further. I have more than paid for my sins, Ōshima-san. Now, I have been blessed with a new life. God sent you with a purpose in mind—to tell me that these dreams are not idle, that they must go on, that they must become reality. This dream is not a bad dream. How can it be a bad dream to work and live together on the land, to make the land produce and to give back to the land what we have taken, to find happiness from a simple life, to create a new civilization of strong and Christian people? I have been foolish and sinful, but the dream itself—it is not a bad one."

Ōshima nodded.

"You are a godsend, Ōshima-san. You alone, out of all these people, believe. Will you help me? Help me to do the work I have not finished?"

Ōshima was moved by my plea. He converted his trucks to carry eggs and built a warehouse to house our shipments. Once again Ichiro began to haul shipments into the city and to leave them with Ōshima. By the end of the year, Ōshima had converted his entire enterprise to selling and shipping eggs.

Meanwhile, the bank's negotiations with José Santos dragged on for many months. I argued with Sawada over the bank's choice of José Santos, but Sawada said coldly, "Up to now, he's the only one who's shown any interest. You don't think anyone in the colony would take you on with what they know, do you?" Sawada laughed.

I then went to see José Santos and tried to convince him to come to some agreement in which he and I might work jointly. "We are already starting to recuperate our losses," I spoke earnestly. "My partner in São Paulo, Taro Ōshima, perhaps you've heard of him. He has a lot of money, and a good business mind. He will guarantee my participation in a business deal with you."

Santos listened but would come to no decision. "My deal is with the bank. There just seems to be too many people involved in this thing, too complicated for my tastes. Really, if you could deliver this thing with only a couple of families, I might consider it right away," Santos admitted. "Well, I have some other matters to take care of first, then I'll settle my mind on this."

The idea that such a man might soon have legal rights to our land and operation was a chilling one. Somehow, I had to find someone to replace José Santos. Taro Ōshima did not have the fabulous means to buy the bank's offer, but perhaps, I thought, if there were two such financiers.

*   *   *

Ichiro drove me over to see the Bahiano, and as usual, he was my interpreter. The Bahiano and Maria das Dores had an enormous house on a ridge overlooking the rolling landscape of their great ranch. If the Bahiano had once pressed his claim on this land with brute force, everything now had the settled appearance of a well-kept sprawling hacienda owned by distinguished country gentry. Gone were the *jagunços* and the old unlawful ways. The Bahiano met us out on his spacious porch. We were served tall glasses of cool passion-fruit juice and large wedges of watermelon. A gracious warmth radiated from his household. The Bahiano listened carefully and shook his head sadly when I described our troubles and José Santos's plans to buy out our debt from the Nibras Bank and dismantle us. "We are finished," I said tragically. "This is the end. What am I to do? The children—where will they go? We will have no place." My eyes watered.

"No," the Bahiano said, controlling the rising emotion in his own voice. "We must find a way. I will personally see to this. I owe it to the memory of Okumura. What is it that you need?"

"We are starting to want for food in the kitchen. What am I to tell the women? Let the children go hungry? Our credit has been cut off everywhere. We don't have the cash to pay. The bank has passed the word all around that my name means nothing."

"Use my credit at the old Turk's. I will talk to Abdala myself. Get what you need for the children. You and I, we will arrange a partnership, and we will make it work. You can use my name, my credit. What do you have to offer?"

"We have made a good beginning with a wealthy businessman in São Paulo, Taro Ōshima. He is distributing our eggs. He will guarantee everything for us," I said eagerly. "I can pay you back everything. Everything," I promised.

"This is good. This is good. Yes. If you can get that São Paulo man—Ōshima, did you say? If you can get him to agree, maybe we can remove this Santos from the picture."

And so an arrangement of sorts was made. The Bahiano and I talked until it was dark, exchanging ideas, creating a great project, a great plan full of great promises. I had found a Brazilian who matched my sense of vision and moving history. He spoke with much excitement. "Now Okumura once said an interesting thing," he said. "He said that the cooperative had to be careful to sponsor new projects all the time, that you can't just stick to one idea. It's dangerous to produce just one product. You have to have something to fall back on or to move on to. I think you ought to think about diversifying your plant, Kantaro."

"I have been thinking along the same lines," I replied. "You know, we have a strain of watermelon that will beat anyone's."

"Is that right?"

And so the talk went, creating a continuing plan that only grew bigger and better with time. As we drove back home that evening, I settled contentedly back into the seat of the truck and sighed. "Yes," I nodded. "The Bahiano is going to save us."

Ichiro was silent. To the Bahiano, everything rang clear and true, but Ichiro thought he had heard it all before and that he knew things the Bahiano did not know. So he felt sadness in the Bahiano's obvious pleasure and exuberance over my ideas. Maybe he remembered his brother Kōichi, still in prison for burning the Tanaka silk barn. He had once felt the same joy the Bahiano felt; where had it all gone? But I was too preoccupied to see his loss of joy, and I did not notice when Ichiro faltered in his love for me.

In the beginning, it did seem that this new arrangement would pull us out of the bank's tightfisted grasp, and perhaps even Sawada had thought that we could make a comeback to pay our debts. The pressure to dump New World Ranch on some entrepreneur like José Santos receded momentarily, and the Bahiano went to court and pleaded our case before numerous small creditors. The Bahiano turned out to be a man of great passion, and he had come to believe fervently in our cause. He spoke eloquently and passionately for us.

"These aren't the people we should be punishing," the Bahiano declared. "Judge, we must give these people time. They are honest people, and they have made a statement declaring that they want to make good their debts. I myself have entered into an agreement with them, and I can pledge my own home and property on their goodwill!"

Ichiro's trips back and forth to São Paulo began once again with the old frequency. I would myself get him out of bed. "Before we go, I want to stop at the Bahiano's," I would announce.

It was usually so early in the morning that the Bahiano was still in bed. "Send him in, Dorinha. Send him in!" the Bahiano would yell from his room.

I would stride into the bedroom as the Bahiano was awkwardly propping himself up. Maria das Dores would serve us each a cup of coffee, and the Bahiano would stir his sugar in slowly while I announced, "Here is a check from Taro Ōshima for our last shipment. Please add it to our account."

The Bahiano looked over the check. "Not bad. We're in business, I see."

"There will be more. Ichiro and I are going to the city today with a shipment," I said, adding, "I am going to see the American representative for the New Hampshire chicken breed. I think this is our chance. Befu is depending on this. I will need money to put down the initial deposit to show we are serious. Then there is that new generator we need."

"This check won't clear for at least a week. I don't know if we've the immediate funds," the Bahiano hedged.

"No problem," I answered. "You make a check out to Taro Ōshima, and he will endorse it for me. It's all in the same family. Ōshima is rich; he can wait for his money to come back to him. Besides, I can get a better deal if I handle this in cash."

So I left Esperança with a check signed by the Bahiano to Taro Ōshima for a blank amount of money. On the other end, Taro Ōshima filled in some amount, endorsed the Bahiano's check, and I cashed it in for money. When the crisp feel of cash touched my hands, I confess it was difficult not to find immediate ways to spend this money.

I ran off to Miyasaka's for a good meal and some idle talk with Mama Miyasaka. "So Kantaro, it's been a long time," Mama Miyasaka said coyly.

I nodded. "How has business been?"

"Not so bad. Papa came down with something, and he was in bed for a week. Now he's better. Back upstairs again."

"Junko up there?"

"Junko? She comes and goes. She has her own game going at her place, you know."

"Have you seen her?"

"Junko?"

"No. Natsuko."

Mama Miyasaka smiled. "Well now, I'm not so sure. What with Papa sick like he was, and so many people only paying on credit . . . The people who talk big are the worst. We wait, but they don't pay up. Old lady like me should be able to retire someday."

I reached into my pocket and drew out my bundle of cash. "That sort of thing is inexcusable, Miyasaka-san. What do I owe you?" I gave her the money.

"They said you've changed. Is it true?"

"Yes. A new man," I nodded and waited eagerly for the news of Natsuko.

Mama Miyasaka had heard that Natsuko had left São Paulo, that she might have gone traveling to Europe. Someone else thought Japan, but Mama thought not. No one had seen Natsuko for months.

"Did she go alone?" I asked.

But Mama maneuvered herself away with her money. "I wonder," she said.

Suddenly all the old smoldering fires were once again fanned into flames. I forgot about the New Hampshire breed and the generator and rushed about in a panic all over São Paulo to discover where and with whom Natsuko had gone. But all the old haunts housed people who were ready to test my rebirth. By the end of the day, the money was gone, and I had a new story for Taro Ōshima. "I have been looking at a new truck for Ichiro. It's about time that we got him something decent. This is a very good deal. If I could put a deposit down to hold this until I got back to Esperança . . ."

And Taro Ōshima wrote the check for what he assumed must be a deposit for a new truck.

"Don't worry, Ōshima-san," I assured him. "We've got a big rancher in Santa Cruz behind us. I'll be back next week with a check from him to pay you back."

So it went, back and forth, the Bahiano signing checks over to Taro Ōshima, Taro Ōshima signing checks over to the Bahiano, and me, Kantaro, spending all the money in between. In a short period of time, I had practically depleted the resources of both men; the fantasy, however, continued for many more months, even when the checks that reached the Bahiano from Taro Ōshima no longer had funds to support them and vice versa. Taro Ōshima must have known of his situation before actually reaching zero, but he continued to foolishly believe in my boast of a rich rancher in Santa Cruz d'Azedinha for whom there were no limits. Also, Taro Ōshima had made a promise to God to abandon his thoughts of material wealth; perhaps this was his great test of faith. But when the Nibras Bank, with whom Ōshima had long banked, began to notice his climbing loans and bad credit, it did not take them long to find the real source of these debts.

The Bahiano, on the other hand, had made a great effort to keep track of my spending, and he knew exactly how much Taro Ōshima owed the partnership, and quite soon, it was a tremendous sum of money. "Who is this Taro Ōshima?" the Bahiano asked. "I think you've got us into a fix, Kantaro. No more shipments to this man until he pays up! If he's got so much money, he can pay it now. We can't run on promises."

"Don't worry," I always said. "I will talk to him today. He's an honest man."

One day the Bahiano himself decided to see just who this honest man was. He wandered into a pleasant neighborhood in São Paulo called Aclimação where well-to-do Japanese immigrants had begun to build their homes. It was a brief meeting. Ōshima's wife sat at her husband's side and wept the entire time while Taro Ōshima's oldest daughter interpreted everything. "My father has sold everything, all his trucks, the warehouse, even the furniture in his office. He has also sold a piece of land he owned in Santo Amaro. He is still in great debt. The only thing we have left is this house. My father realizes how indebted we are to you. He is so ashamed. He knows that it will not cover everything he owes you, but he is offering . . ." the girl's voice faltered, "offering you this house."

The Bahiano heard all of this in great shock. He had gone to São Paulo full of anger, ready, he said, to twist Taro Ōshima's neck, to wring the money owed from Ōshima's very body. He was ready to make his angry speech about the women and children at New World

Ranch who had been cheated by Ōshima's failure to pay. Instead, he
left Ōshima and his house behind. "It is true, Ōshima's house could
have been mine," the Bahiano wrote to me in a letter breaking his
contract with me, "but I did not have the courage. I am unable to
understand how you, Kantaro, did have such courage."

The Bahiano said that he then followed my tracks all around São
Paulo. In some places, he was surprised to learn that his true name,
Floriano Raimundo, was known to the proprietors; I had cashed his
checks there, had left his name, saying, "Charge it to my patron in
Santa Cruz."

He wrote, "I have begun the difficult process of selling my holdings in Paraná, my second ranch in Santa Cruz, all my cattle, my
truck, jeep and farming equipment. Any profits to be realized from
the next coffee harvest will certainly be lost to this folly. I have already emptied all of my accounts. But the most painful thing is that
I will have to recall my daughters from São Paulo to end their schooling. . . I have been broken by this experience in ways that you can
never imagine. This communication will end any further dealings
with you."

I later learned that the Bahiano was able to save his original farm
and home, which was in his wife's name.

* * *

They say Haru returned to Esperança in less than a week. I never
heard any of this until many years later. No one spoke of her absence, and Haru never talked of it. Even now she glares or looks
puzzled whenever anyone makes reference to her having gone away.
"What nonsense. I have always lived here. I have never been anywhere. Only twice I went to São Paulo to Takehashi's place." Where
Haru went or if she even went with Yōgu, I don't know. It was true
that she had never been anywhere outside of Esperança except one
or two trips to São Paulo. Occasionally she went into Santa Cruz
d'Azedinha. She had been to Andradina, to Tietê and even as far as
Bastos, but these were short excursions and did not really count for
much. My wife is a forceful woman in her own element, but she does
not speak Portuguese beyond a very rudimentary and broken form
of the language. Her life has always been on the land, caring for her
children, her kitchen and her garden. It would not have been an easy
thing to venture out of our world. Maybe it happened. Maybe it is a
lie. It is Haru's only secret. Someone said that it was her only holiday,

but women like Haru don't take holidays. One thing I am sure of is that if Haru did go anywhere, she came back because she wanted to.

That Haru was unable to leave seems natural enough, but I always thought that Saburo would approach me with his curt good-bye and stride away down a solitary road. Even Ichiro must have thought it would be for the best. But Saburo did not leave. He stayed because, for all his talk, he was weak. Perhaps Ichiro thought of himself as Saburo's closest friend, but even from Ichiro, Saburo preferred to keep his thoughts to himself. It must anger Ichiro even now to think that he had not been aware of Saburo's pain. Along with so many other events, Ichiro's constant traveling had distanced him from people and life back at home. When he returned from delivering a shipment to São Paulo, he was more concerned about whether he might be able to see Akiko than in seeing his old friend Saburo. He did not even notice that Saburo had been losing weight or that his features had grown dark and drawn. "Emiru," Saburo chuckled, "where have you been? Out trying to make money so that Kantaro can spend it on his personal dream? When will you ever learn?"

I overhead them talking in the bathhouse.

"We are in a bad way," Ichiro nodded, tugging at his shirt and kicking away his shoes.

Saburo sneered and repeated, "We are in a bad way. We are sinking!" Saburo laughed and slipped down deeper into the tub. "I am sorry I won't be here to see it all come crashing down."

"How can you talk about it that way?"

"What is there to do but talk about it? You have all turned your souls over to Kantaro. Is there anyone among this crowd with any guts, any guts to cut out this cancer?" Saburo looked at Ichiro sharply, his eyes dimming and burning through the bath steam. His words filled Ichiro with confusion and fear.

"Why did you come back, anyway?" he demanded. "You never believed in any of this. What good does it do now to say that you were right?"

"What good, Emiru. What good," Saburo nodded sadly. "You are right. I have failed myself. Who am I to talk? The war brought me back here. I waited for it to end, but as you know, it never ended." Saburo laughed again. "I had this idea that I could build a radio station. I talked to Kawagoe about it one time, but it was only an idea. He told me that we had no money to even think of such a project, and Kantaro never listened to me. He has only listened to Befu all these years. Chickens. All those ideas about breeding a pure form of chicken. Maybe he will succeed someday." Saburo snickered and then broke into laughter. It was a hollow sound, Saburo's laughter rolling around the big bathhouse.

Ichiro did not know of his ideas and must have felt hurt that he had not known. He had to admit that even he had often thought that Saburo was an irksome sort whose only reason to live was to oppose me. I had always cast Saburo as a man without vision, a negative and pessimistic force running against the future. Perhaps it's true that Saburo had a perceptive mind, but Ichiro was just as perceptive; and Ichiro had always been a forgiving sort. Saburo could not see without being cynical. For as long as I can remember, my brother had been angry. No one, except Hachiro Yōgu had ever given Saburo credit for his angry energy. Perhaps he lived in my shadow, but who did not? Saburo did not know how to realize his talents. He wasted away in Esperança, his frustrations gnawing a growing tunnel through his body.

Saburo lifted himself from the tub and nearly toppled over. I could hear the scuffle as Ichiro ran to secure him. "Sabu, what is it? What is this? You are skin and bones!"

When Ichiro learned that Saburo was ill, he felt great anger, but Saburo was coldly passive. He shrugged weakly. "I can no longer eat. I'm starving to death," he chuckled. "Starving in Esperança. Starving. Pretty soon you will all be starving," he wagged a finger. "I'm dying, Emiru. That's all there is to it. Everything I eat, I vomit. It's no use. Forget it, Emiru. Forget it."

"Sabu! Fight! Fight back!" he insisted.

Saburo pushed Ichiro aside and pulled a towel around himself, "Emiru, do me a favor."

Ichiro leaned forward.

"Get out of here. Leave."

"Akiko—" he faltered.

"Akiko, Akiko," Saburo repeated. "Forget Akiko."

"I don't care what they say. I'm going to take her away with me."

Saburo began to laugh. "Emiru. Open your eyes. Everyone knows but you."

"Knows what?"

"She belongs to Kantaro. That's why she went to São Paulo. Probably that Natsuko knew someone . . . to do the abortion."

Ichiro looked at Saburo with incomprehension. "No!" he screamed.

"If it makes you feel any better, it wasn't just Akiko. Haru gets up at dawn every day, and every day Kantaro sneaks into the girls' dormitory, just like a rooster in a hen house. Where were you that day when Haru went running in the dorm shouting, 'Kantaro! What are you doing in here?' Everyone saw him jumping out the back window completely naked. That's why the Horiis took their daughters and left. It wasn't because of Jiro; Jiro was just following Kantaro, as always."

Foolishly, Ichiro raged, "You're lying!"

"Why do you think you're put on that truck to run back and forth, back and forth? You're like a chicken who lives under artificial lights day and night, laying eggs without rest. For you, there is no sleep, no rest, no night, no time to think or question what you clearly see. Everyone says that you have made great sacrifices. You think they are praising you, but you cannot see what they really mean." Saburo teetered about and slumped on the bench, exhausted by his effort to talk. He said weakly, "I have thought of telling you this for a long time now, but you are like all the rest of them, so happy in your illusions. Maybe, there is something to all that. Maybe."

I had nothing to say about Saburo's accusations. That Ichiro believed in Saburo's words more than in my love for him pains me as he will never know. I took for granted that Ichiro was as a brother to me—the brother I did not have in Jiro or Saburo. He was better than many of us. Even now I see the question in his eyes. It haunts me. I failed him. It was not only Akiko; it was his faith in me. I see a fuzzy outline of the man Ichiro once believed in and no longer knew. He had thought that his tired mind played tricks with his old resolve, but now he knew that the pain he felt was real. Saburo had said so. I say so. From the time he lost sight of his birthplace and began to see his his life unfold on this new land, Ichiro had seen everything.

A month later, my brother Saburo died.

* * *

The bank sold New World Ranch to José Santos, who immediately sent his executors out to sell off everything they could get a good price for. When people began to see the tractors, the incubators, our small herd of cows and the chickens go, it was impossible to believe in any sort of illusion about our future. Santos earmarked everything for sale; that which could not be sold immediately would be sold in a general auction. The date for the auction was announced and advertised all over the region, but before the auction, Santos got court orders to remove the invaders on his property. Invaders.

I was not at the ranch to receive the signed court injunction that ordered us off the land. I was running around from bank to bank in São Paulo trying to find a bank with resources large enough to buy our debt. Suddenly I became convinced that Umpei Sawada and his bank were too small and inconsequential to handle our great project. The Bank of Brazil was interested. I thought that I only needed time. Meanwhile, Ichiro read and translated the injunction to Befu, who trembled with anger, snatching the document and ripping it up in front of the astonished official. The official looked at Ichiro and shrugged. "I don't make the orders, you know. This is serious. They'll send troops. You tell him. They'll send troops."

The dentist Takehashi was there too. "Befu," the dentist asked, "what shall we do? He said one week. We have one week."

Befu growled, "We are not going anywhere. We will never leave. We will all kill ourselves before that happens."

"What nonsense!" the dentist yelled. "No one is going to kill anyone. We have all heard enough of this talk. We are not children. We all know what this means. We have been led around like sheep for too long. It is time for us to take hold of our own lives."

"We will wait until Kantaro returns."

"Kantaro has lost his judgment and our trust. We can no longer trust him to make decisions."

"You are a traitor, Takehashi!" Befu yelled.

"No," Takehashi answered coldly. "We have been betrayed."

I know that Kōhei Takehashi and Ichiro Terada went to see the Bahiano. I can see Maria das Dores at the door, barring their way, her teeth set and her eyes on fire. "Who is it, Dorinha?" The voice of the Bahiano could be heard behind her. He came himself to the door and looked at Ichiro and the dentist. His eyes filled with sadness, but he spoke firmly. "Ichiro," he said. "What can I do for you?"

Maria das Dores stepped boldly in front of her husband. "Yes, what more can he possibly do for you?"

"There is an injunction against us. If we do not leave within the week, they say we will be forced to leave. We do not have anywhere to go."

I do not know why the Bahiano acquiesced to their plea for help, but he did. I have to respect that man. "I will see this thing to the end," he said. "I have to live with my actions, and I expect to live a long time. You may bring your people to live on my land. However, my only condition is that Kantaro Uno remain behind. He is no longer welcome here." There was no explanation other than that. Takehashi and Ichiro heard his decision. The three of them sat together, unable to speak. What did they think? None of them could put the blame on me alone. They too were responsible; they believed.

*　*　*

That day, I left a meeting at the Bank of Brazil, satisfied that they were interested in my proposal. On a whim, I went back to my old house on that secluded and shady street. I had heard that Natsuko had returned from Europe, but I did not expect to see her there. I sat at the grand piano and ran my fingers along the ivory keys. A thin layer of city soot covered everything and soiled my fingers. Everything was as she had left it: the tidy doilies, the bric-a-brac, the books I had recommended she read, still neatly displayed and unread. And everything was covered with that film of city soot. I wandered into the kitchen and found an open bottle of French wine. I picked up the bottle and looked at its label. Where had I seen this bottle before? The wine within dispersed a fruity aroma. Even I who was not familiar with wine knew that this bottle had not soured but had been recently poured. Suddenly I remembered. The painter Takashi Inagaki had brought such a bottle home from his stint in Paris. He had arrived suddenly in the middle of the night, banging on the door and waking us from sleep. "I'm back! I'm back! It was wonderful. Get up! Let's celebrate. Let me tell you about everything!" Inagaki had yelled.

I snatched the bottle and ran up the staircase. Natsuko saw me there in the doorway, her eyes rounding with shock and her face flushing uncontrollably, as if my presence had enhanced her pleasure. I flung the bottle with a vengeance, the glass shattering against the wall and the French wine showering onto the bedsheets. I pounced on Inagaki, flinging him from the bed. The naked man sprang up wildly, bouncing about the bed and taunting me. I ran in a rage around the bed, but suddenly Inagaki's foot caught me in the eye, an angry spur of light. I staggered backward, my hand covering my left eye. Blood running down my face, I flung myself down the stairs in pursuit of the painter, but Inagaki was gone. I turned to look back at Natsuko, who knelt in a naked slump at the top of the stairs. The memory of her flushing face mocked me, and I ran from the house.

*   *   *

High in the sky from a small biplane I could see Esperança, spread in neat lots across the landscape, the tiny farmhouses, the plantations of coffee and corn, the grazing cattle, the chicken coops and the silk barns. I could see the red fingers of the dirt roads we had carved out, branching through the forest. Passing over the town, I could see the long house where all of us had first come to live in Esperança. That house had been turned over to the cooperative for its offices. And there was Okumura's old house, where Haru's mother, Tomi, still insisted on living alone, and Kawagoe's old house at the end of the road. I ordered the pilot to fly over New World Ranch. The plane circled the land while I scrutinized the familiar landscape with astonishment. The dining hall with its great kitchen was gone. So too the barn and the sawmill and the chicken pens. Most of the houses were gone, but a few remained, although the roof tiles were removed, exposing to the open air the empty rooms where we had once lived and slept. I looked again. The water tower was still there, standing like a lonely pillar on the landscape. Haru's vegetable garden was abandoned beside the old outhouse and the shed. I ordered the pilot to swoop lower, and then I saw the tiny line of activity, the people, carts and Ichiro's remaining truck scurrying away with anything that could yet be salvaged and called our own.

When I arrived on the land provided by the Bahiano, I ran about in anger, stalking the dining hall, now completely rebuilt in every detail just as it was but in a different place. It angered me to see that even Inagaki's paintings were displayed in the same places on the same walls. I had run to the outhouse and found it in the same position relative to the cottage I shared with Haru, which was also in its same relative place. Everything was insidiously the same. Many were still involved in the general task of moving and rebuilding; they scurried past me, busy and devoted to their tasks, avoiding my anger and confusion, intent on their work, as if work could salve their wounds, could obliterate their fears. Far from the dining hall, they could hear me ranting at Befu, "Whose decision was this? Who ordered this? Don't you know I was about to close a deal with the Bank of Brazil? Now everything is ruined! I want to know who the traitors are!"

Befu said nothing. For all his courageous words about killing himself, he had relented when Takehashi and the Bahiano described how military troops on horseback with rifles would come and drive us out. Of course the Bahiano must have exaggerated; he told Befu he had seen troops drive Indian tribes off their land. Befu would not admit his fear, nor would he take responsibility for the move. "It was Takehashi," he said contemptuously. "He made his own arrangements with the Bahiano."

I seethed, feeling the blood seeping behind the bandages of my swollen eye. They all came to the dining hall reluctantly, but they came. They heard me explain with great emotion and thunder that to stay on the Bahiano's land was to give up our freedom, to become slaves. I would not remain under such conditions; I would leave. Who would follow me? Who? "Who?" I screamed. "Stand!"

For a long moment, no one moved. Only Jiro, faithful Jiro, had no thought but to stand. He looked around in bewilderment at all of the others still seated. Then Befu stood, staring sternly at my sister, Ritsu, and their son, Genji, who also quietly joined him. I uttered a painful shudder, wiping away my tears as, one by one, a small group of the loyal awkwardly stood. Haru stood. Kimi stood, commanding her brood of eight to do the same. I saw Akiko standing next to her mother, her eyes wandering toward Ichiro sitting among his brothers, pleading. He looked away.

I looked around at my small cadre, and then I saw my own son Kanzo still sitting, arms crossed and head bowed. I walked up to Kanzo and commanded him, "Stand!"

Kanzo shook his head. He did not have words to defend himself. He was a bashful kid, awkward in the manner of his mother but without the confident bluster. It was Kanzo's first and perhaps last real decision. I grabbed my son, punching and boxing the poor young man, who would not defend himself. As Kanzo crumpled to the floor, I hurled my fist at his right eye. The young man tumbled backward but refused to cry. "Stand!" I screamed.

Kanzo crawled pathetically to my feet and pulled himself up. He stood before me, blood flowing from his nose, his lip bubbling up in a black bruise. And I stared in horror at a mirror of myself so many years ago.

CHAPTER 15: TWILIGHT

I LEFT THAT SAME DAY with a group of about a hundred people. We walked away uncertainly with only the belongings we could carry, walked away out into the countryside like a band of homeless refugees. From this moment of separation, our lives began anew. It was not the last time I saw those people left behind, but the rift between us was complete. Perhaps others did, but I never again spoke with any of them. They blamed me for their difficulties, and I do not deny my failings. I have been a great sinner, a man with many faults. But I lived the life of which I have spoken; I could not have lived another. I have denied nothing.

Now I believe that this parting of ways was a necessary step in our history, a critical parting in which people were forced to choose their destinies. If life had become too easy, too simple, this was a test of true spirit. Those who were not strong enough for what the future would demand of us fell away to their predictable lives of day-to-day survival, their pragmatic ideas of work and money, their common sense. I no longer feel any anger toward these people. They were not made of the same stuff; they had joined us only to survive hard times.

As for Kōhei Takehashi and Ichiro Terada, I can never forget their betrayal. I cannot forget that Ichiro betrayed me, even though I know that he believed until he could believe no more, and for that he will never forgive me. But what is there to forgive? Who can look back on the passage of their lives and tell such stories, speak of such struggles, remember that they were the participants in a great dream, remember that they pursued a life of ideals, lived their lives as a cup brimming over?

I see in my mind's eye even now that scene of my poor band of followers trudging down the dirt road. We pause for moment on a small ridge, and I look among the faces of my people, the purple light spreading across the clear skies reflected in their faces. My thoughts wander back to New World Ranch, which is no longer, back to the old mango groves where we buried Saburo. The trees are flowering now. I hear a voice saying, "Emiru," but perhaps it is only the wind. Twilight spreads across the Esperança skies. I kneel to fill my pockets with fistfuls of the soft red earth and walk on.

Part IV: Genji

Man is born free, and yet we see him everywhere in chains.

Jean-Jacques Rousseau
The Social Contract

CHAPTER 16: THE SILK BARN

I AM GENJI BEFU, nephew of Kantaro Uno. My father is the old egg expert Seijiro Befu, and my mother is Ritsu. I was born nineteen years ago in 1940 right here at Kantaro's place. They say Sei Terada was the midwife who took me from my mother. Anyway, Sei lives with the others. They have their own place now.

No one will talk about the others. It is as if they were all dead or invisible. If we meet them in town or in Santa Cruz, we never speak to each other; we look the other way. It's been maybe about five years since we split up, and we still don't talk. Maybe some people talk, but they never let Kantaro know. You see Kantaro sometimes sitting alone, thinking about his anger, thinking about those traitors. You can tell that he is thinking about Takehashi and Terada and those good for nothing "others" because his eyes become distant and blank and he gnashes his teeth and mutters things to himself. Then Haru will come by and slap him with a wet towel. "Uno-san!" she yells. "Daydreaming again?" And he stops.

But as I was saying, like everyone else, I was born here and have never been anywhere else in my life. My old teacher, Takashi Inagaki, went to Paris. They say that Paris is where you must go if you really want to paint, so I expect that my old man Befu will send me there when we get out of debt. That may be never, so I don't expect that I will ever leave this place.

I have been trying to think of my first memory. My first memory is a rather strange one; I am in a basket looking up at the blue sky. I must be small enough to fit in a basket but not big enough to move around. I am all squashed, with my knees touching my chin. Above me is the sky; I can see the clouds pass from one edge of the basket to the other. I can see the sky change colors. Sometimes I sleep. Sometimes I watch the clouds. A bird passes overhead. I pass an entire day like this. When I have to pee or shit, no matter—I soil myself. For a while it is a good feeling, warm and comforting not to be so alone, but after a while, I feel wet and cold. I feel hungry, and my stomach begins to hurt. So I cry and rock around in the basket. No one hears. I rock around so hard that the basket falls over, and I roll down a hill it seems. I roll and roll. I scream and cry and laugh until the rolling stops with a thud. There are cries outside the basket and footsteps running excitedly. Someone, maybe it is my mother Ritsu, grabs me from the basket and wraps me in her arms. I grab and wrestle with her clothing until I can find her breast. Everyone says I have been spoiled; they say Ritsu never stopped nursing her only son.

For a long time I thought that this memory of the basket and the sky above was a dream, but I found out that it was not. Ritsu used to take me out to the fields and put me in a basket while she worked. Haru says the reason my legs are so bowed is because I was always crunched up in the basket.

One day I painted a picture of this memory, of my view from deep inside the basket, of the sky above and the clouds passing from one edge of the basket to another. I never told anyone the meaning of this painting. They all shrugged and asked me when I was going to finish it.

They all say that when I was little I was very cute. Haru says this all the time. What she means is that she is amazed that such a cute little child should have grown into something like me. On the other hand, there is Tsuneo, who wasn't much to look at as a kid, and look what a strong young man he turned into. I can't see what there is to be amazed at. It is like my old man Befu says: you can predict what a child will be like from its parents. Anyone can see that I was going to end up something like my old man.

When I was little, I used to play with Tsuneo and the others, but I would cry if I didn't get my own way or if I lost the game. If my old man Befu was around when I was crying, he would get mad and tell the others that they didn't know how to play fairly. I would always get my way. Tsuneo and the others tired of this, so they would find a way to go off and leave me behind.

About this time, Inagaki came. Inagaki was one of those artist friends that Kantaro met in São Paulo. There were a lot of them like Inagaki. This place used be swarming with such types, but this was before everything went bad. Then none of them ever came around again. Kantaro said you can never tell who your true friends are until things get bad. I don't know what has become of these artists. We never saw them again, especially Inagaki, but that's another story.

I was about nine years old when Inagaki came around and boasted to my old man Befu that he could teach anyone to draw. Inagaki said anyone could be an artist. My old man said that true talent was hidden in the blood of a person. Inagaki said that this was nonsense, that you could learn to paint as well as you could learn to read or write or plant seeds. My old man said that true genius came from careful breeding. They decided to find out who was right, so they chose me and some others to apply Inagaki's method to. For a while some other children and a few adults took lessons from Inagaki, but they lost interest or had other work to do, and dwindled away, leaving me as Inagaki's only student. When this happened, my old man said that his theory had, of course, won out, as I could only be the product of superior breeding. Inagaki said nothing; he only continued to teach me. Perhaps it's a pity Inagaki didn't have an ordinary child to test his theory, but he didn't seem to mind. As long as Inagaki taught me, we had all the paint, brushes and canvas we needed.

My mother has kept every drawing and painting of mine from that time. My old man likes to take them out and show them to people. He likes to impress people.

One day Inagaki left. He didn't tell me that he was never returning, so I continued to paint the last scene we did together, one of the mango grove on the knoll. I went out there every day and finished the painting. I finished *his* painting too, in the style I thought he would have chosen. I could imitate anything he did anyway. I finished everything and waited for him to come back, but he never did. When Inagaki left and things went bad, they stopped giving me paint and canvas. No money, they said. I had to draw on scraps of paper and pieces of wood with pieces of charcoal from the fire. Once in a while now, I get paper and pencils from Mizuoka, but he forgets unless I remind him. I haven't seen oils and canvas for more than five years now.

When I asked my mother about Inagaki, she shook her head, and when I asked my old man, he said that Inagaki had served his purpose and that I didn't need him anymore. For a while I didn't know what to do without Inagaki; this made my old man angry. He shouted that I was a genius and didn't need any teachers. He ordered me to paint. So I painted the mango groves again, but after I finished painting the mango groves, there was no more canvas. But I was supposed to be painting every day, so I went back to the mango groves with an old painting and painted over it. I painted over several old canvases with the same mango grove scene until my old man noticed all these paintings of the same scene and got angry. He was angry that I had painted over one painting of his chicken barn which he particularly liked and that now he had all these mango groves. He wanted me to paint his chicken barn back onto the canvas, but by then I had used up all the paint.

Anyway, Inagaki never came back. I don't think I missed him. Like my old man said, he had served his purpose. What I missed was being able to paint. They wouldn't buy me any more paint or canvas.

Pretty soon, they wouldn't even consider paper or pencils. My mother scrounged around for old paper and notebooks. She saved the wrappings on packages and made black paint from charcoal soot, like the stuff used for calligraphy. Suddenly, there were no colors; I was supposed to make color from black. I had a tantrum and screamed until my old man had to come beat me up. He told me that sacrifice and suffering were the only road to great art. Already I have had enough of this road.

Then, everything went from bad to worse, and we got split off from the others. Kantaro says it was like the separation of water and oil; those with vision rose to the top. We all left the others behind and, like a bunch of beggars, went down the road to nowhere, led by Kantaro. I was maybe fourteen when this happened. I didn't know why we had to leave like that without even eating dinner and trudge off after Kantaro. I saw Kanzo get beaten up by Kantaro, and I thought, good, Kanzo got beaten up just like me. His face was all bloody and swelling up purple in a lopsided way. I trudged behind everyone, and Kanzo trudged behind me. When we got far enough behind, I turned around and asked Kanzo why he didn't smash Kantaro's other eye in, blind him and kill him right then and there. Kanzo said I didn't understand anything. I said, if he had killed Kantaro, he would be the new leader, and we wouldn't be out on the road like a bunch of beggars with no dinner and no place to go. Kanzo told me to shut up.

When you hear Kantaro talk about this particular day, he talks about when Moses parted the Red Sea and took his people out of Egypt. But it was nothing like that really. Nobody bothered to chase after us, and the Red Sea just parted onto Tanaka's place. This was because, in the meantime, old Jiro had run off ahead to find a place for us to stay. This was the insane mission left to Jiro: to find accommodations for one hundred homeless people. The first place he ran over to was the Tanaka's. He ran into Tanaka's wife and asked if a few of us couldn't stay for just a few days until we could find another place. Jiro had some idea that we could all just be spread around Esperança like manure. Tanaka's wife said she would ask her husband, but while she was wasting her time asking, we all arrived in a big pack. And Haru said, "Please excuse us," and "This is a terrible imposition," and "How can we ever repay you, Tanaka-san," but "The children never got dinner in all this confusion," and "It's the children who suffer." And Haru took over Tanaka's kitchen just like that.

Tanaka was an old baseball buddy of Kantaro's. He got caught up
in the nostalgia of those baseball days you always have to keep hearing about, as if no one can play baseball like those old-timers used
to. Kantaro sat down and wept about it all, so this settled the question in Tanaka's mind. He figured it would only be for a month or
two. He told Kantaro he was expecting a batch of silkworms in a .
couple of months, but he could let us have his barn until then. This
was a pretty nice barn as barns go. It was newly built with the help
of the cooperative after the old barn had burned down. I heard one
of those Terada brothers burned it down and went to jail for it. Fried
all the silkworms inside to a crisp. Now we were going to live inside
this barn.

All hundred of us squeezed inside the barn, got it partitioned with
blankets and that sort of thing and slept all over the floors. We had
always been close, but this was very close. This is when I got into the
habit of staying up at night; I could never sleep because someone was
always snoring or crying or humping around. At first, I would lie
there in the dark all night and just listen, but after a while, I began to
sneak around and look at people sleeping. It was always interesting
to see how people you see in the daylight get rearranged at night. All
the kids, except for me, got rearranged into different families. Pretty
soon, even the five Tanaka kids were sleeping with us, wedged in
here and there. They started to forget that this farm belonged to their
folks.

A lot of people began to forget this detail after a while, especially
when the two-month deadline passed and we were still there in
Tanaka's silk barn. Tanaka put the boxes of tiny sleeping silkworms
in the kitchen so that everyone could see them, but no one said anything about leaving because of a bunch of worms. Pretty soon, those
bugs must have shriveled up, and the Tanakas had to throw the
boxes out. "My, what a shame. What a waste. What can we do to
repay your generosity, Tanaka-san? As soon as we find a permanent
place, you will see," everyone said. In fact, the months dragged on,
and we stayed on. Kantaro was beginning to make big plans for
Tanaka's lands: a chicken operation over here, the incubators over
there, replace the mulberry fields with corn, a new generator, a new
truck, that sort of thing. Kantaro was always around while Tanaka
must have been running here and there, trying to figure out how he
was going to keep a family like this fed. So while Tanaka was out,
people naturally came and talked business with Kantaro, who always had ideas. You could tell that the Tanakas were beginning to

get worried, that the baseball nostalgia had worn off, so to speak. But Kantaro kept Tanaka going in circles, and Tanaka was too nice a man to say no.

It's a wonder how we all got fed in those days. We used up Tanaka's rice pretty quickly. Then the cooperative sent us donations, and Kantaro's newspaper friend Kasai sent us more, which we also used up. Then there was the time when "the others" came around with a truckload of the stuff we left behind and a lot of food to share. It must have been Ichiro Terada who drove the truck over. Kantaro went out to where they were unloading the truck. There were clothes and tools and sacks of food and Haru's sewing machine. Kantaro looked at everything and began screaming and kicking everything and yelling for them to take it away. "We don't want your charity!" he screamed. "We don't need you! Take it all back! We don't want it!" They started to put everything back in the truck, but Haru ran out from the kitchen and yelled at Kantaro, "Uno-san! Go eat your dinner!" I don't know why, but Kantaro went in to eat his dinner, and while he was inside eating, Haru got the stuff off the truck again and hauled it off somewhere.

Jiro and some others started planting stuff on Tanaka's land, and every day, anyone who could work went and hired out as daily labor. Even Kantaro and I had to go out and work in the beginning. We had to weed, hoe, plant, harvest, whatever work we could get. Mostly it was weeding, which I hated. When I complained, my old man said something about weeding being the most important work you do on the land. I thought that if weeds were stronger, they should win out, and we should find a way to eat them. We seemed to be eating everything else: sweet potato leaves, pumpkin flowers, mulberry tea.

Haru said that it was a good thing that Kantaro went out and weeded every day—when he came back at night, he was too tired to complain about anything, too tired to throw a tantrum or something. But me, I could never sleep at night, so sometimes Ritsu had to leave me behind because she couldn't get me up at dawn. After a while everyone thought it was better if I didn't come along because I was so slow or fell asleep in the fields and someone would have to search around to find me every night. Someone said that if Ritsu wanted to bring me out, she should bring me in a basket like she used to. At least, it would be easier to find me at night.

So I started to get left behind with the little kids and the old people. The little kids ran around and played in the mulberries, and the old people just slept most of the time. The old people were my grandparents Waka and Naotaro. Both of them were weak and sick. I think that only one of them was really sick, and the other decided to be sick just to provide company. I could never really tell. Sometimes I suspected Grandma Waka, and sometimes I suspected Grandpa Naotaro. Haru stayed behind to take care of them. She hung some white sheets up in a corner of the barn to partition off their area. She would come and go with food and medicine and bedpans. She came and washed them in the morning. She gave Naotaro a shave and combed Waka's hair. She fed them both soft food with a spoon. She changed their dirty bedclothes. She did everything like they were babies. And they would just lie there side by side in their bed. The reason why I think that one or the other or neither was really sick was because when Haru left and they thought they were alone, I could hear them talk and even laugh. They said, "Poor Haru, she works so hard." They talked about everything, about the past, about some memory or dream they had both had. I know this sounds strange, but they really talked about their dreams as if they both dreamed the same dream. They were like two peas in a pod or two worms on a leaf.

You might hear someone ask about those old ones behind the white sheets, and Haru would shake her head. "Every day they eat less and less. Well, it's old age." Haru tried every sort of remedy on my grandparents. She was always boiling those stinking teas. She made me swallow something every day because she said I was skinny. Then there was this other thing she made me take for my mind. She said it was genius medicine. She made those poor old people sip the same nasty stuff—I bet Haru finished them off by poisoning them. There was this tea she made out of mulberry leaves. I think she invented this mulberry tea because that's all there was out there. It really finished the old ones off. You could hear them complain when she went away.

"What was that stuff?"

"Tea."

"*Yara yara.*"

Well, maybe they weren't poisoned. They were probably starved. The reason I think this is because they always talked about a number of something before Haru came in with their soup. I could hear them say, "Today, twelve."

"Are you sure? Yesterday was twelve."

"I'm sure, but does it matter?"

Then the next day, it would be eleven or twelve again, but usually the numbers got smaller. Finally, it got down to one. Just one every day. I never knew what these numbers meant until I heard Haru say something about how the old ones would only take one sip of soup. By this time, it was too late. They could hardly move and hardly talk, they were so weak. When it was time for zero, they didn't have to ask each other.

All this time, I was drawing pictures on wrapping paper my mother saved. I started a picture of the mulberry grove. Since the Tanakas couldn't use the mulberry leaves for silkworms, the bushes started to get berries, and the little kids spent all day picking and eating the berries. The stuff got smeared all over their faces in big purple patches. I got to thinking that I could make some paint out of this stuff. I grabbed a can of berries away from one of the kids and squished it up with my hands. I never got to paint with this because that little kid, Jun, started crying and his sister Yae started screaming at me and got the others to pelt me with the berries. They came around and threw berries at me until I was splotched with that purple juice. I ran after them and squished the stuff in their faces until Haru came out of the barn and got mad at us. She was standing there with her mulberry tea, screeching at us. Then she sort of sank down and started crying.

I don't know why, but I ran into the barn. I could see the white sheets still hanging around that corner of the barn. They seemed very still, stiller than usual, as if there was no breathing behind them. The old ones were behind there, wrapped up in more white sheets, a little drop of spittle in the corners of their mouths. They must have been dreaming the same dream—that they had both died.

CHAPTER 17: SHIRATORI

I HAVE BEEN thinking some more about my life in the basket. I remember some other things. I remember how it was dark in the basket but also how sometimes light might come through the straw in little patterns. I could watch the little patterns flicker and change, and there was always some prism of color around the edges. And I remember that there was a hole where I could peek out. I could maybe see some part of my mother bent over planting. Mostly I could see her feet and legs trudging about in the earth. Sometimes her feet would get mixed up with other feet. I don't remember my old man Befu ever going out to do fieldwork; he was always with the chickens. So maybe it wasn't his but someone else's feet. I also remember that my own feet always went to sleep and grew so numb that I couldn't feel them. When Ritsu took me out of the basket, I screamed in pain as my feet came back to life, little invisible knives stabbing everywhere. Ritsu would take my little feet and rub them and kiss them. I grew to like this rubbing and kissing so much that no matter whether my feet went to sleep or not, I always kicked and complained.

It is amazing how much you can see with a little light through a tiny hole. Sometimes I think the inside of my head is the same way, dark like inside the basket, and I am looking out through two tiny holes.

*   *   *

Just when Tanaka thought we might be staying forever, we left. But it had already been more than a year, maybe even two. The reason we got to leave was because of Mizuoka. The way I heard it, Haru's father Okumura used to run everything in Esperança. He got gunned down by a death squad on the same night that that Terada brother burned Tanaka's silkworm barn down. Anyway, after Okumura got killed, Mizuoka came out of hiding. It wasn't that Mizuoka was really hiding—although I bet a lot of people were in those days, thinking they might get knocked off by the death squad—it was that Mizuoka spent all his time reading and studying his books or going into the forest to find Indians. Suddenly he stopped everything and came out to run Esperança and the cooperative and do the things that Okumura used to do. By this time, Mizuoka was an old man with no hair and a white mustache. It was Mizuoka's idea to get us off Tanaka's land. Someone said Mizuoka was Kantaro's old teacher and had a lot of influence on Kantaro. Those two got to talking with my old man Befu about chickens and eggs and manure and that sort of thing, and it was as if Mizuoka was hearing all this for the first time, which maybe he was. Mizuoka got very excited and started to make all these plans. You could tell that Kantaro had hooked him good, so Kantaro tossed Tanaka away because Mizuoka was a bigger fish, with the cooperative behind him and all. Mizuoka found a way to buy a piece of our old land back for us; it wasn't as big as before, but it was enough for us. Mizuoka got us a bunch of loans, and we built everything back together the way it used to be.

The way I heard it, Mizuoka got our land back in the following way: An old couple named Kojima in Esperança were retiring; they decided to leave and go to São Paulo to live with their son. Mizuoka talked to them and got them to exchange their land with the Brazilian who had bought our land. The Brazilian thought he was too smart; he didn't want to strike a deal with Kantaro. I think the Kojima land was better anyway. But the Kojimas got persuaded by Mizuoka that Kantaro was a new man, and besides, Mizuoka would guarantee the deal. So now Kantaro sends the Kojimas in São Paulo regular payments on their land, which must be a nice pension for an old retired couple.

We didn't all fly away from Tanaka's silkworm barn at once. We left gradually, a few at a time. The first to leave got things started, building the kitchen and the dining hall back up. It went piece by piece like that. Maybe some people thought that when we split from the others that would be the end of Kantaro's place. Kantaro says that you can't kill great ideals, and this was one of them.

I suppose Mizuoka thinks the same. You can always see his bald head over there talking with Kantaro and Befu about chickens and Esperança. He says that Kantaro can redeem himself by giving Esperança a future in chickens. Besides the land deal with the Kojimas, Mizuoka got us some big loans from the cooperative for incubators and chicken pens and feed and that sort of thing. Kantaro is not so angry and depressed as he used to be. He even seems in high spirits.

Kantaro has not been in such a good way since old Momose came to Esperança. Momose, they say, founded Esperança, even though he had visited here only once or twice. That's when people say Momose made his famous speech about how in Esperança growing people was more important than growing coffee. Anyway, Momose's the one who traveled around Japan and made speeches and signed people up to come to Esperança. I don't know what he told people, but it must have been pretty convincing. That's how my grandparents, Naotaro and Waka came. They signed up with Momose in Japan. I don't know how you can send people to a place you hardly even know yourself. Well, Momose must have wondered the same thing. He must have wondered how we were all getting along after all these years, so one year he finally made the trip himself. By this time, he was pretty old. We had to all go out and meet him and listen to his speeches, all the same stuff about growing people rather than coffee, even though we don't hardly grow coffee anymore. Then there was a special service given at the cemetery. Then he came to Kantaro's place to give another speech, and afterward, he and Kantaro talked a long time about everything.

It took a while but Kantaro told him how he had sinned and everything. My old man Befu sat around and talked too. Kantaro cried and Momose nodded gravely. Then they talked about what Kantaro could do to make it better with God. They decided Kantaro could help poor Japanese students. They wrote this letter. It was a long letter about Kantaro's place and our history and why young Japanese who had no future because of the war could come to Brazil and start a new life.

My father would never admit that Japan had lost the war. They say he only accepted it after Okumura was killed, but even then he wouldn't talk of it. I myself was surprised to hear Momose tell us that Japan had lost the war.

* * *

So then who should turn up but a poor Japanese art student with no future in Japan. His name is Junichiro Shiratori and he came with a copy of Kantaro's letter in his hand and another from Momose saying that this man was answering Kantaro's call. Shiratori is only a couple of years older than me, maybe twenty-one or twenty-two. He is rather tall and thin and his shoulders seem to fold forward like wings that don't work. Shiratori said that all his older brothers were killed in the war. They came home in little boxes. Shiratori said he tried to leave Japan before. He got on a ship to America as a stowaway two times and got caught both times. He said he left Hokkaido and went to Tokyo and Yokohama and stuck around the American bases. I heard that Americans drive in big shiny cars and chew bubble gum.

This Shiratori wants to teach everyone to paint, even the old aunties and uncles. Even my old man sat down the other night to try to draw. Shiratori told Kantaro that everyone should try to develop their natural talents. He said that life and art must be the same. Ordinary people can be a part of art. Art was not something special or separate, it was a part of life. Kantaro agreed. He even agreed to waste all this material. Haru and the other old aunties were showing their pictures and laughing about how they too might be geniuses like me. They told Haru they were going to take my genius medicine.

Everyone was interested to know how well Kantaro could draw, and Shiratori said he did very well. Natural talent, Shiratori said. Life is art. Art is life.

* * *

Mizuoka came by today. He had a letter to show Kantaro. This letter was from the Kojimas. It said that we haven't paid them for three months now. Mizuoka looked worried, but Kantaro said not to worry. "Tell Kojima-san not to worry," Kantaro said. Mizuoka said he would tell Kojima, and then he sat down with everyone to take Shiratori's art class.

After art class, all the aunties like to stick around and try to talk to Shiratori; they want to know this and that about Shiratori and which of their kids has natural talent. They say, "What about Kyoko?" or "What about Sachiko?" They don't seem to care much about their boys, but they ask about their daughters.

Shiratori is also trying to teach us Japanese reading and writing and a little history too. When he is busy doing this, some mother is always going into his room and cleaning it out or gathering his dirty clothing to wash. They wash and iron and fold everything and then send one of their daughters to take Shiratori's wash to him when he is in his room. Or maybe they cook some special food they've heard he really misses or bake some special cake and take it over to him. I never saw such a fuss over any visitor. And the girls act silly around Shiratori. They don't seem to care that he's skinny or that his shoulders fold forward. I'm skinny, and my legs are bowed, but Shiratori is tall.

* * *

After all the commotion over Shiratori's clothing and that nonsense, it seems Shiratori has become attached to Kimi Yōgu. The other aunties are jealous, but they would not admit it; they all think Kimi Yōgu is too refined to live on a farm, even though she has been working on a farm most of her life. She's just a worn-out old grandma like the rest of them. They talk behind her back about her old husband Hachiro Yōgu, who left her behind and became a traitor. I wonder what happened to him; he went crazy and almost killed Kantaro with a kitchen knife. I can still see him running across the table with the knife. That was a long time ago; I was maybe twelve. I ran around the dining hall to see what would happen when the knife went through Kantaro's body, but it never happened.

Kimi wasn't one of those who sent her daughters to clean Shiratori's room or bring him his clean and ironed clothing. Shiratori just heard Kimi playing the piano. He went to talk to her because she teaches some of the children to play the piano. They like to discuss what should be done about the education of the children at Kantaro's place. They say there's a law. The little kids have to go to Brazilian school. Some days they go. Some days they don't. Kantaro thinks this is a nuisance. Japanese is more important. Kimi and Shiratori are concentrating on this. So now you can mostly find Shiratori over at Kimi's place, talking and eating and sitting around with Akiko and Kimi's other kids. Now whenever Shiratori gets a chance, he wanders over to Kimi's house. Sometimes he talks so late he ends up sleeping there among Kimi's kids.

*   *   *

I sometimes see Shiratori walking around at night. He and I are the only ones awake at such hours. I can see the light on in his room. I know he paints during the night. He doesn't paint anything you can recognize, so he doesn't need the light or a scene or a model. During the day, he sketches things like the barn or the side of a house or a field or something, but when he looks at his sketches again at night, he must see everything very differently. Everything is crooked or out of proportion; the colors are dirty. No one has seen these strange paintings. If Kantaro knew what Shiratori was using his canvas and oils for, he might not be so pleased. Everyone has seen the paintings Shiratori does during the day. Shiratori likes to paint the forest or our cornfield with the sky in several different tones of blue and purple. He likes to make the people and the buildings glow.

The other night, Shiratori saw me in the dark, and he called to me and asked me what I was doing. He probably saw me peeping through that slit in my old man's barn where you can see the old cot where my mother and my old man do it. It's one of my usual stops in the night. I told Shiratori that making the rounds at night is an old habit of mine. I didn't tell him that I know how to see into every house and every building on this place. There's no special trick to it. Anyone can hear everything through these wood walls. The brick houses are more difficult, but everyone leaves their shutters open in the summertime. Shiratori said so that was why I slept during the day and missed his classes. Then he said that I should go out and work in the fields like the others. Then I'd be tired and sleeping at night instead of wandering around. Shiratori spoke as if what I do at night was any different than what he does at night.

*   *   *

Mizuoka came around today and told Kantaro that he has heard again from the Kojimas, who said that they have not received payments on their land for a half year. Mizuoka said, "I feel personally responsible for this situation." He took his straw hat off and wiped his sweaty bald head several times.

"It is not your fault, Mizuoka-san. We are having difficulties. Tell the Kojimas we need more time."

"I can't do that anymore. I am going to have to, to . . ." Mizuoka had trouble saying this. He finally said, "To make these payments myself."

Kantaro looked grateful. He said Mizuoka was like a father to all of us. "This is very generous of you. And it will be easier because you understand our situation." Paying back Mizuoka would be like paying back a family member. Kantaro told Mizuoka not to worry.

Then Mizuoka said, "I have to remind you again that you are also behind in your payments to the cooperative. Some people are beginning to talk." He wiped his bald head again.

"Befu is working on a new strain of chickens. He is working day and night. This takes time. When this new strain comes out, we will be making a lot of money selling hatchlings. We will pay you back for everything." Kantaro sounded very sincere.

Mizuoka seemed to understand. He stopped wiping his head and stayed for dinner. He listened to Kimi's students play the piano after dinner. Then he and Shiratori got into a discussion about this old dead writer Shiratori has been trying to teach about lately. Shiratori says it's important because Kantaro's place was founded on something he said. It's very boring.

*   *   *

I see Shiratori and Akiko sometimes together after classes. They walk out somewhere and come back. During the day Shiratori is painting a portrait of Akiko, but at night, he goes back to that other stuff.

I decided to paint a portrait of Kantaro. Kantaro himself thought this might be a good idea, so he agreed to pose. Shiratori told Kantaro that this would be a good exercise for me. I have a portrait I did of Kantaro a long time ago. At that time, I also did a portrait of my old man. They were younger then. Befu's face now looks older, but it's the same face. If you compare the portraits of Kantaro, his face is not the same. Kantaro cannot understand this; he doesn't like this new portrait.

* * *

I wonder if Akiko still thinks about Ichiro Terada. I saw him the other day. He got married to Takehashi's daughter Reiko and has two kids already. Akiko is getting old. No one else has noticed this thing with Akiko and Shiratori, even though all the aunties suspect that Kimi Yōgu has won Shiratori over for one of her daughters. They don't suspect Akiko because they figure she's too old already—more than thirty. They are all resigned to losing Shiratori to Kimi, except for Haru, who is still trying to push her daughter Hanako on Shiratori. Haru doesn't like it when she can't get her way. I think Shiratori made a bad mistake. Haru will be watching.

I have been following Shiratori and Akiko. Today they disappeared into the tall corn on the far north edge. I followed them several miles, but very silently, smelling their trail like a dog. They never knew. They have a special place hidden in a thicket, but sometimes they cannot even wait to get there and they fall into the corn and roll about without thinking. Once they got going on an ants' nest, and before you knew it they were swatting ants from their thighs and buttocks. Shiratori must have come home with a big rash on his poor penis. That put an end to their rolling around for a few days. Now they are more careful, inspecting the ground first. Afterward, they can lie there in the corn for hours, talking and watching the sky. Mostly, Shiratori talks about his home, and his brothers who came home as ashes in funeral boxes from the war, about his mother and father who both worked in the mines, about how he wants to go to America, about how he will take Akiko with him, about how they will travel all over the world. He is a good dreamer. Akiko nods, but sometimes she asks him why he can't just stay here, forever. Akiko is a good dreamer too. I want to butt in and tell Shiratori that Akiko doesn't have the guts to go anywhere without her mother. But Shiratori must be blinded by all the light. If he would pay more attention to all that work he does at night, he would see that his vision is better at night. He thinks he has discovered light. He even thinks he has rediscovered Japan. Maybe he means that because we missed that war my old man was so anxious to fight, we sort of got preserved, pickled in miso until Shiratori came and dug us up. Akiko thinks Shiratori should just burrow down and get pickled with the rest of us.

*   *   *

Mizuoka came over to tell us that Momose-sensei had died in Japan. Mizuoka shared a letter with us. It says that Momose's last wishes were to be buried in Esperança, so Momose's wife will be coming here to bury her husband. Mizuoka has to make all the arrangements for Momose's wife and the funeral. This is going to be a bigger deal than when Momose came when he was alive. Momose's wife has never been to Esperança. Mizuoka is afraid she will be shocked at the sort of place her husband wants to be buried in.

Mizuoka looks really old these days. His eyes look puffy, and even his bald head looks wrinkled. This cooperative he runs and all the other headaches of Esperança must be too much for the old man. Haru has been trying to make Mizuoka drink one of her teas for rejuvenation, but it's about as effective as her genius medicine.

Mizuoka is always wiping his head and talking about our debt to the Kojimas and our debt to the cooperative, and Kantaro is always telling him not to worry, that my old man Befu needs more time, that better times are in store for us, that God will grant us our daily bread, and so forth like that.

I heard Mizuoka complaining to Shiratori about all these problems. Mizuoka said that Kantaro was the special son of Esperança, that Esperança is this place that was built because Momose said people were more important than coffee. In Esperança, they are always talking about how people are more important than coffee. It would be more accurate to say these days that people are more important than chickens or silkworms. Mizuoka says that Momose had a great dream for Esperança. Like my old man says, he and Kantaro had big ideas. Fate. That sort of thing. They didn't come here like other Japanese to get rich and go back to Japan. This is silly when you think about it—we are so in debt we will never be able to go back. Maybe this is what Mizuoka means, that Kantaro has never worried about making money, only spending it. We have nowhere to go. We have to create that great civilization in Esperança because we haven't any choice. I have been thinking about this idea that people are more important than chickens, but maybe my old man would disagree.

Anyway, Mizuoka said that since someone like Kantaro could only have been created in a place like Esperança, Esperança was responsible for making Kantaro. Shiratori nodded like he understood, but he doesn't understand. Mizuoka and old dead Momose want to take all the credit for themselves when Kantaro and my old man are the ones doing all the great civilization work. My old man says that, without us, Esperança would just be another Japanese settlement with just another Director of the Cooperative.

* * *

Momose's ashes arrived with his wife. She was wearing a blue silk dress, and her white hair had this perfect perm that one of the girls had tried once on Haru. It didn't work, and Haru almost became as bald as Mizuoka. Momose's wife came over here and watched everyone take art lessons with Shiratori. Then she listened to Akiko and some other kids play the piano and sing. My old man took her over to the house to show her my paintings. She was very impressed. She said that Shiratori and I should start an art school.

Kantaro talked with Momose's wife about how he hoped more young Japanese students like Junichiro Shiratori would come to join us. She said she would take another letter from Kantaro back to Japan. Shiratori said he had several friends in Tokyo at the College of Art who might be interested. He would also send letters to them. Momose's wife said she would talk to Shiratori's friends.

* * *

Mizuoka was back again after Momose's wife left. He had to get contributions from everyone in Esperança to pay for the funeral and the party and the big marble stone they are putting on Momose's grave. Everyone is mad at Mizuoka because they say that there was money in the cooperative put aside for this, and that Mizuoka has made a mess of things and owes the cooperative this money. Now that the party and all the bowing are over, Mizuoka has returned with his sweaty head asking Kantaro when he is going to start paying the cooperative back.

Mizuoka finally got desperate about everything. I was sitting under the tangerine tree peeling tangerines when I saw him drive up in his truck. He got out, and I could see something bulging in his pocket. Kantaro was coming out of the outhouse, strolling sort of. Kantaro usually takes a nap after lunch; he was going to take his nap. But Mizuoka screamed from the truck, "Kantaro!"

Kantaro turned around and walked over to see Mizuoka. Mizuoka was shaking, and sweat was seeping out from every pore on his face. His whole head was red as a tomato. Mizuoka said, "It isn't because of the money. I'm not interested in the money. It is because I created you. I am responsible for creating you, and you are a monster! I have created a monster, and it is my responsibility to put an end to this thing." He reached inside his pocket and pulled out a pistol and pointed it at Kantaro.

Kantaro turned green, but then he saw that Mizuoka was shaking like crazy. Kantaro said bravely, "You are right, Mizuoka-san. You were my teacher, and I have been a poor student." Kantaro knelt to the ground. "It is unforgivable," Kantaro said. "Please kill me."

So Mizuoka, who couldn't shoot anything if it were two steps in front of him anyway, lowered the pistol and began to cry. Mizuoka was babbling something about a camera and baseball which I didn't understand. By then, my old man and Haru and everyone else ran out, and once again I missed seeing what happens when something goes through human flesh.

*   *   *

Akiko and Shiratori aren't being as discreet as they used to. I think Haru knows everything, and she is mad. Kimi will never stand up to Haru, but she is just as stubborn in a different way. I wish we could have seen some good fights, but Kantaro heard about everything, so he called Shiratori over. Shiratori said, "I want to marry Akiko."

Kantaro got so mad he smashed Shiratori across the face. "Get out!" he screamed at Shiratori. "Get out! I never want to see you again!"

Shiratori couldn't understand this reaction. He was so surprised he just stood there with his shoulders folded over.

Kantaro yelled, "Thirty-five years! Thirty-five years! You have brought down thirty-five years of our history in this one blow!"

This was even more confusing for Shiratori. What's thirty-five? Shiratori's not even twenty-five. He backed away.

"Get out! Get out!" Kantaro kept yelling.

So Shiratori packed his bags and put all of his nighttime paintings in a big bundle. The daytime paintings he left behind, except the portrait of Akiko. Kanzo came out and offered to drive Shiratori to the bus station, which is after all a long distance. Just before Shiratori got in the truck with Kanzo, I ran over with some old notebooks that Inagaki had left behind years ago. Inagaki had these notebooks in which he wrote all his useless theories of teaching art to common people. But I thought about "Life is art; art is life." Maybe Shiratori would like it. "Here," I told Shiratori, who looked like a fool. "Take this stuff. I've got no use for it. If my old man found this, he'd burn it." I didn't have anything else to give Shiratori, not that these things were worth anything. It was just the thought. Shiratori looked at me. He wanted to say something. Maybe he wanted to ask a question, but nothing came out.

I thought that would be the last I'd ever see of Shiratori, but no, he walks his skinny body all the way back from the bus station. By the time he makes it back, it is the middle of the night, and no one sees him except me. I was at my post by the slit of light near my old man's cot when I saw Shiratori tapping at Kimi's door. Kimi let him in. She sneaked over to the kitchen and fixed him some rice balls and pickles. Meanwhile, Shiratori and Akiko ran out into the cornfields to their spot and rushed into each other for one last time. They both cried while they did it and couldn't stop crying afterward. Shiratori kept saying that he would come back for her and made her promise to come with him when he came for her and that sort of thing. He told her he would find a way to write and would she write him. She nodded to everything. Then they walked back, and by then, the sky was getting light, and everyone would be up soon. So they hurried back and got Kimi's lunch. Kimi cried too, but she didn't try to make Shiratori stay. She knows better.

I followed Shiratori down the road a bit, but after a while I got tired of walking. I let his figure disappear like a sliver. I had been following him and Akiko all this time for miles in every which direction, but there are limits. So I turned around and went back home to sleep.

CHAPTER 18: NEW BLOOD

MAYBE IT'S BEEN TWO YEARS already since Shiratori left. I think he wrote some letters to Akiko, but she would never write him back. She was too embarrassed by her poor Japanese, and besides, what was there to write? I wonder where he went. I could write him some interesting news now that the new blood has arrived.

There are four of them. They asked about Junichiro Shiratori. Where was he? They expected him to be here still. Kantaro shrugged; he said something about being weak and causing trouble and a lack of vision. They all seemed to accept this answer. They laughed. "Shiratori was such a kid. Big ideas, but he could never sit still. Anyway, he always wanted to go to America." They thought it was natural he didn't stay long. They didn't know about Akiko.

Well, about these others: First, there is this round moon-faced character named Masao Hatomura. They say he writes movies. Someone suggested he could write a movie about Kantaro. Kantaro likes this idea. Everyone agrees that Kantaro's life would make a good movie. Kantaro wants something in the movie's final scene where we are all trudging down the road to Tanaka's silkworm barn, just after we split up from the others, looking like the beggars that we were. Suddenly we all stop on the hillside overlooking Esperança, and there is a great purple sunset. Kantaro looks out into the distance. His face brightens. "Esperança," he whispers. Something like that. If I had an imagination, I could paint that scene. Maybe Hatomura has a good imagination.

Then there is this couple, Akio Karasumori and his wife Fuyuko. Karasumori and Hatomura are maybe thirty or so, but Fuyuko is very young, not even twenty. Karasumori is a sculptor and Fuyuko is a dancer. Karasumori is a quiet sort who mostly speaks through his eyes. They all smoke cigarettes, but Karasumori never stops. He likes to lean back and blow little circles into the air. He is always smoking. When one cigarette goes out, he lights another. There are small burns in his rough hands, and there are brown marks on his fingers where he holds his cigarettes. His teeth are spread apart and stained brown, so he does not smile much. Nobody knows what Karasumori's work is like. He drew Kantaro some pictures of what he is thinking of doing. He says he needs granite to work. He brought some tools. Kantaro looked at the drawings and nodded. Karasumori asked where he can find granite. I was disappointed to discover that Karasumori needs granite instead of oil and canvas. Since Shiratori left, they haven't bought any more paints.

Then there is Yoshifumi Kōno. Kōno has a large forehead and big ears. Even though he is only maybe twenty-three, you can see he is the sort to lose his hair at the top, so his forehead will get even larger. He hasn't got any artistic talent, but maybe he has natural talent. He graduated from some farming school and was on his way to work for the Sarandi Cooperative in Campinas. But he met Hatomura and the Karasumoris on the plane, and they convinced him to come to Kantaro's place to see what it was like before going to Campinas. He's young and stupid, so he came along. He probably won't be around long. He's got a contract to work for Sarandi. They say he will make a lot of money, and nobody ever makes money here, since Kantaro says that is not what we came here to do.

Fuyuko. I have never seen a woman like this Fuyuko. She has jet-black hair that is cut in very straight lines so that her face is in a perfect box. Her face is white, whiter than you ever see in Japanese women, especially compared to those here, who are always in the sun. It is as if Fuyuko's skin has never seen the light of day. Then there are her lips, which she paints with lipstick the color of bright shiny blood. The first night they arrived, Fuyuko walked around instead of sitting with Kantaro and the others. She stared at everything, looking at each one of us like we were a bunch of ghosts. Suddenly she turned away and stood in the doorway and began to cry. Karasumori just glanced at her and blew smoke rings, but Kantaro stared for a long time. So did I.

The next day, I sketched a portrait of Fuyuko. I sketched in those red lips. I thought about her all night before. I could not forget. Fuyuko would not have sex with Karasumori that night. She told him that she felt overwhelmed by her first impressions here. She asked Karasumori if he didn't feel the same, but he said nothing. She said she felt totally committed to Kantaro from the first moment. She removed all her clothing and slept naked, covered only slightly by her sheet. Karasumori masturbated, and so did I.

* * *

Kōno is still here with his big forehead after a week. He can't make up his mind to leave and go to Campinas, where he is supposed to have a contract and a good job with a lot of money. In the meantime, he follows Befu around looking at the chickens. All day long, they are discussing chickens. Kōno is like my old man, eating and sleeping with chickens.

Hatomura, the moon-faced one, came to talk to me. He asked about Shiratori. I told him what Kantaro says, that Shiratori had no vision. What else is there to say? Hatomura asked me what I meant by that. I told him that Shiratori wasn't able to kill Kantaro. Hatomura didn't understand. I told him it was too bad Shiratori had to leave. Then Hatomura asked me, just like Shiratori, why I didn't go out to the field like everyone else. Why wasn't I out there sweating in the hot sun? The others need something to do, I said. I never liked weeding anyway. Didn't he know I was a genius? The next day, Hatomura went out with everyone to harvest corn. He came back with his moon face soiled and red from the sun. Even Kōno, who hasn't any artistic talent, hasn't gone out to work in the fields.

Then, in the evening, Fuyuko put a record on the phonograph. She called the music "jazz," and the dance that she danced "modern ballet." She wore this black suit which stretches over her body. I watched every part of her body move. Her buttocks are round tight muscles. Her legs are well molded, and she can stretch them open completely, pushing her toes into a point. She made her body slide and wiggle all over the floor. Her straight black hair flew about her face and got pasted to her by her sweat. Karasumori looked on with no expression, just blowing those smoke rings. I felt like doing it right there. Afterward, she sat around as if nothing had happened. No one of us here had ever seen such "modern ballet," but Fuyuko didn't seem to care. That night, Karasumori and I both masturbated again.

*   *   *

Finally, Kōno decided he must leave. So he was supposed to leave today. But then, last night, Karasumori brought out a bottle of whiskey. He sucked his cigarette smoke through the spaces in his brown teeth and smiled. He said he was saving this bottle to celebrate Kōno's last night. So they sat around with Kantaro and my old man and some of the others and passed around this bottle and started talking about Kantaro and the past and Esperança and the future. Pretty soon Kōno is getting rather drunk and confused, and his big ears get very red. Kantaro is saying things like "This is not a calling for just an ordinary man," and "This is not a question of money—it is a question of spirit, of courage, of true vision."

All this makes Kōno very confused, and he drinks more and sweats and runs his fingers through his hair beyond his big forehead.

Kantaro goes on, saying, "Befu and I and these others made a pact among ourselves many years ago to create a new life, a new civilization. This is no dream. It is real. You see it for yourself. This is thirty-seven years of history. Once you leave, you will no longer be a part of this. But we will go on."

Then someone else says, "Kōno, you belong here. You know you can make a difference. You cannot abandon your ideals."

Someone else nods, "You will be abandoning your ideals when you step on that bus tomorrow and leave Esperança."

This drives Kōno crazy, like he has a great itch that he cannot scratch. He looks like a little boy. Suddenly, he breaks down and cries and says, "Yes. Yes. You are all right. I belong here. I will stay. I will stay."

Kantaro breaks down and cries too; he had put great effort into convincing Kōno.

I thought that Kōno will now have to stay, that he will never leave. But Karasumori makes smoke rings and says Kōno can leave any time he wants. I didn't understand this, but now you see that Kōno's mother sends him packages every week from Japan. This week she sent dried codfish and tea from Kyoto. Last week, it was a shirt and two cans of seaweed. They say all this is very fine expensive stuff. Karasumori makes fun of Kōno. "A young brat," he calls him. He says if Kōno's mother stops sending packages, Kōno will rush home to Japan. He says Kōno comes from a wealthy family, while he and the screenwriter Hatomura are poor starving artists. And they're too old now. They have no choice; they can't abandon their ideals.

I thought about Shiratori, who left with only his clothing and some of his dark canvasses. He couldn't go back to Japan. Where did he go and how could he live after he left Kantaro's? And now, there is this talk that I should leave. Only Hatomura says I should stay and work.

Hatomura started teaching school like Shiratori had because he talked with youth who said they missed Shiratori's classes. They say the little kids get Kimi's reading and writing class, but there must be something more. Kantaro says Brazilian school is only good for basic Portuguese. After grammar school, they have to quit. Jiro's daughter Yae, for example, liked Brazilian school. She wanted to go to the next grade, but Kantaro said no. Yae was only ten or eleven then. She cried. Now Yae is going every day to Hatomura's class.

Hatomura goes out and works in the field, then comes back and teaches. He teaches everything. You can see his serious moon face talking and reading. Every now and then I sit in his class. Yesterday, it was something about the American Revolution and democracy. Tsuneo, Jiro's son, wanted to know everything. He kept asking questions about this thing called democracy, and Hatomura answered everything. It got too complicated, so I left.

Karasumori doesn't like Hatomura. Hatomura doesn't seem to notice this and said something about Fuyuko's dancing. Hatomura pointed at my work and said I had captured her dance very well, better than he imagined I could. Well, Karasumori does not like me either, but since Hatomura said that, Karasumori doesn't give me his cigarette butt to finish off anymore. He used to give them to me and then tell me to get lost.

Befu showed Karasumori the pictures I did of Kantaro. He didn't say anything; he just looked and blew smoke through his teeth. He didn't tell Befu, but I heard him say to Fuyuko that I was just an ordinary boy who had some technique. He told my old man to send me away to learn about life.

Karasumori told Kantaro that an artist must suffer to create, and that I would not progress with my art if I stayed here. Karasumori told Kantaro that I had to learn the new trends in art. He said my art was old-fashioned. Kantaro agreed and told Befu that I must leave.

I heard my old man talking with my mother Ritsu. He told her I had to go way. She asked why, and he said because I had to learn about life and new trends in art. My mother started to cry. She said I was too young, even though I am over twenty. She said the other boys didn't have to leave like this. My father said that Kantaro had decided, and he agreed with Kantaro. My mother said I was her only child, and she didn't want me to go so far away. She said none of the other children like me because I'm a genius. She said I was lonely here, but at least I was protected. Away from Kantaro's place what would happen to me? She sobbed. My father told her that Kantaro had decided. Then, he pulled her down and made her do it there on the floor. After that, we all forgot that I had to leave.

*   *   *

Haru sent her daughter Hanako to clean Hatomura's room and wash his dirty clothing. Hanako was doing this every day, following him around like a maid. Hanako hung around Hatomura's room so much that there was some gossip about the two. But Hatomura never had anything to do with Hanako other than letting her wash his clothes and that sort of thing. Hatomura always spends the night with a lamp, writing something he calls a script, and then goes to bed and snores loudly. When nothing came of this, Haru got fed up and sent Hanako to clean Kōno's room.

Fuyuko decided that because Hatomura is teaching, she would teach the dancing she does. Fuyuko told Kantaro her plans, and Kantaro ordered all the girls to dance. The girls feel shy about this dancing, especially since they saw Fuyuko dance in those black things and crawl around the floor. But since Kantaro said they had to dance, they all went, except Jiro's daughter Yae. Fuyuko complained to Kantaro that Yae wouldn't dance. Then Kantaro made Yae go. This made Yae mad. I heard Yae say that she wasn't taking orders from Fuyuko, who is younger than she is.

Yae is living with Kanzo. Everyone knows this. Someone said they are cousins and can't get married. Anyway, Kantaro doesn't like Yae, who never listens to anyone and always says what she wants. Haru does this too, but Kantaro still doesn't like Yae. Yae even told Kanzo that he has to start standing up to Kantaro. After all, Kanzo is Kantaro's son. Ever since Kanzo got beat up for standing up to Kantaro, he never says anything. This was a long time ago. Yae is too young to remember this.

I saw Fuyuko dancing by herself. She was making her body squirm all over the floor like a worm. When Fuyuko saw me watching her, she got mad. Later she told Kantaro that she also thought it was time I leave.

*   *   *

Hatomura doesn't eat next to Kantaro at lunch or dinner anymore. For a while, he sat every day at the head of the long table next to Kantaro, asking him questions about our history. Kantaro told him everything because he wants Hatomura to make a movie. But Hatomura kept wanting to know something over and over, and Kantaro only wanted to tell it one way, even though Hatomura has heard different things from different people. Kantaro got tired of telling Hatomura the same things. First Hatomura sat next to Kantaro, then he began to sit next to my old man. Then he moved down the bench and sat next to someone else until he was way down at the end of the table. You could see Kantaro looking way down the long table, looking for Hatomura's round face. Maybe he was asking everyone questions about our history, but he was really just getting farther and farther away from Kantaro. Now Hatomura moved even farther away to another table in the back. He sits with the youth, talking and laughing. You can see Kantaro look in his direction every now and then, to see where Hatomura is sitting now. It was the same with Shiratori. Pretty soon, Hatomura will not be sitting anywhere.

At night, Hatomura studies some volumes he brought from Japan. Then he goes to Mizuoka's and borrows volumes from Mizuoka's encyclopedia and teaches something every day. Now he is on Volume 4. It will be a miracle if he gets to 30.

Tsuneo is the oldest of the youth, and he is the leader now. Tsuneo looks like his father Jiro, but he is nothing like Jiro in any other way. Tsuneo walks first. He talks first. In Hatomura's class, he thinks first. I don't know how Jiro's kids turned out like this. Kanzo on the other hand is weak. Tsuneo decided to talk to Kantaro about what he thinks. Kantaro doesn't have anything to do but talk, so he agreed. Kantaro likes to talk about his ideas. Tsuneo wanted to know why Kantaro won't let the youth leave to go on to Brazilian high school and maybe even to college. Kantaro said he had plans for a university in Esperança. Tsuneo asked about the ones who want to study now. He asked how long must they wait. Kantaro answered that that is a question of our history. The talking went like that. Tsuneo would ask questions, and Kantaro would answer. Tsuneo was very serious and did not give up asking questions and thinking about Kantaro's answers. Kantaro nodded, raising his eyebrows and smiling every time Tsuneo came back with more questions. Kantaro said Tsuneo was very bright. He said he was proud of Tsuneo, but Tsuneo still did not get an answer. Kantaro said it was a question of our history.

*   *   *

Yae is also nothing like her father Jiro. This is a problem for Jiro. Kantaro is always pointing to Tsuneo and Yae and asking Jiro why he can't control them. Kantaro says Tsuneo is bright, but Yae is spoiled. Yae needs to dance for her own good. Yae went to tell Hatomura that she hates to dance. She told Hatomura that she hates Fuyuko. She said Fuyuko was egotistical and vain. Yae told Hatomura that she wanted to leave Kantaro's place. She wants to learn to cook and sew. She said she couldn't understand art. She said she hates art. "Genji paints, so why does everyone else have to do it? Let Genji paint," she said. "Let Fuyuko dance." Yae asked Hatomura if he didn't think of leaving Kantaro's too.

Hatomura said he would have to leave eventually because it is too easy here. He could not be creative here. He could not write. He is losing his need to write. Nothing changes. Every day, it is the same. Everybody seems happy. Nobody needs change. Nobody needs creativity. He understood how Yae needed change. He realized that she would leave.

Yae asked if Hatomura would take her with him when he left. He didn't say anything. Maybe he didn't hear. He was thinking. He said maybe he was trying to justify his failure. Maybe he was not good enough. He was confused. He thought art and life was an ideal, but you could not force anyone to do it. "Yae, to tell you the truth, I have never been so happy as I am here. I love the youth here. Still, I can't explain it, but I'm not satisfied." He could not be creative. So he would have to leave.

Then Yae argued with Kanzo. "When Hatomura leaves, we will go with him," she said.

Kanzo was silent.

"This is the only way to have a future," she said.

Kanzo was not so sure. He shook his head.

"What are you worried about?" she asked.

"What will I do out there?" he asked. "It's not as easy as you say. Hatomura can go back to Japan. He speaks and reads Japanese. We can't even read Portuguese. What will we do?"

"We will learn," insisted Yae.

"We don't have any money. We will have nothing. I'm too old to start from nothing."

"You are too old to be crying like this. You need to be a man. You can't be a man if you stay here."

"My father started this. I am a part of this history. If I go, it will be the end of everything. He will never allow it. What you are asking is impossible. Kantaro is still my father."

"You need to be strong. You need to be your own man. Please promise you will leave with me."

"Kantaro says that only the weak leave."

"I am not weak," Yae said.

Kanzo didn't want to talk about it anymore. "No, you are not weak," he agreed.

*   *   *

Kōno is sleeping with Hanako. Hanako was bustling around Kōno's room changing sheets and that sort of thing. Kōno came in late. He had spent most of the night talking to my old man in the incubator barn. Kōno scratched his big forehead and asked Hanako what she was doing there so late. Hanako said she had been too busy to clean his room during the day. Before Kōno could say anything, Hanako pushed Kōno on the bed and started to press herself all over him. She is heavier and bigger than Kōno, so she overpowered him. That's how it started. Now Kōno rushes away at night from the incubator barn. By the time he gets to his room, his penis is up. Hanako is always there, waiting to surprise him. One time she was waiting under the bed. She grabbed him by his legs and pulled him down, and they did it under the bed.

On the other hand, Hatomura isn't sleeping with Akiko, but he wants to marry her. The youth like to talk with Hatomura. He always listens, and his moon face looks concerned. Akiko is getting old, but she goes to his classes anyway. At first, she wanted to talk to Hatomura about Shiratori. She had to talk to him in private, so they walked out to the mango groves to talk. Pretty soon, they were going out to the mango groves to talk all the time. Always talking. That's all Hatomura does. He never touches her. He tells Akiko about some movie script he is writing. He explains that he was working on a monster movie in Japan, but this was not serious. He kept working to make money. Then he showed his serious work to the monster movie people, and they laughed. They were not serious. So he left. Now he has a plan to study the Japanese farmers in Brazil and make a film about them. He really doesn't want to make a film about Kantaro; that's just Kantaro's idea. Hatomura explains everything to Akiko. He has some plan to research this film for three years and then return to Japan to get money to make this film. He will be leaving Kantaro's place soon so that he can go on researching. Hatomura asked Akiko if she wouldn't return to Japan with him. Here is another one asking Akiko to go here and there with him.

*   *   *

Hanako is getting even heavier and fatter. Of course, she is pregnant, but no one knows. Not even Kōno knew. Hanako told him last night. He was so shocked his ears turned red. That seemed strange to me because they have been rolling around every night for several months. Kōno spent a long time trying to figure out when it had happened and how long Hanako has been pregnant. "When did it happen? When? What are we going to do now?"

Hanako said he must marry her. This was even more shocking for Kōno. That also seemed strange to me because Kōno had said he wanted to stay at Kantaro's. He didn't seem so sure anymore. He talked the rest of the night about his mother and his family. He looked sad. Finally Hanako asked, "Aren't you going to marry me?" He had the same confused look on his face when Karasumori passed around that whiskey. Hanako cried that she wasn't going to let him go away, then she left the room.

For a while, Kantaro started to buy oil paints for me, so I was able to finish the one of Fuyuko pasted with her sweat to that black outfit. They must have told Kantaro to stop buying stuff for me. I have some paper left in this notebook, and that is all. Instead, Kantaro bought this granite rock for Karasumori. He also bought black stretchy suits for all the girls to dance their modern ballet and a second record player for Fuyuko to play her music.

Now all the men are building a dance stage. This was Fuyuko's idea. Fuyuko and Akio Karasumori drew all the plans. The stage must be larger than the dining hall. Tsuneo was talking angrily with Hatomura. Tsuneo complained that the men were needed for planting. Kantaro ordered all the men to build the stage. The planting will have to wait, Kantaro said. Tsuneo has been reading and studying about increasing production, and he told Hatomura that soon it will be too late to plant. Tsuneo asked Hatomura why we needed a stage, why we needed art. Tsuneo said we could not eat the stage. We could not eat art. Then Tsuneo went to talk with Kantaro again. Tsuneo asked Kanzo to come with him to talk to Kantaro, but Kanzo said no. Kanzo went back to building the stage, and Tsuneo went to talk to Kantaro alone. Tsuneo asked questions, and Kantaro answered. But it was still a question of our history.

Karasumori went somewhere with Kanzo in the truck to find granite. While he was away, Fuyuko had sex with Kantaro. After I take my bath I sometimes go around to the other side of the bathhouse to watch the girls through the high window. I have a rock I step up on to see. One day Kantaro saw this, and now he comes to look too. He's tall and doesn't need the rock. We just look. The girls know we look; they can see our eyes. They know it's Kantaro, so they pretend we're not there. Anyway, Fuyuko was there squatting on the tiles washing her black hair and rubbing soap all over her body. She is darker now from the sun, but her breasts and buttocks are white like the soapsuds. The girls hurried to leave, but Fuyuko stayed a long time. She sat in the hot water and closed her eyes. Kantaro and I waited for her to stand and step out of the tub. The water spilled around her body. I imagined it was her sweat. Kantaro followed her from the bathhouse. I followed too. Fuyuko did not close her shutters. I could see her looking at me through a mirror on her table. She was looking. I was looking. We all came at the same time. Fuyuko doesn't mind anymore when I watch her dance, and she never closes her shutters now.

When Karasumori got back, he started picking with his tools on his granite. All day long, picking, picking. I sat around once to watch. So did the little kids, but he told us all to go away. He says chips of rocks can fly out and hit us. I can't tell what he's doing, but I sketched it anyway. He picked all day at one piece until he made a hole. At night, Karasumori and I always masturbate. Fuyuko watches us in her mirror.

*   *   *

Kōno and Kantaro had a long conversation. After that, Kantaro told everyone that Kōno and Hanako were to marry. Kōno's big forehead and big ears got very red. Kantaro said that Kōno, like my old man and the other old-timers, has found a place to die. He said it all again about not being a contract for an ordinary man, about courage and vision. Kōno puffed up, even though it is Hanako who is pregnant.

So Kōno and Hanako got married. Fuyuko and the girls danced on the new stage. Karasumori gave Kōno a wedding present. It was a granite boat, an ark he said. You know that story about Noah gathering all those animal couples. I thought about all those animal couples having sex in the boat while everyone else got drowned. Karasumori came up while I was looking at his boat. He snickered through his teeth that I probably was not on the boat.

While everyone was eating and drinking in front of the stage, Hatomura and Akiko went walking away together. Kantaro saw them leave the party and went after them. I could see that Hatomura's face was a smooth happy circle from drinking a little beer. He didn't seem so shy, and he was even holding Akiko's hand.

Kantaro rushed after them. He yanked Akiko away and told her to leave. Then he slapped Hatomura across his moon-shaped face. Even though Hatomura is tanned from working in the sun now, Kantaro's hand left a red impression. Hatomura asked what he had done, and Kantaro said Hatomura had destroyed 40 years of history in one day.

Tsuneo saw everything. He was with a group of youth drinking beer. They had drunk a lot by now. They all came in a group behind Tsuneo, who asked Kantaro why he'd done this. Tsuneo said, "Masao Hatomura is my teacher. I can't allow him to be offended this way."

Kantaro yelled, "This is none of your business!" Then he turned to Hatomura, "Stupid teacher! Get out! Get out!"

Tsuneo protested, "Stop, Uno-san! What are you doing?"

Kantaro started to hit Hatomura again. Tsuneo picked up a piece of wood, came from behind Kantaro and hit him across the back. Wham! Wham! By this time, my old man and the others came running and threw themselves on Tsuneo to protect Kantaro. Kantaro fell to the ground but he yelled, "All of you! Get out of here. Tell everyone to go back to the party!"

Hatomura ran away and stuffed his baggage into the car of one of the outside guests. The guest agreed to take Hatomura to the bus station.

Yae found Kanzo and said, "Now you must go with me."

Kanzo shook his head. "You are crazy," he said.

"You must go."

"I can't."

Yae was angry.

"Yae-chan, I believe in all this!"

"You are a fool! What about me?"

"I love you," Kanzo said. "Don't go."

"You do not love me," Yae cried and ran away.

Hatomura got into the car and sped off. Yae ran like crazy to meet the car before it turned down the main road. Only I saw her disappear into the forest to meet the car on the other side. No one but Kanzo and I knew that Yae had left with Hatomura until it was too late.

By nightfall, Kōno was very very drunk. Nobody was interested much in Kōno's wedding. Instead, everyone was whispering about how bad Hatomura was. The women were saying how he was a pervert and how Kantaro had caught Hatomura trying to force himself on Akiko. As for Yae, they said poor Yae must have been forced or tricked into leaving. It was a good thing that bad man had left. Who would have thought he was so bad? Just like Shiratori, he couldn't be trusted. The men said it was just as well that Hatomura left. He was weak anyway.

In the middle of all this gossip, Kōno got up and proposed a toast. He said, "To Kantaro, who tricked me so well." Then Kōno fell across the table, his big red forehead plunging into the giant cake. Haru jumped up and pulled him out. She was mad because she had spent all day baking and decorating that cake.

That night, Hanako with her big belly got on top of Kōno, but he rolled over and vomited. On the other hand, Fuyuko and Akio Karasumori had sex for the first time in weeks. Meanwhile, I could hear Kantaro yelling at Jiro, ordering him to get his daughter Yae back. I went over to Hatomura's old room. He had left a pack of cigarettes there. I smoked one cigarette after another. By dawn, I could make smoke rings.

CHAPTER 19: LIBERDADE

THEY ALL GOT THEIR WAY. They made me go away. My mother Ritsu must still be back there crying, crying.

I am living here in São Paulo in the Bairro Liberdade with Shigeshi Kasai the newspaper man. They found me a maid's closet in the back of the house. The closet can exactly fit a small cot and nothing more. I open the door and climb onto the cot. Then I close the door, and I am surrounded by four walls—it's a small tomb. There is a narrow levered window near the ceiling, but the glass has never been cleaned so I can't see out. Even if I could see out, there is nothing to see but the wall of the house next door. I did not imagine that houses could be built so close together, one against the next. People in this city live like termites.

At night I climb in here and watch the moths spin around the light bulb. This is how I spend the long nights. I have been squatting on the bed and drawing pictures on the wall. I am starting near the doorway and moving slowly to one corner. It is the mango groves, always the mango groves.

I hear them talking. Kasai's wife Teru is saying that all I do is sleep all day. Get him a job, she is saying. Take him to the newspaper office and make him work. Kasai has a better idea. Get him a job with an artist, he says. Genji can work as an apprentice. If he wants to be an artist, he should see what it's like.

I finished drawing the mango groves all around the walls of my tomb. Kasai came to look at my drawing, squinting through his thick glasses. The maid wanted to wash it all off, but Kasai said no. I thought the maid should have washed the walls off, since I had nothing to do at night.

Then I found out that their son Guilherme can't sleep at night like me. He watches television. There was never any television at Kantaro's. Too bad. We sit there in the dark watching the moving pictures, the *gaijin* laughing and crying and kissing and killing. Only they do everything in grey.

* * *

Kasai took me to see Ogata, who agreed to take me on because Kasai is his friend. Ogata knows Kantaro from long ago. He says those were different days. "We were younger." Then he asked me if I remembered Inagaki. He smiled. He said did I know that Takashi Inagaki was in New York? Inagaki has a studio there. Did I know Inagaki taught his wife Natsuko to paint, too? Now she is selling her work in New York also. Maybe she makes more money than Inagaki. Wouldn't Inagaki be interested to know that he, Ogata, had inherited Inagaki's old pupil. He laughed.

Then he asked about that sculptor Akio Karasumori. Didn't Karasumori want to teach me sculpture? He said that Karasumori was here in the city trying to get a gallery to sell his work, but the gallery already had lots of Japanese pots, and besides, they were shipping direct from Japan some granite stuff by a Japanese who's famous already. Who's Karasumori anyway?

Ogata said, "These young upstart Japanese come here and think they can teach us something. I am a pioneer here. Struggled for years, farming, driving a truck, everything to get to where I am. Guys like Inagaki and me know what it is to suffer for art. If Karasumori wasn't good in Japan, he's no good here." Ogata looked mad. Then he said, "Is it true Karasumori's wife is beautiful? I heard he followed her to Brazil."

To get to Ogata's studio, I have to take three buses. Three times already I have taken the wrong bus. The buses are crowded with stinking *gaijin;* I can never understand what they are saying. I can't get off the bus and have been all over the city, trying to get back to Kasai's. The first day, I never got to Ogata's. The second day I was late, and Ogata wasn't there, so I left. Ogata called Kasai on the telephone to complain. Kasai said Ogata had to be more patient; I couldn't talk or read Portuguese, he said. What did Ogata expect? I didn't even know how to use the telephone; it was a miracle that I even got back to the Liberdade.

So finally I am working at Ogata's. Ogata wakes up early and meditates, he says. Then he paints before the street gets noisy. He paints for four hours and then eats his breakfast. Then he goes out to do his business and comes back for lunch. He takes a nap every day after lunch for one hour. Then he meditates again, paints for five hours, and then it's supper. This is Ogata's schedule every day, no matter what day it is. Ogata's wife said that he goes to sleep every day at the same time, wakes at the same time. He must even shit at the same time every day. You can set your clock by him.

When Ogata goes out to do his business, I'm supposed to be working. First, he said, sweep the floor. Then wash the brushes. Then stretch this canvas. Every day, it's something like that. Finally I asked him when am I going to paint. He said painting is a way of life. It requires strict discipline. Something like that. So every day I sweep the floors. Sometimes I do it twice just for the heck of it.

For this I get some money at the end of the week. I looked at the money and wondered what I would do with it. I never had money before. I took this money and got all these boxes of cigarettes.

Ogata complained to Kasai that all I ever do is smoke. He says he isn't paying me to smoke all day. I think he is paying me to sweep up my cigarette butts. He says I'll never be ready to paint. I don't have any character. No discipline. Kasai said Ogata should think of me as a challenge to his way of thinking. He was too rigid. He needed to see life through my eyes. Ogata laughed.

*   *   *

Ogata won't have me back. He said I almost burned down his studio. It happened when he was out doing his business. It was a cigarette butt. It got mixed in with the rags and the alcohol. I couldn't put the fire out. It burned Ogata's two most recent paintings. Ogata's wife came running in and threw water over everything. She told Ogata that I was just standing there watching his paintings burn. Ogata told Kasai that I did it on purpose.

Kasai's wife Teru is saying again that all I do is sleep and smoke and watch television. All day long in my closet sleeping and smoking, she says, or all night smoking and watching television.

Then Guilherme came to talk to me. He asked me if I wanted to go to the university with him. They don't want me to sleep and smoke, so I went. This university is not what you think. Not like Shiratori's or Hatomura's classes. More like a big club. They sit around and talk. They talk and smoke and talk. I just practice blowing rings. Guilherme's friends were all impressed by this. They keep talking about big changes. About Brazil. About the future. About action. About the people. Always about the people. What people? I asked Guilherme about this. He said that I am Brazilian, that I have to start living in Brazil. Esperança was not the world. The Liberdade was not the world. I was the people.

* * *

Kasai took me to the newspaper office. That's where I saw Hatomura. Hatomura was there with his moon face putting little pieces of type into a big plate. Kasai must have given him this job. Hatomura was surprised to see me. I told him they got rid of me, too. I offered him a cigarette. He asked me did I hear from anybody at Kantaro's? Did I hear from the youth? What about Tsuneo? I said no. I asked him about Yae. He told me that Yae had found a way to go to Japan. I wondered if Kanzo knew this. I asked Hatomura why he didn't go back to Japan too. He said he had other plans. It must have been that old three-year plan. I wanted to tell him that in three years, Akiko would be three years older, and she wouldn't go to Japan anyway. She wasn't like Yae.

I thought about Yae going to Japan. Shiratori talked about Japan. He said that they lost the war. What is Japan? Just like Esperança, I thought. Just like this Japanese *bairro,* this Liberdade. But Guilherme said this is not Japan. This is Brazil. You are Brazilian, he said. I wondered if Yae would ever come back. My old man never went back to Japan, so maybe Yae will never come back to Brazil.

* * *

Next, Kasai got me a job in Urashima's grocery. Urashima's is just two doors down from the newspaper office. I'm supposed to be there when the sun comes up and pull the produce off Urashima's truck. So far, I never get there that early. Urashima complained to Kasai. Kasai asked Urashima if he would want me to work at night, since that is when I seem to be awake.

Urashima has a big family. They all work in the store. They all seem to have something to do. They all know what they have to do. All day long, they run around doing something. They look at me smoking and say, "What are you doing?" I can't figure out what I should do. At least I know it's not weeding. What do they want me to do? Sometimes they tell me to sweep the floor. Sometimes to stack things on the shelves. When I break something, they get mad. I dropped a box of apples; they rolled all over the place, out the door, into the gutter. Urashima yelled at me. "Those came from Argentina! Very expensive. Now they're all bruised. I can't sell bruised apples." He made the apples cheaper and sold all of them.

At lunchtime, I leave Urashima's store and go to see Hatomura at the newspaper office. If I give him a cigarette or one of Urashima's bruised fruits, he will tell me something new. He told me he saw Kōno before Kōno went to Japan. Kōno and Hanako have a baby now. Kōno waited for the baby to be born; then he wrote his mother, asking her to send him a ticket to Japan. Kōno said he is going to Japan to explain things to his mother. Hatomura says Kōno will be back in a few months. Kōno promised Kantaro that he would return. Kantaro made Kōno promise to die in Esperança.

Guilherme sometimes comes to the store after work to get me. I go with him to the university. Guilherme is some big shot at what he calls the Academic Center. He spends all his time there, writing things and printing copies of them on a machine. I turn the handle on the machine. Then we go to some corner and pass the stuff out.

*   *   *

Hatomura got a letter from Kōno. It says that Kōno met up with Yae. Yae is working as a waitress in a coffeehouse in Tokyo. Kōno has decided to stay longer in Japan. He says he discovered a new breed of chickens that he wants to bring to Kantaro's place. Something about bringing the future. Kōno thinks like my old man. They think chickens are always the future. But then, maybe Kōno and Yae will never return.

I went with Guilherme again to the Academic Center. We picked up these papers and took a bus to the Praça República. It was packed with what Guilherme calls "the people." There were just a lot of stinking *gaijin*. There were so many, they spilled out onto the streets and blocked the cars and trucks. Someone was yelling into a bullhorn. Meanwhile, Guilherme and I just kept passing out the papers. I ran out of papers, so I tried to get a smoke in. Then, I saw them coming, rushing out of cars. Guilherme saw them too. He threw the papers away and ran into the crowd. The police were all around. People started to push. I couldn't tell what happened. I got punched in the stomach with a stick. People started to run. The voice in the bullhorn was screaming. Then, there were shots like firecrackers and the air stank. My eyes stung. I wanted to vomit. I ran around looking for Guilherme. I tripped over something and fell. When I looked, there was a woman beneath me. Her dress was soaked in blood. I stared at the blood coming from her neck and her chest. It was not like television. I do not have a good imagination. I could never imagine this. Finally, I saw what happens when something pierces human flesh.

When I got back, I vomited all night, but Guilherme never came home. Teru kept asking questions. What were we doing? Where did we go? We were there at the Praça República, weren't we? Did we want to get killed? Kasai went out to look for Guilherme, but he came back alone.

The next day, the police came and asked questions. I was in my closet sleeping. Guilherme still wasn't there. The police left.

* * *

For a week I watch television at night by myself. Still no Guilherme. Kasai can't sleep either. Teru cries at night. Kasai watches television with me now. Then, in the middle of the night, there is this scratching at the door. It's Guilherme. All night, they talk together in the kitchen. Teru makes a lot of food. Kasai says he knows what it is like to run. He had to run away during the war. He gives Guilherme a lot of advice.

There's pounding at the door. The police rush in like crazy men. Guilherme doesn't know where to go. He rushes to the back. I open my closet, and Guilherme gets under the bed. Then I get in my bed. Guilherme never even breathes. I pretend to sleep. The police rush in. They see me sleeping in the closet. They pull me from the bed, but

I am not Guilherme. I sit up on the bed and light a cigarette. I blow rings. They look at the mango grove on the closet walls. They laugh and leave.

* * *

Guilherme is gone. Teru and Kasai will not say where, but he has gone far away. Teru is like my mother; she sits in her kitchen and cries. She says she spent the war alone with three children while Kasai was in jail in Japan. Guilherme was the youngest. Now he is gone.

Guilherme said that "the people" work hard, but they are slaves. People cannot work hard and get nothing to eat. One day "the people" will get angry. You cannot keep them down. I thought about this. I never worked hard; I always got something to eat. Nowadays, I don't care much about eating if I can get a smoke. The dead woman in the street was "the people." Maybe she got angry. Maybe not. They don't want me at Kantaro's place. Now I am here. This is not Japan. This is not Esperança.

Kasai doesn't talk much. He takes off his thick glasses and closes his eyes. He is thinking about Guilherme.

Instead of sleeping like I usually do, I woke up when the sun came up. I went to Urashima's to work. Urashima's truck was there. He was surprised to see me, but he said, "Genji, pull these sacks off the truck." There was a big *gaijin* carrying the big sacks on his shoulders. The sacks were filled with beans. I got into the truck to pull off one sack. I pushed it to the edge of the truck, but I could not put it up on my shoulders. The *gaijin* came and picked up the sack. He picked it up like it was a pillow and dropped it on my shoulder. I took two steps with that sack. All of my bones sort of folded into a pile under the sack. The *gaijin* and Urashima, Urashima's kids and the people on the street who saw, all laughed. A weakling, they said. What did they expect? I was not the people.

* * *

I hear Teru asking Kasai how I can stay in the closet smoking all day. "He will start the closet on fire," she says. "You can see the smoke coming out from under the door."

At night, Guilherme is not there. Television is not the same. It's not the same.

Teru told Kasai that the neighbors are complaining. Dona Carmen next door said she saw me looking in her window at night. She heard that the neighbor across the street noticed someone peeping in his window at night, so he called the police, thinking it was a robber. But Dona Carmen said it must be me. She said she wasn't going to tell anyone, but Teru and Kasai should do something about it.

*   *   *

I still had some money. I went to Urashima's and got three boxes of cigarettes. Then Kasai put me on the bus to Esperança.

Ritsu cried when I came home, but my old man wouldn't talk to me. I sat in the house and smoked and smoked, day after day, staring at all the paintings on the walls. Ritsu had them hanging everywhere, and there were big piles in all the corners. Then I remembered the rags and the alcohol at Ogata's place. I took the big piles of paintings from the corners. I took everything off the walls. I took down all the mango groves, the chicken coops, Haru's vegetable garden, the dining hall, young Kantaro, old Kantaro, my old man, the laundry, the girls' dormitory, the water tower, everything. I put it all outside in a big pile with rags and alcohol. I was down to my last cigarette. That was all it took. Flames everywhere. Orange, gold, yellow, green flames. Ritsu ran out screaming, running around like a chicken without a head, pulling the paintings away. Stamping on the fire. Stamping with her bare feet. I ran around and around the fire. I had the old man's penknife. I saw the woman in the plaza again. I saw her blood. She was the people. I was the people. I stabbed my breast. Stabbed. Stabbed. Stabbed. Flames. Fire. Pain. Pain. Bleeding flames like my paintings. Flames. Flames. Flames.

CHAPTER 20: DANCE

THEY WOULDN'T LET ME kill me. I couldn't carry a bag of beans, but I surprised them all. It took six of them to hold me down. I could tell they were afraid. My old man. Karasumori. Even Kantaro. Afraid of the knife. Afraid of my blood. Red like mulberry juice. Thick like clay. Shiny like oil paint. Only Tsuneo wasn't afraid. He grabbed me from behind. He held my arm. Tsuneo held my arm.

The hospital was far away. Almost as far as the Liberdade. Everything inside was grey like television. Everything. Even the sheets were grey. Even the sky between the bars. Even the liquid in the tubes going into my arms. Even the bandages. Even the needles. Even the pills. Even the food. I couldn't move. They strapped my legs, my arms. They strapped my head down. They strapped my mind down.

My old man came with his long beard, but then I thought who's that old man? I just stared.

He said, "Are you feeling better?"

I said, "Funny, you speak Japanese too? No one here speaks Japanese."

He said, "Your mother wanted to come, but you know how it is. It's a long way, and besides, she's got no shoes to wear." The old man was wearing wooden clogs. Hand-carved. He didn't have shoes either. "What should I tell your mother?"

"How long have you been speaking Japanese?" I said.

"Your mother sent these," he said. "They said you can eat anything." He tore the paper around the package. He put three big mangos on the sheet. We both stared at the mangos. The only things that weren't grey. He took out his penknife. The blood was washed off, but his hand shook. He spread the paper on his lap. He took a mango and cut it along the seed. He cut away the orange-purple skin. He said, "Very ripe. Very sweet. Good crop this year. Ritsu saved you the best."

"This is not Japan," I said.

The old man nodded.

"You got a smoke, old man?" I asked.

He shook his head. He folded the penknife and put it back in his pocket. He picked up an orange piece of mango pulp with his fingers. He held it near my lips. The juice dripped on the grey sheet, on the grey bandages.

I opened my mouth.

*   *   *

The Kojimas came back from São Paulo to visit. Haru and all the aunties made a big to-do. They cooked all day. They made sushi. They killed a lot of chickens. Kantaro never paid them for our land. Mizuoka must have paid them. Some people said that the co-op paid them. Mizuoka screwed up the money. Where did the co-op money go? Everyone blamed Mizuoka. The Kojimas looked old and tired, even though they were retired and living good in São Paulo. Haru kept putting food on the table in front of the Kojimas. Kantaro stood up and made a speech. He cried about how the Kojimas had helped us. How the Kojimas had offered friendship when other people turned the other way. We could never repay their generosity. It was a matter of our history. This for the sake of Esperança. The Kojimas took responsibility for the future of Esperança. Someone who came to the party said, yeah, what is Kantaro's is Kantaro's and what is yours is also Kantaro's.

Kantaro said Takehashi, Terada and those good-for-nothing others don't have dreams, don't have vision. No imagination. Stingy. Always worrying about money. Always busy saving. Saving. Worker ants with no culture.

* * *

Kantaro has a disease. Parkinson's. Kantaro was always left-handed. His left hand shakes like crazy. He spills his soup and makes a mess. Haru has to come and wipe it up. "Uno-san," she yells at him. "What's this mess? Do I have to feed you now?" He takes this medicine—cortisone. He sits around sulking. Someone said God is punishing Kantaro for slapping and beating up so many people, even Grandpa Naotaro. And Kanzo too. Even Shiratori and Hatomura. My old man tried to tell him that it must be from his old baseball days. It was that left-handed pitching, he said. Thinking about baseball made Kantaro sulk more.

Then Yae came back. She just walked in. It was true what Hatomura said. Yae had been in Japan. She got a job in a coffeehouse in Tokyo. Now she had new clothes. She had new hair. She wore make-up. She had things dangling from her ears. Jiro almost didn't recognize her, but Kantaro knew right away. His hand started to shake like crazy. Kantaro said to Jiro, "Your daughter. Look. She's back."

Jiro wanted to cry. Tears came down, but he didn't want Kantaro to see. He tried to look angry.

Yae came with this man called Shintaro Uguisuyama. He is big and tallish with bushy hair that won't stay in place. He has a loud laugh. Uguisuyama owns the coffeehouse in Shinjuku where Yae got a job. "He's my boss," she said.

Kantaro's hand kept shaking. Uguisuyama said, "Your hand is shaking. Parkinson's?"

Kantaro said, "I take cortisone."

Uguisuyama said, "Cortisone's good for sex."

Kantaro paused. This was good news.

"Yae and I are getting married," Uguisuyama said right away. He didn't even ask. He said, "No weddings. I haven't got time for that. Tomorrow, we're going back to São Paulo. I want to see Rio and then Buenos Aires, the Iguaçú Falls. Then I'm taking Yae to Paris and London. It's time Yae saw the world." Then he laughed a big laugh.

Jiro's mouth hung open, but Kantaro's hand stopped shaking. "One day here is not enough time to visit us. You see how simply we live, but this is Yae's humble home. We are a big family, and we have been worried about Yae in Tokyo by herself. We have all missed her. Yae is a brave girl, and we are very proud of her success in meeting such a good man as yourself."

Uguisuyama agreed and laughed again. "I'm a businessman, Uno-san. I'm used to assessing situations quickly, making quick decisions. I have a knack for learning more and faster about things than most people. I have already been scanning your operation, and frankly I think you could use my expertise. Don't be offended if we only stay one day. I'll bring Yae back whenever she wants. We'll be back again."

Kantaro said, "Yae is lucky to find such a bright young man. Yae was always different from the other girls. She has a mind of her own."

Meanwhile, Yae went off on her own. Kanzo was driving the tractor in. He saw Yae. They stared at each other. Kanzo got off the tractor. His straw hat had the same hole it. His clothes were dirty. His nails were black. He said, "You're back."

Yae said, "It was hard to leave, but I did it. I came back to show you that you can do it."

"We are different."

"I didn't forget you," Yae said.

Kanzo nodded.

"I'm getting married."

Kanzo suddenly looked pale. He shuddered even though he was sweating from his work. He nodded again.

"I didn't forget you," Yae said again.

Kanzo walked away.

Yae went to see the dance studio Kantaro had said to build. The dance studio had mirrors and stereo music. All this for Fuyuko's classes. The girls came in from the field. They changed into those tight black suits. They got excited. They wanted to know what it was like to escape.

"Yae-chan, no one else could do what you did."

"I want to get married to a handsome man like him, Yae-chan."

"Did you marry for love? Kantaro says we must all marry for love."

"But no one comes here to love!"

"We will all die here and never find anyone to marry."

"Yae-chan, I envy you."

"Hanako has two babies now. Are you pregnant yet?"

"What about Hatomura? Where is he now? How I miss his classes."

"Yae, I wish I could go with you, but I could never go. No, I could never leave."

Fuyuko got angry. She pretended that Yae didn't have new clothes and things hanging from her ears. She did not like this talk. "You are all late today," she said. "All this nonsense about finding a husband. We need to practice for our tour. This is an opportunity that people who have left Kantaro's will never have."

The girls are called the Uno Dance Troupe now. The Nambei Publicity Management Agency came to talk to Kantaro and Fuyuko. They said Japan wants them. Japan wants to see country girls from Brazil dance modern ballet. They had a list of cities in Japan. Tokyo, Osaka, Kobe, Kyoto. Even I have heard of these cities. They had a list of theaters. Everyone wanted Kantaro's girls. The shows would be sold out. The shows would pay for everything. Kantaro would go to Japan too. He would go to Japan to tell our history, to tell about our struggle. Everyone would be impressed. They would see the girls dancing in those tight suits. They would be impressed.

Fuyuko is training the girls every day. She is working on a new piece with Brazilian jazz music. She is writing to her old teachers in Japan. When she goes back to Japan, she will show everyone. But first, the girls are going to São Paulo to dance. They are going to the Liberdade.

* * *

I heard Junichiro Shiratori finally went away to America, but then he came back to Brazil again. When he came back he was still skinny and his shoulders still folded, but he was in disguise. He had long hair and wire spectacles and jeans with legs like skirts. The Uno Dance Troupe posters were all over the Liberdade. Shiratori must have seen the posters. Probably he remembered Akiko and their spot in the cornfields.

Akiko is an old lady now, maybe forty. Maybe she is still beautiful. I can't tell, but that's what they say. Anyway, Tsuneo, who's now just twenty, must have felt sorry for her. He was still mad at Kantaro for hitting Hatomura's moon face. He apologized to Kantaro for hitting him with the stick, but he was still angry. He told Akiko that he wanted to go to São Paulo to find Hatomura. Masao Hatomura was a good teacher, he said. Akiko agreed. Tsuneo asked Akiko if she didn't want to go with him to find Hatomura.

Someone said Akiko is a demon. But some people say I'm crazy. Akiko is just stupid. She's the people too. Still, Akiko's got some courage, so she told Tsuneo, yes. I hear the girls talk. They say Akiko is getting too old to have a baby. Akiko goes to take care of Hanako's babies. She holds them like they are her own. She plays with them and laughs and cries.

Speaking of Hanako, Kōno is very busy working. He is working so hard that he is losing his hair, and his forehead is getting bigger. He is the new chicken expert at Kantaro's place. My old man retired. Kōno went home to see his mother. I thought he wouldn't bother to return. But then, he and Hanako had a baby. And Hanako made sure she was pregnant again before he left.

Kōno went to Japan and met a real chicken expert named Yuwasa. Yuwasa liked what he said about Kantaro's place. He decided to help us. He sent Kōno back with some of his special chicks and a lot of money. Kōno took his own money and added it to that. Now Yoshifumi Kōno is the Yuwasa Poultry representative for all of South America. Now we are the Uno-Yuwasa Poultry Project. Kōno struts around like he runs everything now. He says he is giving back Kantaro his original dream. He says he will make Kantaro the King of Eggs again. He bought all this equipment. My old man says it's the newest stuff. New incubators, new feeding pens and these egg-sizing machines so the girls don't have to sort different-size eggs into different baskets. Kōno says this is the future. This is progress. He's going to make Kantaro's place a modern operation. Kōno is running around like crazy. Going here and there. Never stopping. This is all for Kantaro. All for Kantaro. Like my old man. All for Kantaro.

* * *

They took me to the Liberdade for therapy. I sat in the first row at the theater with Kantaro. This was the big Uno Dance Troupe debut sponsored by the Nambei Publicity Management Agency. Kantaro said I could go because I like to watch Fuyuko and the girls practice modern ballet. Even Fuyuko said this is good therapy. "Let Genji come." Every day, Kantaro and I are watching all the girls slither around the floor in those black suits. But only Kantaro can take cortisone. At the theater, Kantaro got up and talked about history and vision and the Uno Dance Troupe. He talked about cutting down virgin forest and building Esperança out of nothing. And how the old-timers were great pioneers. But I thought only old-timers get to pioneer anyway. I heard this before, so I left. I went to the lobby to smoke.

Then I saw Junichiro Shiratori. No one recognized him. Like I said, he had long hair and jeans with legs like skirts and these round wire glasses. He was in disguise, but I knew it was him. He was carrying something in a small leather case. Tsuneo was in the lobby too. I saw him watching Shiratori, so he recognized him too. Shiratori went in the theater and sat in the last row. I followed him. I saw him pull out these glasses from his leather case and look through them at the girls dancing. He was looking like crazy. I could see his mouth moving, saying the girls names, "Yo-chan? No. Sachiko?" Trying to figure out who was who. It was a big job. Yo-chan, for example, is pretty big now. Shiratori was looking through his glasses, so he never noticed that Akiko was sitting right in front of him. Suddenly Akiko got up. That's when Shiratori noticed her. Akiko was going out to the lobby. Shiratori got up too and started tripping over people's feet. "Excuse me. Excuse me." He was trying to get out fast, but Akiko got away. Finally Shiratori got to the end of the aisle, but then my old man Befu rushed in.

Befu looked like he used to when he wanted to beat me up. "You!" he growled at Shiratori. He grabbed Shiratori's arm and jerked him into the lobby. "You are the one who ruined my son! You have no right to be here! Get out! Get out!"

Shiratori looked confused. He pushed back his long hair. I wondered what the old man was talking about too. Shiratori didn't know about them not letting me kill myself. Someone had to take the blame. He kept looking around for Akiko. Looking for the toilets. I looked around too. Tsuneo was gone. So was Akiko.

Then, Kōno ran into the lobby. His big forehead was in a sweat. He saw my old man and yelled, "Befu! Where is Fuyuko?"

"Fuyuko? Dancing, of course." Befu made a face. He was still gripping Shiratori's jean jacket.

"This whole thing is a scam!" Kōno said. "We've got to stop it. Did you see any of those Nambei Publicity people? Did you?"

"I haven't got time for those people." My old man was jerking Shiratori to the glass doors.

"Fakes!" Kōno ran after Befu crying, "All fakes! I've been asking around. No one's heard of them. We've bought airplane tickets for everybody to nowhere for nothing!"

"What are you talking about?"

"Who's going to pay for this mistake?" Kōno was getting hysterical. "This will set us back months! Months of work all for this dancing nonsense!"

The old man nodded. He thought dancing was nonsense too. Befu was like Kōno. He liked chickens. He was the old chicken expert. But the old man was tired now. He used to be angrier in the old days. But Shiratori didn't know I was crazy. He didn't know that everything had turned to grey. The old man still sat next to Kantaro, but he never said much anymore. Nothing to say. Only Kantaro got to take cortisone. The old man pushed Shiratori down the stairs of the theater, into the street. He yelled, "If I were younger, I would kill you! I would kill you!"

* * *

Ritsu ran around and around. I looked at her, but I didn't see her. She was trying to tell me something. She was trying to say she was my mother. She was my mother, but she was no one. She was always no one. Always Ritsu. No one noticed Ritsu. Ritsu had no shoes. Ritsu had the same old dress. The other aunties got their way. They got cloth for new dresses. They got shoes. They got books for their kids. Baseball equipment. Haru got a tricycle for Hanako's kids. Ritsu couldn't even get me pencils. Ritsu was weak. Like Karasumori said, she probably wasn't on the ark. But nobody noticed. Ritsu was the old man's wife. Ritsu was Kantaro's sister. At night the old man remembered Ritsu, but all day he only remembered Kantaro. Ritsu found some stubby pencils. She found some scraps of paper. She thought I needed them. But she was invisible.

She went to the mango groves with a rope. I went there too. I took the stubby pencils and the paper with me. She was hanging there with bare feet. She looked like a mango. I drew the mango.

CHAPTER 21: THE DREAM

KANTARO IS DREAMING the same dream every night. He screams at night. Haru almost never sleeps. She's in the kitchen even before the cocks crow. She can hear Kantaro screaming. She rushes in with a rag and slaps Kantaro. "Uno-san! Wake up! It's a dream! A dream!" Then she makes him wake up and gets him out of bed. She makes him sit up while she changes everything. All the sheets are sopping with Kantaro's sweat. She has to change Kantaro and rub him down with a towel. All the time she is complaining, "This is a nuisance! Every night the same thing. When is it going to stop?"

Kantaro shakes his head. "Every night. Every night."

Haru makes Kantaro a cup of tea. They sit together until Kantaro feels sleepy.

"I heard a funny thing," Kantaro said.

"What's that?"

"I didn't understand it. Someone was trying to remember something when it happened. He said, 'You know, it was about the same time when Haru was gone.'" Kantaro stopped and looked at Haru. "I said, 'Haru gone?' and he said, 'Yes, when Haru was gone, because everything was wrong for several weeks while she was gone. The coffee was no good. Old Takeshita didn't get his medicine and almost died.'"

Haru said nothing.

Kantaro continued, "I said, 'What are you talking about? Haru has always been here. She has never been anywhere else.' Then he said, 'Yes, but this was when Yōgu left, but my memory is bad. You are right. I am confused. Haru has always been here.'"

Haru is fat and old. She has thin grey hair in a little bun and funny thick spectacles. Her hair is never in place. When she smiles, her wrinkles go up.

"What was he talking about?" asked Kantaro.

"I don't know," Haru shook her head. "I don't know. You know, Uno-san, I have always been here."

Kantaro nodded. He looked at this old woman. They said he married her for great love. You still have to hear that story about Kantaro's great passion. "You know, Haru, we're old now, but nobody else has a story like ours." Then he falls asleep. Haru goes back to work.

Kantaro tells everyone about his dream. He told my old man. He told him to make him forget about Ritsu. My old man listened carefully. Kantaro dreams about hell. There is a hot sea of stinking shit. Every night Kantaro is swimming in shit, choking in the fumes. He gets thrown out again and again by big waves. He tries to breathe, tries to swim, but he is drowning, rolling and cooking in the hot stinking rot.

My old man had no answer for Kantaro, but Yae's husband Shintaro Uguisuyama came back. He is always saying something smart. He said, "This dream portends great wealth. You can be sure of it!"

After this, Kantaro stopped having his dream, but he still liked to talk about it.

Uguisuyama came back alone for only one day again. He is always too busy. But Uguisuyama had enough time to tell Kantaro that he needed to think about the education of the youth. He said he taught himself everything by reading. He said he can read a book every day. He said the new generation is stupid. We don't have the same education as Kantaro and Befu and the old-timers. We're too stupid to keep things going. Kantaro talked about our history, but Uguisuyama said history would take too long.

Then Uguisuyama went to talk to Karasumori and Fuyuko. He looked at Karasumori's granite rock. Uguisuyama said he didn't understand art. "Can you sell this stuff?" he asked. He said Karasumori better study the market. He heard Karasumori got a bad review from a Brazilian art critic. He laughed. "Maybe rich Brazilians want something else. If you don't sell, what do you contribute to this place? You are both educated. You need to give the youth more than art. They need math, biology, economics, politics, business. They need to have the tools to be farmers and businesspeople." Then he laughed about the publicity agency mess and about Kōno having to pay for everything. "You got into this mess because you only wanted to go back to Japan."

I thought Fuyuko would get mad, but she looked away. It was Karasumori who got mad. He pointed his cigarette at Uguisuyama and said he didn't understand anything about life at Kantaro's place.

"You are an outsider. It's easy to criticize when you don't live here. We came here to live. We left Japan. We don't need to go back."

Fuyuko said, "This is the life I chose. To live my art. When I first came here, I knew I must stay even if he would not." She looked at Karasumori. "But I was very stupid then. I have learned many things. My ideas are different now. These people are my family. My dance, my body, my life belongs to them. It cannot be separated."

Uguisuyama looked at Karasumori. He said, "What about you? Who does your life belong to?"

Karasumori looked at Fuyuko. He looked confused. He said, "This is the life we have chosen. We left Japan to have the freedom to do our art."

"You have your art, but the youth born here don't have a choice. Only you are free to do your art. Well, not just you. Genji too!" Uguisuyama laughed. "You and Genji!" He laughed again. "Free to do your art!"

When Uguisuyama left, Karasumori went to his granite rock with a big hammer and crashed down on it again and again. Pieces of the rock flew everywhere. Fuyuko came out and screamed, "Stop!" She ran around and hugged the granite, so Karasumori had to stop in midair. He threw the hammer far away and stomped off. Fuyuko ran after him. She cried, "I'm pregnant! I'm pregnant!"

Karasumori stopped. He ran back into the house. When he came out, he was holding the mirror. He threw it on the ground, but it did not break. He fell to his knees and looked in the mirror. Fuyuko was there.

*   *   *

Every other week Uguisuyama's books keep arriving from Japan. They come in boxes, one after another. Everyone knows now they are just books. No one has time to see what books they are. My old man opened one of the boxes. He found some book and showed it to Kantaro. Kantaro looked impressed. The book got passed around, but no one read it. The boxes get stacked in the dining hall. Now it's just a wall of books. Everyone ignores it.

I've got nothing to do all day. I follow Haru around. She scolds me, but I don't care. Now she's feeding me that genius medicine again. Maybe it's working.

The old man's beard suddenly turned white. His eyebrows turned white too. His eyes didn't turn white, but they are empty now. The old man looks like a ghost. He doesn't bother about chickens anymore. He never even talks to Kōno. He doesn't care about the Uno-Yuwasa Poultry Project. He stays all day with his orchids. Just talking to his orchids.

For a while everyone on the outside was talking about the Uno-Yuwasa Poultry Project. They talked about how talented Kōno is. They said now Kantaro's place was on the road to success. All because of Kantaro's smart son-in-law from Japan, Yoshifumi Kōno. Lots of farmers invested in the Uno-Yuwasa breed of chickens. Someone said we should be proud of Kōno, but I only hear people here complaining. "Kōno is selfish." Kōnoo is an egotist. He wants all the glory for himself." "Kōno thinks he is the new leader. No one can replace Kantaro." "Who does Kōno think he is? Kōno is an outsider." "He thinks he's better than us. A rich spoiled son from Japan who doesn't know the past, doesn't know our history." "Ever since he bailed Kantaro and Fuyuko out of that publicity agency hoax, he thinks he's our savior."

But Kōno failed. The farmers say the Uno-Yuwasa breed is too weak. They get sick and die. They don't produce a lot of eggs. They won't buy any more chicks from us. Kōno is saying it's not the breed; it's other factors. Other factors. He is blaming everyone for his failure. He says some workers are lazy. They forget to give the chickens their vitamins. They forget to follow the strict diet. Some people don't follow instructions. Details are important. Kōno is working day and night. He is losing hair, and his forehead is getting bigger and bigger. Where are the others? He can't do everything by himself. Some people say that since Kōno did everything himself, then it is all his fault.

Kōno stood up at dinner. He read a letter from the chicken expert in Japan, old Yuwasa himself. Yuwasa has heard everything from other people. He heard the bad news that Kantaro's place had made a mess of his famous breed. Now Yuwasa's chickens have a bad name. He was pretty mad. He was mad at Kōno. He was mad at Kantaro. He was mad at all of us for ruining his reputation. He said we were irresponsible. We had bad debts in the past. We were bad news. He sent public notices to Shigeshi Kasai's newspaper and other newspapers. The notices said his Yuwasa name was being withdrawn from the Uno Poultry Project. We could call our breed whatever we wanted, but it was not his famous breed. Kōno's voice trembled when he read the letter. And when he finished, no one said anything. They all just left the dining hall, left Kōno alone. Hanako came with her babies. She handed a baby to Kōno. He held the baby and cried.

*   *   *

Kimi had been the first to notice that Akiko never returned from the toilets. She ran around the theater searching for Akiko. I knew by now that Akiko had gone with Tsuneo, but everyone was too busy talking about how Shiratori had come in modern disguise and how my old man Befu threw him out. I saw Kimi's face when she heard about Shiratori. She looked like Befu had punched her one. When she told the old man that Akiko was gone, he shouted, "I should have killed him as I said I would!"

But Kantaro just said to Kimi, "You stay in the city with Befu, and you bring her back. Don't come back, if you don't bring Akiko with you." Kantaro gave Kimi one of those looks that was worse than getting punched.

Then they said Tsuneo was gone too. Everyone got very confused. My old man said that it was Tsuneo who warned him about Shiratori. Maybe Tsuneo and Shiratori had planned this together. Tsuneo always liked those upstarts who came around saying they wanted to teach.

Kimi and my old man stayed in the city. They had to stay a long time. They stayed at Kasai's house for weeks. My old man slept in the closet. Maybe the mango groves were still there. They couldn't find Shiratori, but Hatomura still worked at Kasai's newspaper. Kasai found out that Tsuneo had gotten a job in the produce market, and he and Akiko were staying with Hatomura. The old man wanted to rush out and kill Hatomura, but Kimi made him calm down. Kimi went alone to see Hatomura at Kasai's office. She lied. She told Hatomura that if Akiko wanted to leave, it was okay. Akiko was getting too old to get a husband. She made Hatomura promise to take care of Akiko. "Akiko has never been anywhere before. It will be very lonely for her. Please, I beg you to be good to her, not to fail her trust in you. But let me just see her one more time." Hatomura was so stupid. He must have felt wonderful for the last time in his life. He told Kimi where to find Akiko.

So Kimi and the old man went to Hatomura's place. Maybe Befu's an old man, but he grabbed Akiko and pushed her into a taxi and got her on a bus back to Esperança.

When Akiko got back, Kantaro pretended to look sorry. He told Akiko it was all his fault. "I realize after all this time that it is all my fault. I did not realize how much you wanted to have a family of your own, your own children, your own house to care for. You must forgive me. I have always thought of you as a little girl, but time has been passing for all of us. I have been selfish I admit and not thinking of your happiness. But now, I will make it all up to you, and you must forgive me."

Akiko and Kimi both cried. I guess they cried because they are both too old. Then Kantaro told everyone that Akiko and Kanzo were getting married. This was a big surprise because Kanzo and Akiko have never really liked each other.

Ever since Yae left and got married to Uguisuyama, Kanzo doesn't say anything. He does his work and keeps his mouth shut. When Kantaro said Kanzo's got to marry Akiko, he never said a thing. It was just as if Kantaro had ordered him to go plow a field or build a chicken coop.

*   *   *

Yae and Uguisuyama showed up for the wedding. This time they stuck around for several weeks. Yae brought material to help Akiko make a dress. Yae measured Akiko and cut the material. She said to Akiko, "I saw Hatomura in São Paulo."

Akiko said, "Hatomura is a nice man."

Yae nodded. Then she said, "Do you want to marry Kanzo?"

Akiko didn't say. She looked sad. "Kantaro wants this, so I want it too."

Yae said, "Kanzo is a good person, but he is afraid of Kantaro."

Akiko said, "I know what everyone says. I am getting old. Soon I will be too old to get married. Finally, Kantaro has allowed me to get married. I can't say no."

No one said anything for a while. Then Akiko said, "You are married to Uguisuyama now. Are you happy?"

"Yes."

"Do you regret leaving Kanzo?"

"No."

"Yae-chan," Akiko almost whispered, "thank you for my dress."

Yae put her arms around Akiko, and they both blubbered like two babies.

Meanwhile Uguisuyama took the truck and got bricks and cement to build a library. A building to put that wall of books in. Kantaro pointed to the books and said, "There are your books. We didn't know what to do with them. It's a good thing you came when you did. I was thinking of throwing them out." Kantaro said this, but I know he took some books for himself. His eyes get tired, and he never reads more than two or three pages. Anyway, Kantaro would never thank an upstart like Uguisuyama.

Then Kantaro ordered everyone to build the library. Everyone stopped their other work. They had to build shelves too. It got finished the day before the wedding.

Everyone in Esperança was there. Nobody was going to miss this wedding. Lots of food and lots of gossip. Kantaro spoke at the wedding. "These two events, this marriage and this library, signal the beginning of a new era for Esperança. Fifty years ago, we pioneered a new civilization in the virgin forest to begin a new life. Now we have come together through much sacrifice and many difficulties to build the seed for a new beginning for our children and their children. These two young people, Kanzo and Akiko, are the offspring of our great efforts, our great suffering to conquer great odds. They have both chosen to stay here in Esperança to continue the work that we have started. By their marriage, they show their devotion to a great ideal and their love for Esperança. In a sense, the library is their wedding present, a present to their future, to the education of their children, the promise of a great civilization, a great dream."

Akiko was dressed in the long white dress Yae made. She had a lot of makeup on. She just looked down at Haru's big wedding cake. Kanzo was the same, just staring into the cake too. They were both too old now to be staring at a wedding cake. But Kanzo couldn't say no to Kantaro. Kanzo isn't smart like Tsuneo, but Kanzo doesn't have to be smart. Some day he is just supposed to become like Kantaro, as a silkworm turns into a moth. I never turned into my old man. Kanzo is too old to turn into anything. At least Kanzo can lift a bag of beans.

Uguisuyama came by just after the speeches to talk to Kantaro. He said, "I've arranged for a small plane. A pilot is waiting for us at the field now. I want you to inspect some land I am interested in buying in Mato Grosso. By plane, it is very close, and we would be back in time for the evening festivities."

"Land in Mato Grosso?"

"Yes. Land is very cheap in Mato Grosso. I have been investigating everything."

"You are a sharp businessman, Uguisuyama."

Uguisuyama agreed and laughed.

"My idea is that your people can occupy this land for ranching. Call it a wedding present."

Kantaro was really surprised. First the library, now land in Mato Grosso? Kantaro pretended to be calm.

I never talk much anymore, but Uguisuyama gave me a pack of cigarettes. And I had drunk a whole bottle of beer, so I said, "Take me with you."

Uguisuyama didn't mind. He wasn't like Karasumori who still hates me. "Come along," he agreed. Then he said to Kantaro, "Maybe you'd like to take a photo of our new land with this." Kantaro and I looked at Uguisuyama. He pulled the strap off his shoulders and handed a fancy camera to Kantaro. "Nikon F-2. Latest model." He pulled a round leather case out of his pocket. "Here's the wide-angle lens for it. Try it out from the air." Uguisuyama pushed a button and changed the lens. "They call this a fish-eye." He let me look through the camera. Kantaro's face got fat.

Uguisuyama was right—by plane, the Mato Grosso was only a few minutes away from Esperança.

Uguisuyama said, "Before we look at the land, I have a stop to make." I looked down, but I couldn't tell where we were.

Kantaro asked, "Where are we landing?"

"Just over the border. Bolivia." Uguisuyama spoke to the pilot. He couldn't speak Portuguese. He was trying to speak in Spanish or something. The plane landed in a field. There was someone waiting with boxes. Uguisuyama and the pilot jumped out. They hauled the boxes into the back of the plane. Kantaro was quiet. I just kept on smoking. We got back up in the air. Below, everything was thick green forest.

"This is it," pointed Uguisuyama. "There are several thousand acres of land. I want to buy it, if you will agree to send a group of your people to occupy it, plant, build, live on it." He laughed at Kantaro. "Just like those old days you are always talking about, eh? Esperança was the beginning, but this is the future. First thing I want to build is an airstrip. Don't worry. You're not going to be isolated."

Kantaro's mouth dropped. He just nodded. He was thinking about something.

"There is no telling what we will find on that land below us!"
Uguisuyama was pleased.

I stretched my neck to see. The pilot was trying to say something
to Uguisuyama, but he didn't understand. The pilot was getting very
excited. Very excited. I knew the crazy look in his eyes because I
knew the crazy look. I could feel the plane going down, getting closer
to the green forest below. We were falling. Falling. I could feel the
fall in my ears. Everything went silent. Then the plane was just skim-
ming along the tips of the trees. We were bashing into branches.
Crashing into green tangle. Crashing. Falling. Then silence.

* * *

I awoke. It was dark. Boxes were all over me. I pushed them away.
They were Uguisuyama's boxes from Bolivia. I pushed my way to the
front of the plane. I saw Uguisuyama and the pilot and Kantaro.
They were all pushed into the front of the plane. And the plane was
pushed hard into the earth. I crawled to Kantaro and pulled him to
one side. I looked into his eyes. They were open. They were dead.
Uguisuyama's fancy camera was smashed. The strap was twisted
around Kantaro's neck. His body was stiff, but some places were
soft. Uguisuyama's face was already covered with ants. Maybe I had
been asleep a long time. I looked at Kantaro carefully. To remember.
In case I ever got some paper and a pencil. I was the only one who
knew. No one else knew.

I looked in the boxes. I was hungry, but there was no food. The
boxes were all filled with strange metal things that looked like bugs,
like centipedes with long black spines and silver feet. They were in
narrow plastic boxes. Useless. I looked for paper. I stuffed all the
paper in my pockets. I took the pens and the cigarettes from
Uguisuyama's breast pocket. I crawled away from the wreck.

Outside, all around I could see the sunlight dancing. Dancing with
little feet. I remembered being in a dark basket peeping through the
basket, seeing the light flicker, a prism of light flickering through the
straw. But this time, I was not a prisoner.

Epilogue: Guilherme

I saw this delicious but fleeting state in which love and innocence inhabit the same heart.

Jean-Jacques Rousseau
The Reveries of the Solitary Walker

JACIRA RAIMUNDO AND I were married in Europe. We had both been political exiles for more than twelve years and have since returned to Brazil under the terms of political amnesty. My father, Shigeshi Kasai, was the publisher of the *Brazil Shimpo*. He died a year ago at the age of ninety. Although he was almost blind, he continued to write a column for his newspaper until his death. I have since taken over his publishing business. Jacira and I now have two children.

Jacira's father, Floriano Raimundo, is better known in Santa Cruz d'Azedinha and Esperança as the Bahiano. He is a bent old man with an arthritic knee who supports himself with a cane. He is also hard of hearing. He has, since his wife's death, moved away from Santa Cruz and has lived for the past years alone in the forest of the Mato Grosso. Because of his isolation in the forest and his growing deafness, he seems to have difficulty talking. When I first met him, he had emerged on a whim from the forest, as if he knew that Jacira had come home. He seemed amused that my father Shigeshi Kasai was an old friend of Kantaro Uno, but of that episode in his life concerning Uno, he would say nothing.

I had met Kantaro Uno when I was a boy. He was my father's friend, but that was all. I only began to wonder about him when Genji Befu, Uno's nephew, came to live with us. I surmised that nisei living in the rural interior were isolated and followed the old traditions. I lived in the city and was raised a Brazilian. My friends were mixed, many of them non-Japanese. To me, the Japanese community, referred to as the *colônia,* was a confined world. It amazed me that there could be so many thousands of us all over Brazil involved in so many kinds of work, and yet we could seem so provincial, so small.

People in the *colônia* talked behind my father's back, saying it was Shigeshi Kasai's luck to have a radical for a son, but I wasn't like Masafumi who assaulted banks or Sueli, who fought with guerrillas in Araguaia. These nisei joined an armed revolt, while I thought a military dictatorship could be brought down with a pen. I was young, full of idealism, foolishly prepared to struggle for my country. Many of my friends were tortured, disappeared. What was Kantaro Uno's place compared to this struggle? A small insular statement within a confined world. I tried to make Genji see my point of view. Perhaps I confused him, but he saved my life. When I returned to Brazil, I was curious to know what became of him.

It has since become known that Kantaro Uno died in a plane crash in the forest of the Mato Grosso in 1976. This was substantiated by detailed drawings, sketched in ballpoint pen on pieces of paper and scattered in the forest from place to place. The drawings were of a cartoonish nature, drawn out in small boxes to show the sequence of events. These drawings were collected by Indians in the area. An amateur archaeologist by the name of Shūhei Mizuoka happened to see them and recognized the caricatures. He was also able to read the inscriptions written in Japanese. Mizuoka noted that the inscriptions were penned by a rather mediocre hand with a limited knowledge of Japanese. He surmised that these drawings must have belonged to Genji Befu, who was also in the plane at the time and known to have a talent for drawing. From the pictures, it could be seen that the Japanese businessman Shintaro Uguisuyama and the Brazilian pilot were also killed in the crash. Another interesting detail of these renderings were the boxes of electronic materials which seem to have been thrown forward and jumbled in the crash. It seems that the plane was carrying contraband of some sort, probably computer chips.

Stories later filtered through the community about some crazy Indian who spoke an unknown language and who was at loose in the forest armed with a big shotgun. Supposedly, he was the last of his tribe, everyone killed off but him. There was talk of stores of food and cigarettes disappearing, and this pilferage was generally attributed to him. He always left his mark with strange drawings in soot on the walls or on pieces of paper or scratched in the dirt by some sharp implement. Few people, however, could confirm having seen this lost Indian.

Shūhei Mizuoka, who had recovered the drawings from the Indians, planned to make a special expedition into the forest to find the fallen aircraft. However, he was quite elderly and died. His widow put his ashes in a large Indian funeral urn which was said to have been unearthed by Mizuoka from an Indian mound discovered in Esperança proper. This urn is presently displayed in what has become a museum of the artifacts Mizuoka collected over the years. Mizuoka's widow is the caretaker of the museum and will point out the urn if asked. She has a curious manner of addressing the urn, crossing herself, then pressing the palms of her hands tightly together and pronouncing, "*Namu amida butsu pai nosso amen.*"

It is possible to meet the descendants and followers of Kantaro Uno today. They continue to live on the same land in a communal manner similar to the one they have lived in for decades. The simplicity of their lifestyle—the harsh unfinished wooden structures, communal kitchen, dining hall, laundry and bath—may be surprising to those used to urban life and niceties. Despite the rustic quality of their everyday living conditions, the poultry ranch itself is equipped with the most technically sophisticated incubating and breeding facilities. Embedded in the obvious simplicity, too, are certain amenities of the modern world: a television, a video cassette recorder and a Sony camcorder (all used in common), for example.

It is also possible to visit the members of the second commune, which Genji called "the others." Their living style is quite similar. They are located a good distance from the original commune, and their concerns are completely separate. There is obviously a long-standing rift between the two communities. The nature of this rift seems to have been economic in nature—ultimately a disagreement about how to recuperate losses after a bankruptcy which occurred in 1954.

Jacira didn't know Genji, but she knew the people Genji called "the others." This half of Uno's original group lived on the Raimundo family ranch until they were able to buy land of their own. Jacira grew up in the extended family of their commune, playing with their children, and she considered these people to be her family. To me, who had tried to disassociate myself from the *colônia*, this came as a surprise. "I told you I'm Japanese," she laughed at me. She admits her involvement in political events was influenced by an ideal of co-operation she learned from these people. "Self-sufficient with three meals a day," she emphasizes. "In the Brazil of today that is something from which we can learn."

It is not unusual to make comparisons between the two communes, noting that the original commune led by Kantaro Uno seems, outside of its poultry venture, to be involved in artistic pursuits, while the second commune considers itself largely a pragmatic, social and economic experiment and pursues an agricultural objective of diversifying its produce.

Both communities have and continue to receive journalists, researchers, historians, even television reporters with their video cameras, who come to document the lives of these people. Ichiro Terada, who is seventy-six years old and a member of the second commune, says this: "We who came to live in Esperança were a kind of experiment. It's only right we share our experiences. Perhaps we didn't create the great civilization envisioned by our founder Momose-sensei, but we were a part of a great movement of migrant peoples from many parts of the world and within Brazil itself. I think that Esperança was not an end in itself, it was part of something larger."

Until Kantaro Uno's death, youth in the original commune had not received any education beyond middle school. Like Genji, they have probably found it difficult to live and work outside the commune. They have chosen to remain in the commune, raising families and a new generation of children. The second commune has chosen to provide for those youth wishing to pursue college and careers outside and, as a result, grows year by year smaller and more elderly in its membership. Significant, however, in both communes is the strength and vitality of the elderly, who find themselves useful and active to the end of their lives.

Ichiro Terada proudly announced recently that his grandson passed the college exams in agronomy. He feels this achievement personally because he explains, "The Japanese have origins in the land. And having settled virgin soil, our responsibility to the land is great; farming is our contribution." On the other hand, he speaks with concern about his granddaughter, who graduated with honors in architecture. Unable to find steady work in Brazil, she is one of over 150,000 Japanese-Brazilians who are currently in Japan working as menial labor.

Recently, a curious article was forwarded to Jacira by her father from the Mato Grosso. It reads,

> Three days ago, the so-called Indian of the Lost Tribe was found dead, killed probably while helping himself to someone else's food or store of hidden goods. He was described as a very slight, bowlegged, unkempt man with long dirty black hair, thin strands falling in a tangled beard from his face. He was found shot through the head and clutching a rusty old carbine, empty except for the red earth pushed into the tip of its disintegrating barrel.